CW00448386

Horsemen
at the Gate

First published in 2021 by

© Heather Harrison 2021

'Horsemen At The Gate' is a work of fiction. The characters and the story are products of the author's imagination and although some well-known historical figures are mentioned, they are used fictitiously and not intended to change the fictitious nature of the work. In all other respects, any resemblance to actual events, persons or places, living or dead, is entirely coincidental. However, the effects of the political and religious turmoils of the English civil war on local communities were certainly real.

Kindle Direct Publishing at: www.amazon.co.uk/books

Publications

Poetry
'Roots Beneath the Pavement': West Midlands Arts & Common
Ground 1987
'Experience of Landscape': exhibited by Wolverhampton Art
Gallery 1988
'She is Harlequin in Peacock Blue': Kindle Direct Publishing 2019
'Let Me Catch Whispers': Kindle Direct Publishing 2019

Fiction: Published by Kindle Direct Publishing at
www.amazon.co.uk/books, available as paperback and for Kindle readers

Children's Fiction
'The Terrible Tale of the Lambton Worm': Springboard Stories 2013
'The Magpie Runner' 2019
  Vol 1 'Jewel Thief'
  Vol 2 'The Treasure in the Wall'

Non-fiction
'Wor Harry: A Life'

Dedicated to those who lived in The Croft
in the 1640s and 1650s and may
have lived through such an adventure.

Horsemen at the Gate

Heather Harrison

Ride the Vale road
straight
between the merchant towns
straight
between the grazing fields.

Seasons are our business,
weather.
What have we to do
with Kings or councils;
badges or banners,
we who are the fleece-sellers,
who tend the orchard plums?

Until the days
of horsemen at the gate.

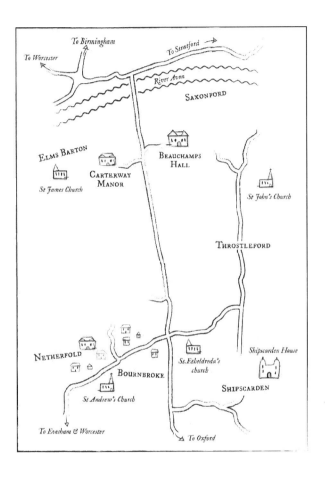

To Birmingham

To Worcester

To Stratford

River Avon

SAXONFORD

ELMS BARTON

BEAUCHAMPS
HALL

CARTERWAY
MANOR

St James Church

St John's Church

THROSTLEFORD

NETHERFOLD

St.Etheldreda's
church

Shipscarden House

BOURNBROKE

SHIPSCARDEN

St Andrew's Church

To Evesham & Worcester

To Oxford

Warrior's Choice

Autumn 1644

Warriors—have ye chosen this place
After the toil of battle to repose
'Paradise Lost': John Milton

It was the noise that woke me. Noise!
Not the usual, the cockerel, the chickens, the dogs. There was shouting, horses, harness, men, my mother.

"Alice! Alice! Lizzie! Now!" Her boots clattered up the stairs. She never ran.

"Get up! Dress yourself. Horses—again!"

"Which soldiers—King or Parliament?"

"Never mind, just get downstairs! We have to hide the stores. Your father's in a rage."

She didn't wait for me. She hammered down the stairs again, yelling at Daniel to get out to my father. She ran outside, hustling Lizzie to grab the cheeses and hide them in the wood store.

I grabbed my clothes, pulled back the shutters and looked out. Twenty or thirty horsemen jostled and stamped in the road outside the house. Some were already in our yard. Tom and Patience in the dairy opposite rolled milk churns away from their front stand for fear the horses upset them. My heart sank.

Not again. Parliament troops, were they? Here into Bournbroke again, demanding quarters on our land and all over the rest of our village.

"Alice! Get down here, girl, now!"

Downstairs they had already carried in two men and laid them on the floor by our fireside. They moaned and squirmed, eyes closed, white faced, bloody. A tall man with long brown curls and a wide orange sash about his waist looked down at them.

11

"Get water and cloths, woman, and see to the wounds of my men here."

I ladled hot water out of the pot hanging over the fire and carried it over to my mother. Lizzie fetched the box of herbals. I soaked a stretch of cloth and wiped away the blood from the gash in a boy's arm. He *was* only a boy,

"All I can do is bind it really tight to try to stop the bleeding." I retched at the sight of the congealed blood but I was heartsore for the lad.

I stared down at him and wondered if my Jack had lain like that on some stranger's floor, wounded and writhing in pain.

"Stop it hurting so much, can't you?" The boy ground his teeth together.

"My mother will have something in her herb store. She's coming."

"Tell her to hurry up, for God's sake!"

"Girl! I'm bleeding here as well. Come here. You've had enough time with him."

Not Parliament troops this time but King's men; long curls, sashes, tattered lace. I ran to the door to look for Mother. Everything was noise and mess. Men pushed and shoved each other aside as they set up their camp all over our orchard, officers and wounded claiming the barn. Three soldiers were wringing the necks of our best laying hens. Others dragged bunches of onions and young leeks from the garden beds. One of them walked out of the storeroom with a whole pot of my mother's bottled beans which she was preserving for winter soups.

My hands were shaking, fearful of these bullying invaders and because I knew how little I could do to help their wounds.

My mother bustled in and took over, bathing and pasting one of her salves on to a linen pad which she strapped tightly round the man's sliced hand. Over her shoulder she grumbled to the officer who stood overlooking her work.

12

"Your men have taken three of my cooking pots and set fires in our orchard to cook stew. They are slinging in half of our harvested vegetables, Sir. Are you thieves, you soldiers of King Charles? Is this honourable?

The officer ignored her and turned away towards the door.

"Is Father…"

"Your father is barely keeping his hands from their throats he is so mad."

"I will cut your father if he lays a finger on our men," the officer said and walked out of the house.

"Oh! Oh!" The soldier with the wounded hand had a musket ball wound in his chest too. My mother was trying to dig the ball out with a crochet hook.

"I must try to get this out or it will fester and your blood will poison, man!"

She spoke sharply because she was worried as well as bad tempered. This was beyond the usual domestic medicine she dispensed to us and our neighbours.

"Is there not an army surgeon you can call on?" The soldier said nothing. He had fainted. My mother ordered me to push back the skin on one side of the wound with the flat of a knife while she prised the ball out. It pinged out and clattered on the floor. We pushed a plug of cloth into the hole to stop the bleeding and I lifted him enough for mother to wind a linen strip around his chest.

"When the bleeding stops, I'll spread some salve over it." She shook her head, "but it will fester. It has been left unclean for too long."

"Get us something to drink," the first boy said, "something hot." My pleading boy was shivering. I thrust the poker in the now hot heart of the fire and drew two pots of ale from the keg on the dresser.

"Crush up some hyssop leaves and put them in it," my mother said to me.

13

"It will put you to sleep, if you are lucky," she said to him. "There's some here for the other one if he comes round."

The boy shouted when we moved him. Mother sent my sister to fetch bread for each of the soldiers and sent me to heat some herby ale. Its comforting smell filled the room. Perhaps it would help them feel better.

"Leave them now," she said and led me out to the yard. It was a tumbled, wretched scene. Our neat vegetable plot had been torn up. Apple boughs had been snapped and thrown to burn on smoking fires. The horses snorted and stamped and left their dung in steaming piles all over our new-swept yard. Mother grabbed a shovel and thrust it at me.

"Here. And grab a bucket. We'll shovel it up and make a midden. It'll feed our poor garden when they've gone."

A hateful, stinking job that one of our garden lads was usually given to do. I worked with a bad grace. As the elder daughter of the house, I was never given such work as this. I resented her, resented these invading soldiers, resented the King and the Parliament for dragging us into their war.

Mother told the soldiers to move the wounded men from the house to the barn on to dry straw and gave them blankets. It was mid-morning before Father called us inside and barred the door. We gathered round the fire to warm our hands and feet. Father sat heavily in his own chair staring into the flames.

We ate our late breakfast without conversation, avoiding each other's eyes. We were all choked by thwarted anger, by fear of what might happen, wondering how long we would have to endure these interlopers on our land and what further wreck they would make of our crops, our animals and the very grass that surrounded the house.

We set about our normal chores with the animals, the garden and the baking. Mother and I set about chopping, pounding and mixing herbs to make fresh balms and medicines to treat the wounded.

14

Late in the afternoon Father brought in two dead chickens and threw them down. "Get these plucked and into our pot before they eat the rest and leave us nothing."

While I set about them, Mother called my sister. "Lizzie. Sit here and bring the writing things. Copy out these instructions for herbal mixtures from your grandmother's old book. And be careful with it, it's fragile." She turned to me. "It will be useful if you have a copy for yourself. I daresay you'll be married one of these days and every housewife needs a healing box, so you'll need the instructions."

"What about me, I'll be married too one of these days. Alice was only seventeen when she ..." Lizzie looked up from her copying.

"Yes, well, at only sixteen you have a few years yet to wait. Time enough for you to make your own housewife copy. Your sister would be married now if Jack Morton had not died at Edgehill. She's young enough to marry still."

"It is not quite two years yet, Mother."

"Long enough for a young heart to heal, Alice. You can't stay alone forever; you are far too good looking for that."

"Thank you for copying my book for me, *Mistress* Lizzie," I said with a smile. She blew a raspberry.

"I hate copying."

"But you are so good at it, your writing is clear and neat. Or would you rather peel the onions?"

As the autumn afternoon grew dark, the officer came to demand bread.

"I have money here, Wife, to pay for your hospitality." He threw some coins down on the table. Mother went on tidying the medicines and salves away into the pantry.

"Have you heard me?"

"Indeed. I have an unerring ear for rudeness, Sir. I had thought your Royalist men would have better, more courtly manners."

"Courtly. Huh! You do not think we all strut about in the King's court in London do you, woman? We are soldiers. We rally to a right cause. We are not all aristocratic fops. Now, six loaves of bread as soon as you can fetch them."

He swept out without a thank you.

While Lizzie wrote her copy, Mother and I set about baking bread, loaves the size of a baby's head for the soldiers and larger ones for our own use.

The evening brought that fraught day to a close and none of us sat up late after our meal. The officers did not bother us again that night. If some of them went off to The Rose Bush Tavern in the village they did not come back raucous, so we slept.

While it was still dark, Daniel and Father went out to milk our cows.

"Make sure we still have five, Samuel, and they have not butchered one, or one of the pigs!" grumbled Mother.

Father grunted something about having to mend the vegetable garden as well, before they could even go up to look to the sheep. Mother sent me with fresh bandages and hot water to see to the wounded men and loaded Lizzie a basket of loaves for the officers to distribute among their men.

I wrapped myself in my heavy cloak and crossed the yard, keeping my eyes down. The soldiers stood in twos and threes, some arguing, some slouched against the house wall. Throughout the orchard campfires smoked and men huddled close to the feeble flames. Some snapped more branches off our apple and our cherry trees in a useless attempt to improve the heat.

Some shouted rude things as I walked past, earning a rebuke from the captain with the brown curls.

Daniel and the farm boys went off to Oxley Fields, already setting about the last of the harvest cutting. Father was in the piggery. I looked over the wall.

"This is not your usual job,"

"I'm not letting them out grubbing today," he said. "Don't want those troopers too close to them in case I find we have one

16

less by nightfall and they dine right royally on our roasted pork." It was a mirthless joke, but I smiled at him sympathetically.

How he hated all these men raiding our land, whichever side they were from.

As I turned back to the house, now yellow in the midday autumn sun on the Cotswold stone, I thought how much I loved Netherfold with its honey walls, its rib of blue lias, the cut pillars of the window edgings, and the grand tall chimneys.

We were friendly with our neighbours opposite: The Wallaces in the Smithy with my friend Miriam and her brothers and sisters, Matt and Will, Rosie and Tamsin; The Waywells in the dairy and further down, towards Lane End Manor Farm, the glovemakers, hatters, shoemakers' cottages and Isaac Lee, the carpenter.

The Rose Bush stood in the centre of the front street and the other tavern, The Waggoners Inn, stood on the crossroads. There, where Simon Morton, the landlord and his wife Leah lived is where I would have lived with Jack when we married. I was betrothed to Jack Morton when I was seventeen but he joined the militia and was killed in his very first battle. How much I cried. The memory of that time was still painful.

"What you got there for me my lass?" A rough voice interrupted my thoughts.

"I'm off to change the dressings of the wounded men," I said without looking at him, pushing against the barn door.

He stretched his arm in front of me. "It's not a broken man, you need, my bonny, it's a good strong un' like me." He pushed his face up close to mine, grinning, showing only one tooth in his upper jaw and one tooth beneath it. Repulsive! I could smell his breath.

"Move aside. I have instructions."

"Oh-ho! Instructions, is it? And who is your *in-struck-shuns* from, lassie, eh?"

17

"Your Colonel!" I snapped at him, unable to remember the officer's name, but it was enough, the toothless soldier let me pass into the barn.

There were ten men now lying in the straw or leaning against the wall. Some stared ahead in silence. Some nursed their wounded limbs. Some rolled about, groaning. There was no one to attend them but me. I took a breath.

The two from yesterday needed their blood-soaked dressings changed and several others had obviously arrived through the night. Not even sure all of them would survive, I did my best to clean wounds and spread the ointment-pads and make them drink the sleeping drafts. My mother came to the two in most pain and dosed them with her crushed poppy seed-potion which deadened pain and let them sleep. That was the best we could do for them. It was our last task of an exhausting day.

At supper Lizzie voiced what was on all our minds: "How long do you think—"

"Be quiet, Lizzie!" my mother snapped. "Don't vex us with useless questions. Your father and I know no better than you do how long they will be here."

"Or if they'll be the last," concluded Daniel. "Eat your supper."

That night in bed Lizzie and I did not have our usual talking time. I could not stop picturing the bloody bandages and flesh-torn cuts and my poor sister hated having so much unpleasant work to do instead of her usual cooking and sewing and copywriting. She liked to read aloud the bible stories sometimes, while we sewed or to listen while my mother told us stories of her girlhood and how things had changed.

Before I blew out the candle, I caught sight of my reflection in the metal mirror. My mouse-brown hair hung, bedraggled about my face. I was too tired to brush it. My eyes were almost black with gloom. Normally I prided myself on my pleasing looks, but tonight I felt scraggy and hunched. All bones. I blew out the candle and tried to warm my feet against my sister's body but she kicked me away. We were all out of spirits. 'Bring on sleep.' I thought.

The cockerels woke me and the neighbour's dogs began their din. Men outside shouted across the yard and I could smell my mother's early bread.

I put on extra clothes and stockings against the Autumn chill and splashed my face and hands. I brushed my hair and covered it with a clean white work cap and was ready to go down.

"Lizzie! Come on! Get up to help."

"Leave me alone, I'm still asleep," she whined and pulled the blankets over her head. I pulled them off in one sweep and draped them over the back of the chair. She called me an ugly name but got up anyway, so I left her and went down to share the chores.

My mother was kneading a vast lump of dough for the soldiers. My father and Daniel were already out among the beasts, and I could smell more bread cooking in the hot oven.

"You must have started early," I said.

"I want to have things ready before they start asking, so I don't get flustered and angry. We want as quiet a life as possible. Take that basket up to Oxley Fields. There's bread, cheese and ham for Father, your brother and the lads. Don't let the soldiers see what you're carrying, or they'll have it off you. When you come back I'll have finished here and we can do the wounded men together."

I set off for Oxley Fields. I could see our neighbours also had soldiers billeted on them. Again. Two years of civil war. Not that it was civil at all. Acrimonious and bloody. Quarrels at every side. Over religion, over the King's Right or Parliament's Right so Father said. It was all about the life in London, I thought, far away from Bournbroke and Netherfold – until they came clattering up our front street and onto our land.

Daniel said we were in the unluckiest place because our crossroads led south to Oxford, and west to Worcester where the

King had his headquarters, but also north and east to Stratford, Warwick and Coventry where the Parliament had theirs.

The first real fighting we heard of was what Daniel called a skirmish, outside of Evesham. My Jack was there. That was when the troops began riding all over the county, camping in gardens and raiding houses.

"I never thought to see a civil war in England again," said Father, "after King James's settled time, when your mother and I were children."

"So, what have they got to fight about now? I thought they fought wars against foreign people, invaders."

"Politics, Lizzie. It's about who has the right to rule." Daniel picked up his news from the broadsheet readers in the towns.

"Whatever the rights and wrongs of it, we are right in the middle of it, here in Bournbroke with our crossroads," Father said.

We had tried our best to protect Netherfold but could not stop them trampling over our planting and our hard work. Disgruntled Parliament men came and went, stragglers and complainers; all millstones about our necks. Now the King's men were here with their bonfires and their bleeding and their demanding ways. We were occupied again.

From Three Corners of the World

This England never did, nor ever shall
Lie at the proud foot of a conqueror
But when it first did help to wound itself....
Come the three corners of the world to arms.
'King John': William Shakespeare

The harvest was almost in. We hurried to hide our stores from the wandering soldier bands as they rode in and squatted in our village, Parliament men and Royalists.

One day Daniel and Father came back from the flour mill, full of the news they had gathered.

"Sir Carlton Trentham is dead. Killed in a skirmish at Worcester. They brought his body back to Beauchamps Hall strapped over his horse."

"Mercy on him for a good man," Mother said, "and his wife left now with that big estate to manage and the children and his aged parents living there as well, I heard."

"They're rich, though, aren't they?" Lizzie asked. "Beauchamps is a big estate. It has been in that family for generations. They collect rents, they have sheep, crops, everything."

"She is a kind woman," Mother went on, "But a Catholic family like theirs has to pay heavy fines and she has two daughters to find dowries for and Thomas Trentham, the son, is away fighting for the King. Your friend, Will Franks is the steward there, though, Samuel, is he not?"

"Yes. We often eat together at the markets. He's a fair man. Works hard," Father said. "I like him."

"The soldier-gangs will be bound to push their way all over there, though," Lizzie almost gloated. "Roasting a whole sheep or two and making beds all over their great hall. Better pickings there than them bothering us here, I would say."

"The King's men might leave her alone," said Father, "Once they know Sir Carlton fought and died on their side and that young Thomas is still under the standard, they will realise she's one of their own."

"She's good to her tenants, though, from what I hear. I am sorry for her trouble, Samuel. When is the funeral to be?"

"Been and gone already at Throstleford, with that St. John's priest that keeps to the old prayer book."

"Catholic priest, some say, just teetering this side of the law. Our Minister Barnes denounces churches and priests like that. I don't care for his ranting, Samuel, I'd rather go to service at St. Etheldreda's in Plovers Hill, even if it is not our parish. Old Vicar Page is a moderate man."

My father stood up. "Time for work. Come, Daniel, let us get on. We have had this matter out before, Sarah. It eats up too much time to walk there and back every time. Just keep your prayers private inside yourself and don't listen to Minister Barnes too closely. I don't."

A week of pleasant autumn sunshine followed. Our trees glowed amber and gold. There was the last warmth of the year in the sun and Lizzie and I were set on raking the piled manure onto the garden to renew the soil after the trampling and plunder. Lizzie, however, was leaning against her rake gazing up into the face of a Royalist soldier who had been sharpening swords with no great energy. He actually touched her cheek and she just stood there, smiling.

"Lizzie! Lizzie! Come over here!"

She glared over to me and did not move. I threw down my shovel and dashed over to her. "Come away, girl! You have no business with these men. If Father sees you…"

"You fuss too much. We were just chatting. He likes me."

"Likes you? He 'likes' any creature in a skirt you silly girl. Just stay away from them!"

The commander of the troop came out of the barn and strode across to the soldier. He ordered him to collect the swords and store them in the barn, his face as furious as mine.

"You stay away from the women of the family here!" he shouted. He looked me directly in the eye, glared at Lizzie and moved off into the barn again.

I bustled Lizzie back to her spreading rake and shovelled more manure over the soil.

"Get busy, or I'll tell Mother what I've just seen." She muttered something rude in my direction but got back to work.

At midday the men began to gather at our door, waiting for the basket of loaves my mother would bring out. My sister and I took the tools back to the shed and went to wash our hands in the basin kept outside.

"Hoy! You there! Bring that to me!" Mother dumped the bread basket and stalked over to a soldier who was coming out of the storeroom with a barrel of salt pork.

"You put that down at once! I have just salted that meat. It is not ready to eat and while I might be glad to see you choke on raw meat, I want that for my own family for the winter."

The soldier still held the barrel fast and looked at my mother as though she had not spoken. She whacked his arm. "Give it back, Sir. Now."

The commander, hearing the noise, looked out of the barn.

"What now, Mistress? I have given orders that the family is not to be interfered with. What is the matter?"

"We have given you everything you have asked for and you have taken more. You have taken possession of this smallholding and whatever we produce for scant payment and no thanks. That meat is not yet fit to eat but neither is it yours to take. I want you off our land, but since I cannot force you out, I expect you, Sir, to put your men under some discipline."

"You are an angry woman, mistress. Take care your waspish tongue does not carry you too far in impudence against me. My discipline needs no advice from you."

"Exercise it, then, for I do not see it here today."

She turned back to the house, leaving the bread basket, now empty, on the ground. The commander looked at me. "Your father has a shrew for a wife, I think. Daley!" he addressed his lieutenant who stood alongside, "Pay the people a few shillings."

Lieutenant Daley threw the coins on the ground at my feet and followed Colonel Calcotton into the apple orchard where the troops were cooking stew over a bonfire, singeing the boughs above it.

I picked up the coins, rinsed them in the water basin and dried them on my apron. Lizzie followed me into the house. Mother was heating pottage for our meal, clattering the ladle angrily against the side of the pot.

"The Colonel sent you this money." Mother looked at the coins in my hand.

"Hmph! Three days' wages for the likes of your brother. Does he think that will suffice for all these men have taken from us? Well, put it in the chest and eat. I'm heating a pot for your father and Daniel, Lizzie. As soon as you have finished, carry it up to Oxley Fields with bread and cheese. And mind you hurry. They won't want it cold."

She was badly rattled by her words with the Royalist commander. Mother was usually the peacemaker in the house. She was seldom goaded to anger herself.

"You can finish the muck-spreading, Alice. Have you much more to do?" I shook my head. "Then you can come in here and we'll get ahead with bread-making for tomorrow. And you, Lizzie, when you are back, gather more herbs for the medicines and salves. The wounds are still infected, I'm afraid. I think that fellow will have to lose his hand."

"You'll never cut it off, Mother!" Lizzie was aghast.

"No. They will have to find a surgeon for that job. It's beyond me."

So, the day went on, full of work and ill-temper.

Across the road, our neighbours grew resentful too. They stood at their doors in hostile knots. Quarrels and fights broke out between soldiers and the village men. Matt Wallace and his father, at the Smithy wrestled two of them to the ground when they tried to walk off without paying for the shoeing of their horses. George Wallace fared badly and had two teeth knocked out and a blackened eye.

A few days later I was in the henhouse when I heard my father shout, enraged. I came out to see him run, faster than he had ever moved, across the yard to grab that same, blond-curled King's man I had seen flirting with Lizzie. He was at it again, even more blatantly, grappling with my sister trying to kiss her mouth. Father lunged himself at the man and threw him sideways into the manure heap. Lizzie staggered, gasping," Father, father—I—I didn't—"

"Get in!" He shoved her towards the house and dragged the trooper to his feet. "Lay hands on my daughter, would you? I will thrash you, sir!"

He slapped his face this way and that with his huge, open hand. The soldier grabbed my father by the throat, shoving him against the wall. I leaped forward, grabbed the straw-fork and cracked it down across his back. He yelled and turned on me as Father crumpled to the ground.

Colonel Calcotton and his two lieutenants raced out of the stable and seized him. I helped my father to stand. He coughed and spluttered, his lip cut and bleeding.

"He will not touch a girl of mine, Colonel. I warn you. You have seized our food and the use of our land but by God you— he —will not seize my daughter's virtue! I will kill him, sure."

"Don't make threats, Yeoman! You would not want to be accused of rebellion against the forces of the King."

"The forces of the King, Sir, would not want to be accused of rape, but I will broadcast it far and wide if this goes on. See to your discipline, Sir, or get off my land and we will furnish you with nothing more. Nothing, do you hear?"

"A threat you cannot sustain, Yeoman," smirked Calcotton's lieutenant.

Before my father could say any more, I gripped his arm and led him towards the house. As I turned to close and bar the door, I saw Colonel Calcotton take out his gauntlet and strike my sister's attacker across the face with such a force he staggered backwards. I did not hear whatever orders the colonel issued, but he was furious too.

It never crossed my parents' minds that Lizzie had flirted with the soldier, encouraging him to think she might be easy. I had watched her loosening the curls from under her cap to fall in alluring wisps. I saw her, more than once, giggling and flashing her eyes his way. What a fool she was.

I shoved Lizzie in the house and bolted us in.

She turned on me. "You always have to interfere in my life! You are not my mother, Alice. You have no right to keep telling me what and what not to do. You are just sour because no one will ask to marry you now Jack Morton is gone. You are too much of a plain-faced goody-goody. You are like one of Minister Barnes' Puritans, all prim and seeing sin and wickedness in everyone!"

"Have you even heard of rape, Lizzie! Have you not heard Daniel's stories about soldiers lying with local girls by force and leaving them saddled with a child they don't want, abandoned, rejected by their families? Is that what you want for yourself? Because you are going about it the right way. That is exactly what was on that soldier's mind for you. He would ride you like a bull to a cow and ruin you for life."

"You never even spoke to him before. You don't know what he's like. He was sweet to me, he never had rough hands or –"

"You are a fool, Girl! You know nothing about such men, who speak one way and act another."

"Oh, and you do, do you? Did Jack Morton ride you like a bull, then? Did you not like it?"

I was on the point of slapping her when my mother came in.

26

"For God's Sake, you girls! You are screaming like tavern women. Lizzie get upstairs! Alice, get down and scrape out the ashes. I want to get the bread bowl on the hearth. Get on, both of you!"

I cried tears of rage to myself and I have no doubt Lizzie was up there crying for herself. This is what invading soldiers can do, cause trouble wherever they are.

"I think, Mother," I said that night, after Lizzie had gone to bed, "we had better keep Lizzie to do jobs inside the house until these soldiers leave. She is at a silly age, wanting to have sweethearts and such."

My mother narrowed her eyes and was about to ask me for my reasons but Father came in and she clearly wanted to avoid more upset so she left it at that.

On market day Father left for Shipscarden to buy a new ram, grumbling we could ill afford it, but we needed another. He set off in no better mood than yesterday, saying no goodbyes to any of us.

Lizzie and I were busy with kitchen work when he came back, full of news for my mother.

"I saw Will Franks at the market. His sister Nell's been taken badly to bed in early labour. Not married. You'll have heard."

"I heard Will Franks's sister had been abandoned." Mother said. "She's ill with it, then?"

"Will can't manage her all by himself so I have offered Alice to go over there to nurse her and Lizzie can go with her to be a help."

"What!" I heard my sister yelp and slam down her chopping knife. "No, Father! I am not going over there to listen to sick people raving and screaming. Let Alice go herself. Anyway, they've got servants of their own. Why do we need to go?"

"Because I tell you to, my girl."

Heaven knows I did not want to go to nurse a sick and shamed girl myself, but I knew this was no time to challenge my father's decisions. I suspected Mother had told him of my suspicion that Lizzie was misbehaving with the Royalists.

"You're already sending Alice over there, I don't want to go and anyway, Mother will need me here if she has to do without Alice about the house. Mother can't do everything herself; I'm not going. Not!"

Father ignored her outburst and spoke only to Mother. "I have already spoken to George Wallace to send you his lass, Sarah. She doesn't do much at the smithy. Tansy can manage over there. Rosie and young Tamsin can help their mother."

"As long as it's Miriam, not Rosie or her young sister." Mother accepted Father's arrangements as she always did.

"You'll train her up. She'll be more use to her mother when they get her back."

"Dare say." Mother banged the tankards on the table, the only sign she was not happy with the changes to our family ways. She glared at Lizzie.

"This all comes from you, fool-girl!"

Lizzie stamped off upstairs, crying ostentatiously to punish Father, but also because she knew Mother was right and because she was ashamed the running of the household was to be so upset. Nor, of course, did she want to come to Beauchamps, sick-nursing at a childbed with me.

Our evening meal was tense. Lizzie sulked. Father and Mother were each in a bad mood. Daniel was grumpy because he did not want to interrupt his work to drive us over to Beauchamps and I resented having no choice about going to nurse Will Franks' sister, however nice father's friend was.

"Alice, follow me out," said Father, after supper. We walked through the orchard and sat on the log seat. He took my hand. "I know this is not your choice, my girl, and of course I am using Will's difficulty as a means to the end of removing your foolish sister from that Royalist mischief-maker, but there is more to my thinking. Sir Carlton Trentham's death gives Will more responsibility than he had before. He says Lady Abigail is a clever and determined woman, well used to taking charge of business matters, but she is struck with grief. The family are at constant risk because they are Catholics and while these armed bands are roaming the Vale claiming quarter hither and yon, they are wary of who might come upon them. Now, Will says he discovered his sister Nell lying in the tavern where she worked, alone and sickly. He wants to do right by all his duties and I am eager to help him and, as I have told him, protect the virtue of my daughters from that popinjay."

I kissed his whiskery cheek. "I understand. I know you are right about moving Lizzie, moving us both if it comes to that."

"At Beauchamps there are many more men on hand to defend you if incoming troopers should try any more of their lascivious tricks."

Lizzie knew better than to cause more argument and next morning, in the dark, she and I made up our clothes-bundles. Mother packed us baskets of bread, cheese, a minced pork pie and a ham to give to Will.

"The man is doing his best for his poor sister in her trouble," she said. "Many a brother would have thrown her out. He deserves a little kindness, I think."

She gave me a rough-hewn box full of salves and herb oils from her store of summer-making, together with some bunches of dried herbs should we need to make more.

"This is especially good to help bring sleep, you might use lots. And this," she held up a stoppered horn. "And this."

"Just give a sip every four hours of or so, for dulling pain. Don't give it too frequently or it will cause vomiting."

"What about the wounded soldiers? There's so much to do for them, how will you manage on your own?"

"Our own neighbours come first. Even if Nell Franks has been caught up in sin, Will is your father's friend. We have done our duty by these soldiers in common humanity but they betray our hospitality rather than give thanks, as we have seen." She glared at Lizzie again.

We packed the strips of bandage we had made from old linen shifts and folded thick pads to absorb blood. She warned me there would be a lot of bleeding from the birth channel if Nell's labour went badly and she would need to be washed and changed like a baby herself for several weeks, if she lived.

None of this made me any happier about doing this nursing or leaving home, but reluctant as I was to look after a stranger, and face all her suffering and blood I would, of course, do what my father told me to do. We climbed into the market cart and set off for the crossroads, anxious about what might lie ahead at the Hall.

Sir Carlton Trentham had been well respected throughout the Vale by yeomen landowners like my father. He had never stood on rank and met all his neighbours in a bluff and friendly way. Father had liked him, even though he, and Sir Sheldon Norton, who owned the adjacent estates around Shipscarden Magna and Plovers Hill were Catholics and supporters of King Charles. Religious differences did not bother us all here, as far as I had ever heard, however hotly such things were debated elsewhere.

My father and Will Franks often met at the market tradings, enjoying their pies and beer together, listening to the news sheets being read out in the taverns. Sometimes Father brought broadsheets home for us to see. That was how we learned about the quarrels between our rulers, the outcomes of their battles, the shifts of their fortunes in Coventry or Warwick, Oxford or Worcester, Parliament or crown. We did not escape the fighting in the end.

"Nothing civil about civil war!" Father used to say. "Violence and vandalism! It's the opposite of everything Will and I give our time to. We plant and nurture. These armed bands gallop about stealing and despoiling, undoing everything we have done."

'And I had been widowed before I had even been wived', I thought. Lizzie and I sat through the whole ride in gloomy silence.

We turned in to the estate road and Daniel drove the cart to Will's gate house. It was a pretty stone cottage with glass in the downstairs windows.

Will came out extending his hand to Daniel, then held out his arms and helped Lizzie and me down from the cart. We carried our bundles into the house. Will and Daniel unloaded everything Mother had sent while I prepared some of our fresh bread and cheese for us before Daniel left for home.

The room was small but the fire was bright enough. The floor needed a change of rushes and the hearth needed a good sweeping and several dangling cobwebs in the beam-corners needed to be brushed away. It was obvious Will had no time to be a housewife on top of all his other work.

"Come and look at Nell." He led me up the narrow stairs and I could hear her moaning before I saw her, her legs restlessly stirring the bed from side to side. Her hair was knotted and bunched round her head, her face grey and slippery with sweat.

"Has the apothecary seen her?"

"Lady Abigail said I could send for him, she would pay, but Nell wasn't so ill as this then, I thought we would manage with the kitchen girls. Then your father offered your help. It was good of him and of both of you."

Lizzie hmphed. I frowned at her.

"Will you see to her, Alice? I have so much estate work to do."

"How long has she been like this?"

"At least a week. Moll Newby the landlady of The Green Man Tavern where Nell worked sent to tell me to take her away because she was sick. She did not say that Nell was expecting a child. By the time I got there Nell was restless and incoherent, obviously in pain. She couldn't stop crying." He frowned at the memory. "I scooped her up and brought here. It was an uncomfortable ride for her. By the time we got here she had lost a lot of blood. I was frightened. Anne Carey came down to tend to her. She made her more comfortable but couldn't get her to take even soup. I thought she would die then. I still fear she will, but I want somebody, you I hope, to at least lessen her pain."

"I'll do everything my mother has taught me, Will. We will do the best we can, I promise."

"Thank you, Alice, whatever you can. Tell me if there is anything you need." He bent and took Nell's senseless hand, kissed it and lay it gently down. "I'll get on now." He looked at me with a sad smile and left us.

I sent Lizzie down to sweep the hearth and clean the room, put water on to boil and fetch me a bowl to wash myself and Nell.

I turned down the bedclothes and my stomach heaved. Nell was drenched in blood from waist to knees. I hardly knew where to start.

"Ugh! Horrible" Lizzie whispered from behind me, peering at the mess.

"Put that bowl down, bring the chest of medicines upstairs, stoke the fire so we can have more hot water and see if you can find some clean bedclothes from somewhere—and a cup."

I spoke abruptly but it was the only way I could get on. If I stopped to think too closely about what I needed to do I might be as squeamish as my sister, and not be able to do anything at all.

I dragged Nell's shift wide open and eased it away from her belly then loosened all the blood-soaked sheeting from around the mattress and drew it away from the bed on to the floor. The straw in the mattress would need to be changed too but I could not lift Nell by myself.

As soon as Lizzie came back with the chest, I took out some fresh cloth and washed Nell's body as thoroughly as I could until the first basin of water was deep red. I wrapped her loins in a napkin with a thick linen pad in it as Mother had instructed. Lizzie came back with fresh hot water.

"Look around for another straw mattress," I said. "Take it off Will 's bed if you must. He can make fresh ones when he comes in. Be quick. She's chilling."

I found a clean shift in a pile of clothes on a table by the window, which I pulled carefully over her head. It was a struggle to pull the sleeves over her lifeless arms, but I did it. I decided I would leave the rest of it up around her belly rather than pull it under her in case it got blood-soaked again before we could wash or find more. I arranged the blankets loosely over her to keep her warm then turned my mind to making her a pain-soothing draught.

I looked at the horn with its thick stopper. It was for soothing pain but Mother warned me not to dose her with it too often. I did not want to make her vomit on top of all her other troubles.

I made up the drink with drops stirred into ale and lifted her head. The liquid dribbled down her chin, so I lowered her head on to the pillow and opened her lips with my fingers, dripping the medicine in a few drops at a time.

Lizzie staggered in dragging a mattress and waited while I dribbled as much of the mixture into Nell as I could. She choked and coughed and spat it out. This was no good.

Leaving that aside, Lizzie and I struggled to get the mattress on the bed frame, shoving it as near to Nell as it would go, then rolling her body, while she cried out in pain, then rolling her back on to the straw and dragging it the other way until she was roughly straight in the clean bed.

"Is the baby still in her?" Lizzie asked.

"I don't know. She still looks swollen, but Will didn't say. We'll have to work as though it is until he comes home." I straightened up. "Lift her shoulders so I can drop some medicine into her." I dripped the medicine down a strip of linen as I had seen mothers do with babies. Drop by drop it went into Nell's mouth as Lizzie tilted back Nell's head. Although she gagged at it, she swallowed some. I hoped it was enough to give her ease.

I washed my own hands and went downstairs to find a laundry bowl. There was one outside the door beside the well, which I lugged back upstairs and loaded all the blood- soaked linens in and carried it down again.

Outside I filled the bowl with water near the well to soak overnight. Tomorrow I would go up to the kitchen at the big house and get a soap ball and some lye to wash it all. Drying it in this weather would, however, be another thing.

Back upstairs, Lizzie stood as far away from the bed as she could looking at Nell tossing and turning, muttering words we could not make out. I decided my sister would be happier running up and down fetching things than standing there looking aghast so I gave her another string of instructions.

I was laying a fire in the small fireplace when Nell screamed. I ran across and took her hand.

"You are safe, Nell, I'm here. We've come to help you."

Her eyes shot open. She gave me a terrified look. "The baby!" she cried. "My baby! Oh, the baby. Where's the baby, where is he? Will! Will, where is he?"

Her cries grew to screams. I struggled to hold her down as she tried to get out of the bed, then she fell back, limp. Another spasm of pain gripped her. I reached for the pain-dulling medicine.

"Here, Nell, some more of this, it will take the pain away. Drink it."

She resisted, spitting it out but I persisted, hoping some of it would reach the centre of her pain.

How I wished my mother was with us. I wished I knew more. I wished someone—anyone—else was in charge of this poor woman and her distress.

We carried the tub of bloody linen outside near the well and filled it with cold water. I pounded it with a nearby log until the water was the colour of whole blood.

"I'm going to be sick," moaned Lizzie.

"No, you're not. We have enough to do. Just look away. Send the bucket down for fresh water. I'll tip this out. Just mind your feet."

I tipped the reddened water out and watched it seep away into the earth. We filled the tub again and swished the linen round.

"We'll let it stand all night and take it up to the laundry stuff at the big house to get them properly clean."

We went back in and I sent Lizzie upstairs to watch over Nell, with instructions she should shout for me if she grew restless or called out again. I set about chopping vegetables for a pot and some chunks of Mother's ham. I mixed some dough and left it in the hearth to prove and sat down for a rest. I could not imagine where we were going to sleep or what more we could do to help poor Nell. When Will came back, we would have to sit down, all three of us and make our plans. Above all I needed to know if Nell's baby was still inside her or already dead and gone. If, in my ignorance, I had to deliver it, I would need advice.

I built up the fire as it grew dark to make a welcome place for Will after his work as Mother always tried to do for Daniel and my father. I left Lizzie up there to watch Nell, now she was calmer and I prepared our meal. As soon as he came home, Will went upstairs to see his sister.

"She is quieter," he said, "You must have eased her pain. I am grateful to you. I'm sure Nell will be too when she recovers."

I made him some mulled beer and served him his supper and we discussed the arrangements of the household and whatever extra needs we had.

"I'll take my supper upstairs and watch Nell," I said. "Lizzie has been up there a long time while I've been cooking. She can take the bread up to the kitchen oven and ask Mistress Carey if she can come down to give me some advice in case I have to deliver the baby. I've never—"

"Nell has already given birth to the baby, Alice. It died."

"Oh, then why is her belly still so big? I need to ask. I am shocked by my own ignorance, Will. Mistress Carey must explain everything about childbirth, well its complications, at least."

"Have you never seen it at home? I suppose you were too young to be there when young Lizzie there was born."

"Yes, I was only four."

"And your brother's wife, their babies— too far away, I suppose. They live in Bristol, don't they?"

"Oh, we haven't seen them since their betrothal when he first brought Susan to meet us all. And it is the same with our older sister, Martha. She has four children but I haven't seen her since her wedding either. I was never there at any of the family birthings. I only know about childbirth in general. Mother never described things in detail. I have seen the animals, of course, piglets, lambing, but that is not enough for me to help Nell."

"I'll make sure Anne Carey comes down to talk to you tomorrow. Don't be too anxious about your ignorance, Alice, all you or any of us can do is try. I'm just glad you came."

He leaned over and stirred the fire. "I have resigned myself to the fact that it is hopeless, that Nell will die. All that bleeding, the fever, her mad confusion. She has been desperate, I think, since the man she said she loved left her." He shook his head. "She was too trusting. Such a fool."

"Surely not wicked, though, as the preachers say. Steeped in sin and such. She told you she loved him."

"I suppose she did. We never talked much. She left the Trentham estate for The Green Man in Hampden. She had a room there. I was Old Sir Felix Trentham's apprentice then. He held the baronetcy with this Beauchamps estate as well the manor at Cheyne St. Paul. When Sir Carlton married Lady Abigail, Sir Felix gave them this place as their home and they brought me up from Oxfordshire with them. I left Nell behind. Perhaps if I had stayed there I would have seen what was happening and prevented her from being seduced. Working in that tavern exposed her to the wrong sort of men—and she was so young. I blame myself. I should have brought her with me. She could have worked here."

He stared into the fire, lost in thought.

"Perhaps Nell was like Lizzie—and would have refused to take notice of you. My sister enjoyed flirting with that soldier who molested her, you know. He made her feel like a woman, and pretty. She is not cautious enough around men. She said she liked his fancy curled hair and his London way of speaking. Perhaps Nell was like that."

Will looked up at me. "What makes you cautious of men, Alice?"

"Some men look at you with an avid look, greedy and with something smirking about the eyes and mouth."

"I must watch my smiles then, for fear I appear to smirk."

I grinned at him and his honest, not too frequent smile then took my share of the stew and went upstairs to relieve my sister.

Nell looked white and chill. I felt her face and wondered if she was already dead, but her breath still rose and fell, although shallow and uneven. I ate my supper and, once finished, rolled back the bed clothes and collected the bowls to change and wash Nell again.

The bleeding was less, which I was relieved to see. I made her comfortable, wrapped her covers close and took clean water to wash her face and hands. I tried to make her drink some hot posset to increase her strength, but she kept her lips tight shut so I gave up. I drank it myself, rather than have it go to waste. I might need strengthening myself before the night was out.

Lizzie and I slept in Will's chamber, while he made up a straw mattress and slept in the downstairs room. That way we were able to take turns to sleep or to sit with Nell through the night.

Lizzie was upstairs watching over Nell after breakfast while I sat at the window stitching when there was a knock at the door. Lady Trentham stood there with Mistress Carey behind her.

"You must be Alice Sanderson," she said. I made my curtsey and held the door open for her. "Unpack the basket, Anne." She sat in Will 's chair by the fire and looked around. "Will tells us you need some talk with Mistress Carey here, so I will leave her with you. But tell me, how is Will 's sister?"

"In great pain, My Lady, and still bleeding. I am afraid I have not been able to do more than calm her a little. "

"Will tells me your medicines and your care have eased the burden on Nell and on Will himself. I am very fond of him. He has been with my family since I first came here."

"He is a friend of my father's too. We were happy to be able to help him."

"Where did you learn your skill with the herbal mixes and the nursing? From your mother?"

"Yes. She has a way with sickness, how to soothe and how to make effective treatments. My grandmother passed on her book of herbal recipes. My sister and I are copying our own."

"You have been taught to read and write?"

"Indeed, yes. My mother was taught and considered it useful for a woman to be able to support a husband's trade or, in our case, help manage our holding."

She heaved a deep sigh. "She is wise. Since my husband and my son left to fight, I have had to take over responsibility for the estate management. Will's stewardship is essential to me. I could not manage without him. So, you see help for his sister helps me too in the way of things." She looked around the room. "You are a good cook too. Your stew there smells delicious. And I see you are sewing. May I see?"

I brought her the shirt of Will 's that I was stitching.

"Are you mending this?"

"No, My Lady. The cloth was cut ready but it was unmade. It is for a Sunday shirt."

Lady Trentham examined the seams and the Spanish black work I was embroidering at the collar.

"But this is really beautiful work, Alice. You sew a fine needle. How did you learn the black work pattern? Was that from your grandmother too?"

"From Grandmother to my Mother, but Mother says I inherited my grandmother's fine touch. She gave me these." I showed her the pouch of sewing materials I had brought with me, including a precious silver thimble and the stitch-designs Grandmother had made and preserved."

"My, these designs are lovely. Even Elizabeth and Isabella cannot sew as well as this. And I have four thumbs, I'm afraid."

"You have an entire estate to run, My Lady. I imagine that does not leave you with a deal of leisure."

"You are right. I am responsible for my parents in law here, too. My father-in-law is almost blind and Lady Eliza is increasingly frail. I fear the time is coming when I would be relieved to have a permanent nurse-apothecary living with us. I might ask you to become one of my women one of these days, Alice. If your mother could spare you."

I thanked her. To work here appealed to me more than raking manure over Netherfold garden plots.

"See here." Lady Trentham stood up and crossed to the table. "Mistress Carey has brought you a share of our coming feast up at the house. There are some spiced meat pies and roasted duck and a jar of plums in wine. I hope you will enjoy them, even if poor Nell cannot join you. I will walk back now. I will leave Mistress Carey to give you her advice."

"Mistress Carey, I know about animals, but hardly anything about women."

"I have seen times when childbirth goes wrong, I mean, the sufferings that can befall women, but I have never heard any midwife or apothecary explain why. You know when Will brought Nell up here and we unwound her linens, so foul-smelling they were—" She shook her head, remembering, "Some midwife or someone down in that tavern had strapped a tiny, shrivelled suckling piglet to her belly! Old wives' nonsense— witchery more like. I do know that whoever attends a birthing must make sure everything within comes out, or fever follows. I think it is this fever that is bringing her down."

"Perhaps grieving for her dead child adds to her suffering. Poor Nell."

After Mistress Carey left I felt I had learned little new, but that few others knew more. I made up my mind that I would make it my business to join my mother attending births when I went home, and by observing, learn what I could. Ignorance was a dangerous thing.

After Mistress Carey left and we had bathed and changed Nell, I told Lizzie that Lady Trentham might want me to stay on at Beauchamps.

"Well, I do not want to stay here. I want to go home to my own friends. There is no fun here. Everyone is too serious. You only want to stay because you will be in the big house mixing with fine ladies and get closer to Will Franks."

I slammed the ladle down and turned on her.

"You need not glower at me like that, I have seen how you look at him. You are sweet on Will Franks."

"That is enough, Lizzie! Your head is far too full of flirting with men. It is all you think about. You are too flighty and stupid! And be careful because this—" I gestured to where Nell lay, "—can be where it can lead you!"

It was a cruel thing to say, and I was sorry for it as soon as the words were out. Lizzie gave me a shocked look and ran down the stairs.

I tried to give Nell more poppy draught but she swallowed none. I sat down to watch her with a heavy heart.

I went down to make our evening meal. My sister went up to take my place, saying nothing to me. When Will came home I showed him the fine foods Mistress Carey and Lady Trentham had brought us.

"What is this?" I asked. "Why all this special food just for us?"

"What day is it, Alice? Think on?"

It was the beginning of December tomorrow. That was all I knew.

"Advent. The family has a feast here because as Catholics they fast up to Christmas. They invite all of the staff to join in meal. Normally I join them all for the feasting but I told them I should stay here, close to Nell," he paused, "and you. This is our share."

Nell was feverish and restless but Lizzie and I succeeded in helping her swallow some of the mixture while Ned spoke to her in gentle tones and at last she became quieter. We felt able to leave her for a while and sit together by the fire. Will had laid out the Advent food to add to the pottage I had made and he served us some mulled ale. None of us had the heart to be exactly merry, but we enjoyed what we ate and drank and told each other stories of happier days.

The hot spiced ale, the good food and the warmth of the flames caused Lizzie's eyes to droop.

"You go up to bed," I said. "If Nell is asleep, I will sit up a while. I will give her a dose of the mixture before I come to bed."

I cleared the supper table then went to look at Nell. Lizzie was already asleep. Nell slept restlessly, her breath coming in shallow snatches. I went back downstairs to mix tomorrow's bread. Will was resting with his feet in the hearth. He poured out the last of the ale between us.

"It is good of you to take all this care of my sister, Alice. It cannot be very pleasant for you. I know it was your father's choice, not yours."

"I will not pretend, Will. I was reluctant to come, but I understood my father. He wanted Lizzie – wanted both of us away from that soldier. It was more than that, though. He often has a brusque manner but he holds friendship and loyalty in high esteem, and he counts you his friend."

41

He nodded. "People would judge Nell harshly, say she was a wanton."

"Not us. My mother agreed with your decision to take her in. She has no truck with sermons about sin and hell and casting the wayward into outer darkness."

"Lady Trentham said the same when I asked her permission to bring Nell here to the gate house. We are fortunate my sister and I, but you are still young and unmarried. It must revolt you to see so much blood and have to clean up a stranger's intimate parts." He looked down.

"We have animals at home, Will. I have seen ewes give birth; calves die. I have, seen cows put to the bull, stallions for stud – I am not ignorant of these matters."

Will laughed. "Well, thank you anyway. Never think I take your, or young Lizzie's efforts for granted. Now, you go to bed and I will clear away."

He took my hand and kissed my fingers, grinning. I grinned back at him but a strike of heat tingled through my arm and warmed me all over.

It was a bitterly cold morning as I walked up to the hall kitchen to collect laundry stuff.

"Sit yourself here by the fire and warm yourself a while," Mistress Carey said. "If you bring Nell's linens up here they can hang to dry in the back of the forge. Dick has rigged up iron drying rails to hang the washing on in the winter."

"Mistress Carey says you do lovely embroidering, Alice." Luce sat beside us. "I want to begin my sewing for my marriage linen. Dick and are to marry. Would you show me how to do some patterns? I could come down to the gate house."

"Yes, lovely. I will enjoy the company, the gossip." We grinned at each other. Suddenly there was a shriek and a clatter from the fireplace. Anne Carey spun round crying, "My hand! I've burnt my hand! Don't touch that pan – the handle! Oh! Oh!"

I jumped to my feet and carried the water pitcher from the window shelf, sloshed some into a basin and thrust Mistress Carey's hand into it. "Leave it in there. Sit down."

Luce and Aimee fussed around her, moving her seat, fetching clean cloths.

"Fill a fresh bowl of cold water. Bring some from outside it will be colder."

"Thank you, Alice. It is easier. You were quick. But the rabbits."

Aimee was already swabbing the spilt stock from the flagstones. "We will see to the rabbits," I said, looking at Luce. She chopped more bones and bits and I filled another pan with water, added some thyme, sage and salt. We set it to boil while Molly cut up the meat for the stew.

It did not take us long to add the vegetables, the pulses, and take the offal away. The rich savoury smell filled the kitchen and Mistress Carey looked more relaxed. She gave me a grateful smile as I left for the gate house, promising Luce my time tomorrow, if Nell was no worse.

Days passed and Nell's crying and calling out faded to whimpers. She no longer threshed about nor even stirred in her bed.

"She seems calmer." Will felt her cheek. "She is not hot now, surely a good sign?"

I was not optimistic. Her eyes seldom opened and if they did, she just stared away at a distant void. I asked Will to fetch Mistress Carey.

"The bleeding is much less," I told her. She shook her head.

"It has gone on for too long, Alice, she is losing strength, not eating or drinking. She is not in her senses, is she?"

Will came in. "I think you should prepare yourself, my dear," she said, her hand on his shoulder. "Your sister is fading away."

"Lady Trentham offered to send for the apothecary. I will go now." He made to leave but Lizzie cried after him. "Don't bring him, Will! Apothecaries bleed people. Nell has lost so much blood. She will not have enough left inside her. He will make her worse—surely, Mistress Carey? Alice?"

"The girl is right, Will. The apothecary will bleed, it is their usage. Nell is too weak to stand it, I swear to you."

"But if he knows that is the right thing to do, Anne, I must try and find him. He will at least advise us."

"Well, you must do as you must, dear. I will pray for her."

Will stood stock still. "Is it come to that?" He looked at me for a reassurance that I could not give.

"Come, girls. We will leave you with her, Will."

We sat together by the fire, waiting. "How is your hand, Mistress Carey? Is it less painful?"

"Bless you, yes, I have changed the dressing every day. I just keep it wrapped against knocks – and the sting of chopping onions. I let the others do the wet work. You were quick to act, Alice."

"I have had to lean on you and your advice, so we are in balance."

"As friends should be, my dear."

Lizzie and I continued taking our turns at Nell's bedside. Her breath whispered in threads as she lay, pale and still. Aimee and Beth came down with Mistress Carey and stood by Nell to pray, taking rosary beads out of concealed pockets in their petticoats. Lizzie and I left them and prepared some hot ale for them before they went back up to the Hall.

"Her Ladyship says she will come down tomorrow. She has sent Will for the apothecary," Anne Carey said.

"But I thought you warned him," Lizzie was shocked.

"Will wanted to go," she replied. "He said he had to try."

It was late when Will came back and flopped into his chair. "I failed," he said. "He had gone to some estate over by Kenilworth, I was too late."

"The others have been here to say prayers for Nell and Lady Trentham is coming tomorrow with her daughters."

44

"Do they expect a miracle? Poor Nell." He covered his face with his hands. I wanted to comfort him but decided he would want to be alone so Lizzie and I crept off upstairs.

Gloomy days followed, heavy with sad expectations. Will sat with his sister while Lizzie and I busied ourselves cooking, cleaning and taking him food he did not eat.

On the third night after his return, Will came up to Nell's bedchamber with fresh logs.

"We have made Lizzie a bed in your parlour, Will. If you want to sit with her, I will leave you or stay, as you like." He nodded and sat down by Nell's bedside, stroking her hair.

"She was such a pretty dancing thing." He was hardly aware he spoke aloud. "My mother taught her old songs from her youth and she would sing and dance for my father and me. He cut a wooden pipe for me and we would play together while she sang. We were happy when we were children. Before the plague came."

"Plague!"

"Our parents died and my—"

"And you went to work for Sir Felix Trentham."

Will sat closed in thought then went on. "At Cheyne St. Paul, yes. But Nell wouldn't stay there. She said the place bored her. My mother's friend, Moll Newby, saw us at the Mop Fair in Oxford and recognised us. When she heard our mother and father were dead she offered Nell that place at The Green Man Inn. I said she was too young, but she wanted to go. 'So many handsome drovers, Will,' she said. I should have known it would end badly. But Moll Newby promised to look after her. I should never have allowed it, Alice. I failed my sister then, and now." His eyes glazed with tears.

"Blaming yourself is useless, Will. Nell told you she would not stay at Cheyne St. Paul with you."

"No. And she would not come with us when Sir Felix married Lady Abigail and they moved up here. I begged her to

45

come but she was adamant. She said that even if I dragged her here she would just run away. I was angry. I called her a stubborn jade and came away. And now this, the baby dead and my happy dancing sister dying before my eyes."

He bent and threw a log on the fire. "You go to bed, Alice, I will sit here."

I woke in a fright. What had I heard? I sat up. The fire was all grey ash. The room was cold. Will was not there. I went over to Nell and she gave a sudden growl which made me jump. That is what woke me. She gave another raking breath, a terrible sound. I ran down the stairs. Will was dozing in the upright chair as the fire blazed and the water boiled.

"Will! Will!" I shook his arm. "Come up! She is worse."

He ran ahead of me and lifted Nell to see if he could ease her breathing. but she sagged in his arms. Her hand fell senseless.at her side She gave out one last long sigh as Will laid her back against the pillow, dead.

I opened the window, went to waken Lizzie and brought a clean white sheet to spread over the poor dead girl. The three of us recited the Lord's Prayer then we left Will to mourn his sister.

"I don't want to sleep in that chamber tonight, Alice, with a dead body in the room. Can't we just go home today? We have done what we were asked to do."

"Dead people can't hurt anyone, Lizzie."

"What about her spirit? That has to escape or something, doesn't it? I don't want to see a ghost."

"Tush! Come here." I put my arms around her. She was, again, that funny little sister of mine who played chase and giggled through our orchard trees. "We will push both our beds close together and spread our blankets over both and we will lie hugged in together tonight and keep each other safe and warm." We both cried, then I took her hand. "Come and look at Nell now. You see how peaceful she is."

46

Will set about the business of Nell's funeral. He rode to Lavrock to make arrangements with the vicar of the National Church there. Apart from his friends up at the hall, he had no one else to tell. Anne Carey came to show me how to lay out a dead body.

Two days later, the estate men came to the gate house with an empty coffin in the waggon. Will, Lizzie and I laid Nell into it and they nailed down the lid. Thud. Thud. A hollow, melancholy blow into Will's heart, and ours, whose work had failed to save her.
We rode to Lavrock church in the waggon, Will resting his hand on the coffin the whole way.

Dick and Luce, Aimee, Beth and Ruth walked behind and Nell was buried alongside the tiny grave of the baby she had lost, with Anne Carey, Lady Trentham, Elizabeth and Isabella standing beside it. And the church bell tolled seventeen times. Nell Franks was buried and mourned by strangers, out of friendship for her brother.

The Bubble of a Robin's Song

When to the sessions of sweet silent thought
I summon up remembrance of things past,
I sigh the lack of many a thing I sought...
But if the while I think on thee, dear friend, All losses
are restor'd and sorrows end.

Sonnet 30: William Shakespeare

After the funeral, Lizzie and I cleared the bedchamber, scrubbed and scented it turning it back into a pleasant room for Will. We carried the laundry up to the wash-house at the hall and while it was boiling we looked in at the kitchen. Everyone there smiled and made room for us at the table.

We sat to warm ourselves and drink the hot posset Molly gave us. I asked about using the laundry room to dry the wet linens and Ruth said she would show me how to heat the hot rails.

"Why do you think Nell Franks died of this baby, Mistress Carey?" my sister asked. "I have been so afraid."

Anne Carey looked at Lizzie and raised her eyebrows.

"Pray go on, Mistress Carey. We have seen things with our animals, but never with women, not so close."

"Oh, don't you be afraid, young miss. Mostly nature just takes its course and babies are squeezed out in their time, albeit with some pain and mess and shouting. There is no escaping the pains. It is God's punishment for Eve's temptation of Adam and our downfall," she said.

"Punishment? For Eve's temptation of Adam?" Lizzie frowned. "Is Nell to blame because she bore this baby without a proper husband? Is that why she suffered so much?"

She looked at me, puzzled. "Is a man not to be punished for behaving so when he has not married himself to his sweet-heart? Whoever he was, he left Nell uncared for. I think he should certainly be punished."

48

"It is the way of the world, I am afraid," said Mistress Carey. "That is why we pray not to be led into temptation."

"You said that childbirth for women can be, as it is with the farm animals we have seen, fraught with complications. It seems to me more a matter of accident at random. Such things are not sent to animals as punishment for sin."

"I cannot explain such things. In the end we must depend on prayer and hope the Blessed Virgin intercedes."

Lizzie took a breath to ask more questions but I gave her a warning look.

"Did any of you meet Nell?" I asked, "Before she fell so ill?"

"No, said Beth. "Will brought her in here that first day while he went to speak to Lady Trentham, but she was utterly exhausted from the journey."

She looked so ill," Aimee added, "She looked as though she had been crying for days and would begin again if we asked her anything."

Molly refilled our cups. "Will said Lady Trentham was happy for Nell to stay with him down at the gate house and would we go there and set fires and warm the bed for her."

Beth went on, "Then two days later Will came up to tell us Nell had gone into labour."

"I went down there," Anne Carey continued, "with Luce and we delivered the baby but it was no use. Nell tried to suckle it. She told me to call it Eleanor after their mother, and I said I would send for the priest, but I knew there was no time. I baptised the babe myself with water from the bedside cup, which I am sure was no sin to do."

"God would understand your kindness, Mistress Carey," I said, "It could only be right."

"Let us have a change from this sad talk," Anne Carey said. "Luce, you said you wanted Alice to teach you some fine stitching."

49

Yes. But I would still love you to show me how to do that Spanish blackwork of yours. I want to make a wedding shirt for Dick, as a gift."

"Yes, let us do that, Luce, whenever we can have some time."

"And are you clever with a needle too, Lizzie?" she asked.

"Oh no, I am bored by stitching. They always give me the long seams. I am no good with fancy stitchery."

"You are modest, Lizzie," I smiled. "Her handwriting is excellent."

Beth looked up. "You have learned to write? Ah. I can only make a mark and that is unsteady. Will you write something. Show me." She scattered a layer of flour over the table. Mistress Carey raised her eyebrows but said nothing. Perhaps she too was interested to see my sister write.

"This," said Lizzie, "Is B for the start, the sound of your name, B for Beth, see?" She drew in the flour with her finger. "You can do it. Here." She took Beth's forefinger and pressed it down in a vertical line. "Then you join a curve to it at the top." She moved to the second curve, "then this, see, a 'B'."

Beth looked around at the rest of us, smiling and tried again on her own. "B!" she repeated. "Then what?" Lizzie wrote out the rest of her name, took Beth's finger to trace over the 'e', the 't' and the 'h'. "The 't' and 'h' presses together to make the 'th' sound, you must write them close together." Beth tried several more attempts with great excitement.

"I will come back with a piece of charcoal and beg some rag paper from Will and teach you some more, when I can."

I could see our time at Beauchamps would be filled with things to do before our return to Bournbroke.

We remade our bed with fresh linen sheets and clean blankets. Lizzie had pleaded with me to let us stay sleeping together but that night Lizzie stood and glowered at the bed.

"I don't want to sleep in here," she said. "I can still smell the blood. Nell died in here, Alice."

"Don't be ridiculous!"

50

"I'm not. We might catch some disease."

"Nell died of after-childbirth fever. You heard Anne Carey. She did not die of a 'disease'. The room is not plague-infected, just climb in. I'm tired and I'm cold."

"One good thing, anyway," Lizzie muttered. "We can tell Will we want to go back home now. He doesn't need us any more now his sister is dead."

"Lizzie! You are a selfish creature! We can't just leave Will the minute Nell has gone. There are things to do. He will need our help. Just hold your tongue."

Huffing and puffing, Lizzie flapped the bedclothes we had so neatly tucked and smoothed and lay still, rigid with resentment. I could have slapped her. I was glad I had been there to help Nell, but even more, I was glad to help Will. I was sorry he was alone with no family, even his baby niece was gone. But perhaps he would no longer want us here, reminding him of this saddest of times. Tomorrow I would ask him if and when he wanted us to go back home.

I got out of bed and peeped out of the shutters. It had been snowing, not much, but a light covering on the fields. I put on all my clothes at once, wrapped my shawl around me and took the ewer to fill with water from the well.

Will was already out of the house to work. I stoked the fire and set out. I decided to let Lizzie sleep, and while I waited for Will's return for his breakfast, I mixed the bread dough for the day, lay it on the hearth to rise and sat warming myself by the fire, sipping some hot rosemary ale.

Will arrived, chill air blowing in with him.

"Lovely fire, Alice. It's so good to come back to a warm house."

We ate breakfast and he talked about the work he had to organise before the frosts and snow stopped the men from digging.

51

"I expect the work at Netherfold is much the same for Daniel and your Father." he said.

"They do a lot of the orchard clearing and pruning, so the storms don't split the trees, and there are always the animals to see to."

"Your father and brother always do well at the markets with the lambs and I never see them without produce to sell."

"We have suffered from the billeting, Will. When the soldiers come to claim free quarter from us they eat up the vegetables, steal the chickens for their pot. Father keeps the pigs locked up for fear they snatch one and roast it."

"Yes, we have them here, of course, like everyone else from Stratford to Worcester. They have to pass our gates. They see the hall and the estate and they assume wealth. The King's men expect the family's support. The Parliament troops want to bleed us dry."

"Us? Are you on the King's side, Will?"

"My loyalty is to the Trentham family. Old Sir Felix, I told you, took me in and trained me. He gave me a station in life and Sir Carlton made me his steward. I owed a duty towards him, and now he is dead I must work for his widow. She is more than kind to me and Heaven knows, she struggles to make the estate prosper. She has to pay the fines they put on Catholic estates, support Sir Carlton's parents and their two daughters as well as the servants and the estate workers. These are not easy times." He paused, staring into the fire and sipping his ale. I looked at his strong hands around his tankard and the way his hair curled at his neck. He looked back at me and smiled.

"What about your family? Do they support one side over another in this war? I have never heard your father speak about a particular allegiance, but he and I don't discuss the war much, other than to comment on the news in the broadsheets generally."

"I expect he mostly grumbles to you, doesn't he?" I said. "At home he fumes at both factions because they trample our land and either undo his work or make more work for all of us. After

52

the Evesham 'skirmish' as Daniel called it, we had six Parliament-wounded in our barn. One with an arm cut off, several with broken heads or shoulder wounds. All writhing and groaning. Terrible. This time we had the King's men. Colonel Calcotton and his men."

"Could your mother help them?"

"She made up ointments and salves, used my grandmother's old herbals-book, made sleeping draughts. She helped some, others were too far gone."

"So, it was she who she taught you how to make up these lotions and salves and things?"

I nodded. "But I need to know more. Mother has set Lizzie to copy out the recipes from Grandmother's book so I can have one of my own."

"You and Lizzie have both been educated, haven't you?"

"We all have. Mother came from a household of girls. My grandfather needed the land-holding business to be done, the rents recorded, the letters, land contracts, beast-buying and selling. So she was taught and in our home she taught us with our brothers. It does not mean I escape from mucking out the animals though."

Will laughed. "It sounds as though your mother could do my job. Sir Felix Trentham taught me all those things your mother did."

"Why was he so good to you, do you think?"

"My father saved his life in a stable fire. Hauled him out and saved two horses. They stayed friends until my parents died in the plague."

"But you did not suffer the plague then, nor Nell?"

"Nell was sick but survived. I escaped it. Then she went to the Green Man, fell in love with Joshua Grey and the rest you know."

We sat quietly again, comfortable together, I thought. When he spoke again, he changed the subject.

"Has your mother got a healing medicine for the plague?"

"No. She says there is no cure. Some survive it. Some never suffer it even if it is about. We just have to try to avoid it, which she says is difficult because no one knows what brings it to the towns. Some say it is in the stink from the middens, some say it is from the running gutters. Some say you breathe in the disease from people who have it, that's why the plague doctor has that beak-mask. But she doesn't know and I certainly don't."

"So do her treatments cure soldiers wounds?"

"Some of them. I watched her take out a musket ball from a deep wound. But she says there is bad blood which goes to poison from a ball or a blade and spreads until—" I stopped and looked at him, still staring down into the flames. "Will, why are we talking about this? Is it your way of asking me if our herbals did enough to save Nell? Do you think I could have done more to prevent her death?"

"Oh no, no! Alice. You did more for her than ever I could have."

"Mistress Carey knows more about childbirth. She said if that afterbirth fever sets in it can be deadly."

He shook his head. "Everybody knows childbirth can be a risk for mother and child. I believe Nell's sadness and shame made her more sickly somehow. Women have babies safely again and again, both rich and poor."

"Mistress Carey talked about the curse of Eve's disobedience in Eden."

"Do you believe that?"

"No. I think the human body is full of mysteries we know nothing about. Mother says even if a barber-surgeon comes to cut off a soldier's damaged leg, or an apothecary comes, they do not know much more than she does."

Will took my hand. "Never think I doubt that you did all that could be done for my sister. I could not ask Anne Carey to leave all her other duties for someone not of the household, even though I know she would, out of kindness, have made time for my sake. I grieve for Nell, for the old times at home when we were children, running happily with the chickens and scaring crows for farthings. I just feel the weight of not having brought her here with me, kept her close, safe. I feel my fault."

He still had hold of my hand, so I squeezed his. He looked at me for what felt like a long time. His eyes were a warm velvet brown, his face, open and gentle then he let go of my hand with a smile that gave me a trill of happiness like the bubble of a robin's song inside me, rising.

Lizzie clattered down the stairs and broke the moment. She huddled over the fire, not looking in the least ready for a morning's work.

"Have you asked Will, then, have you?"

"Asked me what?" I wished Lizzie away.

"If Alice and I can leave you now that Nell is, erm, now you do not need us."

"No, Lizzie, I have not asked him because it is for our father to decide. I will write and ask him or we will wait until Will says he will see him at Shipscarden market."

Lizzie sighed and shuffled nearer still towards the fire. I shook my head at her, embarrassed that she had blurted out wanting to go home without me having prepared Will or prepared myself either. I was angry that she had broken into our quiet talk.

That night I lay in bed, glad of the warmth spreading from my sister's body but too irritated to bear us touching. My mind ranged back and forth over the incidents that had led me to be lying here in this strange house that felt so homely to me and had led me to be warmed by the smile in a man's eyes again. Since I had agreed to marry Jack I had not felt a stir of interest in any other man. I was nineteen then and full of love and excitement. I was ready, with confidence and with desire, to marry him, have his children. I had not thought, for a moment that quarrels between government men in London would break over our heads in Bournbroke like a thunderclap.

Father and Daniel used to pick up scraps of news about fighting, a battle here and there, down south or to the east. It shocked Mother and Father for there had been nothing like it, even in their grandparents' time and London unrest did not trouble them here in our sleepy Vale. Not at first.

One Sunday I remembered our minister, Josiah Barnes reading out a pronouncement from London saying King Charles had set himself up to rule as a tyrant, seeking to do away with the people's parliament and had raised an army against his own subjects and that this was treason. People around us in the church gasped and turned to exclaim to their neighbours. Minister Barnes read out that our men were called on to volunteer to fight in defence of our native rights. He said a lot more besides and ended with a passionate reading from the Psalms about God delivering us from evil men making war.

People left the church in silence that morning. Lizzie and I went home afraid. Mother said she did not like the way the minister bent bits of the Bible to justify his ideas about fighting a war.

When Jack said he was off to fight for Parliament, I was angry with him. "Is it not wicked to fight against the crowned King of England?" I had shouted. "Our vicars have always preached that kings were made by God himself." But Jack would not be swayed.

"We must have a fair rule by a parliament of the people who advise the King, not by a King who, like the Pharaoh of Egypt, holds all power to himself and treats free men like slaves. I must do it for my conscience, Alice, then I will come back and marry you and we will have six babies and be happy all our lives."

He begged a lock of my hair which he tucked into his knapsack and left me with a kiss. I never saw him again.

Almost two bleak years with no hope followed. Then a trooper billeted on us in Bournbroke told us he had seen him fall. I took him to The Waggoners Inn to tell Jack's mother and father. I tried to comfort Leah, thinking we could cry together but she could not even look at me. She sent me away. My girlhood life at Netherfold carried on as though I had never been betrothed at all. All the baking and salting, the smoking hams and the harvest filled my days and tired me sufficiently to help me at last, to sleep.

Mother taught me to sew fine linen. She made me the gift of my grandmother's sewing casket, full of beautiful silk threads they had both hoarded over years. There was the silver thimble too, that I told Lady Trentham about, worked with ivy; silver crochet hooks for making lace, and, at the bottom, the lovely old sheets of designs that Grandmother had drawn herself with motifs to embroider, and writing in strange lettering describing how to make the stitches.

Mother told me that Grandmother had been a seamstress in a grand house near to Hereford. She had such a fine sewing hand that the mistress taught her French embroidering and she was allowed to stitch with the finest silver threads, even with precious gold thread sometimes.

"They taught her how to make lace for altar cloths for their chapel and trims for priestly vestments, very fine." Mother used to tell me She said I had Grandmother's flair for the work, which made me proud.

After I lost Jack my days were uneventful, even tedious. Then the fighting spread and the Vale became increasingly rattled by horsemen riding through the village. Troopers would stop at The Rose Bush or join the riders on the Roman road at Jack's mother's inn, The Waggoners. How she would hate that, I thought. If they were King's troops, perhaps she would empty the chamber pots into their beer.

In that swirl of memory, I passed a restless night and went down to prepare the breakfast ready to discuss our return home with Will.

When he came in from setting the men to work, he opened the discussion.

"I am happy, young Lizzie, to take you home to Netherfold, as soon as you are ready, but Lady Abigail wants you to stay here, Alice, if you are willing. I can speak to your father when I take Lizzie back. The Mistress wants to speak to you up at the house.

"She does? To me?"

"She won't try to stop us going home, will she? That wouldn't be fair."

"Don't be so suspicious, young Lizzie, the mistress is never unfair." Will looked amused, but my sister was not.

"Lizzie!" I was cross with her and embarrassed at her way of speaking to Will.

"Don't call me young! I'm nearly seventeen now. No one ever takes notice of what I want!" She stamped off upstairs, frowning.

"I'm sorry, Will. She is so cross and selfish."

"Do you think I can't remember how Nell was at Lizzie's age?"

Upstairs in the hall, Lady Abigail was sitting between the fire and the table in the solar reading documents, piles of coins set in front of her. I dipped her a curtsey and Will removed his hat and bent his head.

"Ah, Will. I have been looking over the rent rolls and calculating our income for the coming year. These troop movements are increasing. More demands are being made on my neighbours to billet and feed the troops. They will be bound to come here. We will have to assess what it might cost us. And Sir Edward Carter warns me Elms Barton has had priest hunters calling, presenting them with the demand for recusancy fines. I need to know how we can meet it all."

"I will make an inventory, My Lady. There may be timber we can sell."

"Do that, Will. I am so anxious." She turned to me. "Ah, Alice. You find me distracted by these estate matters." She

58

pressed her palms into her eyes. Her brows were knitted and tense. "Is your sister here too?"

"No, My Lady. I have left her at Will's house baking bread."

"Will is full of praise for you both, for your kindness and for your capability. He tells me you would like to be taken back to Bournbroke soon.

"It will depend upon my father's permission and whether the King's troops have left our property, My Lady. He was afraid Lizzie's youth and young soldiers are an evil mix."

"It is not so long since my own daughters were your sister's age. I understand his watchfulness. Will has been with my husband's family since he was a boy. He is a great favourite with us all. We are grateful for everything you have done to ease him through his sister's illness and death and setting all to rights since then. It is right that you and your sister should want to go back home for Christmas. Will tells me he will see your father at the Shipscarden Fair and speak to him. However, I hope we may see you here again, Alice, if your mother can spare you. We have changes afoot at the Hall in the new year. You know Luce, one of my dearest maids of the chamber is to marry Will's right hand man, Dick Page so she will have less time to attend me."

I could not imagine where this news was leading me but Lady Trentham went on.

"My daughter Elizabeth's wedding to Edward Carter is also planned. There will be so much extra sewing and embroidering to do and Luce will not be here to help. I have been impressed by your sewing. You have great skill. I would like to ask your father if he would allow you to come back here to stay with me for a time, not as a servant, but as one of my own women. As well as sewing yourself, I would like you to teach Aimee something of your skill. She is good at homely work, but the family sometimes needs finer embroidery."

I felt flattered by Lady Trentham's confidence and her praise. The idea of living here again and spending more time with the other girls whom I was beginning like was pleasant. And perhaps

I should admit to myself that Lizzie was right, the idea of being close to Will appealed to me more than going back to Netherfold.

"If my father is willing and my mother can spare me, Your Ladyship, I would be happy to come to you again."

"There is also the business of the herbals and the medicines. Will speaks so highly of the way you cared for his sister and eased her pain. I told you how my parents in law are growing weaker. And I have no doubt we will have many more soldiers coming here with their wounded and their dying. We have no choice but to accept and endure them. Mistress Carey has enough work to do running the household and neither I nor my daughters have skill with nursing or preparing potions and salves. It is a deficiency in our education, no doubt. It will help us greatly, Alice, if you would bring that skill here for us and instruct Ruth and Beth in those matters and perhaps Isabella too."

"I will do anything I can."

"Good. You have seen that we are a large family here. Elizabeth and Isabella are a great support to me but, as I said, Elizabeth is going to be married and who knows when Isabella may marry and leave us. My son, Thomas is away with the King's army, God preserve him, so I depend a great deal upon Mistress Carey and Will Franks to help me run my affairs. We constantly have visitors and people of business whom Will and I must meet." She sighed.

"Sometimes I am exhausted by all that is asked of me. And on top of all of this there are the soldiers. We are so close to the road to Saxonford and the bridge over the Avon. Troops on both sides will think we have great wealth, so of course they rein in here to claim free quarters. If only they knew how I struggle for money to survive in this huge place: to pay my estate workers, the house servants, feed the family, meet the taxes charged on Royal supporters, the taxes on us as Catholics for not attending the Protestant services. The money flows out and we struggle daily to make more." She closed her eyes. "I know you owe me no duty, Alice, but as a friend I should be glad of your skills."

"As long as Father agrees, I will be happy to come back."

"Good. I will write a letter to your father for Will to take and we will hope all can be arranged as I wish and we can have you back with us in the new year. I will arrange with Anne Carey to prepare a place for you. The round room, will do very well. It is small but has good light for sewing." She stood up. "Thank you, Alice. I am pleased."

I was happy to stay at Beauchamps. I enjoyed the work I was given to do, now the sad nursing of Nell was over. I would not miss having to look after the animals, help with the garden crops, pull weeds. To sit in this great house sewing fine fabrics, surrounded by rich wall-hangings and carved furniture would be like living a long holiday. And Will Franks would be there too.

There is No Comfort To Be Had

We know that the whole creation groaneth,
and travaileth in pain together.

St. Paul's Epistle to the Romans

Will took Lizzie and me home in the waggon and it was a happy homecoming. Netherfold was free of troops although the family had lots of tales to tell of the soldiers who claimed free quarter on our land and of their sometimes, outrageous behaviour. Mother made Will stay and share a meal with us before he left.

"I've brought you a letter from Lady Trentham, Samuel," he said. "She needs Alice again after Christmas, if you can spare her. The old couple have been sickly over the winter and need nursing. Mistress Elizabeth's wedding must take place before Lent and all her wedding clothes and linens have to be sewn and the wounded keep arriving, as they do here, I'm sure. Could you spare her? I can come back for her after Twelfth Night."

Father looked across at Mother who had, I thought, a strangely satisfied look. He turned back to me.

"Are you pleased to do what Lady Trentham asks, Alice? She cannot require you to go. You are not to be a hired servant, but you can hardly be her companion. Do you not feel awkwardly placed? What do you think, Sarah?"

"There is no question of hire here, Samuel. Her Ladyship says in this letter she thinks highly of Alice's skill. She wants her to instruct the others with the medicine-making and such, as well as giving of her talent as a needlewoman."

"Lady Trentham makes little distinction between kitchen servants and her waiting-women, Father. Everyone at Beauchamps has treated me well. Mother is right. Her ladyship told me what she wanted from me It is nothing menial. I am happy to go."

My father nodded.

"I have done well with Miriam while you and Lizzie have been away." Mother said. "She has turned out to be a good worker and now Lizzie is back we will manage the work together. Lady Trentham's proposal is a fine opportunity for Alice to see how they manage matters in a great house. It will make her a better housekeeper when she has her own home to run and I think there will be some pleasure in watching the manners of ladies. Perhaps she will meet a fine lord and marry into the gentry."

"Foolish woman!" my father laughed. But I knew he was happy enough with the arrangement now and I would be going back among my friends beyond the crossroads.

The New year began and the winter snow came and went. We could relax, then, knowing no soldiers would ride into the village while the roads were so bad. Neither side would fight in the snow or the churned-up mud of the thaw.

One morning as I was feeding an orphaned lamb in the barn, Will Franks rode into the yard. I was so happy to see him again and his face lit up with smiles when he saw me.

We all sat around the table, warming ourselves in the kitchen with hot soup and fresh bread, exchanging news.

Will produced a covered basket he had brought in from the waggon. "Lady Trentham sends you a gift to thank you for allowing Alice to come and help her." He brought out a suckling pig for roasting and a small cask of French wine. It was well received and soon after, with great warmth and fond goodbyes, I climbed into the waggon, wrapped in a thick new cloak, and set off with Will for Beauchamps Hall again.

"Thank you for what you said to Father about Lady Trentham not being about to treat me as a servant. He is too proud to allow me to go back to Beauchamps on those terms. He is jealous of his own rank."

"I stressed to him how she had said she wanted you to teach her daughters. He liked the idea of his daughter 'Instructing the gentry' as he said."

I laughed. "Yes, that sounds exactly like him."

"Just a word of warning, though, Alice. The younger daughter, Isabella might be less than friendly. She protested to her mother about the idea of your coming. She considers it beneath her to be taught by 'an inferior', as she put it. She even tried to involve me, to say your board and lodgement would be an additional strain on the estate expenses that they could ill afford."

"I hope she doesn't think I asked for this sign of favour. It was her mother who asked me to come."

"Yes, yes, Lady Abigail said so," he sighed. "Isabella is not like her mother. She dislikes the way her mother blurs the distinction between Aimee, Beth, Luce and Ruth—even Molly. Yes, they work in the kitchens and clean and polish, bake bread, do the laundry, all of that, but Luce, Aimee and Beth spend a lot of time with Her Ladyship, sewing, talking together, singing sometimes. Elizabeth is happy to be part of that too, but Isabella is jealous of her status as a daughter of the house and, well, she often has a bitter tongue. She endures those three, who are fellow Catholics, with better grace than she does Ruth and Molly who are not. You, I'm afraid she will regard as another—"

"—cuckoo in the nest." We rode on in comfortable silence for a time, a pale sun brightening the fields. I took a breath. "Will, about Nell's death. Are you feeling better about it all?"

He stared at the road ahead, flicking the reins now and then to keep the horse's pace steady. I should have held my tongue, I thought. He resents my prying into his personal life.

"I have thought about it a lot since we buried her. Our parents' death changed everything for us. She chose the tavern life because she said she enjoyed the laughter, the talk. She enjoyed being flirted with and called after. I saw it. When I told her she could join me here at Beauchamps she refused, saying she was happy at the Green Man. I could only accept it."

"But she turned to you when things went wrong for her."

"I told her when I left that I would always make a home for her if she needed me. She did not beg of me, though. Moll Newby wrote to tell me Nell had taken to her bed with melancholy because her sweet-heart had left her and she was refusing to eat or talk. She said Nell was no use to her and I must take her away. She did not tell me then about a baby."

"Poor Nell. I sometimes think we are like leaves in the river, snatched from the quiet shallows and forced into directions we have not chosen, for good or ill. Poor Nell's life took that bad turn while I was swept out of my life at Netherfold and cast into a grand house to sew fine seams."

"And to ride here, beside me." He looked at me and smiled. That robin song thrilled through me again as I smiled back.

I arrived into the kitchen of the hall to a friendly welcome. Everyone was busy but they took time from their duties to give me a hot drink and Mistress Carey told Beth to take me to the round room at the corner of the solar which had windows overlooking the front of the house and the sheep meadow. There was a bed there for me and a worktable by the window with good light for sewing and another table by the small fireplace for my medicine-work, with tools, pots, knives and a pestle and mortar. There was a chest for my belongings and a small box by my bed with a chamber-stick and candles. I was charmed.

I unpacked my sewing box and the medicines recipe book Lizzie had copied for me then tidied my dress and went to present myself to Lady Trentham.

"Alice! I am pleased to have you here." She actually took my hands in hers. "Are you happy with the round room?"

"I am touched by the pains you have taken to make it so pretty. It is a home indeed. I have never had so much room all for myself."

She smiled and took me over to the table. Elizabeth and Isabella were sitting by the windows sewing. Elizabeth smiled and Isabella nodded a welcome. We spent the rest of the afternoon, until the light faded, discussing the first garments they wanted me to stitch and which areas I could decorate with embroidery and which with lace.

Elizabeth asked me friendly questions about my family, about our Christmas feasting and told me about her plans for moving to Carterway Manor after her wedding.

Isabella was different. She made it clear that she regarded me as a servant, not one of her mother's more elevated waiting women.

"Keep your needles and silks in your own sewing box. I like to work with my own. Always put your finished seam-work on my left, so that I can find it easily when I am ready to insert a sleeve."

She sat with her back to me. I was never going to be able to teach her anything about embroidery, herbs, medicines or anything else, despite what her mother said.

I went down to the kitchen to ask where I should find the herb stores and to look inside the medicaments chest to see what was already there and what I thought we would need to deal with any wounded soldiers who might arrive. The other household women greeted me like a friend returned and made room for me at the worktable as they prepared the day's food.

I asked for a paring knife and joined in the preparation of the vegetables. I noticed Ruth and Molly exchange a smile at my willingness to help with the less refined work.

"Alice, don't for goodness' sake cut your sewing fingers with that knife when you have fine embroidery to do!" Aimee was not, I noticed, chopping or handling the soil-covered vegetables.

"I think I can do both," I said. "I am happy to sit here with you."

"I expect you found it rather solitary at the gate house, caring for Nell Franks," said Beth.

"My sister was with me, of course, but I own it was rather a melancholy vigil between us."

"Poor Will. We like him a great deal, Alice, Will Franks."

"Has he a sweet-heart or anyone?"

"If he has," Ruth dropped her voice, "we have heard nothing of her."

"It is not one of us, that's certain, sadly." Molly pulled a rueful face.

"Do you pine for him, Molly Parker?" teased Beth.

"No, of course not. He does not even notice me—or any of us, does he?"

"I think he is dedicated to Lady Trentham and the estate. He is not one for holiday days. I think you have discussed the poor man enough now. Talk about other matters, lest he come in and hear you."

They all grinned in such a way that I could see they were not afraid of Will, or of Mistress Carey either.

"I would like to be as useful as you all seem to be when I am not sewing, so will you show me where I might find everything. I do not want to be always asking."

They were all eager to learn more about the mixing of medicinal draughts and wound-healing salves. They crowded round the copy of my grandmother's herbal book and passed it from hand to hand to look at the drawings of the plants that Lizzie and I had made.

I did not see so much of Will now that I was no longer living in the gate house and I missed our evenings alone together. But he would stop and make friendly conversation if ever we passed each other with some time to spare. Now and then I would look up and catch him watching me. Sometimes I would watch him then, if he caught me, blush and look away.

The whole household ate the main evening meal together, the family and all of us, save for the estate workers who lived with their own families in the cottages about the grounds.

I hesitated on my first evening there, unsure of where to sit. Lady Trentham had said I was there, not as a servant, but 'one of her women', but I did not want to push myself forward.

Aimee saw me hang back and beckoned. "We all eat together, Alice. The Trenthams make no distinction."

After that, Will would often show me there was an empty seat beside him. We enjoyed quiet conversations together but we had no time alone. How sweet those private talks at his own fireside had been.

The work I had promised to do for Lady Trentham was pleasant. The mornings passed busily in the warm kitchen with Beth, Aimee and Luce, Molly and Ruth. We sang and gossiped but we all worked hard. As well as my medicines, I cut up old bed sheets to make bandages to increase our store against the arrival of wounded men once the battle-weather returned. I helped with the cooking, the breadmaking and the laundry. I did not mind this mix of servants' work and my work for Lady Trentham. It was no different to the shared work of the other girls. Mistress Carey was exacting but pleasant with us and the food was good.

Most afternoons I spent up in the solar, stitching new undergarments and embroidering nightgowns and linen sleeves, household bedcovers and lace.

I felt almost like a lady of the manor then, sitting sewing in those beautiful surroundings. The fire was always bright, the wooden panelling rich and polished, the floors sweet with lavender and there were wonderful portraits full of colour.

One afternoon, after I had been there about two weeks, I was sitting with Lady Trentham and her daughters embellishing the decorative designs I had drawn on to Elizabeth's trousseau; forget-me-nots and rosebuds between trails of ivy. Elizabeth asked me good natured questions about our land at Netherfold and about my brothers and sisters. Isabella stitched on in silence looking at me every so often as though I had brought the whiff of pig-muck into the solar clinging to my skirts.

At last, without looking up, she spoke. "Your home lies in the parish of St Andrews in Bournbroke, does it not?" I agreed. "I have heard that your priest there is a fierce opponent of the King and a stiff-necked Puritan. Is it so?"

"Minister, he insists on being called *Minister* Barnes. Yes, he certainly stands with the strictly biblical Protestant church."

"And do you and your family find that compatible with your own faith and worship?"

"Isabella!" Lady Trentham intervened. "You know my wishes. I will not have our people here subject to inquisition about matters of religion. Heaven knows, we Catholics have suffered enough from such questioning and harassment."

"We cannot know if Mistress Sanderson is discreet among us. As you rightly say, Mother, we live in constant risk among Protestant antagonists. We must have a care that we do not harbour informers who watch and wait for opportunities to betray us. Do you not agree, Elizabeth?"

I put my stitchery aside. "You cannot believe such unkindness—such treachery from me. Your Ladyship, you cannot believe I would be guilty of such duplicity, that I am not to be trusted at your hearth."

"Hush, Mistress Sanderson, Alice, please. I entertain no such misgivings. I would not have invited you here to help me and be so close within our family circle if I did not feel total trust and amity towards you. Isabella, beg Alice's pardon. I insist."

Isabella sat, her lips tight pressed, her eyes narrowed.

"I beg your pardon, then, if I have offended you with my zealous care for the safety of our life of faith here. As my mother says, we suffer for it. We need to be watchful with strangers." She stood up and, leaving her work behind, walked up to her chamber.

"Elizabeth. Follow your sister and ask her to go and read to your grandparents, or play her lute. It will calm her to do something for them. Leave all the work. Go now. Alice and I will collect it all."

I could not check the hot tears that spilled over and ran down my cheeks. I was furious, insulted and at a loss what I should do. Could I continue to stay where one of the ladies of the house regarded me as some sort of dangerous spy? I began to fold away the sewing. Lady Trentham put out her hand to stop me.

"Leave it, Alice. Just sit quietly a moment. Let me talk to you. Isabella spoke badly to you there. She was unjust. I have no such misgiving about you or any of the Protestants here."

"I understand that Catholics are persecuted, Your Ladyship. I know there are laws and punishments. Our Minister Barnes preaches harshly against your church and its ways. But it is not how I or my family thinks."

"I have no doubt of it, Alice. Forget what she said. She is more preoccupied with her religious duty than the rest of my family." Looking troubled, she absently folded and refolded the linens. "Isabella has spoken about becoming a nun, but here in England that is impossible. It makes her unhappy. I have tried to interest her in the idea of a holy marriage, of children she can bring up in the faith but she will not hear of it. Not yet." She paused and drew a sharp breath. "I just wish I could find a good husband to please her, a good man as much like her father as possible. I would arrange it at once."

She fell silent, her thoughts taking her far away. I picked up my sewing again as she began to speak.

"My husband's father and my own father were old friends. Their estates were adjacent. A match between Carlton and me was always talked of. We were fond of each other as playfellows, so it was natural to me that we should become man and wife. Our neighbours here, Edward Carter in Elms Barton and Henry Norton in Shipscarden Magna have never shown any interest in Isabella, nor she in them. When I saw the fondness grow between Edward and Elizabeth and he asked for her hand it pleased me, but Isabella..." She fell silent and turned her face away. "I despair, rather. I wish Carlton had not left me with so many problems." She began to cry. I fixed my eyes on my sewing. She stood up and went to the window. I could see her shoulders shaking as she struggled to control her tears.

I pushed back my chair and packed up the sewing, wanting to save her embarrassment, and leave her but she spoke again.

"This war! It makes widows of us, Alice." She came back to the table, calmer now. "Will told me you lost your betrothed at Edgehill."

"Yes. I thought at the time that I would never recover from the sadness of it. I saw his death as the loss of all my future."

"But you are happier now. You are young, you must have hope."

"I had so little time with him, really. You had the loss of so many years to mourn."

"You look happy here with us. I hope you are."

"I have been made very welcome."

"Welcome, yes." Again, she paused. "The help I am given is welcome. Will Franks is my right hand. The estate would flounder without him and without Anne Carey running the house in such perfect order. The church requires me to accept what God sends and not rail against His will."

We each went on with our work, each with our own thoughts. My grief for Jack had lost its sharpness. I struggled now to recall his face. He came to me sometimes in my dreams and now and then I would I recall incidents, a sunlit memory frozen like an image in a church window, pretty but barely real. He was the sweet romance of my youth. But he was gone and I was older.

The silence of the room was interrupted by the sound of horsemen galloping up to the house. Lady Trentham sprang up and looked out.

"Some official business for Will to manage, I think. He is out there with them, exchanging documents." She sat down again. "You know my son Thomas is with the King's army in Oxford. Ever since my dear husband was killed, the sound of horsemen coming to the house makes me fear bad news; that Thomas is

wounded, or worse. How could I bear to lose them both? I think
a hurt to Tom would defeat me utterly, Alice."

One sunny morning early in the year I was clipping thyme and
rosemary in the herb garden. Snowdrops were opening under the
tree boles. They made me smile, as they did every early spring. I
lingered to enjoy them.

I heard shouting. Shutters banging. Horsemen!

I ran back to the stable yard to see two of the estate men
locking the barn doors.

"Master Will says you'm all to get indoors. Soldiers is
comin'."

"King's or Parliament's?"

"Didn't say. Just to lock the barns and shutters and run back
here."

The men and their dogs were driving sheep into the
wool -barn and barring the doors. I hurried into the kitchen and
shut the door behind me. My hands were shaking. Again! Again!
The horses, the neighing, the jangling harnesses.

Mistress Carey hurried in ahead of everyone, issuing
instructions as she came. Aimee, Ruth and the others ran about,
hiding pies and jars of preserved fruit behind concealing
cupboard-backs and hiding holes within the pantry walls. The
kitchen men lugged beer and wine from the cellar to hide in the
game store.

"Cover it all with the turnips," Anne Carey shouted after
them, "and firewood!"

I could hear the men, urgent in the stable yard. Will's deep
voice gave orders, which men relayed to those further off. Luce
ordered all of us into the hall with the family, bringing small-
beer with her for the men. She told us to water wine if the
officers demand wine and to bring bread, cheese and a ham with
us.

We scurried around and somewhat shakily carried everything
in, not knowing who or what we would see. To my amazement,

there stood Colonel Calcotton, his two lieutenants and one other officer. Their coats and plumed hats were even dirtier and more battle-torn than when they rode into Netherfold.

"I hear you have ridden here from Bournbroke, Colonel." Lady Abigail nodded as he bowed a reverence to her, sweeping off his hat. "I am surprised you felt the need to stop for rest again so soon."

"We passed through Bournbroke without stopping this time, My Lady. I have orders to join an attack on Rowcester. The Roundheads are laying waste to the place. They have desecrated the church, using it as stables."

"Fouled it with horse-droppings, My Lady," Lieutenant Daley added, "Cooking on fires where they tore the altar down!"

"Smashed every coloured window glass and attacked the citizens in their homes."

"So, what is it you want from me here in Beauchamps, Sir?"

"We are bloodied and tired. We need quarter here for a day and a night and help for our wounded in the King's name."

"Very well. But understand, Colonel—"

"—Calcotton, My Lady."

"Understand, Colonel Calcotton, my estates are sadly stretched. I have a large family of dependents and you must know how much money I am forced to pay for Catholic and Royalist fines."

"You will, however, be eager to lend your support to the forces of your King."

"The Trentham loyalty cannot be in question, Sir. My late husband—"

"—I knew Sir Carlton, My Lady," Lieutenant Daley said. "I was in the Worcester fighting."

"Did you see him killed?" Her eyes were on his face.

"I saw him after he had fallen. His men lifted him with great respect. I can tell you they revered him greatly."

"Thank you, Lieutenant. Colonel, my steward, Master Franks here, will give orders for your grazing and the bedding of the men in the Copse Barn. Mistress Carey, here will arrange for hot stew, fresh bread and cheese to be doled out at the kitchen door."

"Will, tell Dick and the men to set up trestle tables in the Copse Barn for them to eat at. They can find barrels and logs to sit on, I daresay." She turned back to Colonel Calcotton. "You and your officers put your beds down in our guest room and join my family tonight for supper. "

"Most grateful, Lady Trentham."

"How many officers, Colonel?"

"Myself, Captain Bond and two lieutenants: Daley here and Charlton."

"And your wounded men, Sir?"

"Seven. They are in the waggon. There must be a barn with warm straw for them."

"Direct the waggon driver to the Larch Barn, Will. Alice, go with him and see what medicines and salves you might need. Ruth and Molly can help. I will tell Mistress Carey to send water jugs and basins to you."

I hurried to do as I was told, fearful again of the upheaval, the blood, the soldiers' demanding menace. But I took some comfort from my father's comment that there were more men to defend us here at Beauchamps than I had around me the last time I saw these same troops.

Everyone went to work. Beth and the girls went back to the kitchen to prepare food for the officers and the family.

I followed Will out to the front to face more blood, torn limbs and suffering men.

Soldiers were leading their unsaddled horses in to graze in the sheep field. One of the soldiers, bare headed with his fair curls blowing across his face, heaved his saddle off his mount and almost knocked me off my feet. As I straightened up, I saw the Royalist soldier who had caused my father to send Lizzie and I here and whom I had brayed with the straw fork.

"Why, here is the hellcat of Bournbroke!" he exclaimed, setting his saddle down and moving closer. "I did not think I would be fortunate enough to see you again, sweet-heart. See her, Marcus?"

He leered at his friend and grabbed me. I dashed him away with all my strength.

"Get off me!" I was shouting and felt myself undignified.

"Hoity-toity," the trooper sneered at me. "Were you jealous that I kissed your pretty sister instead of you, eh? I can put that right, now!" He lunged at me, grabbing my waist.

I twisted and writhed to get out of his grasp. "Sour old maid! Come here!"

I could smell his stale mouth as he pressed his wet lips over mine and dragged his kisses down my neck. I wrenched my head from side to side. His hands were over my body, pressing me into his groin. I pulled one hand free and cramped my fingers around his hair and tore at it.

I thought I had freed myself but other hands were hauling him backwards. I stumbled and straightened up to see Will wrenching the trooper this way and that. He threw him to the ground, striking his face. Grunting and swearing the soldier staggered back up, lowered his head and crashed into Will.

The two of them fell together, rolling and punching.

Will clambered to his feet, half dragged, half lifted the soldier toward the horse-trough by the sheep field fence and threw him in the water, headfirst.

"Cool your lust, you pig!" he shouted and drew aside, gasping for breath. There was a bleeding cut near his eye and he had a burst lip. I sat against the wall, sobbing in a fury. This is what it meant, having coarsened ruffians billeted on homesteads; not just the seizure of foodstuffs and demands on our time and care. They wanted to rape us, as well as our land.

"Alice." Will came closer and opened his arms. He closed them around me, helped me to my feet and held me, soothing my hair with the palm of his hand. Yes. I was safe with him. I was sheltered here. We stood wrapped together until I was calm again. Reluctantly I drew away.

"Thank you." I was determined not to cry. I looked down so I could not see his eyes examining my face. "It was the one who attacked Lizzie at Netherfold. He recognised me. He remembered I set about him with the rake and decided to take revenge. If you hadn't come—I pulled—pulled his hair but he was too strong. I'm so glad you—" Then I cried.

"You go to your chamber, bathe your face, rest a while. I will tell the others in the kitchen."

"It is shaming, Will."

"You need feel no shame. It was all his doing. If these troops behave like beasts they must be given discipline. I will see to it."

As he left, I gave him what I hoped was a brave smile but was, I fear, pathetic. I wished I could have just stayed there, safe in his arms. I stumbled back into the house, avoiding everyone. I was ashamed that I had blamed my sister so readily for this same whoreson molester kissing her. He was not one to be fought off easily. I soaked a cloth in cold water and held it to my aching face.

I kept to my room. Mistress Carey would send for me if I was needed I thought. I just wanted to be alone. I was sure my face was swelling already and my salves were all down in the kitchen. I would have to go down among them looking monstrous.

Later, Aimee tapped at my door and asked me to go into the hall, Lady Trentham wanted to see me. Aimee stared at my face. I knew how ugly it must look. I bathed my eyes and held the cold pad to my cheek and followed Aimee downstairs.

By the hearth stood Lady Trentham, Will, Elizabeth and Isabella, Luce and Beth and Mistress Carey and, worse, Colonel Calcotton. The only consolation was that the trooper who had set about me was not set in front of me too.

Lady Abigail gave a sharp intake of breath when I lowered the face-pad to curtsey.

"Alice, my dear! You see, Captain, the result of your man's handiwork on my woman here. This is disgraceful!"

"Indeed, My Lady, it is a bad business but I must tell you this young lady struck my man when we were billeted on her father's land."

"Because, Sir, he made the same disgusting attack on my young sister, then struck my father who intervened to defend her."

"All this behaviour is the work of ruffians. Men without honour cannot be engaged to uphold the honour of our King, Colonel. I give you notice; you are not welcome. I will sanction no open hospitality to you and your men but my steward did right to uphold the honour and safety of Mistress Sanderson. I cannot stop you from seizing what you need, but after this I will not allow you and your officers to sleep in my house and we will lift not a finger to further aid you. And, Sir, see that—that maid-molester is sent to sleep in the pigsty where he belongs!"

She turned away from him and left the room, followed by her daughters. Mistress Carey led the others into the kitchen and I went after them to nurse my sore face and my sore pride.

Later, as we sat sewing together, Elizabeth and Isabella began discussing the attack on me. I kept my mouth shut, wishing they had chosen to talk about it when I was not there. They were eager in their praise of their mother's angry reprimand to Colonel Calcotton. Isabella looked askance at me then said, "I hear Alice has been involved with that soldier before, at her father's croft. That is why she and her sister were sent here in the first place."

I was angry but could hardly defend myself from Isabella's insinuation without decrying my sister. I did not speak.

"You occupy a peculiar position here, don't you? Partly kitchen maid and partly our instructress."

"I do whatever Lady Trentham asks of me. She has always been kind."

"Of course, she is kind. It is my mother's way. With all the servants." Isabella stood up. "I will take a turn around the garden, Elizabeth. Will you come? It is a lovely afternoon. I do not think I wish to be taught anything more by Mistress

Sanderson just now." Without waiting she left the solar and went downstairs, leaving all the sewing tumbled about the table for me to fold away.

Elizabeth said, "I think my sister is harsh towards you, Alice, but we worry about my mother. She has so much to trouble her. Perhaps I will join Isabella in the garden. You can work a little longer, I think." She paused at the head of the stairs. "The embroidery you have added to my wedding dress is beautiful, Alice. You have my thanks."

My tears welled and dripped down onto the linen in my hands.

Elizabeth's wedding day arrived and the family travelled in the carriages the short distance to the church at Elms Barton. Because Sir Carlton had been his old friend, Sir Lockhart Carter played host to the wedding breakfast at Carterway Manor. Ruth, Molly and I offered to stay at Beauchamps with Philip and Jake in case the troops tried to enter the house and make mischief. The family and the rest of the household came home late in the evening in high good humour. Even Lady Trentham looked carefree and happy. I looked at Isabella to see if she joined in the general happiness but there was no change to her expression.

One afternoon Lady Trentham's parents in law were in the solar with me. Old Sir Felix was sitting in the sunshine of the bay window, peering at his missal. He held it up close to one eye, squinting, trying to angle it to catch the light.

I was sewing near to Lady Eliza who liked to watch the emerging patterns.

"It is no use, Felix," she said. " You cannot see to read it and I cannot read the lettering. Put it aside until Isabella comes. She will read it to you."

He turned to me. "Can you read letters, young mistress? My eyes fail me."

I took the book from his hand. It was a beautiful page of Latin, illustrated at the margins with flowers, birds and strange beasts.

"This must be very old, Sir," I said. "It is written and decorated by hand."

"Yes, yes." His voice was papery. His breath wheezed as he spoke. "My father gave me this when I was twelve. We did not have to hide such things in those days. We were all one in faith. I thought that is how it would always be but, oh dear, dear, in these modern times, nothing in that way is safe for us now."

"Hush, Felix. Try not to dwell on sad things. We are all safe in this house with dear Abigail. Do not fret, dear."

I turned the jewel-coloured pages of the old missal. I had never seen so beautiful, so valuable a book.

"Find the Nunc Dimittis, for me. Could you read it, Mistress Alice? My poor wife was never taught to read."

I turned the pages. I could read but I had never been shown any Latin. I could recognise 'Nunc' though and found the page. I held it out to Lady Eliza who looked at the illustrations.

"Yes, that is the prayer. Can you read that, Alice?"

"I can read the way the letters look together, but I have never learnt Latin so I am afraid I will shock you with my wrong pronouncing of the words." Sir Felix gave a little moan of disappointment so I said, "But I will try Sir, if you will forgive my mistakes."

"Read what you can to me, Alice and I will recognise it as you say it, so I can correct you. You will need to speak up so my husband can hear. We will try it together. We'll see if we can make you happy, Felix dear."

"I'm sure Isabella will be back soon, she will be able to read it to you properly, Sir."

"No, I don't want to wait. I want to hear it now."

His wife shook her head, part in sympathy, part in irritation but I held the book up and tried my best. Limping from error to English error, pronouncing 'pace' as if in English and 'faciem'

79

as 'face-y-em' but with Lady Eliza's corrections I improved at the second time of reading and Sir Felix began to nod in recognition. Looking more peaceful.

Nunc dimittis servum tuum, Domine Secundum verbum tuum in pace:
Quia viderunt oculi mei salutare tuum
Quod parasti ante faciem omnium populorum:
Lumen ad revelationem gentium, et gloriam plebis tuae Israel.

I was reading it for the third time with more confidence, when Isabella came in.

"Mother wants me to take you both to your chamber, Grandmother. The Protestant Assessors are coming for their fines. What are you doing with Grandfather's missal, Alice?"

I opened my mouth to explain, but Lady Eliza stood up and smoothly taking the missal out of my hand before Isabella could snatch it, which she certainly intended to do, her eyes narrow, lips tight shut.

"I asked Mistress Sanderson to help your Grandfather and I, my dear, which she kindly did."

"Very well, but you and Grandfather should not sit here in the drafts. Come away now, both of you. Let me move you."

She took the old man's arms to lift him to his feet then held out a hand to Lady Eliza.

"We were enjoying the feel of the sun on our faces, Isabella, and your grandfather insisted Alice to read him the *Nunc Dimittis*. He would not wait for you."

"Heretics have no business reading such prayers. You should not even have touched a Catholic missal, Alice. It is precious. Holy."

I stared at her but said nothing. To argue would have been useless. She just did not like me near her family.

Isabella steered the old couple towards the staircase. "Come away to your chamber, Grandmother. You are both tired out and befuddled. Grandfather, take your precious missal back. Keep hold of it. Come away."

I wondered if she would come back and chastise me further but she did not refer to it again she just avoided me as much as she could.

Later, Lady Trentham came to find me alone and thanked me for reading her father his prayer.

"My mother-in-law told me how you struggled to pronounce the Latin properly for him. It was kindly done, Alice. I know Isabella was rude to you about it. I fear her religion gives her too much rigidity and not enough grace."

One hot day in high summer, Lady Trentham ordered chairs to be carried out on to the lawns in front of the house. All the windows and doors stood open and the air was fragrant with roses and honeysuckle. She asked Isabella to play some music on her lute and she suggested to Will and Anne Carey that the household should enjoy supper out of doors in the cool of the evening.

With a great bustle we all helped carry tables and benches outside. I helped fetch and carry the food, my eyes straying across the table to where Will sat next to Dick, laughing with him and with Ruth alternately. She looked up at him with shining eyes. 'Ah!' I thought, 'does she care for him? Does he—' I looked abruptly down at my plate. I must not fall victim to jealousy. Heaven Knows I had no right. Will and I were—what were we? Friends, certainly, but that did not explain the desire I had to be with him, to listen to him talk, to make him laugh. When he looked worn out, when the frown lines between his brows were cramped with worry, I wanted to smooth his face, calm him, walk with him. I often wished everyone else away, so we could be alone.

I remembered the nights we sat alone in the gate house, when Lizzie and I were nursing Nell. Then I could imagine us, almost as if together in our own home. I stood up and began to clear away the used plates and left-over food stuffs, shaking away a useless trail of dreams.

The summer meal passed in music, singing and laughter until long after a blazing sunset.

Next day the happiness of the previous evening vanished like the dew. Edward Carter rode across to us from Elms Barton with news for the family. Lady Trentham, Isabella, Luce and I were in the solar at our sewing when Aimee brought him in to us.

"I have bad news, My Lady," he said. "I have had a messenger come from Worcester, the mayor has yielded up the city to Cromwell's siege army and Oxford has fallen to Fairfax and the Parliament army there. We are defeated."

"And the King? What of His Majesty?"

"Better news there. He has escaped by God's grace and gone north to seek protection from the Scots."

"Holy Mary and the Saints of Heaven protect the King."

I could see tears well into her eyes so I left them to mourn together and stole into the round room by myself. I had not been in there long when I heard Anne Carey's voice calling for Lady Trentham.

"The Parliamentary Assessor has arrived to collect the estate's fines and the 'Charges to Government'.

I opened the door and joined the others again.

"Master Franks wants someone to go and help him carry the rent rolls into the hall with the money chest and the estate ledger. Do you know where Dick is, Luce?"

"I'll find him." Luce hurried down the stairs.

"I know where the rent rolls are kept, I will go and fetch them," I said, and followed her.

I was drawing the rolls out of the cupboard when Dick rushed in and picked up the money chest. "Will has already got the estate book. He is with the assessors in the hall."

In the hall a smartly dressed Puritan stood at the table in front of Lady Trentham, his hat still on his head. Will took the rolls from me with the faintest of smiles and asked Dick to stay to help him with the chest and bag up the coins as needed while he drew up a receipt for the Assessor to sign. Later they came into the kitchen and sat down. Dick blew through his teeth.

"That was a heavy set of charges, Will. The mistress looked quite pale as he made all their demands."

Will spoke to everyone. "They want an inventory of all the tenants and the rents they pay, all our incomes from wool, beasts, brewing, timber and hay. That will be my work for days."

"And they have demanded one twentieth of the value of the whole estate!"

"But that is enormous!" Anne Carey was horrified.

"Much more than they charge Protestant landowners, from what I hear'" grumbled Dick.

"It is up to the limit." said Will, "and no appeal."

"We will have to sell—"

"Yes, sell something. I will have to do some assessing myself." Pulling a gloom-laden grimace, Will left the kitchen for the estate office.

I did not see him again for several days as he locked himself away organising what Parliament required to meet its levy. Occasionally I saw him in close consultation with Lady Trentham, their faces serious, their voices hushed. They always talked well away from the old couple and the rest of the household but an air of anxiety pervaded the Hall.

The old lady and gentleman had to be told the sad news of the King's defeat again and again. Straggling knots of Royalist soldiers came, stayed a night and left. I was kept busy binding wounds and giving sleeping draughts and poppy medicine to dull the pain of those worst injured. We buried two men across the way at the Elms Barton church, which was the nearest graveyard.

One mealtime Will appeared in the kitchen and sat to eat with us for the first time in days. He was unshaven and looked ill-slept.

"All finished?" Anne Carey asked as she served him his pottage, some ham and fresh cheese.

"Yes. I have copied out all the information they have asked for and negotiated the sale of an acre of timber from Wreykham Woods."

"So much?" Dick was shocked.

"Reluctantly, yes, so much." Will shook his head. "Wretched business, but it means we can pay the levy they want for the army and the Recusancy fines and leave something over in the chest against their fresh demands."

"Will My Lady approve the sale?"

"I am going up there now. with the details and letters for her to sign." He took everything up and left. When the household gathered for supper that evening he and the mistress came down together, still talking business. She looked pale but frequently nodded her agreement and finally sat to her meal.

On my way upstairs to my bed that night I passed Lady Trentham's chamber. The door swung open in a sudden draft. I closed the landing window and as I turned back I saw the mistress hunched in her fireside chair weeping bitterly. I hesitated. It was not my place to intrude on her grief, but I could not walk by. I stood with my hand on the door and spoke softly.

"Do you need help, My Lady?"

She looked up, wiping her face, her breath coming in gulps.

"Shall I fetch Mistress Isabella to you?"

"No, no one. There is no one" She wept again, silently, her shoulders juddering. I stepped closer, my hand over her shoulder. Could I touch her? Was that too familiar? It is what I wanted to do, for where words fail, sometimes the touch of a kind hand shows us we are not alone.

"My Lady, forgive me if I intrude, but no one should weep alone."

"I am defeated, here. Weak. Hopeless." She covered her face with her hands. She sobbed with tight gasps, her hands bunched into fists against her forehead. "I cannot bear all this alone. I do not want this, any of it. I want my husband here. These troubles are unbearable without him. How can I maintain the estate in the teeth of so many demands on our income? How can I preserve it for my son?"

"Shall I fetch Mistress Carey for you, she knows you so well, she—"

"No! No one can see me so."

"I am sorry I did, if it pains you."

"Oh, Alice!" she shook her head.

I stepped away, still uncertain. It was callous to desert her.

"I want my husband to tell me what to do. No one here understands what it is to lose the man you love. I cannot speak to my children about their father, about my own loss." She crumpled into more desperate, choked-in weeping.

"I do." I said, coming closer. "I lost my betrothed. I grieve for you," I said. "But you work so hard, with such strength and dignity. I am sure your husband would be proud of you."

She did not notice I had spoken. "I pray," she said. "I try to keep my faith always, but it is so hard. And I must not despair It is a sin. Isabella would tell me that." She wiped her face and turned to me. "I am sorry you have seen me so lacking self-control. Please tell no one." There was a small silence. She wanted me gone. I could say or do nothing more.

"My Lady." I nodded my reverence and closed her door behind me.

It troubled me that Lady Trentham should suffer without comfort. In the end I told Anne Carey that I had overheard the mistress weeping.

"She said I was not to tell her daughters. She is so unhappy but says she believes despair is sinful."

"She would be helped by a priest, but as we are placed here we cannot fetch one. I will say nothing but I will watch over her."

I felt I had said enough. Philip came in soon after with a trader's deliveries which I helped to unpacked.

I carried a delivery of paper and ink powder to the estate office and found Will standing with his back to the door, swearing.

"Will, what is it?"

"Look what I have done!" he cried. He stood away from the table and I saw a whole page of his written columns awash with red wine. "So poxing stupid! What an oaf I am!"

He looked around wildly for something to mop up the spill.

"Here! Don't try to wipe it, everything will smudge. Leave it!" I snatched at his hand. "Don't touch it." I ran into the washroom and found a fine muslin cheese cloth and ripped it into three, rushed back into the office and lay one length gently over the wine. I watched it soak into the cloth. I folded the second piece double and let that absorb the wine too. I laid the last piece of cloth and pressed it gently. I did not want to absorb the ink too and lose everything.

Carefully Will and I lifted the cloth away, hoping it would not lift the paper with it but it was too coarse and heavy. Will peered at the writing.

"I think it is still readable, just. I can rescue it. I'll just have to copy the whole thing again. He groaned and rubbed his eyes. "I'll have to leave it for now though. Dick and I have to ride to Coventry about the timber deal. Thank you, dear girl." He kissed my cheek, his lips lingering there. That kiss was worth the work.

"Safe journey," I smiled back.

One afternoon Elizabeth came to visit her mother. We were sitting in the solar sewing with Luce companionably when we heard two of the estate men run in downstairs calling for Will.

"There's Parliament Army men coming up the estate road."

Everyone was busy with the usual rush to hide what stores we could and lay out such food and ale as we commonly gave to billeting soldiers.

"Lock all the doors after me and close the shutters," shouted Will and ran out to the front.

Anne Carey called out her instructions. "Aimee, Alice, come with me and bring the wine and cups for the family. Aimee, you take refreshment up to Sir Felix and Lady Eliza. Tell them there might be a troop of Parliament horse soldiers so they had better stay in their chamber where it is quiet."

"Alice, come with me."

"What is happening, Anne? There is a commotion. I heard shouting."

"More horsemen, My Lady, Roundheads. Master Franks has gone down to them."

Lady Trentham sighed and drew her hand over her eyes. "I do not want them here, to boast about their victories. It is bad enough we have lost hope for the King's cause. I would be spared their gloating."

"That is the very reason Master Franks has gone, to direct them away from the house and into the barns."

"I'm not sure he will be able to do that, Mother," said Isabella. "What is one man against a company of soldiers? They will be here, thrusting themselves into our faces at any moment."

"Isabella! By the saints, you are no comfort to my mother!" Elizabeth stood and put her arm around Lady Abigail's shoulders.

"There is no comfort to be had in these times, Elizabeth. You cannot keep pretending all will be well for us. We will be made to suffer, for our allegiance and for our faith."

"Enough, Isabella!" Lady Trentham shrugged Elizabeth's arm aside. "I have enough to contend with without listening to my daughters quarrelling. Everything you say may be true, Isabella, but we cannot dwell on what we cannot change. Your father, rest his soul, gave all he could for his allegiance, his faith and his king. He made his sacrifice. Whatever sacrifice we are called upon to make within Beauchamps we will make. If we must face those ruffians again, insulting us and our religion we will bear it as a wound, as your blessed father did. Now, Mistress Carey, have all the usual precautions been taken downstairs?"

"Yes, My Lady, everything is stowed that may be, and modest refreshments laid out."

"Good. I will come down to the hall and wait for them to arrive. Elizabeth, I am sorry you are trapped here while this happens. Go up with Isabella to her chamber and stay there unless I send for you. Alice, stay with me. We will need your box of medicines, no doubt."

Down in the kitchen Will was standing with an officer of the Model Army, still wearing his helmet, his coat streaked with blood.

"Alice, this is Captain Purdy. He has a musket ball in his chest. He needs help."

"She hasn't been with the plague victims, has she?" His voice was a strained whisper.

"No, nowhere near."

The soldier sank into the hearth chair, his head drooped to his chest. I took off his helmet and opened his coat. Blood had soaked his shirt.

"Help take this coat off, Will. Cut it if necessary, and the shirt. Philip, the medicine box is under the dresser, open it here. I need hot water and cloths, Ruth, please."

While everyone helped assemble what I needed, the captain's body sagged.

"He has fainted. Lay him on the floor. I will try to get the shot out while he is stupefied."

I concentrated on the memory of my mother cutting the musket ball out of that soldier's wound at Netherfold. Then I had just watched. Now I had to do it. Ruth knelt and mopped away the blood, rinsed the cloth, mopped again as I probed and found the ball. Using two short meat skewers I poked and pressed, substituted one skewer for a knife and eventually prised the shot out.

"Grab it!" I hissed and Ruth rolled it out. Captain Purdy came round, groaning. At my final thrust he screamed and pushed me away. Will and Philip seized his arms and held him down. He kicked out in his pain and fear.

Mistress Carey pushed a flask into my hand.

"Brandy," she said. I poured some over the wound and pressed a clean linen pad against the wound with all my strength.

"Try to drink some brandy, Captain. The worst is over now."

He gulped some down but burst out groaning and gasping again while Will and Philip held him down.

I spread my most powerful salve on to a thick linen pad, pressed it into place and bound his chest as tightly as I could with linen strips.

"Find a board in the yard, Philip and we will carry him out to the Larch Barn while his wound is fresh," said Will. "Once the heavy bleeding stops—"

"—*if* it stops," I murmured.

"When it stops, he will need to be kept still. Have you finished with him, Alice?"

"I will give him some poppy medicine when he is calm enough to drink it all down. I will come over to the barn when you have settled him."

After they carried him out, Will and Philip came back to the kitchen to find Lady Trentham there, waiting for him.

"What has happened, Will? Are they here, on the estate? How many? Do they want to speak to me?"

"No, My Lady. There is only a small band of about thirty. Battle-weary. Quiet. I have told them there is a possible plague victim in the house, perhaps more than one, so they have agreed to stay confined to the barn and stables."

"Plague?"

"Master Franks ran to the gates and tied a sheet and made a plague cross flag of it. I ran out from the gate house carrying Will's fowling gun and a powder horn in case they made trouble but they made none," said Dick. "They demanded quarter here, saying they were back from Worcester and had wounded men. They wanted the gates opened. I asked them if they could not see the plague sign, that we feared one of our drovers brought it here from Stratford and they had better move on and even avoid Stratford too. But the captain said the wounded officer was bad and would not last much longer. He ordered his men to break down the gates."

"I said there was no need for that. Philip and Dick let them in and I told them they must stay in the barn, not enter the house."

"You all did well there." Her Ladyship smiled at the men. "I will not see them unless I have to, but if they demand it, send me the officer you judge to be the most reasonable. How is the badly-wounded one?"

"Alice was like a true army surgeon, removing a musket ball from his chest."

"Gracious Heaven! How were you able?"

"I helped my mother do it. It has left a deep wound, though. There may be infection within. I am not sure he will live."

"You were an astonishment, Alice," said Will. "So calm and careful. I would be happy for you to doctor my wounds any day."

"Thank you, all of you. Now, Alice, come with me. I want to consult you about some sewing."

I followed her up to the solar and she led me to the window seat by the worktable. The sewing materials were there but she made no attempt to touch them.

"Sit here, Alice. I have had no opportunity to thank you privately for your kindness to me when you found me so distraught. I am glad you said nothing to my daughters. It is important that I seem strong to my family. You are the only one who has seen me so weak."

"My Lady I will not—"

She held up a hand. "I am confident of your discretion. I think you understand the role I must be seen to play. My private grief has to remain so."

"There is no shame in mourning."

"No, but it is seemly to keep it under control before others."

"You did not choose to lose control before me, and I did not choose to be there and overhear you, it was chance. The wind blew the door, I was passing, there you were. I should have walked by."

"But you cannot pass by a wound without seeking to bind it. I thank you for your quiet company in my distress."

The last weeks of Autumn burned with late sun. The estate harvest was done. Lady Trentham roused her spirits and, somewhat reluctantly and against the wishes of Isabella and her grandmother, agreed to the old tradition of the Harvest Thanksgiving supper.

"I think, my dears," she said, "we must show by our lives that we trust in God's grace to bring us out of this grievous war as safely as we have gathered in our harvest."

We held the feast with music and singing and to my delight, Will and I sat together.

"You seem well settled here, Alice. You are happy, are you?"

"Yes, almost all of the time. Isabella does not like me. She is the only one who resents my being here. She thinks because I am not a Catholic I am somehow a threat to the family. It makes me angry, Will. She has no reason to suspect me of any such thing."

"Isabella is never happy. Strange, though, she does not accuse me of being a Protestant danger, or Ruth or Molly."

"She dislikes my presence in the solar, dislikes her mother treating me as of equal status to the family. My station is that of a yeoman's daughter, she is the daughter of a baronet. When I sit alongside her and her mother asks me to instruct her, she finds it intolerable."

Will covered my hand with his own warm one. "Try to dismiss her lack of charity. She is sour somehow. You have so much more gentleness and favour. Everyone here has taken you to their hearts."

A thrill stirred through me as he said that. Had he taken me to *his* heart? Is that what he meant? I looked up at him. His eyes were dark and deep, his smile steady. But I could read no clear intent.

"I have to go to the Mop Fair at Stratford on Friday. Lady Trentham wants to employ another kitchen maid. Also, Dick and I and Philip have farm materials to buy and Luce wants wedding favours for their marriage celebration. Would you come with us? I have already asked the mistress's permission and she has agreed. She needs silks or some such. She will tell you."

"I would enjoy that, Will. I used to go every year with Mother and Father and my brothers and sisters, but these last two years have been rather sad."

"But you are ready for some frivolity now?" He gave me another of his warmest smiles and I embraced the prospect of a holiday day with Will. I went to bed wondering.

The Mop Fair

Gloves as sweet as damask roses
Masks for faces and for noses
…pins and poking sticks of steel;
What maids lack from head to heel
Come buy of me, come buy, come buy
'Autolycus' Song': William Shakespeare.

I was up and ready before dawn on Friday and after our breakfast we wrapped in our warmest cloaks and Will, Dick, Luce and I climbed into the waggon among the knobbly sacks of market wares and Philip Drake drove us into town. I was light-hearted as our ride passed through Saxonford without sight of any roaming bands of soldiers. Only now and then, as we passed a rotting horse carcass in a ditch, were we reminded of the war.

The nearer we drew to Stratford, the more crowded the road became until Philip was forced to steer a stop-and-start pathway through droves of bleating, mooing and cackling animals, merchants carting their produce, pedlars staggering under their packs and labourers and maids carrying their brooms or shovels to show they wanted work.

Philip tethered our waggon outside the livery stable, so we all knew where to find him again. Will and Luce went to the hiring ring to find a new kitchen maid.

I set off with my basket, pleased with myself for being in sole charge of the purse for spices, French embroidery silks and fine threads for the wedding clothes. I had never bought such luxurious stuff for us at home, but I had eyes in my head. I had looked closely at the decorative trims on Elizabeth and Isabella's sleeves, the stitchery at the yoke of Lady Trentham's gown. I knew what to look for. I lingered over the mercer's stalls, feeling the skeins, sorting through the rich crimsons, pale violets, saffron and rose.

I hesitated over the prices they asked, as I did at the spice stall, hazy with the smells of nutmeg and cloves. I had the money and the responsibility of spending it wisely. I traded and bargained, jingling the purse of coins at my wrist as a lure.

The midday bell sounded. I tore myself away from a troupe of jugglers and a dark-eyed dancer in a scarlet skirt playing a tambourine and went towards our waggon. Will came to me at once, smiling.

"Have you enjoyed your morning, Mistress of The Needlework?"

"A wonderful morning, running my fingers through silken rainbows and the given coins that I was free to spend. Have you found a good kitchen maid?"

"We have found two. Luce is speaking to each in turn. I have made a choice; I am off to see if she and I agree."

While I waited for him to come back I walked over to the broadsheets pasted on the walls of The Bear tavern.

By Order of Parliament
Papists, Recusants who will not attend the Established Church are required to pay fines charged by acreage as demanded by the Commissioners Rightful Appointee.

There was another beside it, half ripped away which read:

All furnitures and objects of the
Popish Religion
shall be confiscated or destroyed.
These are declared **illegal**.

Beside that was an ugly woodcut drawing of a king and a pope sticking forks into a boar's head stuffed with holly while the devil stood behind them, leering. It read:

Pagan Yuletide
an Abomination

It was daubed with mud pellets and the word 'abomination' was streaked over with cow muck.

As I turned away, I could see Will through the thinning crowd. He was handing the shilling to the young girl he and Luce had obviously just hired, sealing their bargain. I approached them.

"All our business is complete so shall we go to see the pleasure parts of the fair? I can hear music."

"There is a stilt-walker!" Luce exclaimed, pointing. We were interrupted by the Town Crier's call and the ringing of his bell. He led a small procession through the crowd. There was the Mop Master followed by four Puritan officials in their black coats, white collars and tall-crowned hats. One of them mounted the steps of the old preaching cross.

People drifted closer to hear him.

"We the chosen elders of this parish are come to announce the decisions of Parliament. First, hear you, the Book of Common Prayer established by Archbishop Laud—" at his name there was a smattering of booing and catcalls. "Is to be abolished, for this book stinks in the nostrils of God!"

He paused for effect and a few people cheered. Others shouted them down. There was some pushing and pulling in the middle of the crowd. Will reached out and drew me close to him. Dick led Luce further back, calling the new serving girl to come after them. The elder carried on.

"Hear you, Christmas feasting has been declared a sacrilege. All exchange of gifts, gorging and dressing in fine clothes is now forbidden."

The farm labourers in front of us raised their staves and shook them at the elders. There was an outcry.

"Bishop and King!"

"God save King Charles!"

"Cromwell for the people!"

"I'm for Parliament!"

The godly and the ungodly abused each other ever louder, cursing and tearing into their neighbours of only an hour ago. One red-faced, toothless giant in front of me grabbed at the preaching elder and pulled him to the ground. Others tore into the melee, some pulling off the attackers while others wrestled the Puritans and pulled off their hats.

The Town Crier rang his bell wildly to call order until a woman with huge hands wrenched it from him and threw it in the horse trough.

"Save the prayer book!"

"Save our Christmas cheer!"

"Popes to the devil!"

"Kings to the devil"!

Punches were thrown, tussling men fell to the ground, locked together. The mayor gathered his gown about him and ran towards The Bear Inn, followed by the parish elders, falling over their feet. Squashed vegetables flew over my head and splattered on their neat coats. Men picked up horse dung, mud clods, sheep muck and pelted the Mayor. He shrieked at the landlord to bar the door behind him.

"Lock it! Lock it after me! Keep them out—ouff!"

The last steaming clod struck his head as he slammed the door shut and more filth slapped against the wood and slid down into a stinking heap.

Women scooped up their children and ran. Blood was drawn and screams overtook groans and swearing.

"Out of this!" Will grabbed me and propelled me towards our waggon-tether. Bodies bumped into us. Someone plucked at Will's cloak and spun him round. "Run on, Alice!"

I dithered between helping him and doing as he said. He wrenched free. We stumbled through upended stalls, skidded on spilt fruit and shoved terrified sheep aside. Geese hissed and flapped their furious wings, attacking everything in their way.

At last, we reached the edge of the market where the smarter merchants and more sober Stratfordians were already making their escape in pairs and family groups.

Agitated and panting, Dick shoved Luce and I up into our waggon. Will helped the new girl, who was white and wide-eyed. Philip already had the reins in hand.

Dick untied a bundle of fence-staves and gave one to each of us. "Grab one of these and if any of the ruffians come near us—"

"—we will clout them roundly, dear, don't you fret!" Luce looked braver than I felt.

"Mad lot!" she exclaimed. "Are you hurt?"

"No, just frightened," I gasped. "I have never been in such a turmoil—not even when we had soldiers ride over our land."

As we moved off, a gang of youths waving sticks and bits of broken market stall, ran past us chasing a man in a velvet cloak shouting, "For the King! For the King!"

Philip hurried the horse and drove us away leaving the clamour behind us.

"What a day!" said Luce, straightening her cap.

"Is anyone hurt?" asked Will. He turned to the new maid. "This is a terrible introduction to our part of the world, Jane Martin. Stratford Market is never so rowdy, so violent. I am sorry you had to witness it. We were lucky to escape with our noses unbloodied."

"Without broken bones, even!" Philip smacked the reins over the horse's rump in his indignation.

"I am pleased the men found you, Jane," I said. "You must have been afraid, for we were all strange faces to you, and the market was in chaos."

"I did not stray from the hiring place," she said, her voice quiet, trembling a little. "Master Franks said he would come back

97

for me but I was worried he would not know me again, nor I him."

"Well, girl, you had a cruel start with us. You will feel better once we have you safe to Beauchamps among us kindly people." Luce smiled at Dick for being one of them.

"Master Franks told me it is a Catholic household."

"Does that trouble you?" asked Luce.

"Are you all Catholics there?"

"Not all," Luce said. "Lady Trentham never refers to any differences between us, whether of religion or of position. We eat together, we share the work."

"My father is fighting with Oliver Cromwell's army. Should I keep that a secret from the mistress, if she is a Catholic and a Royalist."

"Her Ladyship never confronts any of us about our allegiances. All she looks for is good work and loyalty to the Trentham estate. And we give it with all our hearts," said Will.

Philip decided to avoid the main Stratford road to Saxonford and took the quieter lanes around Foxley Ash, in case of more trouble. As we rode along, I noticed the patch stitched into Jane Martin's blue cloak. I lifted it to examine the stitching. "This mending is very fine. Did you do this lovely, neat stitching?"

"Yes." Her voice was eager now. "I love to sew, even if it is just mending. My mother took in sewing for others. She taught me because she said it was a useful skill, like Dorcas, in the Testament."

"Good. Me too," I smiled. "It is work, but pleasurable."

Jane Martin said, "I told Master Franks, I have no skill with animals or dairy, but I am always willing to learn new things. I can cook simple food," she said, in a rush as though she was reciting a lesson learnt. "I work well under direction and I would do well in an orderly kitchen."

"Mistress Carey would expect that," Luce said and looking at me, went on. "Do you know how to make up herbal medicines and salves? Alice, here is our expert but we always need more.

Soldiers are always coming back and forth, you know, needing their wounds mended."

"My mother taught me some simple things, but I can soon learn more." She gave out a sigh. "I just want a secure place to live and work."

"It's Mistress Carey, the housekeeper you will have to please. She is exacting but motherly," Luce finished with a grin. Jane Martin thought for a moment then gave a small smile back.

It was dusk as we approached the Hall, the candles already winking through the window glass. It was surprising that this grand house should feel like home to me but it did, and never more so than after the threatening riot at the Mop. I was glad to be back whole.

The estate men helped Dick and Philip unload the marketing while Luce took Jane Martin in to Mistress Carey for her approval. Will helped me down.

"That was terrible, today. You are sure you were not hurt?

"You were the one more likely to be hurt, that fellow who grabbed you. Did he hit you?"

Will shook his head. "We tussled a bit, but I threw him off and went to fetch young Jane. I thought she would be terrified, in a strange place, just employed by strangers. She is a timid creature but she speaks sensibly about the work she can do. I'll go in and see if Anne Carey is satisfied. I'm sorry our pleasure-day was spoilt." He rested his hands on my arms a little longer, keeping me close, then led me into the house.

The kitchen was warm and welcoming after the fright and the waggon ride. I put the spices to the dry store cupboard and helped with the preparations for the evening meal which we all gathered into the hall to eat.

Everyone wanted to hear about the Mop Fair riot.

"The Elders have declared a ban on celebrating Christmas. That's what started the crowd shouting."

"What?"

"Impossible!"

People exclaimed all around the table.

"No fancy food, no drinking—"

Ruth spluttered out her ale, "People will never obey that one!"

"Pagan abomination they called it," grumbled Dick. "Ridiculous!"

Lady Abigail looked around, shocked. "Will they send officers into every house, great or small, to examine them at their dinner on Christmas Day, then? Cannot be, surely. Will?"

"Judging by the outcry in Stratford, I think they would be thrown out of almost every door in Warwickshire." Luce looked around for the agreement of the others.

"But there's worse news yet, My Lady. The Parliament are sending commissioners to ride around to call for recusancy fines again."

"But Will, we already pay fines enough!"

"And holy images and crucifixes are declared illegal and must be destroyed."

"Oh, how weary I am of this." Her Ladyship looked despairing. Isabella drooped. There was a stir of unease around the room, of anger simmering."

"There was an outcry at that in the marketplace, though. Some jeered in support but there were other voices of protest, shouts of 'Keep our Christmas!' and 'Leave things be!'" I said. "I think people like the old ways, the old things in the churches, don't you?"

Will agreed. "How can the Parliament enforce it wholesale? People will resist it. They did today. I nearly had my head punched."

"Were you afraid, Alice?" asked Aimee.

"Yes. I was. And I was afraid for Dick and Will, and afraid Philip would be dragged off the waggon and we would be upturned. It was terrible!"

Mistress Carey clattered the spoons and plates together. "Why in God's name can they not leave people alone? We have feasted our Christmases, brought in our holly and ivy for generations. Where is the harm? And what—no mince pies, no roasted goose, no pig? Is winter to be one long ordeal of ice and darkness? What do these men want of us?"

"They want to ban the Protestant prayer book as well," said Luce.

"But King James himself called for that, and he comes from the strict Scottish Protestants. What can they see wrong with that?" Philip slammed his tankard down, spilling his ale.

"Half of the Stratford crowd were angry and the other half in support of it so they fell to blows. My cloak was ripped away and poor Jane Martin here must have wondered what sort of neighbourhood she had been hired into."

"Then we should talk of other things," said Lady Trentham. "Where are you from, Jane?"

"Stoten End, My Lady, in Gloucestershire. "

"And are you family there still?"

"My mother died and my father left to fight in the war."

"For whom, Jane?" Isabella asked.

Lady Trentham spoke across her daughter. "So, you no longer had a home. Of course, you need a new place. Your dress is plain. Were your family Puritans?"

With every eye on her, the poor girl shrank in her chair, her eyes wary. I felt sorry for her.

"Protestants have always celebrated Christmas as heartily as any." I said. "My family certainly have: the gifts, the evergreen, my mother's cider brew."

"And mistletoe, I'm sure," Will joined in to help me. "There is not a man here who would want to ban the ancient Christmas mistletoe tradition." Dick and Philip banged the table and the mood shifted, lightened. Will actually winked at me.

Lady Trentham rose and, asking Aimee and Beth to help her elderly in-laws up the stairs. Isabella followed and the talk among the rest of us turned to laughter as Will and Dick

101

recounted the story, much embroidered, of the flying horse dung landing on the mayor.

As the company dispersed to complete their evening tasks, I went over to Jane Martin who sat with her hands folded, looking about her.

"I have not been given anything to do."

"Well, I will sit here with you," I said. "Will it content you here?"

"It is a place. Comfortable."

She sat for a while, silent. Then she said, "We did not celebrate Christmas when I lived at home. My father did not agree with it."

"It will not offend you, though, if they invite you to join in here?"

"I suppose not. I must do as I am bid if I am to keep my place. Will you be here?"

"No, I am to go back to my own family I think. You will find you have come to a kind place. No one quarrels about religious differences here."

"What about the young mistress, the severe one?"

"Mistress Isabella? She is a strict observer of her faith, but you will find you have little to do with her. She stays in her room mostly. Come with me to the kitchen. We will find a job for ourselves. There is always something."

Molly took Jane pot and plate scouring and I was sent to the cellar with the empty beer keg. As I came out again and turned to padlock the cellar door, I heard a horse gallop into the yard. A single rider reined to a halt, dismounted and hammered on the garden room door. I ran to him and fetched him into the kitchen calling for Will.

Whatever questions Will and Mistress Carey asked the finely dressed newcomer in his lace-trimmed velvet and his feathered cap, his answers satisfied them and they took him upstairs to find the mistress.

Aimee came in, having settled Lady Eliza and her husband to their bed. "Who is it that has come? Is it trouble? Is it about Thomas?"

Mistress Carey bustled in behind her. "Go up and prepare the south guest room, Aimee. Jane go with her. The late master's nephew has just arrived to stay. He needs food and wine. Ruth you arrange that."

"Is he a soldier?" I asked.

"No." I had never known Anne Carey say fewer words. She left us and went back up to the family. I did not think one visitor, even one unexpected, would make our housekeeper look so flustered.

I had to pass through the solar on my way to bed in the round room. I walked around the edge of the room so as not to disturb Lady Trentham but she was so intent on her nephew she did not look my way. Luce had followed close behind me with the family's night- chamber candles.

She bent surprisingly close to the young man and addressed him with an air of reverence that surprised me. I thought he was a stranger to the everyone in the kitchen. Perhaps I had misunderstood.

As I shut my bedchamber door I felt a chill breath of air. The very house seemed to have been disturbed by the day's events.

Feast Before Fast

And the door stood open at our feast
When there passed us a man
With his back to the East

'Unwelcome': Mary Coleridge

Next day Lady Trentham and her nephew spent the whole time together. I saw them walking in the garden talking intently and in the afternoon when I went into the solar to join the ladies for sewing, he was there with her again. Sir Felix and Lady Eliza were there too.

"Alice, this is my husband's nephew, Francis de Paul."

"And my grandson," Lady Eliza beamed up at him and grasped his hand and kissed it.

Master de Paul bent to give me a half bow, grinning at me.

"Alice is the daughter of a neighbouring landowner, Francis. She is a great help to us here." She gestured at the sewing.

"Mistress Sanderson is improving my handling of fine lace, cousin. She is talented with her needle, and with bandages." Isabella inclined her head my way. Francis came round beside her and examined the needlework as though it was his greatest interest and grinned at me again.

That night the family dined privately upstairs. The rest of us gathered around the kitchen table.

"What have they been talking about up there, Alice? You were with them all afternoon," Ruth asked.

"They grumbled about the quartering of troops here. Master de Paul asked what happened when Parliament troops came, were they violent, did they destroy things, did they search the house?"

"I heard him earlier," said Will, "telling them about his ride here through Warwickshire. He came through Stainsby and the talk was that Roundheads had taken over Stainsby Court and

104

made camp all over the house itself and declared they were staying there for the whole of the winter!"

"What about the family then?"

"The Lyttlejohns? Gone to stay with relatives in Staffordshire, Anne. And he said there were Scots soldiers riding south under the King's banner to carry on the fight."

"The King is not completely defeated then, like people were saying?"

"I was at the Elms Barton mill today," said Dick. "They were saying there that the Scots were riding south, taking over all the farms around Birmingham, butchering the sheep and roasting them!"

"What! Sheep stealing got you hanged at one time."

"Some folk think it should be brought back again, Philip. All that and drunken soldiers in Lavingham, fighting with the locals."

"It wasn't just the Roundheads behaving badly, what about that king's lot here, Calcotton and them? If the King is bringing foreigners to help him I'll fight them too and be glad to if them wild Scotsmen try their games with me. Fancy a King depending on louts and foreigners!" He swigged his beer.

"The Scots are not foreign, Philip. King James joined us together, after all."

"Kings! Princes!" He set down his tankard and went out saying something about the stables.

Anne Carey and Luce between them took the table talk in another turn but our usual air of fellowship was in disjoint.

As people moved, some to tasks, some to sit nearer the fire, Will came and sat close to me.

"Don't move your seat just yet," he said, laying his hand on my arm. I sat down again, my arm alive to his touch.

"Are you worried, Will? Things seem to be worse everywhere, even here in the house. The soldiers are more violent on the farms, and there is all this talk of rules and bans. The whole country is becoming more stiff-necked, nastier."

"I'm not so worried. We have not been much troubled with violence and as for the strict rules, the commissioners cannot march into every house on Christmas Eve to see how we eat our dinner." That made me smile.

"Those Royalists were violent, Will, that one you fought with after he attacked me."

"Yes and you were brave enough to fight him off before I laid my hands on him."

"I was not so much brave as angry, Will, and disgusted. He was so repulsive." I shuddered at the memory of his raking kisses.

"Shh. Don't think about it again. That was not my intention, Alice, I just wanted to say I admired you over that business."

"But I cried all over you, like a weakling."

"Nothing weak about tears after a bad experience. And you may cry 'all over me' any time you need to."

We were staring at each other. The voices in the room, the plates and tankards faded away. The colours and the candle flames swirled into a fine mist until all I saw was Will, his face, his eyes, his mouth. I thought he would kiss me. I thought I would kiss him, if I dared, if we were not sitting in a room full of people. But he broke his gaze, stood up and touched my arm, leading me to join the others in the gossiping circle.

At the end of the evening, as I climbed the staircase to my round room above the front door, I crossed the solar and found Francis de Paul sitting by fire, wine cup in hand. He was beautifully dressed in his silk suit, his lace, his frilled cuffs. Seeing me, he stood up and made me a courtly bow then put down his drink and left to climb the stairs to the bedchambers. No lordling had ever bowed to me before. He knew my father was just a yeoman without large acres and I a woman working at everyone's direction but my own.

I climbed into my bed and thought, not about a lordly bow from a lace trimmed gentleman, but of Will who, tonight, had almost kissed me.

Next day was All Hallows. We did not mark it as a religious festival at home. Minister Barnes had preached against the Popish doctrine of Purgatory and unredeemed souls, but here in Beauchamps we were all busy preparing the fish and baking spiced soul cakes dotted with currants.

"We won't be dressing up here or carrying them about to our neighbours like we did when I was a girl in Birmingham," said Anne Carey, "but you'll taste one tomorrow."

These were innocent pleasures. I could not see why Minister Barnes and his like were so enraged by them. I would have thought they would approve of praying for the souls of the dead.

Beth and I were grinding spices for the soul cakes, when Luce came in to say Lady Trentham wanted me to join her and bring the new silks I had bought at the Stratford Mop.

Up in the solar, Lady Trentham and her nephew sat close together in the window seat. His face was turned from her and she looked to be whispering in his ear. He saw me and stood up at once, bowing politely but with none of the flamboyant courtly flourish of last night. Then he grinned to let me know he recognised the difference. I smiled back, acknowledging it was so. I rather liked his mischievous look.

"I hear you are an expert at wound dressing as well as embroidering lace, Mistress Alice," he said.

"I came to nurse Master Franks' sister as a favour to my father's friend and because Lady Trentham kindly gave me and my sister safe haven from some boisterous Royalist troops."

"Safe haven," he repeated. "Indeed. Beauchamps can be relied upon to offer safety to fugitives."

"Francis!" There was an unusual sharpness in Her Ladyship's voice. "Take yourself off and have a healthy walk about the estate. I have domestic matters to discuss with Alice."

He bowed to each of us and left. Lady Trentham moved to the table and signalled me to join her.

Since I had mentioned my sister and our reason for being here, I thought it was a good time to ask Lady Trentham's leave to go back home.

"I would like to go back to my family for Christmas time if you can spare me My Lady. I can easily have your sewing finished by Advent."

Her face showed neither disappointment nor irritation. "Of course, I understand, Alice. You will be missing your own family. I am sure you will want to celebrate Christmas with them " She paused. "You do keep the old traditions of Christmas don't you? Luce tells me there were posters in the Mop Fair banning the whole festival. She said the Puritans in Parliament are calling it pagan."

"We keep all the old customs at home. My mother keeps to a middle way in those matters and Father refuses to take sides. He just wants to keep our land prosperous."

"Has your holding been in your family for long?"

"Father's family has lived in Bournbroke for generations. He is proud of our history on the land. My grandfather had a small plot but he made money from skilful sheep rearing. When he married, my grandmother, she was an only child, so she brought Oxley land with her. He made more money selling timber and wool and bought more land adjoining hers, planted our orchards and established Netherfold. My father inherited the holding and a yeoman status he is proud of."

"With land like that, fields and orchards, you must have had your share of soldiers demanding to be quartered, as we have."

"It has driven my parents to fury, whichever side—forgive me, My Lady—rides in."

"It is easier for me to make the Royalist men welcome, as my husband fought for the King's cause. Perhaps your family feels that about Parliament's soldiers, in their way."

"Not at all. My father says his loyalty is to his own fields and orchards, not to a London quarrel between the factions of great men."

I thought she was going to say more but she made an abrupt change of subject. "You know I am happy to have you here but I would like you to move out of the round room up to the attic chamber with the others women."

"Of course. Today?"

"Thank you, Alice, yes. My nephew needs a place with better light, for his work."

It was such a pretty room, I was sorry to leave it, but I had had the feeling recently that people, maybe Francis de Paul, had been in there. My belongings had been moved. My bed looked as though it had been lifted about. They clearly had another use for it, and it was their home, not mine.

Lady Trentham called Anne Carey and ordered the move to be made. I went up to the attic chamber where all the waiting women slept. Ruth was already there arranging a mattress for me and blankets and everything needful. I looked out of the window.

"You can see for miles from here."

"Do you feel you have been banished up here with the rest of us?"

"No, of course not. I am quite happy to be here with you. I thought my place in the round room was rather fine. I suspect—" I had not thought of it until now. "I suspect Isabella has not been happy with my being there for some time. I have seen her going in and out several times. Francis de Paul too. They need it for his use."

I sat down on the mattress.

"Comfortable enough?" asked Ruth. I looked back at her and smiled. "Yes, comfortable enough for a fine lady, never mind just me." Ruth grinned. She gave me her hand and hauled me to my feet. "Wedding preparations downstairs, Alice. Lots to do. Will you come?"

"Gladly. I love a wedding."

The household was abuzz with preparations for Dick and Luce's wedding, which was to take place the week before Advent Sunday.

I was in the solar, sewing when Dick and Luce came in together.

"You asked for us, My Lady?" Dick said.

"I would like to hold your wedding breakfast here in the hall so that the whole estate and all the families can celebrate with you. Would you allow me to arrange it?"

Dick looked at Luce. "We would be delighted to have all the families united and take it as an honour for you and yours to share our feast."

Whatever sadness she felt at the news of the Royalist defeats, Lady Trentham engaged with Anne Carey, with Will and all of us to prepare for Dick and Luce's wedding. The kitchen baked and brewed and roasted. We girls stitched lace trimmings and ribbons to everyone's wedding caps and collars. We collected dried flower heads and crimson berries to decorate the wedding arch outside the church door.

The day before the ceremony, Will carted Dick off to Shipscarden Market and Dick's mother kept Luce busy so a gaggle of us were free to invade Dick and Luce's cottage and decorate it for the bedding ceremony.

We made up the bed with fresh sheets which we strewed with lavender and thrift. Lizzie and I tied sprays of dried roses at the head and foot of the bed and scattered dried rose petals all over it and over the floor. We placed oranges, stuck with cloves, a gift from Lady Trentham, around the room filling it with their spicy scent and laid fires in both rooms, finishing with apple twigs and lavender stalks so there would be a fragrant burning on a cold December night.

The wedding day arrived and we made our procession to Throstleford church. Stephen Barkswell, their minister, stood under the flower arch waiting for us.

Dick and Luce walked through the lych gate, hand in hand as a fiddler played a merry tune and we girls ran ahead of them, scattering petals and dried marigold heads.

Dick gave her a pretty blue-stoned ring. They exchanged their vows then we all crowded into the church to hear the prayers and drink from the marriage cup. I looked away from the newly married Master and Mistress Page beaming their happiness on all their friends and family and felt a twinge of envy.

I looked around this church of St. John of the Cross, at the statues and the gold crucifix, the silver cups and plates on show. Even the altar was still in its place covered with fine lace. There were candles, even incense. I thought all those things had already been banned. The local elders must not be troubled by the legislation and were not enforcing it. I thought it all looked pretty and as it used to when I was a little girl.

As the wedding party turned to leave the church, I was shocked to see how all the Trenthams, and Aimee and Beth knelt before the altar and signed themselves with the cross, seemingly unafraid. I had never seen that in St Andrew's. I caught Will's eye but he just smiled his open smile.

Lady Trentham hosted the wedding breakfast in the great hall for both families and the whole household. We feasted and drank beer and the family offered the wedding toast with French wine.

Francis de Paul sat with his cousins. He smiled and talked to Isabella and Elizabeth and Edward with great freedom. Natural enough for cousins, of course, but he caught my eye across the table once or twice and nodded with a grin. I thought this man was enjoying flirting with every woman in the room, high or low. 'I'm not sure I would trust him,' I thought. 'I'm glad that sister of mine is not here.'

As the table was cleared, the village band arrived. They fiddled, piped and sang. There was even some ring-dancing and some jigs. Will offered me his hand to join the 'Rufty Tufty!' and although it was ages since I had danced, the steps came back easily and the others pulled me about in the right figures, with lots of laughter. When Will threw his arms around me for the final turn and jump, I hugged him tightly so as not to fall. I did not want the music to stop.

At last, he led me back to my seat, both of us gasping for breath and laughing. I had not felt so completely happy for years. As I took a welcome drink I felt a twinge of regret that I would be leaving him soon and leaving Beauchamps, even though it was to go home.

At last, the lanterns and torches were lit. We wrapped ourselves in our cloaks and, with the band playing ahead, led Dick and Luce up to the cottage and up the stairs to their bed, raucous with laughter and catcalls and joking, banging their chamber door on our way out.

'What a happy day!' I thought. 'The marauding soldiers, the war and the religious quarrels were far off worries. For today.'

We were all back at our duties next day when Anne Carey called to me.

"Alice, Lady Trentham wants you to take your sewing box upstairs. She is waiting for you."

Isabella was sitting with her mother at the work table.

"Ah, Alice. I have a piece of work I would like you to do." From the dresser drawer she took the finest piece of linen I had ever touched. She spread it out on the table. The lace border was as wide as a man's span and it was already decorated with lilies and leaves.

"I have asked Will to take you back to your father's house on Saturday. But first, this cloth. As you can see the lace has been worked but I would like you to devise a design for each corner and embroider it. And I want you to use the fine silks you bought at the Stratford fair."

She took a packet out of a casket by her elbow and unwrapped a fine lawn handkerchief. Inside it were the bleached white silks and the skeins of spun silver. I stroked them with my fingertips.

"I have never worked with anything so fine."

She smiled. "I'm sure you can create something beautiful." She moved the polished wooden casket closer to me. Inside was a pounce-pot and a bodkin for transferring the powder and catching the design on to cloth. I repacked the precious threads into the casket and collected the paper and charcoal she had ready for me to use.

Just then Francis de Paul came down the stairs and joined us.

"Look at this lace, Francis. For Christmas. Alice is going to embellish the design."

Looking at her nephew, Lady Abigail put her finger, almost casually, to her lips. I could not think there was anything secret about the work unless she was planning it for wedding lace. He bent over it.

"Did you do all of this, Alice?"

"No. I wish I had. But I am delighted to work with it. I hope what I do will please Your Ladyship."

"I am sure of you, my dear," she said.

The pair of them left together and went into the round room, my old room. I wondered why.

Isabella began to fold up her work ready to follow them. I went to the dresser, washed my hands in the bowl of rosemary water kept there and came back to examine the lace. Isabella stood watching me. Conscious of her, I nevertheless put my charcoal to the paper. I drew a trailing vine of leaves, echoing the pattern of those already woven into the lace, then created a spray of leaves with lily-of- the-valley flowers curling in posies around it and at the base a burst of lilies with wild roses clustered at their base.

As I prepared to prick and pounce my first design onto the cloth, I moved my work nearer to the window for more of the morning light. Isabella stood still, her hand on the door latch of the round room. She followed my eyes as I looked at the stained-glass image in the window. It was of the Virgin Mary carrying a spray of lilies. The lilies looked familiar. I went back to the table and spread the cloth open. There! The Virgin's lilies were woven into the lace. This cloth I was to embroider looked more like a church cloth than a wedding garment.

"I would prefer you to keep that folded," Isabella said in a tight voice.

The ranting of our minister and of the elders in the marketplace at Stratford, denouncing popish decorations, echoed in my ears. I was being asked to embellish an altar cloth.

Late one afternoon when the light had faded Lady Trentham was sitting with her parents in law as Isabella and I packed our threads and linens away when we heard a hammering on the front door.

"What's the matter, now?" Isabella sprang up to look out of the window. "Soldiers!" she said.

"Parliament or King's men?"

"It might be priest hunters," Isabella muttered and seized the cloth and folded it over to bury the Virgin's lilies. I caught up the silks and passed them to her. She hid everything in the dresser and lay plain serving cloths on top.

We ran down into the hall just as Aimee opened the door. Roundheads.

Mistress Carey sent Jane Martin to fetch bread, cheese, ham and small beer to be set out on the hall table before the officers came searching for it. She did not send for wine this time, not even watered wine.

The officers stood in front of the hearth.

Lady Trentham came down the stairs with her family.

"Captain Heywood, Madam. Where is your husband? Is he off fighting in the tyrants cause? For if so, he has lost the war."

Lady Eliza cried out. Her husband turned his head this way and that. "What is it? Who is there? What are they saying about my son?"

114

"There, there, Father-in-law. These soldiers need my attention. Isabella, take your grandparents up to their chamber, they should not have followed me. Keep them in their chamber. I will have their supper sent up to them. You stay and eat with them, keep them company. Do not come back down unless I send."

Lady Trentham turned back to Heywood. "My husband is dead, Sir, having fought for his King and his conscience."

Heywood stood frowning at the holy images in the window glass, which were lit up by the candles. "Well, the King's armies have been swept out of Worcester and face defeat everywhere. We have only the sprouting from that branch to cut off and our work is done. Tell me, can the bridge at Saxonford be crossed? Is there a force occupying the town? Who here will know?"

"My people have not been abroad today. You had better send your agents on ahead to enquire. It is not far to ride – another two miles or so. I wonder that you felt obliged to stop here on my land when you could have answered your question with your own eyes in such a short time."

"You have a sharp tongue, Madam. James! Call the officers in and we will eat. Her Ladyship here has so kindly prepared food for us. And, as Her Ladyship advises," he gave a mock acknowledgement, "order Lieutenant Clarke to send two men ahead to Saxonford to examine the bridge and look out for an armed band of Scots. Tell them to take only daggers. Be clandestine. No swords, no helmets, no buckskin."

Lady Trentham made no move. Anne Carey placed herself behind her mistress's chair, glaring at the Parliamentary soldiers, willing them to choke on the food we had provided.

"Did you hurry your relations out of the room because you think we make a habit of attacking old people and violating Catholic maidens, Madam?"

"Or bite off their heads!" shouted one.

"Their maidenheads!" guffawed another to general laughter.

One officer, dressed in deep Puritan black, his wide-brimmed hat still on his head, walked across to the stained-glass window and peered at it closely. He lifted one of the candles and held it close to the glass, examining the images. Very deliberately he replaced the candlestick, blew out the flame and lifted the handle of his sword.

Looking intently at Lady Trentham, then back to the window he beat the windowpane with the handle of his sword again and again.

"Thou shalt not make unto thee any graven image or any—thing—that—is—in—the—earth—BENEATH!" With each word he struck the glass. He smashed the saintly figure into a crazed star. Another strike and the glass fell to pieces inside and out. He went on and on smashing every coloured pane until each figure lay in splinters inside and out of the room.

Silence. Lady Trentham gripped her hands together, her face white and furious.

Anne Carey bent to the hearth, picked up the fire tongs and struck the Puritan officer with all her force.

He stumbled against the dresser. Several pewter plates crashed to the floor and rattled, spinning, spinning. His hat fell to the ground. Beth picked it up and threw it into the fire, where the flames flared over it. He grabbed at her arm but she wrenched free.

"Enough Brother Levens! You, Woman!" Captain Heywood hauled Anne across the room by the arm and pushed her towards the kitchen door. "Get out there. Know your place!"

Beth and Ruth rushed after her' We could hear their raised voices through the door.

"Brother Levens!" Heywood, turned back to the Puritan officer. "That was badly done! Go out to the horses. Organise their stabling."

"She is a Catholic whore and this house a den of wickedness! The Lord God is not mocked. He—"

"Out! Jenkins! Take him out!"

The officers left at the table, grabbed the last of their food and drained their beer. They knew they had reached the end of all hospitality here at Beauchamps.

Heywood turned to Lady Trentham. "His abuse was excessive and the damage. I am sorry for it."

"Wickedness is not the prerogative of Catholics I see, Captain. I want you out of here as soon as may be."

Dick Page's face appeared in the gap of the broken window. "Is anybody hurt here, My Lady? Do you need me?"

"It is as you see, Dick. Damage but no blood spilt. Tell Will these officers are to sleep in the barn with their men. I will not have them in my house. All the beasts can lie together."

He was angry but Captain Heywood bit back his words and left the room through the front door to find Dick. Aimee stood rigid at the hearth, with the long poker in her hand.

"I'm glad you didn't attack one of them with that. They would have hurt you."

"Just ready if needed." She pulled a grim face but I admired her. I had just stood there, frozen.

Lady Trentham sank into her chair, her face in her hands. Will ran in from the kitchen.

"I should have been here to defend you. "

"Aimee found a broom and swept up the broken coloured glass with great care. Will brought a pouch and collected all the pieces. "We will have this mended, My Lady, and defy them."

He went outside and collected the rest then put up the shutters over all the ground floor windows where the remaining glass was prettiest.

"All secure, Your Ladyship. Is there anything else I can do?"

"Nothing more tonight, Will. Just keep all the servants in the kitchen together all night, to eat and sleep. You too, Alice. For safety's sake."

Francis de Paul came in through the garden room door. Lady Abigail started. "Francis! Where have you been? For pity's sake get upstairs. Quickly. Say nothing!"

He caught her alarm and ran up the stairs two at a time. Lady Trentham followed him, taking a rosary of pearls out of her pocket.

I wondered why they were so afraid. The soldiers were out of the house.

We did not see any of the family again that day. They ordered their meal sent to their chambers.

It was barely light when we woke to the soldiers' shouting and the horses' complaints. I peeped through a crack in the shutter.

"Yes, they are leaving." Will, Dick and Philip were out there already, following behind them. Each carried a pitchfork or a staff.

"They will drive them out if they don't move fast enough."

"Good riddance to them! Devils!" Anne Carey spat in their direction.

Soon we had a good fire blazing, the shutters open and the breakfast prepared for ourselves and the family. There was no sunshine, but the day was brighter for the soldiers' leaving.

In the days following, Will travelled to Stratford to find a glazier skilled enough to mend the broken casements. In Anne Carey's kitchen we were all full of busy preparations for the Advent feast and laying down meats and puddings for Christmas. I joined in the peeling and chopping, the baking of pies. We minced pork and stuffed chitterlings, soaked dried plums in some of Lady Trentham's rich red wine and killed and plucked the geese to hang in the cold store.

Everyone was cheerful, looking forward to some merriment to cheer the damp and dark of winter, although there was no better news for the family about King Charles's cause.

Lady Trentham urged her parents in law and the others to rally themselves. "We must prepare ourselves for the Advent fasting and the honouring of the Nativity."

Elizabeth, having been told of the image breaking at the Hall, came to console her family. They wept together a little, Lady Eliza still full of fear, Sir Felix hardly understanding what he heard.

"It will hardly be a happy feast this year. Edward and I are as afraid of harassment as you are, Mother. And I worry that my brother's whereabouts are a mystery and we hear of nothing but defeat for the King's forces."

"I hope we will can enjoy something of the season, dear. We are surrounded by people of goodwill in your household and ours, we must find comfort in that."

I looked around at them all, anxious, weary-looking and I thought how carefree, in comparison, my own family Christmas festival would be. I would be glad of that. I would leave Beauchamps with some regret, because I enjoyed my work, especially the embroidery, and I liked being near to Will.

On the first day of Advent we were all called into the hall for household prayers. Will came in with the King Edward Prayer Book. His cheeks were red from the outside chill and his dark hair was tousled, tumbling over his eyes.

He read the collect for Advent and the season's prayers of course, then the Trentham family, with Anne Carey, Aimee and Beth went upstairs together. I supposed they were going for Catholic prayers of their own.

I had finished sewing my lace border. I folded it with great care so that the lily design was shown to best advantage and when Mistress Carey came back to the kitchen I told her my lace cloth was ready.

"Shall I take it up to Her Ladyship?"

Before she could answer me, the mutton haunch that was roasting on the spit began to hiss and the fat flared up in the fire.

"Jonathan you scallywag! Where are you boy? Come and turn this spit! The meat will singe!"

"Here I am, Mistress, here!" He ran over from the corner, grabbed the handle and began to turn the spit wildly.

"Slower, boy! It needs to cook evenly, not whirligig about!"

I did not bother her with any more questions but went upstairs to find Lady Trentham. I expected to see the family finishing their prayers in the solar but the room was empty.

A log shifted and fell into the hot centre of the fire. It flared and crackled. The sewing things lay strewn about on the table. I tidied them and collected my own belongings into my work box. The silks were tangled and as I lifted them my grandmother's silver thimble dropped to the floor and bounced against the door to the round room. It rolled into the gap between the door and the jamb. I held on to the door handle to bend and flick the thimble free and the latch lifted. The heavy door swung open and pulled me forward into the room.

I struggled to my feet and looked up to see the whole Trentham family turned towards me, faces full of alarm.

"Forgive me, I fell. I was looking for my thimble." My words dwindled away.

Lady Trentham was on her feet. The others sat in rows facing the table. In front of the table by the window Francis de Paul stood, wearing a long silken band around his neck. His eyes were fastened on me. He looked severe, even angry.

Sir Felix began his anxious questioning, straining and squinting to see what he was no longer able to see. "Who is it? Who has come?"

"Alice. Come away with me." Lady Trentham took my arm and propelled me forward.

"Is it pursuivants, Abigail? Are they come again?" Sir Felix whined.

"Hush, dear. There are no pursuivants any longer. All in the past, remember? We are all safe now." The door closed on his wife trying to soothe his fear.

"I am sorry, My Lady, I did not mean to disturb your family's prayers. It was my thimble."

Lady Abigail steered me towards the fireplace in the solar. Someone shut the round room door abruptly behind us.

"Thimble? Do you need it this moment?"

She looked uneasy. I was embarrassed that I had stumbled upon them worshipping illegally. No wonder she was frightened, they had turned the round room into a chapel. What I saw was not just family prayers, it was a Catholic Mass. Francis de Paul may be her nephew but Lady Trentham was sheltering a Catholic priest.

"You have seen what I would rather you had not seen, Alice. You have us in your hands now. Keeping my nephew here, and he a priest, celebrating the Mass means we are breaking the law. But we are forced to. The ban is cruel."

"You pay all your fines, as Catholics, Will told me. You keep that part of the law."

"But they do not allow this." She gestured to the round room.

Francis de Paul came out. He confronted me. "What has she said, Abigail? What will you do, Alice?"

"Alice will say nothing to hurt us, I am sure."

"You know I will not. I will never speak of it. I will never endanger any of you."

"You speak lightly, Alice," de Paul said. "You have no idea what the persecutors do to force the truth out of witnesses."

"That is enough, Francis. I trust Alice. I took a foolish risk, celebrating Advent like this. We must dismantle everything, return the round room into a sewing chamber, an office, something. Hide the crucifix and chalice. And you must be more the nephew and less the priest."

"This Protestant has us at her mercy, Abigail."

"I can do nothing more than give you my word of honour that what I have seen will remain secret with me. I cannot unsee it but you must believe what I say."

De Paul looked from face to face then turned and went back into the round room. Lady Trentham moved to the table and saw my needlework.

"Ah," she sighed, "the altar cloth. "She lifted it to her cheek and began to cry. I moved away until she spoke again. "Do you regret doing it, now you know its purpose?"

"No. I was proud to do it for you. Your faith is a matter for you, it is not my business."

"That is not the law of the land, sadly. You can see our trouble." She folded the cloth. "I will hide this away. Perhaps a happier, a safer time will come and it will have its day."

I went up to the attic room and packed ready for our morning departure. As I came back down and made my way to the estate office to leave my baggage for loading, Francis de Paul stepped out of the shadows. He seized me by the wrist and steered me into the cold storeroom, all his former manners and charm gone.

"My aunt tells me to trust you, but forgive me, I am doubtful. I have seen the gross cruelty inflicted on my fellow priests and on those who shelter them. She tells me you are leaving. How can we know you will not tell what you have seen to your people?" His grip was tight over my wrist. I tried to free myself.

"You have no need to threaten me. I am a loyal friend to the Trentham family. I can say no more to you. I can only prove it to you if I am tested and we must hope it never comes to that. Forget I saw the chapel or you. Please."

Whatever he was about to say stopped as he drew breath, for the door swung open.

"Will!"

"Master Franks. My aunt sent me to find Alice here."

I pulled my wrist free and, passing Will, hurried to the estate office, wondering how to explain what Will had seen without giving away the very secrets they wanted me to keep. But Will did not come after me.

I churned all that had happened over and over in my mind. Francis de Paul's sudden abandonment of his charm shocked me. I resented his roughness, his suspicion, even though I understood it. I had seen the cruel drawings stuck to the walls of the Stratford taverns lampooning the Catholic Mass with the devil on an altar among the candles and crucifixes. I had read broadsheets that denounced them as spies for the Spanish king and that papists would spear our children on long toasting forks. These friends of mine could not be traitors or agents of the devil. It was all nonsense. Except the men in power did not think so and it cost people their land and their lives.

I kept my distance from the family and helped in the kitchen with the preparations for the Advent feast. The day passed in a whirl of work. At last, everything was ready. Candles stood on every nook and shelf. Ivy, studded with hedgerow berries glowing crimson, trailed from the window ledges, When Anne Carey was satisfied that everything looked beautiful, she gave Will the signal to strike the bell that summoned everyone to the supper.

Once the family, including Elizabeth and all the family from Carterway Manor, were seated, we all took our places, the men and under maids, the estate workers and gardeners, their wives and families. It was a merry crowd.

Will, having satisfied himself he had done all he had to do, settled close to me and poured me cider. I wondered if he would ask me why Francis and I were closeted in that way, but he said nothing. Perhaps Francis explained it away. I felt a wave of relief when Will looked into my face and covered my hand with his own.

"I will miss you when you go back to Bournbroke, Alice. Seeing your bright smile every day. Indeed, I already miss coming home and not finding you there at my fireside. When you were there, looking after Nell, you gave the place a homely glow I had not known, not even when my wife was alive. I have always had a spartan house, not a home. You changed that."

"Your *wife?* I didn't know you were ever married."

"Nobody does. I have been single as long as your father has known me. I came up here with Sir Carlton as a single man. I never talk about Prudence. She and I were educated together by her father, who was a Puritan minister in Hampden. He believed in educating women and intended Prudence to help him with the financial side of parish business and help manage their small farm." He looked into his tankard, twisting it this way and that.

"Don't talk about it if they are sad memories."

Will shook his head. "No, it does not distress me. It was a long time ago. We were almost children. Her father became convinced he had been called by God to travel the country and preach. He sold everything, gave his money to the poor, packed a knapsack with a bible, a cloak and some bread and cheese and set off to spread the gospel."

"So abruptly? What did Prudence do, and her mother"

"Her mother meekly took up a bag and followed him but Prudence would not go. Her father accused her of disobedience to God and to him and just abandoned her. My mother and father were disgusted. They brought her in with us and when Prudence and I were sixteen, my father thought I ought to marry her, young as we were."

"Were you happy together?"

"Happy enough, I suppose. I knew nothing about love. Then the plague came. My parents died and Prudence died too."

"And you were not even ill."

"No, by a miracle. But by then armed bands were roaming around Oxford and the nearby villages. The King raised his army and Royalist soldiers crammed the taverns. Sir Carlton and his brother joined the King, much to Sir Felix and Lady Eliza's dismay, even though were loyalists. James was killed almost at once so Sir Felix insisted Carlton leave the army and take possession of Beauchamps Hall in his brother's place. But Sir Carlton obeyed his father, married and came here. As soon as the Royalists occupied Worcester he left Lady Abigail and me in charge of the estate and joined the King's army again."

"Sadness has rather overtaken your life, then, since you and Nell danced together as children."

"I didn't break my heart over Prudence, Alice. It was a passionless marriage and after her death I was too busy with the changes and the duties that fell to me. And here I am, as you see me – a rather dull fellow."

I am not sure what I was about to say to that, but a burst of laughter around the table broke the moment. The talk rose and fell. No one took notice of Will and I sitting with our heads so close together, until Francis de Paul stood up, looking straight at me. I thought he was coming to speak to me but he bent close to his aunt and spoke in her ear, then went up the stairs. I turned back to Will who was still speaking to me.

"I worry that the mistress lives under a risk of course. The religious quarrels flared up after the Powder Plot against King James and they have never really gone away."

"Do you fear for their safety?"

"I hear worrying things. You know Stainsby Court, outside Dryden? There were Powder Plotters in their family and the gossip is they still hide priests there in secret holes behind chimneys and such, even that they hold the Mass in a private chapel. They could be hanged for it."

My stomach rolled. My mouth was dry. "And here?" I whispered. "Do they have such things here?"

"God's blood, Alice, I hope not! But I do think the family is watched."

I said nothing.

"You saw those Puritan inspectors, some so full of hate. The Royalists are defeated everywhere. Cromwell is going to win this war. Lady Trentham's husband and her son fought for the King. She will be watched. It was no random visit, that Puritan, Levens, who smashed the stained-glass window."

"I never saw such hatred in a face."

"I should have been there, Alice. I would have knocked him down."

"Mistress Carey tried it with the fire irons. What I hate is how they force their quarrel upon us, eating up the stores, squatting on the land, and worse. I struck that Cavalier soldier, you know, the one that came here. He was wrestling with my father That's why he was so angry when he saw me again."

He beamed at me. "And you fought him again, I saw you. Brave Warrior Maiden!" He raised his tankard in a mock toast.

I smiled back. "I didn't feel brave, just furious. You had to pull him off me."

"And right glad I did." He kissed my hand.

Elizabeth and Isabella stood up and moved nearer to the fireplace with their lutes. The talk fell silent as they began to play. I smiled to myself because Will kept my hand in his.

After Elizabeth and Isabella, two of the gardeners took up fiddles and played old country songs as the others joined in, singing.

A movement at the door of the garden porch caught my eye. Edward Carter's groom came in with someone newly arrived. Both men spoke confidentially to Edward. Whatever message they delivered, it was important enough for Edward to tell his parents and Elizabeth to leave. He crossed to Lady Abigail and repeated his news to her then went out after his family.

Almost at once Lady Trentham rang her bell and brought the singing to a halt.

"I must thank you all warmly for making our Advent feast so delicious and for your music and your good fellowship." Everyone rapped the table, stamped their feet and clapped.

"I have just been told that Cromwell's army is poised to overrun our neighbours in Shipscarden Magna. The Royalist garrison in Shipscarden House is threatened. My daughter's husband and his father have gone to help defend the Nortons. Troops from one side or the other will doubtless ride in here tonight or in the morning. I must ask you to disperse and prepare to defend our livestock, goods and property. It grieves me to end our pleasant evening this way but thank you for everything you do."

Everyone got to their feet, and scurried this way and that to carry, lock away and remove food, wine, pewter, cheeses, everything we wanted to hide from incoming troops. Isabella helped the old folks up the stairs and Will stood to direct matters when Lady Trentham came over to us.

"Will, Alice, I have a task for you." She took us into a quieter corner. "I am aware there is danger in what I ask. Just before dawn, I want you to take the small coach to Shipscarden House and bring Sir Sheldon Norton's wife and daughter here away from the fighting. Kathryn is intended for my son. We must help them. Our families are old, dear friends. Their son Henry is away with the King's army and Sir Sheldon will naturally stay to defend his property. They need our help. Will you go? And Alice would you take your medicines chest in case in case of need?"

It was never in question. "Get your cloak and come into the yard." Will hurried off. By the time I joined him he had the small coach harnessed and ready.

"Are we going now?"

"No, we will go to the gate house together and leave well before dawn, before the soldiers start to move about. From my house we can drive through the copse, well away from them." I collected the medicine chest and climbed up beside Will.

In the gate house, Will refreshed the fire and we sat together on either side of the fireplace warming our toes, as I had seen my mother and father do all my life.

"Are you tired, Alice?"

"Yes, but I am happy to sit here with you. I am warm and comfortable."

"Comfortable." Will reached for my hand and drew me to him. He closed both hands around my face and kissed me, his lips tender but with the power to overwhelm me. We clung together. Logs crackled. We kissed again. I had no thoughts. Only Will's arms. His hands on my neck, over my hair. He gripped the tops of my arms and stood back looking deep into my eyes.

"I promised you my honour, Alice. I..."

I stepped closer and wound my arms around him. This time *I* kissed *him*. He sat me back down, knelt in front of me, holding both my hands and we kissed again, gently. He held me away from him. I tried to read his expression. Seconds went by, charged with words I hoped he would say, that, perhaps, he wanted to say, but then, it happened again—the London world intervened in my sweet country life. Horses rode up past the gate house towards the Hall.

"Soldiers already? This time of night? Run upstairs and bar the chamber door."

I did as he said then opened the window and leant out, craning to see who had come. How many. There were only three horsemen. Not a troop, at least.

I sat up as long as I could, but at last I undressed to my shift and climbed into bed, shivering. I had a restless sleep crowded with confused images; the family in their secret chapel, Francis de Paul as a clandestine priest, Will's warm hands, his kisses.

The sound of the front door banging shut jolted me awake. I lay there, listening. The fire grate was empty, the bedchamber cold. I heard Will moving about downstairs. I wrapped myself in my cloak, unbarred the door and went down.

"Who was it? What has happened?"

"Two of the King's officers have come from Oxford with news for Lady Abigail, about her son." I looked across the room. His face was buried in a towel as, stripped to the waist, he washed himself.

"My God! He is not wounded, is he?"

"They would not say anything. They insisted on seeing the mistress, so I had to rouse Anne Carey."

He threw the towel down and stared at me standing there in my nightgown. I looked back at him, his chest bare, his arms strong and inviting. Whoever moved first, we folded around each other. He filled my world in a moment. I ran my hands over his back, feeling the cool ridge of muscle, the dip of his waist. His

128

face was in my hair. We kissed and there was nothing else, just our kisses and the bond of our arms.

All I wanted was for us to climb into the softness of the bed, lie close, closer and love one another. He groaned softly.

"I promised you, Alice. I have to consider your father. He trusts me."

"My father is not here, Will. He is not on my mind. Only you. Am I shameless? I feel shameless." I reached for him, drew him in to me. We kissed again, long and slow.

At last, he took my hands and kissed them. "Go to bed, Alice. There will be time. Go now."

We stood together, unable to move, reluctant to part. But after another long-held kiss, part we did. I ran upstairs. 'There will be time,' he said. Time for what? When?" I wanted to ask him outright. Hear his answers.

I closed the bedchamber door but I did not bar it. 'I am as shameless as young Lizzie,' I thought. I lay sleepless in the empty bed, turning this way, that way, finding no peace without Will beside me.

The Great House Burning

…from these flames
No light but rather darkness visible
Served only to uncover sights of woe
'Paradise Lost': John Milton

Will tapped on the chamber door. "Time to go, Alice. Come."

I splashed water over my face, dressed and hurried down. We ate hastily and left by the back door. Will drove at a slow pace past the sleeping hall, through the copse and out on the east track towards Shipscarden Magna.

The fields spread around us grey-white under the ringed moon. The hedgerow grasses were frosted into stiff blades. Drifts of cloud now covered, now revealed the waning moon. Silence lay over the Vale. Will sat, stiff-backed, steering our way through the frozen ruts and ridges ahead. I thought of things to say, to ask, but left them unspoken. I had expected him to kiss me this morning, to talk about love, about that future time he spoke of as we parted. 'There will be time,' I thought. We understand each other, our longing, our loving. Yet today Will was reticent again and that made me so. Did he regret all we had said and done, not done? What was it held us in this grip of unspeaking?

The back of my throat was stinging. Tears pricked the corners of my eyes. 'Don't let yourself cry' I thought, 'Too weak, too clinging. We have work to do. Danger, perhaps 'There will be time.'

A white owl dipped, soundless across our path. The horse tossed its head, snickered. The moon clouded over. The horse plodded on, making the only sound. A pair of deer started out of the woodland and ran ahead of us. The sky lightened to grey. A fox sloped towards us, swerved and dropped head-first into the ditch.

"Are you afraid, Alice?" His voice breaking the stillness was a relief.

"Not yet."

"This is another hard favour the Trenthams are asking of you."

"Yes, but a woman had to go with you."

"Lady Abigail would have asked Aimee or even Isabella, but I wanted you. I know your courage and we can speak as equals if there is danger."

"You could not order Isabella about."

"And you are saying I can order you?"

"Well we have been able to count on each other in troubled times."

"Certainly." He took my hand and tucked it between his body and his arm. "Also, it meant I could have you to myself, for the ride."

It was just light enough to see his smile. I felt warmer now. Safer.

"After we have collected the Norton ladies and taken them to Netherfold, I will take you to your father's, however reluctant I am to let you go."

"Are you? Reluctant?"

The horse crunched through iced puddles, snorting.

"I said last night there would be time for us, Alice, but the future is uncertain. I have duties to the estate. We have each had our troubles and our losses. We need a surer, more settled time to speak of promises."

"I wanted to say, 'Speak of it anyway, speak to me of love, let us make promises.' But I did not. It was a decision I later had cause to regret.

Will rattled the reins and the horse picked speed up to a trot. Shipscarden Magna lay ahead. The sky streaked sunrise; *red sky in the morning, shepherd's warning.*

Candles lit the first cottage windows. The great iron gates of Shipscarden House were shut against us with a huge bar rammed

131

across them. We rode further along the wall of the estate to the lodge. Will handed me the reins, jumped down and knocked at the lodge door.

I assumed it was their steward who answered. After some discussion he came out and unlocked a tall side gate through which Will led our coach. We followed the steward to the back offices of the house. He left us in a kitchen, empty of people, food and fire and disappeared further into the house. A well-dressed man with sword and pistols at his waist rushed in to us.

"Master Franks! My message reached Beauchamps, thank God." He shook Will warmly by the hand.

"Sir Sheldon. We are sent to rescue your ladies."

He offered me his hand too and steered us into the great hall.

"Yes, yes. So grateful. "Wait here."

It was a massive place with arched beams, tapestries, carved furniture.

"My wife and daughter are ready to go with you, their belongings are packed. They are reluctant to leave me, of course, but you must insist, Master Franks. You have my permission to be stern. I want them away. Enemy campfires are already lit along the Cotswold ridge." He gestured out beyond the yard. "My men are ready. The battle is coming. I expect cannon fire at any moment."

He left us in the hall and reappeared with his wife and daughter, carrying small bundles. "This is Mistress Sanderson, a companion of Lady Trentham. She has sent her and Master Franks to take you to Beauchamps. You must leave with them now. No complaints. Do as I bid you, darlings. I will come for you when I can but I must be sure you are safe."

They did complain, of course, through tears, but Sir Sheldon pushed them with some force, towards our coach and helped them in.

"Tell Lady Trentham I am grateful for this help."

Royalist officers rushed into the yard, shouting orders, warnings, directions for groups of armaments. A drum in the field beyond beat out a muster and soldiers ran from all directions to a flag that fluttered on a bending pole.

Will climbed up and took the reins, turned the horse and drove us away from the gathering fight.

The red sky was brightening to daylight as we turned away from the gate when huge fire-flashes exploded behind us. The horse screamed and reared as a salvo of cannon fire shattered the stillness. I twisted in my seat and saw roses of gunfire blooming from the troops massed along the ridge.

Bursts of stone and splintered timber erupted from the house. In the distance I could see a wave of horsemen careering down the sloping fields. The Royalist defenders returned fire with their muskets and cannon. Hell's thunder broke all around us. Will drove the horse on through the narrow streets now choked with merchants in a panic to escape with their laden carts, drovers poking at their herds with sticks, terrified sheep scrambling over each other's backs to get away; families, carts, screaming women, wailing children. Shipscarden was heaving with shouting, bleating, roaring bodies. Cannon balls arched over the roofs and brought down branches.

The main street was jammed. There was no escape that way. Will strained at the reins to change direction and drove up a side street towards the church. We were thrown against each other as the coach almost overturned, teetering on two wheels. We came out by the great Shipscarden House gates. Lady Norton let out a terrible cry.

"The house! Look at the house! Oh, it is burning! Your father! Master Franks, you must stop. Stop! We need to rescue my husband."

Will shouted over the din, without turning to her, "Your husband ordered me to get you away from here. I must do what he said."

Sparks flew by us, burning fragments of wood rattled against the coach and fell away.

We passed the church. The lych gate had been torn open and hung askew. Cannon-shot tore into the graveyard sending up spouts of earth and smashed headstones. Royalist horse soldiers galloped up behind and overtook us.

Lady Norton hung out of the coach window, straining to see her house. "They are leaving! They can't leave us undefended! Look at the flames, Kathryn, they are burning through the roof."

Will clutched me to him and covered my head with his arm until we rode out of the range of the flying debris. Our horse, terrified by the rubble falling around it, was in a panic, jerking and tossing between the shafts until I was sure we would be thrown into the ditch in a mangled mass of bodies and splintered wood.

Will swerved again, this time into the woods. "This will be a rough ride. It is just a footpath, but it will keep us away from the soldiers."

He slowed our horse to a standstill and climbed down to stroke and soothe it. Inside the coach, the Nortons were holding each other and crying. There was nothing really helpful I could do. I delved into my medicine chest and for the sake of doing something, gave each of them a sip of brandy. "For the shock, My Lady. It will revive you a little. Have you taken any cuts or blows? I have salves with me."

"No salve for the grief we feel for my husband, my home." She wept again.

"Master Franks is taking us a safer way now. And your forces were escaping, you saw them."

"But have they left my father behind to die?" sobbed Kathryn.

There was nothing I could say.

Will remounted and I climbed back beside him. We plodded through the wood until we reached its edge and the road to Beauchamps and Stratford lay ahead. It was blocked with waggons, horses and Shipscarden folk on foot carrying bundles seeking refuge in Lavrock or Foxley Ash.

Lady Norton leant out of the coach and hailed a soldier hunched over his horse's head. "You, officer! Have you come from Shipscarden House? Why are the King's forces running away? You should be there to defend it."

He lifted his head. "I have shed blood here. I am done. The force is done. They say Prince Rupert himself set the fire, him an' the Lord Dalton, ran about with torches."

"In God's name, why?"

"Prevent Cromwell settin' up his quarters in the house. Sir Sheldon himself said that."

"I don't believe you!"

"If princes and lords ain't defendin' the place then why should I stay there to die in it?"

He turned his horse away. "Clear out yourselves afore them Roundhead bastards come for you."

"Master Franks! My husband would never give an order to burn the house. You must go back and find him."

"I cannot, My Lady, it is impossible. Rest assured it is Cromwell's guns that caused the fire. Now we must do as your husband asked, not add to his troubles. He wants you safe."

Ignoring her pleading, Will urged the coach through the throng. We were jostled and clutched at. People tried to climb beside us begging to be taken along.

"I'm getting out of this, Alice. We will go across the fields. We will have to walk or the wheels will bog down in the mud. "

He turned and nudged across the tide of refugees to a narrow sheep track leading into the Beauchamps estate.

He helped me down and I walked ahead as he led the horse. Our boots were clogged with mud, our legs heavy with the effort of sinking in and pulling ourselves out of it. My dress was soaked and filthy at the hem. What a relief it was to see the Hall in the risen wintry sun, offering a peaceful welcome.

In the safety of the stable yard Mistress Carey, hearing the coach arrive, ran out to help the Nortons down. Lady Trentham stood at the back door, waiting, her arms open. The friends fell into each other's embrace, sobbing.

Will steered me around the back of the coach and, out of sight of the others and took me in his arms. He held me close.

"Terrible," That was all he said.

Even before we could clean our boots, we were seated by the fire and given hot food and ale. Everyone crowded round to hear about the attack on Shipscarden House, rumours having already run into the estate as people knocked at Dick and Luce's house and the neighbouring farm cottages. begging refuge.

"Shipscarden House in flames!" they exclaimed.

"A huge line of Roundheads riding down from the ridge! How many?"

"Did you see people killed?"

"What, the church? That beautiful church! Have they fired it too?"

"How did you get out of it, Will? All the explosions—the panic!"

"His driving was masterly," I said. "For every street was blocked."

"Flocks of sheep, horses in a stampede. It was like a scene from the doom. The great house will burn to ashes, depend on it."

"Oh, that beautiful house." Anne Carey was horrified. "It is almost new, from King James's time—all those fancy chimneys and stone fol-de-rols. How could they burn?"

"Well, it was a vanity, if you ask me. Better gone," said Philip. Jane Martin, sat beside him, admiring him, nodding.

"Lady Norton stopped a soldier on the road and asked him why they were running away," I said. "He told her Lord somebody or other made Sir Sheldon set fire to it himself."

"Why on earth would they do that?"

"To stop the enemy using it for glory," Dick said. "Or maybe just to stable their horses in. That's what they did at Stainsby Court I heard tell."

136

"From what I could see the cannon fusillade was more than enough to set the place burning. Don't you think so. Alice?"

"Yes, Will is right. It was hellish. The noise. I felt the end of the world was come upon us."

"You must have been terrified, my dear," Mistress Carey said.

"Yes." I burst into tears.

Christmas and a Long New Year

"Then drink to the holly berry
With hey down hey down derry
The mistletoe we'll pledge also
And at Christmas all be merry."

Traditional

Will and I could not leave for Bournbroke as we had planned. The household had to be rearranged to accommodate Lady Norton and her daughter and they pleaded with Will to ride back to Shipscarden and enquire after Sir Sheldon.

Dick and Will went together on horseback. I stowed my belongings in the garden room and found kitchen chores to keep me busy and distract me from worrying about Will's safety.

"Is it true," asked Molly, "that Sir Sheldon Norton set the fire himself?"

"Jake says he heard it was Prince Rupert," said Ruth.

"What did they say, Alice, the ladies?"

"It was all confusion. They were sure of nothing more than that their home was burning down and Sir Sheldon was staying there to fight."

In the afternoon, Mistress Carey sent me to the cellar to collect vegetables from the storeroom to accompany the fast-day fish. The basket was heavy with turnips and onions so I set it down in the arch of the cellar doorway to turn and secure the door. Francis de Paul was walking back to the house from the fishponds with Philip Drake. Philip took both fish creels away to clean and cut the catch. I was just about to pick up my load and go back to the kitchen when a horse galloped around the corner, almost crashing into Francis de Paul who flattened himself against the wall with a cry.

The rider shouted. "You, Sir! Ho! Help me here!"

"You nearly rode me down, man, who are you?"

"Father Barkswell from St John of the Cross in Throstleford. I want Lady Trentham to give me sanctuary. Take me to Her Ladyship at once. She belongs to my parish. We are fellow Catholics. She knows me." He threw himself across his horse's neck and fell, ungainly, out of the saddle.

Francis grabbed Father Barkswell's cloak. "You can't come in here." The priest struggled to break free.

I shrank back into the shadow of the cellar arch. De Paul would not want to know I was a witness to a quarrel between priests. He distrusted me already.

"I need to get in there. Let me go. Shipscarden is in flames. The Roundheads have overrun the town and are riding into Throstleford to sack the church—image-breakers, desecrators! They will kill me. Let me go in!"

Francis shoved the panic-stricken priest against the stable wall and pressed a hand over his mouth.

"Hold your noise, man! You will raise the servants. The place is full of strangers. You must go elsewhere. My aunt is in no position to help you."

"Let her be the judge of that. Your aunt, eh? I have never seen you in my church with the family. In any case I cannot ride further. There are soldiers everywhere. And I have these." He slapped the two sacks tied to his horse which clanked and jangled."

"What is that?"

"Silver from the altar of my church. Look. You are a King's man, I can see that. You must know what the enemy will do with holy images, with the chalices, the Holy Monstrance with its relic of Saint—"

"Stop! Stop, man. What are you saying? You want her to hide a Catholic priest and bring precious plate from a church altar to the house? Are you mad? If my aunt is found with you and with such illegal stuff in her house they will arrest her. Take it away! Go!" He grabbed him as though he would lift him bodily back on his horse.

"You cannot treat me like this. I am a priest. I demand to see Her Ladyship. She will help me. I need—"

"—I will tell you what *I* need, what my aunt needs. We need you gone, for your own safety as well as hers. Look. We cannot risk hiding two priests here. She already shelters one."

"Another priest, a Catholic priest? Why, who?"

"Me."

"Is there trouble here, Master de Paul?"

Will and Dick rode into the yard at that moment and drew close, dismounting. I crept behind the cellar door and pushed it almost closed.

"I need to see Lady Trentham. You, Master Page, are one of my congregation. You know me. I need protection from the Roundheads."

"Now, now, *Father* Barkswell, I will help you with your horse. Will, you and Dick, is it? You go indoors, I will see to our visitor here."

I peeped through the crack in the door. Francis dragged Barkswell and his horse towards the copse.

"Keep quiet, Barkswell. Now they have seen you I will have to take you in or it will raise suspicion. We will move you on as soon as maybe, tomorrow, but we must hide this altar plate among the trees. We cannot risk that in the house as well as your head." He pushed the horse's rump and shoved Barkswell in the back, less gently.

I watched them retreat into the copse, hoisted up my vegetable basket and hurried indoors, my mind in turmoil. Two Catholic priests and a hoard of illegal religious objects here! And Father Barkswell's agitation would add to the fears of a household already in turmoil over the attack on Shipscarden.

Will and Dick came back into the kitchen, having told the Norton ladies everything they had found out about their husband and their home.

"Was the house totally destroyed?" Mistress Carey asked.

140

"The walls were burnt black, the roof beams charred and all windows were agape, empty of glass."

"And you did not find Sir Sheldon?"

"No one could tell us anything," said Dick. "Will and I split up to ask whoever would speak to us, but there were so few king's men to be found. The grounds were swarming with Roundheads setting campfires. Wounded from both sides were being dragged into people's houses."

"Dick had the good idea of trying to find what we could learn from Throstleford, thinking people had run there. We knocked on doors but no one would answer."

"What about our church, Dick?" Aimee asked. "Have they wrecked it?"

"Smashed every window. I went in to look. Horse dung all over the floor. Horses tethered to what was left of the rood screen. They tore the rest down for campfire wood and the altar upended."

"They chased us off with threats and pelted us with their horse muck."

"Holy Saints! We are surrounded by hellhounds. Defilers!" She slammed the fish platter on the table and threw down spoons and knives. "But eat. Eat."

We were all too tense and miserable to taste the fish. The turnips were bitter, the onions tough.

"This is a penance of a dinner," Dick complained.

Anne Carey glowered at him and called for bread and cheese.

"Then clear it all away," she said.

Will took me aside. "I want us to leave from the gate house again before dawn. I must be back on the estate quickly in case more soldiers arrive for quarter. Get your belongings. I will wait out at the waggon."

I was bringing my things down from the attic rooms when, passing through the family corridor, Isabella called me from her open chamber door.

141

"In here," she said. Her bedchamber was a cell-like room with a crucifix, rosary beads hanging from it; no fire in the grate.

"My mother sent me to find you."

She threw a drawstring purse on to the table between us. "My mother asked me to give you this. She says it is payment for your 'excellent additional work'.

"I helped your mother with my needlework out of fondness for her and because I love sewing, not as paid work. And I nursed Nell Franks as a favour to my father's friend."

"Oh, you are all goodness and charity, 'Mistress' Sanderson. I see you as a hired servant, however my mother regards you. She says it is a gift. I think it is your wage."

"As your mother's gift I will accept it."

"Make sure you remember your indebtedness to her when the Catholic persecutors come back among us."

"I will never betray this family Never."

"I hope not. Perhaps once you leave here you will not come back." She held open the door and I left.

In the solar, I opened my sewing box to put the purse away and saw the velvet space for my grandmother's silver thimble was empty. In the sudden shock of blundering into the family's secret chapel, I had held up the thimble to explain my intrusion. I must have dropped it again, in there. I wondered if it was safe to go back there and find it. I tapped on the door. No reply. I opened it. The room had been rearranged. The table was placed like an altar opposite the window-wall. Kneeling, with his back to me was the Throstleford priest.

He twisted round, eyes, wide, and clambered to his feet.

"I'm sorry, Sir, I have come for my thimble."

"Thimble? What are you talking about? Thimble? Where?"

I could just see it, by the candlelight. Someone had left it on the window seat.

"There it is."

"Get it and get out!" He lunged for the door and flung it open. "Say nothing about me to your kitchen skivvies. The Trenthams
are followers of the true faith. Do not threaten their safety."

"You do not need to remind me of any duty I hold to the Trenthams, Sir."

"Get out, then and keep your mouth tight shut." He shoved me out and shut the door.

I staggered, tripped on the hem of my dress and fell to the floor. As I struggled to my feet there were hands at my elbows. Francis de Paul lifted me up.

How could he be there so suddenly? I know I had been alone in the solar. He stepped away from me and pressed himself against the panelling.

"Grovelling on the floor again, Mistress Sanderson. What have you mislaid this time?"

I put the thimble into my sewing box and fastened it.

"I have collected all my belongings now. I will be off."

"Safe journey back to Bournbroke, then. Beware of the wild Scots. They are rallying to the King's side, I hear. Very fierce men. We should all be aware of the danger we might find ourselves in. Don't you agree?"

"Go or stay. There is risk everywhere, I fear. I hope there will be no incomers here to take advantage of Lady Trentham's hospitality and put her in even greater danger, Master de Paul. We must all have care for our friends."

"We are at each other's mercy, then." He regarded me closely then gave me a chill smile, fingers to his lips. Half caution, half kiss. "I hope you will keep silence."

I turned from him to see Will standing at the top of the staircase.

"Here you are, I want us to go." He turned back downstairs and I followed. How had de Paul appeared so suddenly in the room like that?

143

I hurried out to Will at the garden porch door. The waggon was fully laden, which surprised me.

"What is all this?"

"Nothing really, makeweight logs and corn-sacks, in case we are stopped by soldiers, so I can say I am on my way to make deliveries. I do not want awkward questions which might bring them to poke their noses into Beauchamps."

Back at the gate house we settled ourselves at Will's fireside watching the logs burn low.

"You look ill at ease, Alice. What is it?"

"That stranger you saw in the yard, with Francis de Paul—"

"Does he bother you, de Paul? Does he flirt?"

"No." I tried to sound amused at the suggestion.

I was tempted to confide all my fears to him to tell him that Francis de Paul was a Catholic priest, that Barkswell was too; that the family used the round room as a chapel to celebrate the illegal Catholic Mass and that I knew that Barkswell had hidden sacks full of altar silver somewhere in the copse by the fishponds. Any and all of these things could result in arrest or worse for Lady Trentham.

I was tempted but afraid. If Will knew nothing, or only just suspected, and was interrogated, he needed to be able to say in all honesty that he knew nothing of such things. I could not put him in danger too.

"Oh, Philip Drake was grumbling that Vicar Barkswell who has come here from Throstleford is a clandestine Catholic claiming to be a priest of the National Church."

"Philip Drake is turning into a bigot. He never used to bother himself with religious matters."

"He and Jane Martin are very close I think."

"And is that all?"

"I had an uncomfortable farewell from Isabella," I wanted to move the subject away from Francis and Barkswell. "She dislikes me. Lady Trentham gave her a gift to give me as I left.

She almost threw it at me, and said she hoped I would not be back."

"Mistress Isabella has rather a cheerless heart. I think it is her manner, not a fault in you."

"She said I was just a servant in her eyes. She does not like me being treated as a lady at her mother's worktable. Perhaps she felt envious watching me sew wedding garments for Elizabeth and not for her. Is there an intended match for her or someone she likes?"

"I wondered," said Will with a glint in his eyes, "whether she might view her cousin Francis as a husband. They are both very religious. They might make a good match. Perhaps that is why he has been brought to the house."

"What Isabella and Francis de Paul!"

Will was grinning now. "Which do you think is more likely to forward their love match, her stiff and serious manner or his 'charm-this-way frown-that-way' manners?"

"He will never be a match with Isabella!" I instantly regretted the vehemence of my reply but Will spoke on, partly in jest.

"I don't trust him," Will said. "Why is he dallying here with his aunt?" The fun died from his eyes. "He is young enough and strong enough to fight for his family's cause. He is Royalist enough as far as I can tell, yet he stays as a leech on Lady Trentham's hospitality and does nothing useful in return. And I didn't like the way he huddled together with that vicar of Throstleford. If Philip is right and Vicar Barkswell is suspected as a Catholic, his presence here is a threat. I don't like it, or him—either of them."

I did not dare to say a word. 'Keep your mouth tight shut' were Barkswell's last words. 'Silence', was de Paul's.

Will stood and helped me to my feet. He kept hold of my hands. "I like to see you here at my fireside, Alice. I know I am a solemn old stick. I had a few sweet-hearts when I was young, but I can't say I was ever in love. My marriage with Prudence was a shallow sort of love and after she died, well, I never learned how to speak fair to women or make myself charming."

He let go of me and bent over to rake the ashes. "You told me you were cautious about men. I recognise caution over 'sweet-hearting' as you called it. But, for me, the times you have been here in my house, and lived in it, the times we have shared here, alone have been the happiest I have had. I wish you were not leaving my hearth."

Words trembled on my tongue. 'Ask me, Will and I will not leave, I will never leave you again.' I waited for him to say more, to say he loved me, ask me to stay, to marry him. But he stood, tongue-tied too. His courage failed him. Will, the cautious 'solemn stick' and me, burdened with secrets not my own, dangerous to him and the house of Trentham and too wary to be unmaidenly, to break custom and be the first to speak of love.

"Time for sleep, I think." He led me to the staircase, kissed my fingertips, turned into the scullery and closed the door.

In the dark, cold morning we huddled in our cloaks and set off for Bournbroke. Flakes of snow drifted in our faces and settled on our knees to melt.

"I hope you get back before it snows in earnest."

We talked in short bursts, wondering if Sir Sheldon Norton was dead or had escaped; how long his family would stay at the Hall; what Will thought of Jane Martin. While we talked on quietly we heard the clatter of hooves behind us, coming at a lively pace. Men of Cromwell's army caught up with us. Will pulled in near to the verge to let them pass. They took no notice of us at all.

"Battles and manoeuvres usually come to a stop in the winter weather. I don't know why they are riding about now. I hope they don't intend to stop in Bournbroke. I don't want to celebrate Christmas with them glooming at us for being pagans."

146

It was almost daylight by the time we arrived at the Bournbroke crossroads. We turned in, past The Rose Bush and along the front street. All was quiet. No soldiers at all.

We rode into Netherfold. Mother and Lizzie hugged me. Father shouted of Daniel and they came into the house to embrace me. The room was warm and welcoming and Mother laid breakfast before us.

They were agog with the news of the burning of Shipscarden House. 'Had we heard about it?' they asked. 'It was rumoured Sir Sheldon Norton had been burned alive in his bed,' they said. And once we told them we had been right there in the mayhem, they insisted on hearing the whole story, which Will and I took it in turns to tell.

Father was dumbfounded. "Well! I am glad you saw him, Will, and he was still alive. I am right sorry for his house, though and the nigh destruction of Shipscarden town. It will mean no wool trading and no lamb sales in spring if the merchants all ran to save themselves."

"The farmers drove their flocks out, you say?" said Daniel. "The whole place will fall to ruin."

"The Norton ladies are at Beauchamps. Will went back yesterday so see if he could hear news of Sir Sheldon but there was nothing."

"I daresay they will send me again in a day or so to ask again. If I hear news of trading, Samuel I will call back here to tell you."

"Grateful to you, Will."

"Do you think the great house can be repaired? Where will they live?"

"When Dick and I saw it, there was barely a wall left standing. The roof was all over the ground."

"Dear, dear and it was so beautiful," Mother sighed.

"Did you see Prince Rupert there?" asked Lizzie. "They say he is so handsome and brave. He has moustaches like silk, they say."

Father choked at his ale.

I groaned. "No, I did not see any princes or fine lords, Missy. My eyes were streaming tears from the smoke and fright at the cannon balls."

Lizzie pulled a face at me but I kissed her cheek. "I am very glad to be here and safe among you all."

"This girl of yours, Samuel, is one brave lass. She tells you she was frightened but she made not a whimper, despite the uproar. She doled out brandy to the fine ladies cowering in the coach."

"Why were you even there, Alice?"

"To help the Nortons escape."

"Hmph. Fine thing if you had helped them to safety and ended dead in a ditch with a cannon shot in your lap."

"Don't be annoyed, Father. I was a volunteer recruit, no one ordered me to go."

Mother's jaw was set. "Your father is quite right."

"She just wanted to go through fire with you, Will," Lizzie laughed. "Did she hold your hand? Good excuse."

"Lizzie, stop!" I knew I blushed but Will just laughed and winked at my sister.

Father, Will and Dan went out together and I realized Will and I would have no opportunity for a private goodbye. After a little while he put his head back around the door and smiled at me.

"Have a merry time at Christmas, Alice. Thank you for everything. I will see you as soon as I can in the new year."

"Don't ever be a stranger, Will. You know how welcome you are here, my dear," Mother said."

"Goodbye, Will. It has been my pleasure, all my time at the Hall and in the gate house." How could I say all I wanted to say with my family watching?

He lifted his hat to us and, climbing into the waggon, drove away. He dragged half of me away with him.

By supper time I had given myself a shake and settled to enjoy being home. We exchanged news.

"Have you had more soldiers quartered here?" I asked.

"We had a shoeless, ragged company of Cromwell's men that gobbled everything they could find. They stayed in the village for three weeks! There were about a hundred of them, beggars almost. They raided Nick the cobbler's—took his whole stock. They went about pinching and stealing from right inside people's houses!" My mother was scandalized.

"Minister Barnes had five of them in his house because he thought they were pious Puritans but they got drunk at The Rose Bush and came back and wrecked his parlour and spat on his floor!" Lizzie giggled over it. She loved the thought of Minister Barnes being discomfited.

"They raided Jack's mother's kitchen at the Waggoners," mother went on, "and went off with her cooking pans for their campfires. It's going to cost her money to replace them."

"I suppose Simon Morton gave out a few black eyes and bloody noses for that."

"It is no laughing matter," grumbled Father, "People's hard-earned prosperity, such as it is, the homes they have made. Lord knows life is rough enough without strangers rampaging in like that. No discipline! The officers did nothing. And the other lot are just as bad."

"We had six king's men through here at the end of the autumn." Mother stopped eating, remembering. "Such wounds they had. Two of them died the same night they arrived. They lay here, crying and moaning. My poppy potions were not strong enough to help."

"What about the others?"

"Lizzie was a great help with them." She looked fondly at my sister. "I think she learned a great deal with you in her time at Beauchamps, Alice. She has been a good daughter altogether."

Lizzie smiled. There was, indeed, a softness about her face that was not there before. She had lost that discontented scowl. "Grown up," I said.

"Well," Father shifted from the table to his fireside chair and stretched out peacefully. "With luck the snow and ice and mud will keep them all quiet in their camps for the winter and give us all a bit of peace."

"Peace, yes. That is something to wish for. We saw some of the Roundheads on our way here. I did not think they would be moving about or changing garrisons in depths of winter."

"We haven't seen much of the King's men lately," said Daniel. "The rumours are they are suffering defeat everywhere; north and south. The King was captured again. You heard about that, surely? But he threw himself on the mercy of the Scots."

"Did a secret bargain with them, they say. He thought they would raise an army and march south with him against Cromwell." Father and Daniel took turns to tell me the news that they had picked up in the taverns and from the criers in the markets.

Father continued: "The Scots betrayed him and gave him over to Cromwell after all. No honour in any of the parcel of them!"

"And now the poor man is imprisoned in one of his own castles."

"I expect Minister Barnes will have plenty to say to us about it all once he stops chastising us for persisting with Christmas," said Lizzie. "Let's talk about something more cheerful."

"Right," said Mother, "Daniel, tell your sister your good news."

"I'm going to be married at Easter, to Joan Fletcher from the farm."

"Lane End Manor Farm? When did that start? You and Joan! You've known her all your life."

"I've always liked her and we were dancing at the Harvest village feast." He paused and looked down at me, smiling his crinkly smile, "Suddenly I didn't want her to go home and thought it would be very nice to have my own home with her in it."

"There was a big family meeting," Lizzie chimed in, full of the importance of it. "I went down there too, into their huge parlour room with all their grand furniture. They are really rich, you know."

"She brings two acres with her, and a cottage on the manor land," Father grinned.

"And a nice fat dowry,"

"Lizzie! Stop that. I am not marrying Joan for what she will bring me."

"They have fallen in lo-o-ve," Lizzie crooned.

"Charles Fletcher and your brother and I had a good discussion. We could see the benefits of uniting our two families, there is no doubt about it. We can share stud management and the animal husbandry and sharing some of our tools we won't each have to buy two and three of everything."

"And in the end," Mother joined in, "Joan Fletcher and Daniel's children will inherit Netherfold and look after us in our old age."

"Lizzie and I will do that, Mother, of course we will."

"Well, look at where your brother Luke fetched up, Bristol. And our Martha with Henry Steele in Hereford. You and Lizzie cannot know where you will marry."

"So, with all this 'good business', dear brother, does love enter the bargain at all? Poor Joan! At the moment you all sound like merchant-traders." I knew not all marriage contracts were founded on romantic love, but for me today, it was the only bearable condition for marriage. Oh, Will!

"Yes, my love-charmed sister. Joan Fletcher is my heart's desire."

"You are a lout!" I laughed and threw the pot cloth at his head. "I wish her joy of you with all my heart."

"And I can have your bedchamber when you leave us." Lizzie rubbed her hands in delight.

At the end of the evening, they all went up to bed. I was still restless from Will's kisses. The sinister business with Father Barkswell and Francis de Paul gnawed away at me.

Father stood up, stretching. He opened the window shutter to see the stars. It was a clear night, sharp and cold. I stood beside him watching the tilted moon silver the tops of the evergreens as the stars winked in their patterns.

He put his arm around me. "We are glad to have you home, girl. Will told me you were splendid, not only in Shipscarden but particularly with his sister."

I waited, breathless, to hear what else Will might have said to him.

"And he said Lady Trentham was impressed with your needleworking. She had you teaching her women and her daughters about the medicine-making and those herbals of your mother's. In fact, he talked on endlessly in your praise. Everything you did has been well done. He thinks so and so do I. You have made me proud, girl. He thinks Her Ladyship will want you back there. Were you happy with them all?"

"Very happy, most of the time. But it is good to be back with all of you. There are no mysteries here. No risks."

"Risks? The soldiers, you mean. I told you. Battling will close down for the winter."

"Not only that. I'll tell you sometime."

"Living with Catholics, you mean?"

"Yes. I had not fully realised the dangers before—all the laws against them and their fear of being discovered."

"Being discovered at what?"

"Oh, I tried not to enquire but there is a tension. And their son, Thomas is with the King. They have no news of him."

"Were you afraid?"

"I always felt safe with Will nearby."

"Ah, yes, Will. He's a fine man, young Alice." He said nothing more but kissed my forehead and went up to his bed.

In bed that night, I asked Lizzie if she too had a found a sweet-heart while I was living at Beauchamps.

"No one I want to name to you," she said, "You will only narrow your eyes at him, whoever he might be, and tell me he is not good enough."

"That would only be to protect you."

"Everyone keeps thinking I need protection, but I am sixteen already. By next year I'll be the same age Mother and Father were when they married."

"Yes, you are right. But you have plenty of time to discover your heart's fancy and now I am home I can watch over you, whether you want me to or not. Goodnight, Lizzie."

She kissed my cheek. "Goodnight, Alice and welcome home."

The Sunday before Christmas, Minister Barnes preached a fierce sermon denouncing the pagan tradition of bringing holly and ivy into the house. He said it belonged to the ignorant worship of tree gods and our God was a jealous God and forbade us from bowing down to any other.

"Neither should you give yourselves over to the feasting that leads to drunkenness and debauchery. The Bible does not say one word about the day of Our Lord's birth. This festival of Christmas springs from ancient Roman days, full of wickedness and idolatry. You need prayer and fasting, not singing and spiced mince pies. Dress yourselves soberly and repent of your sins."

On and on he went. My mother pursed her lips. I knew she was thinking of all the good things she had prepared for us to eat and drink. She—we—would not give up the old-fashioned merry Yuletide.

Christmas came indeed and we enjoyed ourselves mightily, even making fun of Josiah Barnes' ranting, drinking a mock toast to him with Mother's special cider.

On the last evening of the old year, all our neighbours gathered round a bonfire that George and Matt Wallace built for us in front of the smithy. We speared apples on sharpened branches and toasted them in the red embers. We nibbled on them and burned our mouths, laughing. Tom, the fiddler from The Rose Bush came and played jigs and reels. We lined up to dance the 'Rufty Tufty' and the 'Greenwood' till we ran out of breath.

At the height of the moon, the men took up burning branches and each family walked around its own house chasing away the evil spirits to make ready for the new year. Minister Barnes would have been horrified at such pagan ways but he was not here and we were full of merriment.

On the first morning of January, we sat at our breakfast wondering what this year would bring.

"With the King in prison and all his armies surrendered," Daniel began, "and Cromwell's men in charge everywhere, what happens next will be the Parliament's choice—for all of us."

Father drained his tankard. "The tavern-men say there are cities up North with fighting and riots going on between factions everywhere. They don't need armies with flags, they just fight. The whole country is divided and angry." He stood ready to start work. "All the people I talked to in the market before Christmas say how sick they are of war; sick of the soldiers riding all over our homesteads; sick of the drunkards, thieves and lechers. Our villages used to be peaceful."

Mother looked so fierce I think she would have been happy to lead a force herself to re-establish good order "Someone should take charge and organize companies of constables to arrest the rabble-rousers. Enforce the peace."

"I think you'd take your soup ladle to crack their heads open if you had the chance, Mother," Daniel laughed.

"Don't laugh, you Daniel! We local folk have put up with the despoiling long enough. It has to stop."

"Heaven knows the winter months are hard enough as it is," Father said.

"Mind you," Mother was stirring her pottage, thinking. "I can't help feeling it goes against the natural order of things, for a country to put its own king in prison. I feel no good will come of it. Who will take his place? His son?"

"No, Parliament wants nothing more to do with royalty. They say they've chucked the ordinary Parliamenters out and just left the ranting ones that support the army."

"Will they make Cromwell into King, then?" I asked.

"That can't be right!" Mother was shocked. "What right could he possibly have? Being the victor does not make him a fair ruler."

"The right of arms, Sarah. Power. If you have it, you wield it."

"It's not fair, though, is it?" I smiled at Lizzie using her old girlish grumble over so serious a matter.

"Whatever is decided in London and the Parliament, we just have to put up with it. We have no choice."

"We never have a choice about anything."

"We have no voice, woman. No power to choose who rules us or how. The great men in London and in castles up and down the land are the ones who choose." Father shook his head. "I can be as angry as you are, Sarah, but it is useless. The broadsheets and the posters talk about the rights of the people. *We* are the people, but we cannot stop even one soldier from bedding in our barn, eating our chickens or mauling our daughters."

Lizzie's head dropped. Poor girl, she did not want to have that incident cast back at her.

He stood up and crossed to the door, ramming his hat on his head." That's why I would not go to war and why I forbade you to go, Daniel. Our land. Our home. Our family. That's our war. And the cows don't milk themselves and the pigs don't get rid of their own shit, so let's get to it." Out he went.

155

Lizzie left the table, subdued. Mother and I stood to clear away. Yuletide merriment was over.

At the beginning of February there was a mild, dry spell of weather so Father decided he and Daniel would take the cart to the Stratford Market. He needed seed and twine and some new tools. He asked Mother what she needed. She said she would rather come herself so Lizzie and I asked eagerly if we could come too to buy some trimmings for our clothes for Daniel's wedding.

We set off in good spirits just as the sky was beginning to show a pale dawn. The cart plodded its way along the Roman road towards the river bridge at Saxonford. As we passed Beauchamps Hall I craned my neck to see if anyone I knew was out in the sheep fields or on the road through the estate towards the house. I was disappointed. I missed them all, the Trentham family, the girls in the kitchen, even Anne Carey's sharp tongue. And especially, I missed Will.

The wintry sun had risen by the time we drove into Stratford. Mother, Lizzie and I climbed down and walked off among the market stalls and heaped goods.

We had our list: a new pair of gloves, a cap for Mother to wear at Daniel's wedding, a bale of linen to make a new shirt and nightshirt for Daniel and trimmings for our wedding clothes.

Lizzie wanted a new cap for herself. I decided to use some of my money-gift from Lady Trentham to buy one for her.

I left the others at the spice stall and chose a pretty cap for my sister and one for myself and a bundle of lace and blue satin ribbon. I looked forward to seeing Lizzie's face light up at her gifts. I bought a skein of black silk too, to embroider some Spanish blackwork designs on to the collar of Daniel's wedding shirt, one of the fancy skills I had practised at Beauchamps.

It was a happy day, after which the snows fell. For a while Bournbroke and Netherfold looked beautiful. We huddled indoors. When the logs were nearly used up, we had to stamp out to the store with our skirts hitched up to help Father and Daniel carry more inside to dry, stacked in the hearth. The animals needed to be fed, watered and bedded in fresh straw, whatever the weather, and we had to break lumps of ice from the water ewers to melt in the kitchen.

Daniel struggled down to the Lane End Manor farm to help his future father-in-law dig several snow-bound sheep out of the farthest pasture. He stayed down there, sleeping on a pallet-bed in their parlour, because all his clothes were sodden with the deep snow. Winter gripped us all.

At last the world turned, and with the primroses and the trembling catkins came more warmth in the sun and into our hearts. We prepared for Daniel's wedding to Joan Fletcher.

Mother, Lizzie and I stitched new shirts and nightshirts for him to take to his new home. I sewed a lace trim to the collar of his wedding shirt and stitched my blackwork.

We brushed down his best chestnut brown jerkin, damping away the marks we found.

I embroidered Lizzie's new cap with sprays of forget-me-nots and added a bunch of blue ribbon curling from a lover's knot on each side. Her face lit up when she saw the gift I had made for her and hugged me to her. I trimmed my own Sunday dress with bows at the shoulders and at last everything was ready.

All brushed and festive, we picked posies of primroses and violets, fastened with our last lengths of ribbon and we walked up to St. Andrew's church together. Father and Mother fixed blackthorn blossom in wreaths around the church door together with fresh arcs of branches in green leaf.

Minister Barnes came out to greet the bride and groom, frowning, at the pagan greenery. Daniel and Joan walked up the church path together, beaming with joy, Joan's mother and father on either side of the couple, ready to give her away.

In spite of the minister's dour looks, the service went off well and we walked inside to complete their marriage vows so all could hear them and witness the holy kiss. He declared them man and wife and they led our procession around the village and down to Lane End Manor for the wedding feast.

Lizzie and I had taken down the blossom to carry with us and the four parents followed waving the branches of green.

In their large kitchen we sat down to a grand wedding breakfast of hams, roasted chickens, rare, white manchet bread and broke into two wheels of their delicious cheese. We drank beer and sweet cider, which my mother had helped Joanna Fletcher to make.

It was the merriest day we had all enjoyed since Christmas. As I walked home, I mused on how much I would miss my brother in Netherfold.

"How will you manage all the work, Father, without Daniel?"

"I've had a good talk with George Wallace. Matt is his eldest and George is training him to join him in the smithy. I said I would bring young Watt over here and train him in the farming side of the work, managing the oxen and the horses. He can help with our digging and planting and the care of the orchards. That way he can make more use of the land behind the smithy and I get a strong pair of hands to replace Daniel. He's a good lad, young Watt."

"Do you like Matt, too? Because I think Lizzie is growing fond of him."

"Has she said anything to you, Alice?"

"Nothing special. But I have eyes in my head, Father."

He laughed. "Yes. Your mother has said something similar. We have to be ready for both you and your sister to leave us for your own households and husbands. I told your mother, if we make good money selling the lambs, we could pay another hand and a maid of all work to help her."

"Lizzie is a lot nearer to marrying than I am," I said. I had seen her and Matt kissing at the new year bonfire and I knew they took the longest way to walk home together every Sunday after church.

As for me, I could not imagine my own future. I ached for Will, his gentle smile, the touch of his broad hands, but I had no prospect of seeing him. The demands of his duties at the Hall meant he could not pay visits and I could not choose to visit him, so there it was.

My life at Netherfold resumed its pattern. I was restless, eager for news about my friends only a few miles along the road but miles out of reach to me. Of course, my future was unforeseeable. Jack Morton was a long lost love affair. A distant memory. Perhaps Will would be lost to me too.

Jane Martin

My friend whom I trusted
Which did eat of my bread
Hath lifted up his heel against me.
Psalm 5

One hot afternoon, Mother, Lizzie and I were sitting in the orchard shade shelling peas for storage, when a cart turned into our yard. My heart turned over. I stood, eager to see. It was Philip Drake. Disappointment doused my smile as we all went to bid him welcome and give him some refreshment.

"I have letters," he said, "from Lady Trentham. One for Master Sanderson and one for you, Alice."

"My husband will be some time in the fields," said Mother. "Have you time to stay for supper? You will certainly see him then."

"Ah. Lady Trentham hoped I could bring Mistress Alice back with me."

"What, today?" Mother's eyebrows shot up. She looked at me.

"Everything is in the letters, Mistress," said Philip. "But it is urgent."

I broke the seal and read my letter.

"It is her son, Thomas. He has been held prisoner. She has just now got him home with a serious wound, unhealed. She wants me to go."

"If the wound is serious, Alice, he will need a barber-surgeon"

"Beg pardon. Lady Trentham has sent for the surgeon but he is away at Stow. She does not want to wait."

"If Lady Trentham asks me, Mother, I must try to help her. Is Watt somewhere in the orchards? I will ask him to fetch Father. I will pack some things, Philip. I know Father will allow me to go."

If my mother wondered at my eagerness, she said nothing against my going. She and Lizzie followed me into the house and prepared a meal. We were already eating when Father rushed in.

"What has happened? Ah, Philip Drake, it's you. Is there trouble?"

Philip, Mother and I all spoke at once. Father shushed us and sat down to read his letter from Lady Trentham.

"Seems no one will do to help Her Ladyship but our Alice, Sarah. Are you willing, girl?"

"Yes, of course. Can I take some of your herbals, Mother? They may have run down their stores since I left."

She and Lizzie helped me fill a basket with what Mother thought would be needed, giving instructions while she moved about. At last, we were ready to go. I hugged my family, who followed me out issuing warnings and advice.

"When did Master Thomas come home, Philip?"

"Just three days ago. Will brought him back in the waggon. He is in a bad way, been held prisoner in London since before Christmas."

I remembered the horsemen arriving on the last night I spent at the gate house and the messengers arriving with news for Lady Trentham. So that was their news!

"Why was he in prison, Philip? Has anyone talked about it?"

"Something to do with plots down London way, after the King's defeats. Don't know any details."

I had always found Philip more talkative and friendly than this. His taciturn replies puzzled me. We travelled on in silence. I turned my mind to Will and the tremors of excitement I felt about seeing him soon. How much time would we be able to spend together? Would he remember everything we had said and done last December?

161

We turned into the Beauchamps estate road and Philip drove us into the stable yard. Anne Carey opened the door as soon as she heard our wheels.

"Alice Sanderson! How relieved the mistress will be to have you here! Come in, come in. Thank you, Philip. You have made the journey in good time. There is ale for you when you have seen to the horse." She led me into the house and pointed out the herbal chest set waiting for me.

"Aimee, find the mistress and tell her Alice Sanderson has arrived and ask for her instructions. Alice, Lady Trentham is beside herself with worry about Thomas, she will want you to see him straight away. He is—well, you will see for yourself."

I sat at the familiar table and ate and drank. Jane Martin smiled at me in her quiet way, filling a pitcher with hot water and collecting basins and clean linen for my medicine box.

"Are you enjoying the work here, Jane?"

"It is all as I expected. I am quite content."

Philip came in and joined me at the table but it was not me he looked at. His eyes rested on Jane Martin's pale round face. She gazed back at him with more warmth in her smile than I had ever seen from her. 'Ah,' I thought, 'This is a romance in the bud.' I realised Philip was now wearing all black with a white Puritan's collar. He smiled less and did not join in the kitchen banter.

"You are welcome back," said Aimee. "We might get some better treatment for our oven burns and cuts. Poor Philip sliced half his finger off with the gutting knife. I made a poor job of mending it, did I not, Sir?"

"It was wrapped enough. Perhaps it was a judgement on the persistence of fasting here, calling for fish days at all," he grumbled. Jane Martin nodded her approval.

'A Puritanical love affair, then,' I thought.

"Jane." Mistress Carey handed her a knife and a basket. "Fetch me the cooking herbs; rosemary, thyme and parsley, lots of that for the Friday fish."

162

Philip stood up, even though he had barely started his food. "I will walk with you, Jane. I am on my way to catch the fish. Come through the garden porch while I collect my nets."

"There is no need to hurry yourself, Philip." But he did not even hear the housekeeper. He was already out of the room.

"Foolish girl. She is so heart-struck by Philip Drake she has forgotten the knife. On your way up to My Lady, take the knife to Jane, Alice."

I looked out of the garden door, about to call her when Stephen Barkswell bustled out of the stable and collided with Jane.

"Mind yourself, wench! Out of my way."

"There is no need for you to speak so roughly, Vicar Barkswell, we go about our work here," Philip said, steadying Jane and holding her arm.

"Hold your tongue, Drake. You are the servant. I am the guest here. You step aside, not *into* my way. And I am not a vicar."

"Call yourself 'Father' then, do you, as the papist priests do?"

"Get out of my way—and keep out of my sight."

Philip spat on the ground at Barkswell's feet and turned away. "Traitor," he hissed.

"How dare you, you Puritan cur!"

I thought Barkswell would strike him but he shoved his hand into Philip's chest pushing him aside and stalked off towards the house.

Jane reached up her hand and caressed Philip's cheek, her eyes
shining in admiration.

"Our time will come, you popish devil!" he shouted as Barkswell slammed the door.

"He is wicked, is he not, Philip? He should not be in this house, the ungodly with the godly."

Philip took her hand in his. "How many here are ungodly! It is we, the godly who should not be here, Jane." They walked off into the copse, talking with their heads close together.

I had never seen such bad feeling in this house. Then I remembered the knife. "Jane!"

I held up the knife and waved it. She came back for it and took it without a word. I went on up to Lady Trentham and Thomas.

"Alice, thank you for coming. Thomas is back with us. When you see him, you'll see how ill he is. He looks broken."

"What happened to him?"

"After the defeat at Oxford, all the King's officers were imprisoned to forestall a counter attack. The prison conditions were harsh. They were moved to London and eventually he was released but rioting broke out soon after. There were rumours of a plot to murder members of the Parliament and free the King. Somehow Thomas's name was spoken. They tried to arrest him again and in the fight he was hacked down. His friends dragged him away and smuggled him up here. His wound has been left unattended for the whole of their flight. So now his arm is infected. He cannot move it."

Tears filled her eyes. Her face was drawn, her cheeks hollow. "Isabella and I sit by him day and night. I've bathed and bathed the wound but I cannot get rid of the foulness or the swelling."

Isabella was sitting by his bed, her rosary in her hand. She nodded in my direction and stood away to let me near her brother.

I could smell the infection before I unwrapped the bandages. He was restless with fever, his face grey, his hair unwashed, tangled and thick with sweat.

Beth and Aimee stood behind Lady Trentham looking anxious. "Beth," I said, "make a cold-water pad for his forehead. Aimee, pour hot water in the basin and bring me fresh cloths."

I tried to unwind the cloth around his arm but the least movement caused him to cry out, so I took up scissors and cut it away, dropping it into an empty bowl.

"There is poison there, so wash yourself after you have burnt it."

The deep gash in Thomas's arm oozed pus. The edges were inflamed, and the surrounding flesh was puffed and rigid. There was more poison here than I had dealt with before. I was afraid whatever I did would be too little, too late. I was uncomfortably aware of my own ignorance. Mother had warned me when we worked on wounds before, the danger of infection lay in its spread through the body. It caused brain-fever and death. I did not want to be the one to warn Lady Trentham that her son might be beyond human help and Isabella's prayers their only hope.

I worked on, trying to conceal the shaking in my fingers as I bathed, mixed and spread a hot poultice of deadnettle and groundsel on the putrefied wounds. I hoped the heat would draw some of the poison to the surface and away from travelling further up his arm.

"He will not eat," said Isabella, looking over my shoulder. "Surely we must nourish his strength to fight the fever."

"It is more important that he drinks," I said. "He is sweating away so much he will dry out. Food will not lower his overheating."

"Do you know that?"

"We must bathe his body in cool water to reduce his—"

"Too much of a shock, surely?" Isabella interrupted.

"Cool water, not cold, to reduce the fever."

I ignored her. Isabella would not trust me, whatever I said. I felt the weight of anxiety in the room.

Beth, Aimee and I cut away his shirt and carried out a routine of soaking, soothing, rinsing and soaking again until we had bathed all his upper body. I refreshed the cold pad to his forehead several times. and gave him a fresh sheet and a cool pillow. I mixed an infusion of plantain to give him some liquid which might also combat the fever, then I left him to rest.

"I have done all I can, My Lady, to make him more comfortable. My understanding is there are three things to do; reduce the fever; make him drink liquids and seek to reduce the terrible infection at the wound. I will change that hot poultice for a clean one every hour."

"Will it be enough to save his arm, Alice?" She searched my face. Her hands were clenched together.

"Hope and pray, My Lady, as I will."

"I will sit with my brother," Isabella said, moving her chair back near Thomas's head.

I arranged with Beth and Aimee to bring pitchers of water to Thomas's chamber so I could heat a constant supply during the night to mix the poultices. I settled myself by the fireside for a long vigil.

'If only Will would come quickly,' I thought, 'and bring the surgeon with him.' I wanted him to take the responsibility of saving Thomas away from me. But Will did not come. The surgeon did not come.

"You go to your bed, Mother. I will send for you if there is any change." Isabella opened her prayer book and turned her back on me.

"Good night then. Thank you."

I looked at Thomas, stirring his head from side to side. He did not look at all comforted. It was going to be a long night.

I renewed cooling pads to Thomas's forehead and bathed his face and chest. I changed the hot poultice over the wound every hour and tried to give him sips of healing infusion. Occasionally he muttered or called out a name. Then Isabella and I would start up and lean over him.

"What do you want, Thomas? What are you saying?" But nothing he said was clear.

Every time I unwrapped his wound it was still angry and swollen. Isabella moved away to let me near her brother then sat

166

back in her place by his head when I finished. Sometimes she held his hand. She whispered prayers into his ear and laid her rosary over his wound. Perhaps that did as much good as my uncertain efforts.

"I have faith that God will heal him," she said, "if it is His Will." My faith in myself was less sure.

At first light, Dick came to help with Thomas's personal needs. Isabella and I went down to the hall for breakfast. We sat apart but before she began to eat she looked at me.

"You have been very good to my brother, Alice, and nursed him with great care. The family is grateful to you."

"I wish I knew more than I do. I wish I could *do* more. I hope the surgeon comes soon."

"Of course." She examined my face. "You have nursed wounded soldiers Have you ever had to deal with wounds as bad as my brother's?"

'Never as bad,' I thought, but I did not want to add to her fear. She had never had a good opinion of me and she was afraid for Thomas. I was too, come to that.

"I have helped my mother care for terrible blade cuts and shot-wounds. I know you have to rid the area of infection or it spreads around the body and you must get the fever down. But I have never stitched a cut. I have watched my mother do it and I think I could, but I cannot do it until all the infection is clear or I would seal it up inside, I think."

She searched my expression, desperate for reassurance. "Do you believe he will survive this?"

"The surgeon will know better how to answer that. I can only do my best and hope."

"I will pray for him," she said.

"Both your brother and I have need of your prayers, Isabella." She turned away and picked at her breakfast. Silence fell between us.

As soon as I finished I left the hall and went out into the gardens. I lifted my face to the sun's warmth and breathed in the sweetness of the honeysuckle and the roses. I walked into the copse, enjoying the leaves' whispering, the freshness of the green. In the distance the blue-grey line of the Cotswold ridge marked the world beyond my own; a place where Will was.

'Where are you, Will? Bring the surgeon. Bring yourself. I will feel safer then.'

I drew close to the fishponds where the rings made by the fish nosing up to catch the hovering flies spread wide and interwove. Like consequences.

I sat on a felled log and tried to quieten my mind. An old weeping willow drooped its summer hair into the shallows. Its roots upheaved the ground. Thick weeds grew between them. Fresh growth had sprung up around the tree bole in the fresh soil heaped there. Fresh? Fresh soil?

I went to look. The ground surrounding the willow was hard-packed, grassed over. It had been undisturbed for years, yet someone had been digging where I stood, for no tree-managing that I had ever seen. Only weeds had grown to thrive all through the spring and summer.

A scene flashed into my memory as lightning makes a night-room bright—Francis de Paul and Stephen Barkswell leading the horse into the copse here, carrying those clanking sacks. My stomach turned over. They could not have decided to hide two sacks of illegal altar silver here on his aunt's estate! Surely Francis de Paul would not put her safety at such risk? Yet, someone had been digging here. Digging and burying. I could not ignore this. It brought danger on the whole house, especially Lady Trentham. Who could I speak to about it? Francis de Paul himself must know that to have such things found hidden here risked fines or imprisonment. I had to do something. On an impulse I dragged leaves, twigs and scattered them between the weeds, trying to cover up the fresh soil from the curious, from prying eyes. I had to think.

I hurried back towards the house. Barkswell and de Paul must not suspect that I had stumbled on the hidden altar stuff. They had been furious with me when I saw them in their chapel. They already doubted me enough. This was knowledge I did not want to have, but how can you un-know what you know?

I went back to tend Thomas. Dick had finished his care and the young man looked and smelt fresh, the bed linen new and smooth. I prepared a hot poultice and changed the dressing over the wound.

"Does it look less red and swollen to you, Dick?" I hoped it was not just my wishing that made it seem a little better.

"There's a lot of foul stuff come out onto that dressing, Alice. That has to be a good thing."

I gave him a grateful smile and set about bathing and cleaning the still-gaping gash. Thomas moaned and opened his eyes. "Mother?" he whispered. "Elizabeth, is it you?" Then he fell silent again. I bathed his forehead and he opened his eyes, blinking. "Will this pain never ease?" he whispered.

It was the first time I had heard him speak with sense since I arrived. His eyes roamed between our faces and the window-light then he would screw them tight in pain as I touched his arm. Assuming he could hear me, I told him what I was doing and why then I bandaged his arm again and mixed two infusions, one to act against infection, the other to ease his pain.

"It will make you sleep," I said, "but it might make you feel sick. It would be better if you could swallow a little gruel so that the medicines are not the only things in your belly."

He grunted, which I took to mean he would try, so Dick went down to the kitchen to fetch it.

I finished the dressing and gave Thomas sips of the herbal mix.

"Am I really at home? How long have I been here? I thought my mother was here."

"Your mother and sister have been sitting with you, night and day. I will tell them you are awake. They can explain everything."

"Who are you? Do you work here?"

169

"I am a friend of Will Franks. I came to help your mother with the medicines and such like. Let me fetch your family."

Lady Trentham and Isabella hurried to Thomas's bedside. Francis de Paul was with them. I left the room, hoping they were not being too optimistic about Thomas's recovery. The wound was not better, just no worse.

I went down to the garden and walked among its fresh scents to rid myself of the smell of infection. I sat down in a quiet spot enclosed by shrubs, closed my eyes and enjoyed the play of the sun on my face. When I opened them, I saw Jane Martin walking back through the herb garden. She waited where the copse edged the garden and presently Philip came to her from the fishponds with his creel and nets. He put them down beside her basket full of herbs and took her hands. They stood for a little, gazing at each other, then exchanged a modest kiss. Tenderness between them, yet speaking to Father Barkswell with such hatred. It sat awkwardly, I thought.

At midday Aimee, Ruth and I carried their fasting-food up to the family gathered in Thomas's chamber. As we came out and crossed the solar we heard horses approaching the house. Aimee looked out.

"Roundheads."

She ran back upstairs to warn Lady Trentham and as we made our way down to the hall, Stephen Barkswell hurtled down the stairs with Francis de Paul and into the solar.

Downstairs there was no panic, no rushing to secrete our stores. Troops had come and gone too often. The household had made their cache-places for foodstuffs permanent in the cellars and cupboard-backs. Only one day's supplies were kept on view these days and two men worked permanently in the kitchen gardens near the chicken coops and piggeries to safeguard our animals and produce.

The commander dismounted. "Will you call the master of the house and say Captain John Purdy sends his respects and claims space for billeting tonight. I have a hundred men here."

"Wait there. Dick! Come here! Aimee, fetch the mistress."

"She is with her son," I said.

"Captain, Lady Trentham is mistress here. She is a widow caring for her son who was injured in the late fighting." Anne Carey drew the officer into the hall. "You add to the troubles of the house, Sir."

"I will keep out of her way, and yours, so long as we can have bread, beer and bedding space for the men. Send your man to direct us where to pitch camp and tell us what we can take from you for our meal."

Mistress Carey did not come back. Dick went out of the front door. "Philip, take the captain to the barn for his officers and direct his men to make camp in the north meadow. Ruth, go to the gardeners and ask them to take two barrows of vegetables for their cooking. Molly, will you ask Mistress Carey for bread? It is more than I dare do."

"I will go with you, Philip," said Jane Martin, picking up an ale jug and two mugs and carrying them out.

They led Captain Purdy to the barn, Jane Martin talking eagerly to the soldiers. I had not thought her able to speak more than two words unbidden. Had she changed so much since the first days after the Mop Fair? She and Philip stood close together while the officers inspected the barn and, as they were left alone I saw him bend and kiss her cheek. Her head fell in her drooping-flower way, then she gave him a smile from under her lowered lids, and ran back to the kitchen.

"Shall I begin to bake the bread?" she asked.

"Are you housekeeper here, missy?" Anne Carey was rattled. "Oh, get the bowls out, I suppose we must get to it."

I joined in and we mixed and proved and baked for the rest of the afternoon. As our mealtime drew near, I went to refresh Thomas's dressings. Lady Trentham left and went down to speak to the Roundhead captain. Isabella sat with her brother, who was asleep.

"Is it a peaceful sleep?" I asked.

171

"Not so disturbed as he has been. He seems to be suffering less pain, although when he did speak he said the pain was terrible. Has the surgeon come?"

"No, a large company of Roundheads. A hundred, to camp for the night."

"Not more wounded?"

"No. On their way to Worcester, Dick says. Their captain is polite."

"Hmph! Fair words do not always speak fair deeds. I will leave you to your work."

I wondered if she included me in that doubt.

I collected everything I needed and examined the wound. Still infected, still swollen and red, still exuding and his head and body still overheated. I repeated all I knew to make him comfortable. 'If I am doing him no good,' I thought, 'at least I am slowing down the worsening of his sickness.'

I woke him long enough to make him drink more of the cool plantain liquid and he fell heavily asleep once more.

I cleared up and stood looking out of the window at the soldiers arranging themselves in groups about the sheep field, building campfires, stretching themselves to rest. Summer evenings, though long, were quite pleasant for sleeping under the sky.

More of their carts trundled up the estate road in front of the house, full of equipment.

I sat by Thomas, wondering if someone would bring my supper to me. Eventually the latch was lifted and Isabella came in.

"You are to go down for your meal, Alice. I will stay here with my brother."

I saw she had her small prayer book and a rosary.

In the hall the supper was almost over. The old couple were not there, only Lady Trentham sat with the staff. Everyone was discomfited by the Roundheads' presence, but not so set by the ears as in earlier days. The Model Army men were better

172

controlled and, I supposed, their late victories over King Charles made them less aggressive now. The Royalists, and we who belonged to their house, were subdued.

The evening was drawing to a calm close when two horsemen rode to the front door. Anne Carey went to open it. It was Will. Will and the surgeon.

"Praise be to God!" exclaimed Lady Trentham, jumping to her feet. "Come up, come up at once to my son. Anne, prepare supper and lodging for the doctor-surgeon. Come!"

She hurried him up the stairs. Will sat heavily on the nearest chair, rubbing his face with his hands. I wanted to run to him, soothe his exhaustion, bring him food and beer, but it was not my place.

"Will, dear soul!", exclaimed Anne Carey, "You look worn to your bones. Here, drink this."

She put a tankard of beer in front of him and sent the kitchen maids to bring his pottage, ham and fowl. Jane brought a bowl of hot water and a fresh cloth. I watched him wash his hands, resting them within the bowl, breathing deeply.

"I found Doctor Chivers easily enough," said Will in answer to the questions that came to him from every side. "But the way from Stow was choked with retreating King's men. There were so many wounded on the roadsides, the surgeon insisted he had to stop every half mile or so to tend to some poor man who was screaming. He helped where he could but it was impossible. He had not the means to mend wounds or stop bleeding and I told him we had no time. We were paying his fee, after all. He kept saying, 'Trentham is just one man. Here are many who need me.'"

Will sat back and looked around at us all. His eyes rested on me, at last. His face softened into that smile I had come to cherish.

"Alice. I said they should fetch you. I had no idea how long it would take me to find the surgeon. How is Thomas?"

"Poorly. The gash in his arm gapes open, it's full of poison. He is feverish and in great pain. I think all I have managed to do is stop it growing worse. But I'm not sure."

"You have been a great help, girl," said Dick. "He was raving and threshing about before you came. What you have done has, at least, calmed him. I think, you've lessened his pain."

"I would be happy to think so, Dick. I am just sorry I don't know more."

"We have soldiers billeted again, I see." Will gestured to the meadow behind him.

"Yes, a bit better behaved, this lot," Anne Carey told him. "Just as well, mind you. I don't think Her Ladyship could bear another crisis. She looks worn threadbare."

They went on comfortably exchanging tales of Will's journey and of the household's doings in his absence. I stayed Anne Carey with my hand and cleared Will's plates myself and went to fetch him some fruit and cheese and refresh his beer, just to be close to him again.

The kitchen door stood open and in the yard Jane Martin was talking to an officer in the full Puritan garb of black, white collar, tall, black hat. At first my heart squirmed. I thought it was the insolent Brother Levens, who had smashed the images in the hall windows, but this man was a stranger. 'This is forward behaviour on her part,' I thought. 'She is usually such a shrinking blossom. She is fond of Philip Drake, though, she cannot be flirting, especially not with a visiting soldier, even if he is a Puritan. What could she be finding to talk to him about?'

I took Will his fruit. He gave me a long look and closed his hand over mine, just briefly, but it was warm and strong. Together again.

Later that evening Lady Trentham brought the surgeon down to the hall and Ruth took him his supper. They called me in to tell him all that I had done, the herbals I had given and what I had used for the wound-dressings.

"You have done well, Mistress Sanderson, although I have told his lady mother here, the wound is still infected and his fever has not abated but, if you had not treated him as soon as you did, the poison would have spread throughout his body. He would have died."

Lady Trentham covered her face with her hands then looked up at him again, eager for reassurance.

"I will stay here until I see the infection properly healing. Once I am satisfied, I will leave him to Mistress Sanderson, but I recommend the local apothecary then visits him every week. However, I will not leave until I am sure I have done enough because if it does not soon heal and poison spreads I will have to amputate his arm."

Lady Trentham wept quietly. I felt a great, undigested dread.

"Now with your leave, My Lady, I will go up to my bed. I have endured a long and uncomfortable journey with your steward."

The mistress roused herself and rang the bell which stood on the dresser. "Goodnight, Sir, and many thanks. Goodnight, Alice."

I nodded my curtsey to them all and went back to the kitchen. I knew the others would be waiting to hear what the surgeon had said about the young master.

Next morning we had the satisfaction of watching the Roundheads break camp and leave without incident. We all relaxed a little.

As long as Doctor Chivers stayed I worked under his instruction, watching what he did, how he searched other parts of the body for any spread of infection, learning from him.

At last the day came when he called the family in to Thomas's chamber and gave them the good news that the infection had gone.

"Now the wound is clear and the swelling has subsided, I am going to stitch the edges of the gash together. I warn you, young man, this will be painful. I ask all the rest of you, save Mistress Sanderson, to leave the room. Alice will assist me and I will need two of your strong men to hold Master Thomas still."

I would rather have left the room with the family. Will and Dick held Thomas down at top and toe. He shouted and groaned so loudly I wondered how much worse it would have been for him if Dr Chivers had had to cut his arm right off.

It was done at last, strapped and bandaged still. I gave him some of the poppy draught and we left his mother, his grandparents and his sister to pray over him.

I sat on the window seat in the solar, my hands shaking. I opened the window to smell the freshness of the day. Dick went away but Will came and sat beside me. He took my hand and kissed it. "That was bravely done, girl."

Doctor. Chivers came down the stairs. "Ah, steward. I have told Lady Trentham I am leaving now. I have many urgent calls on me as you will all understand. I am sure Mistress Sanderson here will do whatever needs to be done before your master is fully recovered."

Will, having brought Doctor Chivers to Beauchamps, took him back to his home.

Lady Trentham and I were sitting at the table with our sewing, but Her Ladyship's hands lay idle. I heard boots on the stairs and Will came to us in the solar.

"After I left Doctor Chivers, I rode through Stratford, Your Ladyship, and I found these broadsheets spread all over the town. It is bad news. They claim to have uncovered another plot to raise an insurrection against Parliament. There is a list of suspected rebels posted at the Town Hall. Thomas's name is on the list."

"No! Impossible!"

"They say he escaped from prison, so he is subject to re-arrest."

"Holy Mary!"

"All the officers that escaped from Oxford are on the list. It is not just your son. They are so determined to stamp out this plot that they are sending Commissioners to search all known Royalist and Catholic houses and they are calling Catholic priests traitors also subject to arrest. Priest-hunters are to be sent out too. They will come here, My Lady, depend upon it."

My mind was in turmoil. Here was Thomas lying trapped in his bed; Stephen Barkswell, Francis de Paul Catholic priests in the house and buried silver altar vessels, in the grounds. Beauchamps Hall stood under the threat of prison bars or the gallows. The silence hung heavy in the room. Will signalled to me with a look. We left Lady Trentham alone.

At the bottom of the stairs, I plucked Will's sleeve and steered him into the estate office. I closed the door.

"What if we took Thomas to Netherfold, telling no one but his mother? You know my mother would nurse him. It is not far for him to travel. If anyone asks them, my parents could just say he was a wounded Royalist left behind after the last local skirmish. That is not far from the truth."

"There is hardly time to seek your father's permission."

"I will answer for him but I will stay here. I will write a letter and tell my mother all Doctor Chivers has said and done. If I am here, no one will suspect he has gone to Bournbroke. It is a good plan, Will."

"Yes, it is. I will tell Philip to ready the waggon. He can take him."

"No! Not Philip Drake. I don't trust his loyalty. He was with you in Stratford, he saw the poster, he saw the list. He should not know where Thomas is. Believe me."

"Well, I need Dick here. I will get Jake to do it, he is a good lad."

We walked into the kitchen to find Philip holding everyone's attention.

"There are posters everywhere. More plots by the Royalists and papists to overthrow the people's parliament, to steal

Cromwell's victory and set Charles Stuart to tyrannise over us again."

"You have said enough, there, Philip," Will exclaimed. "Such talk here. This house—"

"—harbours Thomas Trentham, named as a rebel right here." He waved the broadsheet in Will's face. "We should think shame to collude in sheltering him."

"It is you who should think shame, Philip Drake! Have you no loyalty to this family that has been your secure employment and your home for these last years? You owe them—"

"—I owe nothing to them, or to such as you, a papist and king-lover, though a servant. Lady Trentham's family and you and your ilk should obey the laws like English folk."

"Like English folk! What do you mean?"

Philip pointed in Anne Carey's face. "She will not defend you when the Spanish bring their invaders, their Jesuits, their burnings of the godly to England's shores."

"Enough!" Will grabbed Philip and thrust him towards the door.

"You! You lickspittle, you have been in thrall to Lady Trentham since your boyhood. You should be ashamed, Will Franks."

Will was white with anger. I was sure he would knock Philip down. He seized him and frogmarched him into the yard.

Jane Martin got to her feet and stood tall.

No longer meek, she stood, defiant. "Philip is right. This is a family of idolators. 'Thou shalt not bow down to any graven image,' yet they do, I have watched them. They worship the foreign pope. They whisper their wickedness in corners. I see them. But the Lord's Elect are not mocked. God's plan cannot be thwarted by a nest of traitors."

"Out! Get out after him!" Anne Carey shouted. "You have no place here. I want you out of my kitchen."

She glared and made to follow Philip.

"Prepare yourself to leave your place at the end of the week. I will not keep you here until Lady Day."

"You must ask the mistress before you can dismiss me and I will want my wages paid fair."

"Pay you? Jane Martin, pay you? Thank your good fortune if I do not throw you out tomorrow. Ingrate!" Anne Carey snapped her oven cloth in Jane's direction.

"You will find the Lord's righteous servants will triumph over evil-doers," Jane said, slamming the door back against the wall as she went out.

The shrinking maiden I had first met at the Stratford Mop shone with a zeal I would never have expected. She ran out to find Philip and a tumult of outraged talk erupted in the kitchen. I hurried into the estate office and scratched a letter to my parents.

Will looked in at the door. "Alice. Come." He led me to the side of the house where a waggon was ready, padded with straw mattresses and blankets. Will, Isabella and her mother half helped, half carried Thomas through the garden door and into the waggon, covering him with blankets and sacks.

I handed Jake my letter and he rode away.

In the half-light of dawn, I forced myself to wake from a dream tormented by shouting, horses stamping and neighing, someone hammering on the door.

I was back in Netherfold and besieged by soldiers again. I sat up, not in Netherfold, the clamour was real!

"Horses," said Ruth and ran to the shutters. We looked out.

"The stable door is hanging open, this early!"

" Look, Alice, Jane Martin's bed is empty. She has rolled it all up and taken her things."

We dressed and hurried down to the kitchen. There she was calmly mixing bread flour while Mistress Carey pummelled the first batch of dough.

"So early. This is usually our morning task."

"Couldn't sleep." Mistress Carey slapped the dough and ground it into the board. "Jane Martin here was out in the yard with no business to be abroad so early. I had to call her in."

"We heard horses moving outside," said Ruth. "We thought there must be soldiers. We came down to help."

Jane stopped mixing. "Philip was out in the stables grooming."

"That will not stop him being reprimanded today, or you either, Missy. If I had my way you would both be sent from here today but I fear Her Ladyship has too soft a heart."

I took the water carrier out to be filled and peeped into the open stable. All the horses were there, except for the oldest one that the men seldom used, and one of the saddle-hooks was empty. There was no sign of Philip Drake, grooming or not.

We were busy with the breakfast when Will ran in, breathless. "Trouble," he said, "Priest hunters have just ridden past the gate house. They will be knocking any moment now. Warn the family. I will open the door. If they walk in unhindered they might do less damage."

Just as he made for the hall, the kitchen door banged back against the wall. Four Parliament Commissioners strode in. One stood guard while the others hustled us forward into the hall, pushing Will ahead of them. The others, priest hunters, stood at the fireplace, all in black, like Brother Levens and just as hostile.

"Is there no end to this?" cried Aimee. "What has happened to our peaceful Vale?"

Lady Trentham and Isabella came down to the hall, helping the old couple, holding each other's hands, the rest of us ranged around them.

"You are come upon us early, Sir. I can see that you are not soldiers requiring a quarter here."

"This Catholic household breaks so many of the rules our victorious parliamentary government insists upon, you cannot be surprised that we are here to investigate you."

"Who are you, Sir? Show me by whose authority you come into my home without my leave."

"Gideon Ellison, formerly Captain in Parliament's Army. I do not need your permission to come in or go out from any place, Madam. I have the authority of the Lord our God, to whom these pagan images that surround you and the plots you make against the enemies of England are an abomination. I am here to root out sin wherever I find it and I find it here."

Lady Eliza began to moan and her husband plaintively repeated, "What is it, Abigail? What do they want? Who are these men. Oh dear, dear me, oh!"

Will stepped forward, with Dick at his side. "What is it you want? I am the steward and I can assure you the family has paid every penny exacted from us in fines. I have the documents if you want to see them."

"Documents! I have no time for that. Or for money. I am searching for plotters, for Roman priests and those who protect and hide these servants of the Antichrist."

Lady Trentham and Isabella crossed themselves, so did Aimee, Beth and Luce. Lady Eliza began to mutter a Latin prayer. This inflamed the Puritans who shouted curses and strode about the room breaking dishes and striking the portraits with their staves. Their chief shouted above the noise.

"Brothers! Concentrate upon our duty. Madam, we will search your every room. If you want to preserve this place from destruction, tell us now where the Catholic priest is hidden. We know for certain one is here."

Will faced him. "You are misinformed, Captain Ellison There is no priest here."

Ellison shook his head with a bitter smile. "I do not expect to hear the truth from you Papist hangers-on. We will search the place for ourselves. Be assured we will find the priest holes. I have seen them built in all the houses we have visited—Stainsby Court, Lavingham House, Brayburn. We know every trick, every hollow panel, every secret cupboard, every tunnel under stairs."

He confronted the mistress. Will took a step forward, his fists ready. Dick moved to the other side, preparing to defend her. Anne Carey edged towards the fireplace. She had her eyes on those iron tongs. Ellison thrust his face close into Lady Trentham and shouted,

"Will you give up your Popish priest?"

"How dare you! Move away!" Ruth crashed a water pitcher across the back of Ellison's head. He staggered sideways, his hat at his feet. Two of his men grabbed Ruth and dragged her away. "Catholic bitch!"

"She is no Catholic!" cried Isabella, "Leave her!"

"Shall I come for you, then, Mistress, instead?"

Will stood in front of Isabella as Molly helped Ruth out of the room. "Follow me, Captain!" He shook his keys at Ellison. "Search, if you must, then get on your way! I will conduct you myself."

"I will search where I please, Steward. Give your keys to me." He wrenched them out of Will's hand.

Will grabbed a fist full of Ellison's coat, lifting him off his feet but two of the hunters seized Will's arms and threw him aside. He sprawled across the floor, cracking his head.

"Coulson, Hickston, follow me," rapped Ellison. "We'll search the cellars. Selby, knock at every wall panel in here." Off they went, one of them kicking Will as he stepped over him.

I ran to Will and helped him to a seat. He was white with fury.

Lady Trentham stood quivering.

"Mistress Carey, take everyone into the kitchen. Aimee, go with Isabella, take my parents in law back to their chamber and stay with them in case those people search there."

"I'm sure they will, My Lady."

"Yes, well, we must endure it. Do not let your grandparents pray aloud, Isabella Make them keep their beads hidden. Keep silence for God's sake. Do you hear me, Mother Trentham? Do

182

not pray in front of them. Put away your crucifix and your prayer book."

As they left she turned to me and whispered "Alice. We are completely at your mercy."

"Thomas is safe. I will never open my mouth about him."

"No, not that, not Tom. No, it is the other things you have seen here, our chapel, the Mass."

"Shh! Mistress. There is nothing to tell them. I lived in the round room as my sewing chamber. I stitched wedding lace for Lady Elizabeth. I have met your cousin and your visitors. That's what I will say if I am asked. You can trust my loyalty absolutely." I glanced at Isabella. I wanted them both to believe me.

Lady Trentham sat down to wait for the priest hunters to come back. I knew she was praying, although she neither moved nor spoke.

Will gave me a long grim look and, rubbing his swelling brow, strode off to see what Ellison's men were doing. I left the hall and went out to the yard to keep out of their sight. While I stood there, worrying, I heard movement in the stable. A swish of hay. Harness. I hid behind the wash house door, wondering if the priest hunters were still searching the cellar. The kitchen door was standing open and Jane Martin came out. She must have heard the same noises I had.

As we watched, a horse emerged from the stable. A figure, cloaked and hooded, crouched low over the horse's neck and set off at a quiet walking pace towards the track through the copse-trees.

Jane ran back into the house, shouting "The priest! It's the priest!" "Ho! He's escaping! He's into the trees! Philip! Captain Ellison! Captain, he's here! Get him!"

Philip ran from the kitchen and chased after Stephen Barkswell, lunged up at him and pulled him off the horse's back. They rolled together, wrestling, swinging wild punches. Boots clattered down the stairs and out to the yard, shouting.

Two of the priest hunters pulled Philip aside and dragged Father Barkswell indoors, his riding boots gouging the floor. Philip followed, straightening his clothes. I ran in behind them.

"Leave me, leave me! I am no priest! It is not me you want! Let me go. I am no one."

They threw him on to the hall floor in front of Captain Ellison and Lady Trentham, like a maimed fox.

"Sneaking away to warn his plotting traitor friends, Sir," said Philip. He kicked the whining Barkswell who was alternating between protests and tears.

"So, Mistress, no priest here, yet, here we are, one snivelling cowardly priest, skulking in your stable, escaping on your horse now, here before your eyes. Oh dear. Lie upon lie and treachery right here. Proved! There is nothing you can say. Take him out, Coulson. Tie him to your saddle. He can run to Warwick behind us, until he can run no further. Out."

He looked around the room, stopping again at Lady Trentham. "You can expect a further visit from us. Your plotting here will be punished, but I will examine that priest further first. I am sure our means of persuasion will force him to tell us all your secrets."

"Her Ladyship was not hiding the priest," said Will. "The man was in plain sight. He is just the parish vicar of Throstleford, down the road. He came here after the destruction of Shipscarden, his benefice. He had nowhere to go."

"He *should* have nowhere to go. I would that all such priests were driven out and back to Rome."

"But he was not being hidden in any secret holes in walls. This house is innocent of any plot."

"We will see what truths the jabbering fellow tells us on the rack, then we will return." He made for the door.

"Who told you to look here for a Catholic priest?" Dick shouted. "Who sent you fishing here?"

Ellison slowly turned. "We would not tell *you*, any of you in this hornet's nest, about our loyal informants, but I told you I have searched half the Catholic houses of Warwickshire and bagged myself a string of prey. There will be no escape from God's grinding wheels."

He left. The front door stood open after him. We saw them mount and ride off towards the Roman road, hauling Barkswell behind them, howling.

"We do not need Ellison to tell us who informed on Barkswell." Will's voice was thick with rage. He looked around the hall. "Where is Philip Drake?"

"He was just here."

"You think Philip betrayed Her Ladyship, Will? Perhaps it was just a routine search as he said." Luce was aghast.

"No one in the household would speak about having a priest here. None of us would put you at risk, Mistress," said Dick.

"I thought I could vouch for everyone in my kitchen," Anne Carey said, "but that outburst from Jane Martin and Philip Drake yesterday proves it. They are our enemies."

"I saw Jane Martin just now," I said. "She was standing outside and she saw the priest leaving from the stable. She shouted of the priest hunters, warned them. She shouted of Philip too," I said. "They are together in this."

"I saw she had folded up all her bedding. She intended to leave us," said Ruth.

"So she should, I told her to leave. She hung about because she wanted her wages. I should have made you drive her off the estate last night, Will." Anne Carey was in a rage. "I should have dragged her out myself. It might have avoided this."

"It is as if she knew the priest hunters were coming," said Luce. "Perhaps she had already told them there was a priest here. Maybe she and Philip Drake plotted it together."

Without waiting for us to finish speaking, Will and Dick ran out to look for them.

"Here!" yelled Dick. "They are here!"

We all crowded out to see. Jane Martin already mounted on a horse in the stable yard and Philip struggling to haul himself up

185

to the saddle behind her. The frightened horse wheeled and tossed its head as Philip hopped about, desperately trying to mount. Will ran to grab him but Philip threw himself head first across the horse.

"Go, Jane!" He whacked the horse's flank "Go!"

Dick threw himself at Philip's legs but the horse reared and plunged away. Our men were left standing.

"Horse-thief! We'll have you hanged!" Dick shouted after them.

"Got away! Damned Judas!" Will panted.

"What could you have done?" gasped Luce, "short of beating them senseless, man and maid both?"

"I will go and tell Her Ladyship," said Will, straightening his jerkin.

Anne Carey stood in tears. "My people, trained here; working among us. How could they treat us so?"

"She changed Philip," Luce said. "Remember how he spoke after he saw those broadsheets about the plots."

We wandered back into the kitchen, subdued. Will came in, sat heavily at the table and dragged a hand through his hair.

"I am wretched, Anne. My judgement has been seriously at fault to bring that two-faced Jane Martin amongst us. I endangered the mistress—all of us."

"How could you know, Will" said Anne Carey? "People change. I blame myself too. I should have seen the signs before this. I should have run them out of the house at once, not waited for morning or wages or anything."

Francis de Paul came in. "Alice, my aunt wants you upstairs with your medicines. My grandmother is taken ill."

Upstairs the old lady sat, pale and short of breath. She complained of a pain in her head and that her legs were too weak to carry her.

Isabella sat upright, earnest. "I think we should leave here at once, Mother. Uncle Edward would welcome us at Cheyne St.

Paul. We would be safer there. Those men will be back. They mean to destroy us."

"Your grandparents could not bear the journey, Isabella. And what if they sent commissioners to follow us? We should put your aunt and uncle into danger with us."

"We could make Grandfather comfortable and Grandmother could even stay—"

The old gentleman wept openly. "No, no, no Isabella, Abigail, don't say you will leave Eliza here and take me away. I cannot be parted from her."

"Hush, Father, dear. No one will take you anywhere. Isabella look at your grandmother! She is prostrate. Alice is doing her best but the poor soul is ill. We need to help her into bed not into a draughty coach for a hundred miles of bone-shaking discomfort."

"Then take them to my sister's. That is just across the way. The family would make them welcome and we can get away to the south."

"How can Carterway Manor be any safer than here?"

"Because they are not sheltering Francis here."

Francis stopped her. "You have said enough, cousin. Help me upstairs with Grandmother." Sir Felix burst out crying again, begging not to be separated from his wife and Lady Eliza moaned and cried.

As they helped the frail old couple to their chamber, Anne Carey spoke up.

"In my opinion it is a good idea, Your Ladyship. I think at least we should prepare. I could ask Will to organise the estate affairs, your documents and money and I could make preparations for the journey. That way you would be ready."

"You do not usually forget your place and tell me what to do, Anne."

"I read your exhaustion, My Lady, I have looked after you and yours for enough years to be presumptuous in your interest."

"Dear soul," said Lady Abigail. "I will consider the matter but do nothing for the present. We must pray for Father Barkswell in his time of trial."

In the kitchen, Anne told Will all that had been said and that she thought they should make ready in case Her Ladyship agreed to leave for Cheyne St. Paul.

Francis de Paul came in to find her, asking for some hot posset and wine for his grandparents.

"My aunt told me of your advice, Mistress Carey. I agree with you, she would be safer in Oxfordshire so it would be well to make some preparations but do nothing overt. We must not seem to disobey her, she has worry enough, but it is not safe for us all to stay here. Thank you all. I will pray for us."

I watched Will as Francis left the room. He scowled after him. "Perhaps it would be safer here if *he* were to go to Cheyne St. Paul."

Mistress Carey's calming measure was to call for cider which she mulled and served to us all for our comfort, which it was, a little.

Anne Carey allocated tasks for packing and preparing in the event the family were to leave. Will spent all morning in the estate office. Molly and I filled the medicine chest with herbs and bandages and lotions for them to take to Oxfordshire, if that was Lady Trentham's choice.

I wondered where my place would be. Was I to stay or go back to Netherfold? Would other people, other circumstances separate me from Will again?

Unbidden Guests

'Unbidden guests
Are often welcomest

'Henry VI': William Shakespeare:

Next morning Aimee carried the breakfast up to Sir Felix and Lady Eliza and ran back down again calling for help.

"Lady Eliza has collapsed. I found her on the floor with Sir Felix trying to rouse her, crying her name."

"God have mercy! Is she dead?" Anne Carey was already on her way up the stairs. Ruth and I followed.

Mistress Carey bent over her. "Thank God she is still breathing. Alice, help me to lift her back to bed."

I felt her limbs to see if I could feel any broken bones. She groaned but I could find no points of disjoint. Sir Felix held on to her, uselessly, his hands shaking. She did not open her eyes or speak, she just moaned.

Lady Trentham hurried in. "Oh dear, and the surgeon is long gone. What must we do, Alice?"

"I do not think it is a matter for the surgeon. In any case he will be in Oxford by now. You had better send for the apothecary. It might be an apoplexy, such as my own grandmother died of. The person is struck dumb and the face twists, and there is a paralysis."

"Holy Mother, save us. Trouble upon trouble! Can you do anything?"

The old gentleman seized his wife's hand and wept over it. I set a chair for him at her bedside and Lady Abigail and I retired outside the door.

"I have no experience beyond the care of wounds and pain; that was the only nursing I did for Nell Franks and Thomas and the soldiers. If it is an apoplexy or if her heart has failed her, I will not have enough knowledge to cure her. I can only try to keep her comfortable until help comes."

"Very well, I will send someone to Stratford for an apothecary. Do what you can, Alice, to help her."

Mistress Carey came out of the bedchamber. "That settles the plan, then, we will not be packing up and leaving for Cheyne St Paul. I will tell the others."

It rained all day. It was cold and a low fog hung over the meadow, the trees dripped gloom. I sat with Lady Eliza, watching for change. She lay still, unseeing and silent, except for the dragging of her laboured breath. Sir Felix could not be persuaded to leave the room, so Ruth and I heated rosemary infusions for him.

At last Lady Trentham came and led her father-in-law into her own chamber to eat their supper together and rest. Isabella kept vigil at Lady Eliza's bedside and sent me down to the kitchen for my meal.

Will came in once and took my hand.

"No change," I said. "I cannot even tell if she has a paralysis. She does not speak. Her eyes are shut fast."

"It is not the plague, is it?" I shook my head.

"None of the signs."

"But she still breathes?"

"Painfully. Every breath is a hard labour. I cannot think of anything to do for her, Will. Did they find the apothecary?"

"Dick went but he is not back yet. Do you think she is going to die, Alice?"

"I cannot tell, but I fear so, Will." He leaned over and kissed my hair. Molly saw. She smiled and turned away. No one remarked. The day weighed too heavily on us all.

By next morning there was still no change in the old lady's condition. She wheezed as she breathed, not sleeping in a normal way. She looked somehow locked in.

They made up a bed for me behind a screen in the sick room so that I could take over most of the nursing.

"Perhaps you and Isabella would prefer to watch over her, My Lady, since I know of no treatments to help her."

"I'm afraid," said Lady Trentham, "my father-in-law has taken to bed. He won't eat or drink. He just weeps all the time and repeats his wife's name over and over. I fear for him now too. I will send Dick to sit with him and Isabella and I will divide ourselves between the two rooms until the apothecary comes." She gave a deep sigh. "I am so pleased Tom is with your mother, Alice. Three invalids are more than I could face."

Lady Eliza became more restless but her eyes stayed tight shut. She could not drink anything I prepared.

I fell asleep myself until Isabella woke me for my nursing turn. I applied cool-water pads to the old lady's head and bathed her face and hands. She lay inert. Her face frozen in a grimace. Now and then she mumbled undistinguishable words.

As I refreshed the scented bathing water, the chamber door opened and Lady Trentham came in. She sat in the chair by her mother in law's head, took out her rosary and wound it around her own hand and Lady Eliza's wasted fingers. I turned away and stirred crushed lavender into the bathing water.

"Alice," Lady Trentham spoke low. "Do you think she will recover?"

I put a finger to my lips. The sick may give no sign of life but Mother had told me many stories of how agitated they become if they hear their death spoken of across the bed. I soaked a fresh cooling-pad and laid it across the old lady's forehead. "There is always hope."

She nodded. "Just sit with me. How tired I am of all this pain and sickness and constant fear. When they brought my dear Carlton's body back to me, I thought I could feel no greater suffering. But it goes on and on." She stared into the fire, burning yellow and low. "I have hardly had the peace to sit and contemplate my widowhood, to grieve as I should for my husband's death. My daughters have their own concerns.

Elizabeth is happy in her own home with Edward Carter and Isabella, well, she sits closed around her own thoughts. I loved their father for so long. Our families always intended the match. I think I told you."

"And you liked your father's choice for you?"

"Always. Carlton was my dearest playfellow. He made me daisy chains. He picked bunches of buttercups and field poppies for me. He wove me May Queen crowns. He was my dancing partner when all the children we were given lessons together. He would constantly say to me, 'Abigail, when you are my wife we will do this' or 'When we marry I will do that'. We wanted lots of children and were blessed with three alive." She paused. "Our son is still alive, even though my husband has been wrenched away from me."

She shook her head to dispel her train of thought. "Has your father made a marriage arrangement for you, Alice?" I did not speak.

"Ah, am I prying?" she asked.

I hesitated. If I began to talk about Jack Morton and his death I would be leading her back to thoughts of grief and loss. "I think I told you I was once betrothed to a family friend in the village but he went away to fight for the Parliament and was killed."

"You too. Yet you and Will seem to be fond of each other."

"Ah, yes." I paused. "I have known Will—he has been a friend of my father's for a long time."

"Do you think your father would approve a marriage between you?"

"He has never said such a thing. My parents' marriage was a love-match. I think they hope proximity might lead to something." I tailed off. I could not reveal myself further for Will had said so little to me of love or marriage.

"You know how highly I regard Will—and you, Alice. I would look on such a marriage with great pleasure if ever you felt able to give your heart again after the death of your betrothed. I will never marry again."

I stood to refresh the cooling-water, feeling uncomfortable. Was I heartless, faithless to have forgotten Jack completely and to fall in love with Will Franks?"

By morning, when Aimee came in with breakfast for me, I asked her to help me lift and change Lady Eliza. We prepared fresh linen and a washing bowl and made her as clean and comfortable as we could. She was no more at peace than before. Her breathing was more congested and laboured, wheezing and short.

I made a bowl of steaming lavender and mint water. We raised the old lady and covered her head to make her breathe the fragrant steam. I hoped it would give her ease, but soon her body sagged and she slumped forward. We took away the bowl and propped more cushions behind her.

She passed a day and a night in that position, unmoving. Dying, I thought.

At last the apothecary arrived. Aimee came to tell me, bringing more candles.

"Thank God! Is there any improvement with Sir Felix?"

"No. Dick thinks he is failing. He keeps asking about his wife. As soon as they have told him she is just the same, he asks again, the same question, in the same words. So sad."

Anne Carey brought in the apothecary and Lady Trentham followed. He asked me questions about all that I had done and had observed then I left him to his work.

I went to walk in the garden to smell the fresh, chill air. There was a brittle setting sun. The frost had lingered in the corners all day long, on the edges of the paths and on the dead flower heads. I strolled through the twiggy bare rose garden towards the house—and stopped dead. There were three priest-hunters at the garden door, watching.

"You again! Does Master Franks know you are here?"

"We know our way around this place. Just stay where you are."

193

"We have sick people here, Sir. Lady Trentham is nursing her aged father-in-law, and his wife is sick and dying. Surely you will not subject us to searches again!"

One of them strode forward and yanked me by the arm towards the garden door.

They marched me into the hall and held me there while they split up and ran up the stairs, shouting instructions to each other to search the bedrooms, look into the chimneys, look into every cupboard—all as before. I heard the raised voices of Lady Trentham and Isabella. Ruth rushed down the stairs calling for Mistress Carey and for Will.

It was Ellison again. He spoke to each of his men in turn then faced Lady Trentham. "No priest holes! No more priests in hiding! You are fortunate, Madam, if you have no second traitor in your house."

"You, Selby, anything?"

The last priest hunter came down the stairs and threw Lady Eliza's rosary of pearls with its silver crucifix across the table. "Just these popish trinkets, Brother Ellison."

"Tch! Tch! You are aware these objects are forbidden, are you not? You deliberately flout the law."

"My mother-in-law is old and dying, Sir. She has had these about her since her youth when the practice of her religion was permitted. She needs the comfort now in her last days."

"Comfort! Items of this sort must be confiscated. Put them in the bag, Selby."

Will intervened. "So stealing is permitted under Puritan law, is it?"

Ellison wheeled round on him. "Are you another Papist in this traitors' den?"

"I am a Protestant who stands by what is right, and what you do is not right; and there are no traitors here but you who betray good Christian spirit."

Ellison struck Will full in the face. Dick darted forward and grabbed him.

194

"Captain Ellison!" Lady Trentham was more angry than afraid this time. "For God's Sake leave off this brawling! Is there something else you need to do, because you have done your searching and found no one If you need to ask me anything, ask it. If you need money from me, demand it. Then, for the love of God, go away and leave us to look after the dying."

Ellison, still glaring at Will, rubbed his hand. "It is necessary to make many visits to the home of Romish families to see if more priests have crawled out of their worm-holes since we visited last. You may look for us again. We will not rest until we have made sure you are not part of any plot against the Commonwealth and its true religion. You are not safe from arrest, Madam. Look for us again."

They marched out.

"Thank you, Dick, Will," said Lady Trentham. "There is no speaking to these fanatics." She and Isabella went upstairs. The rest of us moved into the kitchen. I bathed Will's face and pressed a cold pad on his bruising cheek. Mistress Carey unlocked the dresser and brought out brandy. She gave each of us a small draught. "To settle our nervous humours," she said.

"Take this up to Lady Abigail and Mistress Isabella," she said, "They will need this as physick too."

I went up to them. As I opened the door to Lady Eliza's chamber I saw them all standing close around the bed. Lady Trentham, Aimee, Luce and Francis de Paul.

I looked at him more closely. He was wearing the long purple silk around his neck and moved his hands reverently between a small group of silver cups and candle sticks. He smoothed some liquid on the old lady's closed eyelids and on her lips as he whispered prayers. I was watching a priest performing a Roman rite I could not follow but I prayed in my own heart the priest hunters would not swoop back in now.

Lady Trentham was slumped in her chair with tears on her cheeks, deep shadows under her eyes.

Francis de Paul completed his office. I bowed my head and said an English prayer in silence. She had been a kindly old lady and I wished her speedily into heaven.

Anne Carey took charge of the room. "Come, My Lady, you look quite ill yourself. Isabella, help me take your mother to bed in your chamber and stay with her. Luce, you and Dick sit with Sir Felix and Alice, you and Molly watch over Lady Eliza. Come now, I have brought a little brandy to revive you." She eased the distress we all felt by telling us what to do.

I touched de Paul as he was leaving. "Wait." I dropped my voice and I steered him out of the room into a corner. "Listen. The priest hunters have gone, but they will be back. Father Barkswell is a coward. If they torture him, he will betray you, and the altar silver you have hidden in the copse."

Aghast, he stared at me. "How do you know about that?"

"I saw you and Barkswell take it into the trees and I happened upon its hiding place beside the fishponds. It was an accident. But Barkswell will tell his torturers where to look and your aunt will be arrested, you can be sure."

"Yes, yes. I know the risk to her. I am at risk from you now also."

"Get rid of it, then. If I do not know where it is I cannot tell them anything. I cannot threaten the family or you and if Barkswell tells them and they find nothing he will have been proved a liar."

"Say nothing more. I will deal with it." He removed his purple silk and thrust it into his sleeve.

I walked out after him and straight into Will who was turning into the corridor "I thought I saw de Paul just now, has he gone into the chamber?"

"No, I don't know where he is. He passed me a moment ago. He must have passed you."

The solar was empty. De Paul had vanished once again. I was ready to stay and talk to Will but he gave me a strange look and said he had work to do. I went back to watch Lady Eliza. Night fell. I slept sitting in the chair beside her bed.

I woke with a start in the small hours. The candles had burned down. The fire gave only a meagre glow from its remaining ash. Lady Eliza's hand and cheek felt cold. I replaced the candles and added fresh kindling and logs to the fire. Was the old lady breathing? I bent closer. Suddenly she drew in a loud, harsh breath. I started back. Her rasping breaths dragged in and out and in, then stopped. The silence hung in the air until I was alarmed and touched her face. She drew another tortured breath and the macabre rhythm began again.

In order to do something, I poured some warm water and bathed her face and hands. She gave a sudden loud gasp.

I jumped, thinking I had hurt her, but she lay rigid still, her face closed up. I waited. And waited. She did not breathe in. The chamber filled and filled with a silence that I waited for her to break. But the silence did not break. She did not breathe again.

With trembling fingers, I scratched at the pillow's seam and drew out a feather. I lay it under her nose and held the candle closer. Did the feather move? Did I imagine it moved? I took the candle and went to rouse Aimee.

"Is she dead?" asked Aimee?

"I can't tell. Her loud breathing stopped. I cannot see her breathing at all. Look, I put that feather there. Does it look as though it moves?"

Aimee bent nearer. "No. She is dead." She felt her cheeks and brow. "Cold, already."

She crossed herself. "I will go for Lady Trentham and Isabella."

I straightened the bedsheets and tidied the room, without attending to anything I did. The warring factions had brought more death to our door. More grief.

The others crowded round the bed, including Anne Carey and Beth.

197

"Isabella, fetch Francis. We will pray for her departed soul. Open the window for its flight."

I said I would go to watch over the old gentleman while the others prayed for Lady Eliza. "Don't tell him, Alice," Lady Trentham said. "I will do it in the daylight."

We sat in the kitchen at our breakfast, the family staying in their chambers. Will had to go to Carterway Manor to give Elizabeth the news. I followed him out to the stables.

"I'm sorry that I could not keep Lady Eliza alive, any more than I could save your sister. I did not know enough. And Lady Trentham depended on me."

He closed his arms around me. "You saved Thomas's life. Lady Eliza was old. It was her time."

"Will! Alice! Here! Good God! Come back!"

We dashed into the kitchen. Isabella stood there, distraught. "Bring something to revive my mother, Mistress Sanderson. Quickly! Mistress Carey. Bring brandy. Something!"

She turned and ran back through the hall. Will and I looked at the others. Molly had come down with Isabella. She stood there, aghast. "It's her grandfather now. He is gone as well,"

"Gone! Dead? I was with him last night. He was not so ill as that. Just afraid for his wife."

"The Mistress has just told him that Lady Eliza was dead. He just clutched his hand to his chest and fell dead at her feet. Now Her Ladyship has collapsed beside him. Get up there!"

"Is there no end to it?" cried Ruth, running to the stairs. Will ran too and Mistress Carey followed. Molly brought me the herbals box and I found some hartshorn in vinegar for her to inhale and took it up.

"Is there any further blow God can inflict upon our hearts?" Lady Trentham sobbed. They helped her to sit up. I knelt and moved the reviver close to her nose. She cried and coughed as Isabella and Anne Carey lifted her to a seat.

Aimee neatened Sir Felix's clothes, so loose and baggy on his wasted frame. She folded his hands and wound a rosary around them.

"The window, open the window for his poor, poor soul," the mistress sobbed. "Bring Francis here. My father-in-law had no time for his last rites. Francis must sanctify him. Will, go to Elizabeth with the news."

Will hurried away, leaving the rest of us standing together in a fog of sadness, waiting until there was something else to do.

It rained and rained. The family carriages rode to Elms Barton parish church behind the waggon carrying both coffins. It was drenching weather to stand at the burial of people who were loved.

Anne Carey, Aimee, Beth, with Dick and Luce, as Catholics, joined the family at the funeral. I stayed behind at Beauchamps with Ruth, and Molly to prepare refreshments for their return. The rain poured on, rattling on the barn and stable roofs, making huge puddles in the yard. Foul out and foul underfoot. They would be glad to get into the warm and dry. I stoked the fire to a fine blaze and set soup to heat.

They came in dripping; gusts of wind and rain swirling in behind them. I collected the wet cloaks as they all clustered round the fire. Will brought wine up from the cellar for the family. We set their meal out in the hall and were about to go back to the kitchen for our own meal when there came a battering at the front door.

"Not again! Not now!" exclaimed Lady Trentham, "Francis!"

Jake went to open it. But at the same instant, the door from the kitchen burst open.

Two priest-hunters marched in at the same instant as Jake unlocked the front door and the other four, led by Captain Ellison, pushed past him into the hall. He stared at the family in their funeral clothes.

"Oh! Plain and modest dress for once. Do you mean to persuade me you have left off your pomp and vanity? If so, let me tell you I will never be convinced. I know Papists. I smell them." Jake slammed the door behind him. The nearest of Ellison's men grabbed and held him.

"Captain Ellison," Isabella got to her feet. "You see us in mourning, Sir. We have just come back from burying my dear grandparents. You disturb our grief."

"Dear, dear, so I do, indeed."

"Do you intend to search my house again?" Lady Trentham asked.

"No, no need for searching any more. We have come for the other traitor-priest there, at your hearth." He looked around us all. "What was it the prisoner told us? Oh yes, a tall fellow with a weak chin under a pointed beard." He crossed to Francis de Paul. "Hair in cavalier curls." With a swift upward movement he grabbed a fistful of de Paul's hair and yanked his head backwards. "And a fine silken suit." His free hand seized de Paul's wrist. "Such priestly-soft Papist's hands."

"Your informer could not mean me, Captain." He tried to struggle free. "I am no priest, just My Lady's nephew. You will not arrest me for that I think."

"If I believed you, but you lie. You have been denounced most thoroughly by one who knows you very well."

"If you mean that Jane Martin, she did not know Master de Paul at all," Anne Carey interrupted. "She was a new servant. She knew nothing of this family."

"Heighty-Teighty Mistress Cook, keep out of this business or I may arrest you too for abetting this priest with his foreign name."

"The cowardly Throstleford priest has confessed everything to us—that he was hiding here, that he and you, Sir, celebrated secret popish Masses in a forbidden chapel, which, believe me, we will find, and that you, *Monseigneur de Paul,*" he sneered, "are the other priest that this houseful of traitors and plotters keeps hidden. Take him!"

Two of the men stepped towards Francis de Paul. I don't know why I did what I did next. I did not think about it. I sprang forward and threw my arms around de Paul and kissed him passionately."

"He is not a priest!" I shouted, "He is my lover, my bedfellow! We are going to marry and leave this place. He is not a priest! Tell them, Francis, tell them!" I pressed kisses on his face and neck. He resisted, almost set me away from him, but I opened my eyes to him, full of alarm and awkwardly he put his arms around me.

It was only as I turned back to face Ellison and gauge the effect of my performance, that I saw Will standing at the open garden door, wine jug in hand, looking at me in disbelief.

"Of course, Francis is not a priest." Lady Trentham suddenly followed my lead. "He is of my husband's family who lately fought in the King's army. You cannot arrest him for that, or you must imprison half of England."

Ellison looked around the company. I could see a doubt had crept into his looks. Anne Carey joined in this scene we were acting out. "Alice Sanderson! You should be ashamed, to so betray the hospitality we have shown you. And you, Master de Paul, how could you take advantage of one of my waiting women in such a way?"

He looked wildly from Mistress Carey to his aunt, to me and desperately thought of a way to join in the sham.

" Erm - W-w-way of the world, Mistress Carey. Youth is lusty, eh?" de Paul twisted his face into a smirk and looked about at the men then to his aunt. "Forgive me, Aunt, you must be angry with me but—Captain Ellison, the priest of Throstleford is a coward. You saw that when you took him away. He would pretend, confess anything to save himself, blame anyone under torture. I cannot believe so shrewd a man as you, Captain, would be fooled by his lies. Barkswell is as weak as he is stupid."

We all stood there, tense, watching. Ellison examined my face, then de Paul's. Had I weakened his conviction?

Will walked into the hall. He set down the wine jug and reached for one of the open estate ledgers.

"Wait! You must know what a whining coward Father Barkswell is, Captain. He would plead anything to save his own skin, de Paul is right. I have long known him and his reputation. I am sure he tried to bribe you. He certainly tried to bribe me. Look at this."

He pointed to an entry in the book.

"See that? Barkswell begged me for money to make his escape. He said if I did not pay him, he would find you and tell you Her Ladyship's nephew was a Catholic priest. Look at it." Ellison bent and looked. The silence was intense.

Captain Ellison straightened up. "And you paid his extortion?"

Will nodded. "To get rid of him. He was endangering the estate."

He looked at the ledger again then slammed it shut. "Fool! He betrayed you anyway." Ellison turned from Will to me. "Harlot!" His spittle hit my cheek. "And you!"

He shoved de Paul in the chest. "Priest or not, you are capable of all the immoral whoring I would expect to see in such a household." Belligerent, he pushed up closer.

"I will go now but enquire further locally. Be sure, I will come back and screw you to the rack myself if I find further evidence to incriminate you. And My Lady, I will come back for you. You will end your days in Warwick prison, or on the gallows." He nodded at his men "Look for us again."

At first no one spoke. Then everyone began to talk at once. At last Lady Trentham raised her voice. "What did you show him in the book, Will?" Everyone fell silent. "Did you indeed pay Barkswell to leave?"

"Of course not. It was money I had paid to Simon Baker for flour. I just noticed his initials, SB, and thought I could make use of the coincidence to help you."

"SB, the same! How clever of you."

My cheeks burned with shame at my public pretence. They must all believe it was pretence, surely. Before I could say anything, Will gave me a look that tore at my heart, turned away and walked out. He could not have believed what he just heard me say. I had to make sure they all understood.

"My Lady! You must know that I was play-acting to protect Master de Paul, and you!"

"Alice," Francis exclaimed, "That was quick thinking. You saved me. She saved me, Abigail."

Mistress Carey nodded my way. The others stared, wide-eyed. Isabella looked with a curl to her lip. She clearly believed I lusted after her cousin, the priest.

I had to find Will. He had looked so stricken. The estate office stood open and the ledger was back on his table but there was no sign of him. I thought of running down to the gate house to look for him but Anne Carey was calling my name. I did not want to see her or any of them. My heart was racing. Will must have believed what he saw. Had I ruined his good opinion of me? Surely he could not believe what I said!

I sidled out of the office, darted out to the yard and into the stables. I hid there, among the heaps of straw and wept into my apron while I heard them calling for me inside and out.

I cried myself calm and tidied my hair, picked the straw out of my skirts and braced myself to go back to the house.

Mistress Carey was supervising preparations for the evening meal. Ruth fuelled the fire and the others prepared the food. Will did not come in. All my friends gave me such wan and wary smiles I could not tell what they believed of me. Surely they knew me better? Will knew me better.

Anne Carey came over to me. She grasped my hand and kissed my cheek, her smile warm.

I could have collapsed into her arms, I was so grateful that she knew I was no fornicator. "Lady Trentham is asking for you."

I clung on to what dignity remained to me and went up to the solar. Isabella was seated by the fire. Francis de Paul stood near to the mistress by the window.

"Francis assures me there was no truth in what you claimed to Captain Ellison. Naturally, I believe him."

I glanced at Isabella but her eyes were fixed on the breviary in her hands. Francis brought his chair nearer to us and leant forward.

"It was the cleverest thing you could have done at that very moment, Alice. It fuelled the Puritan's belief in our immorality." He sighed. "Abigail, I am bringing even greater danger to you now than in all these recent weeks. I must leave."

"You are right, Francis. You cannot stay here. They will be back. If not Ellison himself, then just such another."

"We should leave too, Mother, and go to Cheyne St. Paul. Why do you hesitate? You could come with us, Francis. There will be fewer priest hunts there. We will all be safe."

"I have a plan." de Paul looked round at all the doors. "But it is safer if I do not tell you what it is. All I will say is I intend to leave England. Ask me nothing, then if the hunters come here asking, you can honestly plead ignorance. They cannot arrest you for what you do not know."

"They can torture us, Francis, or throw us into prison for no other reason but our faith."

"Well, I will do what I must and leave our safety to God's mercy." He left us and Isabella went after him, calling his name.

"Alice, wait. I have another favour to ask of you," said Lady Trentham. "About my son. I must see Thomas. It is weeks since he went into your mother's care. If I am to leave for Cheyne St. Paul, I must see him. I understand Dick is taking you home tomorrow, I want to come with you."

"Of course, but the rain will have flooded parts of the road to Bournbroke, My Lady, it happens every time we have a deluge for days and days like this. It will be a slow journey."

To see my family again was the comfort my aching spirits needed. Will did not appear for the evening meal. I asked Dick, but he had not seen him either. Next day the rain poured down and cloud hung low over the trees as Lady Trentham and I stood in the hall ready to leave.

"Horsemen!" Francis called us to the window.

There was urgent knocking at the front door. "Model Army men, not many, four. One hunched over."

Lady Trentham clutched her daughter's arm. Isabella went beside him to look. "Go, Francis! It is not Ellison back, is it, Anne?"

Anne Carey stood ready to open the door but waited. Francis disappeared.

"Wait, Anne. I will see no one from choice. You and I will go to our chambers, Isabella." They went up the stairs as Mistress Carey opened the front door.

Will came in with four Roundhead officers. He drew them to the hearth where they stood dripping. Two of them supported one who was hunched over, wrapped in a sodden cloak. Mistress Carey, Beth and I watched and waited.

Will came in ahead of them. "These men knocked at the gate house. They are claiming free quarter. The roads are flooded."

"Major Richard Skelton, Adjutant to Colonel Sir Bartholomew Elliot, Oliver Cromwell's deputy. I take it those here are supporters of the King but we must throw ourselves upon your mercy. We are only four, as you see, but the Colonel here is sick. As your steward says, we cannot cross the Saxonford bridge. The river threatens to burst the arch. We need dry shelter and rest for tonight at least."

The wet-cloaked colonel sagged at the knees and fell. The men crowded round him, removing his heavy cloak and boots. They chafed his hands, loosened his breast-plate.

"Not plague, is it?" Mistress Carey peered down. "Where have you come from?"

"Wales, going north. We have passed no plague. He has a fever."

"Not wounded?" I asked. "We have had so many."

"No, sick."

"Very well, then, Beth, fetch blankets and a pillow. Make a bed in the recess by the dresser. We can move him tomorrow, when he has rested."

"Is he vomiting, Major, or are his bowels in flux?" I asked. Skelton hesitated, frowning. "I ask so that we can decide what dressings, what medicines he needs."

"Just because this is a Royalist house, Sir, do not suppose we want to help a Roundhead to his death," said Will. "You can answer her. Be confident of our help. Are there more of your troops to come?"

"No, we are the forward party, but were caught up in these floods. I am Lemuel Jayston, Major. Do we need permission from the master of the house?"

Anne Carey spoke up. "The master of the house, God rest his soul, is dead, Major, fighting for his King. And pray do not discuss the rights and wrongs of our several loyalties. You have come demanding quarter. We are bound to give it. Let that be enough. Master Franks, the steward here, and I, as housekeeper, have all the authority you need."

"The family is in deep mourning, Sir," said Will. "Lady Eliza Trentham and her elderly husband both died within the week. The family are not long back from the burial. They are exhausted and grieving."

"We will sit here quietly and be grateful for anything you do towards our Colonel's comfort, and for ours."

"Hmm. Polite requests and gratitude have not been our experience from soldiers in these last months."

Anne Carey looked closely at the colonel. "But perhaps you are gentlemen. Come Beth, Alice, let us collect provisions and bedding. I suppose you will all want to stay here in the hall together, for fear we slit your gizzards in the night."

"Hush! Mistress Carey," said Will, "Remove your jackets and wet boots, bring chairs around the fire. Your food will come soon."

It looked as though my journey home was going to be delayed. I sighed and set to, bringing bowls of water, hot and cold, to bathe his face and chill his head. I mixed an infusion of lettuce and ribswort to subdue his fever. I tilted his head to make him drink it down in sips. He spluttered and spat some out but gradually I got most of it into him and hoped it would help him sleep. At least he was not in a torment from wounds or pain.

"Major Skelton." I called him over. "One of you must be alert all night. Refresh cold pads for his head to cool his fever. After an hour give him more of this medicine to drink. If he thinks he must get up and leave, keep him still. Sleep and a reduction of the fever is what he needs. If he begins to cough, or struggles to draw his breath, call for my help. There is a bell there, on the dresser."

Will gave me a searching look. I thought he was going to speak, but he said nothing. He spoke quietly to the soldiers then withdrew to the estate office without saying goodnight, either to Beth or to me.

I had no summons through the night, and as the others busied themselves preparing breakfasts, I went into the hall to examine the sick man. He was still feverish, but no worse.

After breakfast Lady Trentham came down to speak to the Roundhead officers. She looked unrested.

"I hear the Colonel is ill," she said. "Is he any better this morning?"

"He is certainly more comfortable, Madam. Your people have been kind. But I am afraid we must trespass on you for longer. He is in no state to resume our journey."

"Trespass! We are not used to soldiers, from either side, apologising for their 'trespass'. Hundreds at a time have ridden here over my land and made free with our produce and forced our hospitality."

"It has been a long war, with suffering at every side, I agree."

"Suffering for ideas, Sir. For arguments. No one is fighting off foreign invaders. I hardly know how all this has come about. My husband, like many, is dead for this. My family and I have been harassed by Puritan fanatics, hating us for nothing but our faith. The last priest-hunters terrified my mother-in-law so gravely she died and my poor father-in-law, her husband, burst his heart with grief. I lost half my family at one stroke. I have been accused of treachery, of plots and every kind of evil, when all I have tried to do is live my life according to the law and in accordance with the will of God. I cannot see we differ so much in that, except you carry the swords and seek to force the world to do it your way. I and mine are powerless before you all."

Major Skelton frowned and looked, not angry, but ill at ease. Major Jayston cleared his throat. "About the billeting of soldiers, Madam, their seizing of your produce and such. Did you know that Oliver Cromwell has invited the folk of Warwickshire who have laboured under these demands to place a request for reimbursement? You can claim moneys from the Parliament for this. Notices are posted in Warwick, Stratford and Evesham."

"Really? I am astonished if it is so. I will ask my steward to look into it. It would be more than welcome. We have our accounts. I will go to find Master Franks. You can explain it all to him.

"Thank you for your hospitality, My Lady," Skelton said. "And for your servant's nursing of our colonel."

"She is a family friend, Sir, not a servant. My housekeeper tells me the floods and the colonel's sickness mean you will need to stay here for a few more days. I will arrange for him to be moved to a guest room. Alice, ask the women to move the other officers' bedding into the round room, which is empty, then come back to me in the solar."

I was relieved to hear Her Ladyship say the round room was empty. There would be no more secret chapel services to increase her risk of arrest.

She stopped at the top of the stairs. "Have you seen Francis anywhere today? I cannot find him. He always tells me where he will be."

Of course, I had not seen him. If she herself did not know which of the secret hiding places he was in, then where could he be? I wished the priest-hunters would come searching now. They would find no priest, no secret chapel and five officers of their own persuasion established in the house.

The aristocratic Roundhead colonel coughed, sneezed, and shivered. I made infusions for him to inhale to ease the congestion in his chest. I watched anxiously for his breath to become less laboured. On the third night his condition reached its crisis. I propped him up with pillows and covered his head so he could breathe a concentration of hot minted steam.

He slept most of the next day and when I came to dose him that night I found him much improved. Another night and a day and, weak but better, he went down into the hall to his men.

Later, Major Jayston came to find Anne Carey in the kitchen and asked if Lady Trentham was at liberty to meet Sir Bartholomew Elliot.

She came back to say the mistress would come down to join him, as long as he was free from all infection and not overtired.

I carried a tray of wine into the hall and there he sat, dressed in a buckskin tunic and white shirt, not in Puritan black like Major Skelton.

"Alice, stay here in case I need to send for anything. My daughter did not feel able to join us, Colonel Elliot. We are in mourning, as I think you know."

"My regrets, Your Ladyship."

"You are Sir Bartholomew Elliot, they tell me. A nobleman and a Roundhead." She inclined her head and sat to face him. "I have not met many gentlemen who support the rebel cause."

"We Elliots are from the border country. We have a long history of opposing tyranny, My Lady, and I am a fervent believer in the rights of members of Parliament to share in government. The Stuart King sought to deny those rights—*my* rights. I know you are loyal to the King so we will not agree about his innocence or guilt, but I must tell you, Lady Trentham, it was he who raised his sword against his people. He has resisted any compromise. Only last year I was with Oliver Cromwell when we tried to negotiate new terms by which we could achieve a fair rule by Parliament under the King's cooperation."

"But an anointed King under God, Sir, how can there be negotiation?"

"Ah, well, as I said, we will never agree. I beg to discuss some practicalities now. My men have told me all the circumstances of your house and I apologise for forcing ourselves upon you during your distress. I have ordered Jayston to ride out and see if the flooding has subsided so we may go on our way and leave you in peace."

"Peace! That would be a fine thing indeed. These wars have dragged on and cost so much blood and loss. I wish you could assure me there would be peace, and soon."

"Indeed, fervently to be wished. Now, your steward came to see me this morning to ask about Parliament's offer of reimbursement. I have explained the terms to him and he will proceed with the request on your behalf. He has all the proof of accounts, the seizures and expenses. I am sure you will receive some help."

"Despite this house and land, Sir, we are not a wealthy family. You know, God save you from offence, we are Catholics, and your Parliament has near overwhelmed us with the charges made upon those of my faith. After a time of calm under the rule of old King James, the persecutions have begun again. Not only demands for money, Sir, even worse have been the insults, the destruction, even in this hall, of images in our windows, accusations of treason, pursuivants, as in the old times, turning our house upside down."

"I could argue with you about the useless vanity of those images, their contrariness to the Commandments, the abuses of your church in former times, but I am too grateful for your kindness to quarrel. Knowing your suffering, I would not have been surprised if you had shut your doors against us, being only five and not a forceful company. But you and your people have been hospitable."

"I do not believe the way we choose to worship God or the way you choose to do it should prevent us from behaving with common humanity towards each other. I wish you could be here if those priest-hunters came back among us with their insults and threats of violence." Tears filled her eyes. "Their abuse killed my parents in law—the shock and fear of their ranting. They had done nothing to deserve such a death."

"I am sorry for that, Lady Trentham. I am distrustful, myself of extreme views. I have had my quarrels with the Levellers in this army. Does that surprise you? I defend my own land and I uphold a Parliament that seeks only the good of the people."

"Catholics and Puritans or Presbyterians alike, Sir, do you think? For it is not my experience."

Major Jayston and Captain Hepworth came back, dragging cold air with them.

"No more rain, Sir, and the road to Stratford and the North looks passable. The bridge at Saxonford has survived the flood."

"Good. Richard, you stay here with me. We will progress tomorrow at first light. Jayston, you take Captain Hepworth and ride back towards Gloucester until you join our forces. Tell Lieutenant General Littleton to make no stops for billet here but speed on to Stratford. They can quarter there. Too much time has been lost with this weather. Oliver needs me. I must move on."

Sir Bartholomew stood up. "If we may, we will spend one more night here, Lady Trentham, then we will leave." He bowed towards her and went up to his chamber.

"A gentleman, Alice. God be praised. Now, to our own plans. If the road to Bournbroke is clear Dick will take you home and me to visit my son. You will be pleased to be back with your family for the Christmas feast. We cannot celebrate in the same merry way this year, since we mourn, but it will be a joy to see Thomas and know he will be back with us again soon, I hope. Can you make yourself ready to leave the day after tomorrow?"

Of course, I would be ready. What else was there for me here? The people I had been brought to nurse were all dead. It looked as though Will had withdrawn into himself and away from me. I had ruined our growing love in my attempt to save a clandestine priest. It broke my heart that Will showed no faith in me. A bleak winter stretched ahead.

At last the Roundhead officers stood ready to leave. Major Jayston asked if we would all join Lady Trentham and attend the Colonel.

Once we were all gathered, Sir Bartholomew Elliot took off his hat and bowed to Lady Trentham. He held out a document to her.

"There are things in your past treatment I cannot rectify and there are events that lie ahead which will cause you more distress. I have prepared this letter commanding safety be afforded to you by all followers of Oliver Cromwell and the Parliament."

"Believe me," he went on, "I have the authority of Lieutenant General Cromwell himself to order this. The seal on this document will protect you. Let your steward take it with him when he makes your claim for compensation. It will be given to you without delay. And, if those priest-hunters come upon you again, show this to them. It instructs that you be left in peace to the enjoyment of your estate with no further blames or harassments. I hope it will do you only good."

"I hope tormentors like Captain Ellison will be obedient to your command, Colonel Elliot. I will then indeed be grateful to you for such ease."

"If you encounter any resistance to it, write to me,"

She held out her hand. The colonel took it and bent his head over it.

"We have been kind to each other, Sir. I thank you. And, even if you may not like it, I will pray for you."

He gave a nod and the ghost of a smile then mounted his horse and left at a canter.

Lady Trentham handed the document to Will. "You had better take charge of this and keep it safely with the receipts and the accounts. If the hunters do come back we will be more than glad to thrust it under their noses."

"If you trust this surety of safety," Isabella said, "and you are determined not to fly to my uncle's for refuge, then perhaps you can bring my brother home with you."

"Not until the certificate has been tested. Thomas has been through enough. Until I am sure, Isabella, we will wait."

Will read it and looked up, his eyebrows raised. "Look, My Lady, at the seal."

"Mother of God be praised!" she exclaimed, "Look!" She held it out to Isabella.

Set in wax was the portrait of the leader of Parliament himself. "See. It is indeed Oliver Cromwell's seal!"

It was resolved that Lady Trentham and I would leave for Bournbroke next day. It would be my last in Beauchamps. I sat to an early breakfast with my friends talking over yesterday's revelation.

"One of Cromwell's own circle here, in this very house! Who would have thought it?" Anne Carey exclaimed for the third time that morning. "And he was so pleasant. And grateful. And polite."

"Did you expect him to have devil's horns?" asked Dick.

"A head of the army that made war against the true King? Yes I did. His men killed the master, wounded Master Thomas and kept the warfare going on and on. He and his master are the authors of our misery—so much of it, at any rate."

"And yet," I said, "he has done this kindness to Lady Trentham. If it saves her from more torment from Puritan persecutors, we must think kindly of him."

Will came in from the estate office, dressed for travel. "I am riding to Stratford with the estate's claim for reimbursement, on Sir Bartholomew's advice."

"You've got his letter with you?"

"Yes, Mistress Carey, that I have and will thrust it under as many noses as I need to, with great satisfaction."

"Have you asked for enough money to cover every mob that has been here billeted, eating their heads off at our expense? I hope you have."

"Yes and made a case for the reduction of the money we have had to pay to stop them sequestering the whole estate because the Trenthams are supporters of the King. I have argued how many family members she has had to support over the war years and how many Parliamentary soldiers we have quartered and healed of wounds, including one of their own colonels in chief."

"God speed, then, Master Franks. Ride safely and come back to us with a sack full of their gold."

Will grinned and even kissed Anne Carey on the cheek.

I waited, hoping he would kiss me farewell too, but no.

I thought, 'Dear Will, come back to me. Never mind the sacks of gold.' I could not bear to think this was my last sight of him, parting without a word. Not caring what the others thought of me, I ran out to the stable after him.

214

He had his back to me, stroking his horse as he secured his case of papers to the saddle.

"Will." He glanced round but did not stop what he was doing. "Is this the way you leave, without a word? I thought we cared for each other. You have not spoken to me once since that business with the priest-hunters. You cannot believe that what I said to protect de Paul was true, you cannot! I know we have not spoken openly but Will, I love you."

His face looked as though it had been carved from stone. His stern look gagged me. He went on fiddling with the horse-straps until I wanted to strike his hands away.

"Speak to me, won't you? Do these last months we have spent together count for nothing to you?"

"Did they count for you when you thrust your kisses on de Paul, when you declared you loved him before the household? Did they prevent you from saying you had shared his bed! God's blood, Alice! I have struggled to honour you. I held back. I knew you wanted me to love you. I thought you loved me. But you— you and de Paul? How could you? You humiliated me, broke my heart. So do not ask me for a tender leave-taking. It is destroyed. You destroyed it."

He climbed into the saddle. I grabbed the bridle, holding back the horse.

"You do believe it! Will. Francis de Paul *is* a Catholic priest. I have seen him perform a secret Mass in the round room. I watched him perform the last rites for the old couple on their death beds. He hides somewhere in this house. If the priest-hunters find his hiding place and his vessels for the Mass, they will hang him, and imprison Lady Trentham. They will confiscate the whole estate. What I did was all I could think of at that moment, to save his life, and everyone else's. My God, Will, how can you not see it, not understand what I did? I never, never had anything to do with the man. It was a ruse to save him and Lady Trentham. If she can see it, if Anne Carey can see it, all of them, why can't you?"

He looked away from me, his face hard. He dug his heels into the horse and left me standing.

I stood unable to move until I heard Dick calling for me. The mistress was ready to leave. Everyone lined up to hug me, which brought me to tears. Lady Trentham was already climbing into the old carriage and arranged the rugs around her, leaving space for me.

Anne Carey took me aside. "We in the kitchen are not blind, Alice. We have seen you and Will grow fond of each other. I have known him so long. I admire him. I would be pleased to see him happy. His pride was wounded by what you said but I understand what you did," she whispered. "I will speak to Will and make him see how good you are for him. He just needs to see it for himself again and trust himself, and you."

I nodded, unable to speak. I climbed into the coach. How was I going to endure this ride with Lady Trentham when my mouth was stopped up with a rag-ball of misery?

Dick urged the horses on and we turned out of the estate onto the Roman road. It was awash with puddles, heavy with mud. This would be a horrible journey to suit my unhappiness. Lady Trentham said nothing, but she took my hand in both of hers and pressed it. I began to cry again, forcing myself to make no sound.

As we reached Bournbroke crossroads she spoke at last.

"I will never forget the debt we owe you, Alice. Not only for nursing my parents-in-law and my son, but your brave action to rescue Francis. I can see Will is heartbroken. He is a proud man. He walked into the scene quite unprepared. He was shocked, of course, shamed, too, I think. I will find a time to speak for you, dear and hope, with all my heart, matters can be mended."

"Thank you." I could not say more.

Dick drove into the yard. My mother, flustered at the sight of a carriage, rushed out of the house, her apron flying.

"Dick Page! Have you come for Master Thomas? Oh, my glory! Alice!"

We threw ourselves into each other's arms. I felt my tears but forced myself under control.

"Here is Lady Trentham, Mother, come to see her son."

Dick jumped down to help the mistress out of the carriage and Mother led them into the kitchen, shooing the cats off Father's fireside chair.

"Sit here. Warm yourself. I will prepare some dinner for us all. I hope you will share what we have."

"Delighted, Mistress Sanderson. Is Thomas well?"

"Yes, fully recovered. He is helping my husband straw sheep in the barn. He is so good, helping us. He says he cannot sit all day, idle. I will—"

"Sit still, Mother, I will go."

I found my father, Thomas and Watt Wallace turning out the old straw and spreading new, as the sheep nudged and barged into them.

"Your mother, Master Thomas, has come here to see how you do. Father, will you come?"

"Ah, Alice, my girl!" He held me to his chest then looked at his hands. "I will disgust Lady Trentham with these hands. And you, Master Thomas, we had better wash before we go into noble company."

"Hardly noble, Master Sanderson, but a lady, I'll grant you."

After their first greetings, my mother hustled my father and me out into the scullery to leave mother and son alone.

"Go and cut down a ham and slice it thin to offer Her Ladyship. Alice, find a keg of the Christmas cider and a jar of plums. Where's your sister?"

"Over in the dairy," said Father, " she went for cheese."

"Good, we'll have that too, the fresh one."

I was laying the table when Lizzie ran in.

"Who's here? Have we officers, or—Alice! Alice! Are you home for Christmas? Lovely! Thomas, do you remember my— oh! Lady Trentham."

217

She bobbed a curtsey and flustered over the cheese at the dresser, looking for a board and knife.

"I have come to see if you have healed my son, young Mistress Lizzie. I see how well you have succeeded. You have been so kind," she said to my mother. "He tells me your herbals have made a new man of him. And you, Master Sanderson, I thank you for allowing him to stay in safety here. We have been harassed by Puritan Commissioners searching, first for plotters then for priests. I was afraid of what might happen to him if he was found lying sick in my house." She shuddered. "We have had a great many tribulations in these late days. I'm sure Alice will tell you all in due course, but she may not tell you that not only do we owe Thomas's life to her, but my own. She has been brave, resourceful and loyal beyond what anyone might have expected. I am forever in debt to your family."

"We have been happy to help you, Your Ladyship. I must tell, I saw your nephew today in Shipscarden. I would not have known him, but I do know the Norton family from our business dealings. I must tell you Young Henry was with him and introduced your nephew to us. It seems I, as the father of Alice Sanderson, am held in high regard among them." He smiled, eyes twinkling.

If Lady Trentham was astonished at the news that her nephew was in Shipscarden, she did not show it.

"Ah, Henry Norton, yes. Our families are old friends. Thomas is to marry his sister," she said.

"Why is Cousin Francis staying with the Nortons" Thomas asked.

Lady Trentham laid a hand over his. "He has a plan to travel," she said. "I will tell you all about it." But she said nothing more. Thomas looked puzzled but asked no questions.

I was relieved that Francis de Paul had kept his promise and already left Beauchamps, hopefully never to go back.

We sat together and enjoyed my mother's winter soup, the new cheese, smoked ham and plums while the talk ranged from indignant tales of quartered soldiers to the surprising generosity of Cromwell's deputy. To my relief, not a word was said about priest-hunters or Stephen Barkswell's violent arrest. My seared heart was not healed, but I felt it soothed a little by being back home.

The Sword Unswayed

Is the chair empty?
Is the sword unswayed?
Is the King dead?

'Richard lll': William Shakespeare

Thomas and I watched his mother's coach ride away to Beauchamps.

"You must wish you were going home with her," I said.

"My mother is too worried for my safety to have me back yet. I am being obedient to ease her mind."

"They were talking about moving to your Uncle's estate near Oxford. Isabella insists it will be safer from priest-hunters there."

"I don't know why she would think that. They are everywhere. My mother will not go. She says it is too far to travel, the roads too foul and they are in mourning."

"If your cousin Francis has really left the house, she will be safer. You know Father Barkswell informed on him. They will come searching again."

"She said you intervened against the priest-hunters at the vital moment."

"I acted on impulse, to save your mother. I was lucky they believed me but I don't want to talk about it inside. It was awkward. Let us go in. I am cold."

Christmas came again to Netherfold. We ate, drank and were merry enough. Thomas did not mourn his grandparents unduly and we never mentioned his family's troubles. The men of the village were clearing the ashes from the new year bonfire when we heard a soldier's voice shouting orders at a band of Parliament's soldiers. They rode into our yard, dismounted and led their horses straight into our orchards to graze, without a by-your-leave. My heart sank.

220

Mother saw them moving in and hurried Thomas up to his bed, bidding me follow with the medicine chest and a pot of the strongest-smelling salve.

"They will probably search the house," she said. "Best be careful." She unbandaged Tom's arm and spread the ointment thickly over the wound. "It will sting and turn red," she said. " It should convince them you are still too badly wounded to rejoin the fighting. I will tell them you were left here when the last lot fled."

We dashed downstairs again, scooping Tom's cup and plate into the dresser drawer.

The soldiers moved about our land quietly. They organised their bedding in our barn, tied their horses securely and gathered around a tidy fire in the yard while we supplied food and ale. They thanked us, talked quietly together and the officer was respectful towards my father.

"I thank you for this respite. We have ridden long and wearily from Wales, although we were victorious, I am proud to say."

"Will you stay here long?" Father asked.

"We are ordered north to face the King's Scots supporters who plan to ride south and fight to set him free but we will drive them back over their borders and the war will be over. We will see victory and the end of all monarchy in England. I daresay that will please you, Yeoman."

"If I think the war is truly at an end Captain—"

"Harker."

"Captain Harker, I will praise God if the warring is over. We on the land suffer by it. I will be glad to see every last soldier away from Bournbroke and far away from my croft here."

"We must search the house, mistress. Enemy soldiers are often left behind."

"Yes, there's a wounded Royalist up there in a bed, Sir. The last troop left him behind because he is useless. His arm is too damaged to fight again. He just wants to go home."

"Let me look at him."

I took him up to Thomas, who lay in bed making a good performance of looking stupefied. The captain put his hand over his nose.

"I am not surprised he lies there out of his senses. That ointment smells worse than whatever wound it heals!" He bent closer to Tom. "Ho, Trooper. Grip my hand."

Thomas groaned and held up a limp wrist. He made a pathetic grasp and flopped his hand back down again.

"Show me the wound."

I rolled back the sleeve to reveal the gash, only just beginning to knit together and red raw at the edges.

"Where did you get this?"

"We were at Shipscarden," he lied. I was there when the great house burnt down."

"Ah yes. We had the victory there."

Footsteps mounted the stairs and one of the Roundhead troopers came in. "The saddler is here for his payment, Captain." He stopped and looked at Thomas, frowning. "Did I hear you say wounded at Shipscarden? Where else have you fought? Your face looks familiar. Were you at Oxford?"

"Yes, but we escaped."

"He is in no position to fight against us with that useless hand. Come away."

Later, we were all at our chores when Lizzie stuck her head around the door and called to me. She grabbed my arm and dragged me into the washhouse and shut the door.

"I just overheard one of the troopers say that when they overran Oxford he was part of the detail that rounded up Royalist officers for prison, or ransom. He says he's sure Thomas was one of them."

"What did Harker say?"

"That they would take Thomas with them."

I groaned. " We have got to get him away then."

"They are all over here, whatever we try to do they will stop us."

"Shh! Let me think!"

At dusk, Father came in. Lizzie and I barred the door and told him what she had overheard.

"They will leave at first light," he mused. "It leaves us little time to get Thomas away. The captain has taken a couple of horses, including his own, across to George to be fresh-shod. I told him that I needed to go to the mill early tomorrow but I would not leave while they were on my land."

He sat thinking then said, "The soldiers are expecting us to take the cart out to the flour mill so could hide Thomas in the cart under the grain sacks but we would need to get him away while it is dark, before the soldiers stir. Would you be afraid to drive him away, Alice? That way, I will still be about the place, as they are expecting."

Mother had been listening intently. "He will not be safe at Beauchamps either, Samuel. Where else could you take him, Alice? What about Shipscarden. You said you were there when it was destroyed. The Roundheads will have no need to go back there."

"Yes!" Father was on his feet. "The Nortons are his friends. They will take Thomas in. I will help you through the back path to the glebe and into the wood. It climbs so it will not be easy driving, but it will be free from soldiers. Would you be afraid?"

"I know the way. I'll do it. They will come for him."

" I will say he sneaked off in the night."

Father woke me after midnight. All was silent in the soldiers' camp. We helped Thomas out through a back window and into the cart and covered him with the grain sacks, logs and bundled canvas. Father took the horse's head and walked us down the track towards Lane End Farm, skirted Woolastone Mill and doubled back into the southern end of Beeches Wood which brought us at last on to the Shipscarden Magna road. I strained to

223

hear the sound of following horsemen, but all was quiet as the winter morning light crept in.

The dawn sky was burning red as I pulled the waggon to a halt on the outskirts of the once rich wool town. Householders had moved back in. Everywhere there were signs of carpentry, stone workings, heaps of thatch ready for new roofs. Already laden horses, barrows and carts moved in and out of yards. Market traders were setting out their stalls. The smell of hot bread filled the air. How hungry I was!

Shipscarden House was a sad ruin, its roof timbers blackened stumps, the walls blasted into jagged gaps between broken casements and its doors hung drunkenly by one last hinge.

Thomas struggled out of his nest of sacks and clambered to the seat beside me.

"Phoo! What have they done to that lovely house? Poor Kathryn. Her father will be nigh broken by this wreck."

"Father says the Nortons have moved into the old Mercer's Hall behind the high street, past the sheep market."

I drove into a wide square yard, glowing like honey in the risen sun. The steward ran out to help Thomas into the house, calling for Sir Sheldon.

The family were at their breakfast and to my surprise so were Lady Trentham, Isabella and Francis de Paul.

"Come in! Come in and welcome."

Sir Sheldon Norton embraced Thomas and insisted I join them for breakfast while he sent one of his men to see about my father's business at their local flour mill.

"We all eat early, Thomas, for your family are readying for their journey."

"Journey? Mother" Where are you going? How is it you are all here?"

Francis de Paul stood and closed the door. "I am leaving England, Tom. The last priest-raid on my aunt's house forced me to accept that my life is in danger, hers too. They have interrogated Father Barkswell, tortured him I expect and he denounced me and your mother for harbouring me so I left."

"And you've come here, bring the danger to our friends?"

"I have not been living here in the house and I am not staying now. This is but the first step of my journey."

"Where to?"

Francis hesitated. "France."

"I am leaving too, brother," said Isabella. "I am to meet Francis on the road and we will travel abroad together. I am entering the English convent in Louvain."

Thomas looked from his sister to his mother. "A nun. You have decided."

"I am called to it. I must." She paused, looking at me. "Master Franks is riding with me to Cambridge."

"I thought you said you were travelling with Cousin Francis?"

"Not at first. I have a visit of importance to make before I leave England," Francis said. His eyes strayed to me.

"Master Franks is here now, preparing the pillion horse for the journey," Sir Sheldon said.

"You are going at once, Isabella?" She nodded. Thomas took her in his arms and kissed her forehead. She left the room to ready herself.

Will came in to say the horse was ready. He took the glass of wine that was brought for him and the talk between them all rose and fell but I heard none of it. My gaze turned again and again to Will. Only once his eyes caught mine, rested on me a moment but quickly looked away. Would we ever be comfortable with each other again?

At last the travellers were ready to leave. Francis de Paul was dressed as a travelling merchant, a battered hat pulled low over his brow. He embraced the family then with a small gesture of blessing he mounted and turned his horse south. There were heavy sacks strapped to both sides of his saddle. He was taking the incriminating church silver away with him.

Isabella came back to embrace her family and, warmly cloaked and hooded, she climbed up in front of Will. They rode away without a backward look and a knot of stone settled in my heart.

Lady Trentham turned away from the company to hide her tears.

I caught Sir Sheldon Norton by the sleeve. "I had better take my leave now and go before the floods swell up again." But before anyone could move or speak the door flew open again and a cavalier tumbled in, his cloak and hat dripping wet.

"Sir Sheldon Norton? Sir. I bring you an urgent letter from Lord Dalton, our commander in Oxford."

"You have had a long wet ride, Sir, you need—"

"—Pray, Sir, read the letter with no delay."

"Louis Dalton! Sheldon, he was the officer in our house with the Prince Rupert, was he not?" Lady Agnes was anxious. "What can he have to do with us? Is it bad news about our son?"

Sir Sheldon broke the seal, scanned the contents and looked up at us all, his face ashen.

"It is the King! He has been tried by a parliamentary court for treason!"

"What? Treason? How can they say that?"

"Treason is *against* the King, not *by* him! It is impossible!"

"Listen!"

Everyone fell silent. He read on.

"He was found guilty of making war against his people, so failing in the duty of a monarch to protect his subjects." His voice cracked. No one protested, no one cried out. We all watched him. There was a weight of deep silence.

"He was sent for execution. The King is dead."

We stood there, horrified. The future, swooped into the dark. Nothing would be the same.

Lady Abigail ran into Thomas's arms and Sir Sheldon Norton threw down the letter, weeping openly.

"They cut his head off, Tom; cut off his poor anointed head."

Thomas spoke to the messenger. "Is there to be no uprising? Who was loyal? Where was the Prince of Wales? Where was Prince Rupert? My God, where are all the noble lords to avenge him?"

"Defeated," the cavalier said. "All fled."

Sir Sheldon picked up the letter again. "Dalton sends a warning. There are riots in London, St Alban's and Oxford. Parliament is afraid of a Catholic-led rebellion. They are searching Catholic houses, arresting priests as Spanish spies. Persecution is rife again. God's Blood! Will they come and burn me out of this house too?"

I stood there, unable to decide what to do. They were all horror-struck, heartbroken. I was intruding on their distress.

I walked out unnoticed to the cart, now loaded with the flour and drove back to Bournbroke in the bitter rain.

Feather or Leaf

1649-50

"I am a feather for each wind that blows"
'A Winter's Tale': Shakespeare

As I rode into our yard the family crowded to the door to ask me what had happened since we left and had Thomas and I arrived in Shipscarden without incident? No sooner had I reassured them than Daniel said, "Have you heard the dreadful news about the king? I just brought this back from Evesham. They are all over the town." He handed me a broadsheet.

The **Trial and Judgement** *against*
Charles Stuart King of England.
He standeth **convicted and condemned**
of High Crimes and put to
Death
by the Severing of his Head from his Body.

"Yes. A messenger came for Sir Sheldon while I was there," I said. "It is shocking."

"I expect they were all heart-struck," my mother said.

"They were by turns angry and overwhelmed with grief. Thomas was crying vengeance. The Nortons were weeping. The Trenthams were there too. Will had brought them to see their cousin Francis who's been staying there. I felt in the way—all their hopes struck down. I just slipped away. They did not even notice me go."

"Ah, Will, good. So you have seen him, are you friends again?"

"No, Mother, we are broken apart and he has left to take Isabella Trentham to the east coast." I turned the subject back to the king, asking them what they thought about the rights or wrongs of the execution.

"I hate this tearing down of our old values," Mother said. "We have been ruled by monarchs all our history. How can men decide to end it?"

"They claim the law, Mother, his misuse of power, his extravagance, wasting our tax money then demanding more!" Daniel said. "In the town they argue that they did it so that the likes of us should not be ruled by a tyrant."

"And do you believe that? I ask myself who wants this?" Father asked. "Do the farmers here, the shepherds, the wool merchants and blacksmiths? Take it further from Worcestershire, do the fishermen and sailors want *not* to have a King?"

"I want to have an end to war, Father; an end to you and I doing our work on the land and soldiers riding in and trampling over it so that we have it all to do again."

"So, are you for Cromwell then, against the King, Daniel? You never wanted to join the fighting? I was happy that you and Father and Luke did not go to war but Thomas and Henry Norton chose to and with so much conviction. They took wounds for it. Sir Carlton Trentham and Jack Morton, men we know, died because they each believed in their side so passionately."

"I am like Father," Daniel said. "I felt it was a London fight among great men wanting power. I resent that our lives here have been torn this way and that by their decisions, decisions we had no part in."

"Then there is the religious quarrel," I said. "They are raiding Catholic houses again, searching for priests and plotters. Thomas is still at risk."

"You have done enough for that family now, Alice. You have done all you can. You are back home with us, so try to put their problems out of your mind. They survived without you before.

They will again." Father rose to close up outside, putting an end to the discussion.

"You have been a long time with the Beauchamps people, dear girl. I am glad to have you home again." My mother reached over and gave me a kiss.

"And I am, Alice!" Lizzie put her arms around me and kissed my cheek.

I settled into my home routine; happy enough with my family. But even being home and being busy with the lambing did not take away the sad ache in my heart for Will. One midweek February day our normal working was interrupted by the ringing of St Andrew's church bell.

We feared more bad news. The village households and the fields emptied as people made their way to the church. Minister Barnes stood at the porch door urging us inside.

When most of the village was present, he spoke to us in his usual scraping tones:

"Brothers and Sisters, you all know that the tyrant Charles Stuart was tried and executed by Parliament's godly justice. We, here in Bournbroke, suffered from the war that he began. That war is done. The tyrant is overcome; Praise be!"

A few of the congregation said "Amen." He nodded approval and went on.

" I am directed by Parliament to tell you that your neighbours, Aaron Parminter, Wilfred Gray, Jacob Larkins and Isaac Felton have been appointed as church officers for this parish. Every parish is henceforth granted the right to decide on its own form of service. These, your Elders, have decided to revive the decision of Parliament taken three years ago to grant a 'Certificate of Worthiness' to all the godly and faithful. These Chosen will be welcomed to take Holy Communion which I shall administer. However."

Here he paused for effect and swept his arm across us all, his eyes hot with zeal. "Any of you found to be Unworthy or given

230

over to wickedness and unbelief, will not be granted the right to share the Lord's Supper."

He looked pleased at the shocked murmur his words produced. Perhaps he thought the 'godly and faithful' in the building agreed with him. It sounded more like suppressed anger to me.

He went on announcing the parish business. "The tithes you have all been ordered to pay to the church will be collected on the first day of September. There will be times when you will be ordered to pay more as Parliament requires funds to support its army for the protection of the Commonwealth. A table of charges will be posted in the church porch in good time."

He made no pause for comment or questions. We all sat there dumb and mostly resentful.

Master Barnes raised both arms and looked up into the roof, heavenwards I suppose he would say, and declaimed:

"Wait on the Lord and keep His way,
And He shall exalt thee to inherit the land."

This time very few of our neighbours echoed the Amen. There was a stolid silence as he disappeared into the vestry, followed by the Elders.

The rest of us looking uncomfortably at one another, stood up and shuffled out of the building.

We had all heard these embargos on the old traditions before; we should not celebrate Christmas, nor Easter, nor the Maying. People liked to hear the beautiful words of the old prayer book and now it too was banned, and I was sure the idea of a Certificate of Worthiness would be very badly thought of by most of the village.

Not one of our neighbours asked for this certificate. My father, certainly did not, but Elder Parminter, called on us one day and presented him with a document which named all of us Sandersons as 'Worthy'. Father took it without a word and handed it to Mother who pushed it into the folds of her shawl. She took down the box that held the family deeds, the estate

231

accounts and the family bible and shut it up in there, right at the bottom.

The night before May Day, Matt Wallace and his father came to see my parents and formally asked for Lizzie's hand in marriage. We were all very happy with the arrangement. It was a love match we had all watched grow. There were handshakes and hugs all round and we trooped out for the May Festival with special delight.

Lizzie radiated joy. I had never seen her look so lovely. She wore the ribboned cap she had trimmed for Daniel's wedding and Matt never left her side nor let go of her hand.

"You must find a husband, Alice," called out Tansy Wallace. "A pity my Watt is too young. I would welcome another Sanderson daughter in law."

I gave her a mock curtsey. "Thank you, Mistress." Then I hugged her. "That was a lovely thing to say, Mistress Wallace. I hope I may find as good a man as your Matt for myself."

"You can't go on feeling yourself tied to Jack Morton forever, you know," she said.

"No, it is not that. Not any longer. It is just that I have not found anybody right."

"Yet," said Matt's mother.

"Yet," I agreed. But, in spite of myself, I thought of Will.

Despite Josiah Barnes' warnings and bans, the village men cut and prepared a maypole for the green outside The Rose Bush. We women and girls tied streamers and a crown of May blossom to its top and it was hoisted amid cheers and toasting to celebrate the arrival of summer and the coming season of fruiting and plenty. The girls took a streamer in hand and danced around the pole in the old way, crossing them at the top, reversing and unwinding them again. Lizzie grabbed my hand and whirled me into the circle.

"You are not too old to dance the maying, Alice!" In and out, bob and turn; I was delighted I remembered the steps that I had danced since my childhood and laughed with my sister and felt again the promise of summer and sunshine.

The Minister came out in his black hat, climbed up on a mounting stone and began to read from the Psalms, exhorting us to 'Stop these lewd pagan practices!' but Tom the Fiddler and his friends surrounded him and played the old country tunes with redoubled vigour, drowning him out as the men came out of the tavern and roared the choruses until the landlady's boy, lurking behind the stable, threw a well-aimed stone at Vicar Barnes's hat and knocked it flying. Cursing us all as ungodly, he snatched up his hat, rammed it back on his head and stalked off, followed by the cheers and jeers of the revellers.

I wandered over to Father and joined him under the chestnut tree, slightly apart from the music and dancing. We watched them winding in and out, turning in their circles.

"Have you seen Will Franks at the markets anywhere lately? You haven't mentioned his name."

"Yes. He was at the Sheepscarden Magna lamb sale and the Restitution Call in Stratford."

"Did you talk to him?"

"Yes. He was just the same as usual, busy with estate matters."

"Is Will worried about the family? Did he say anything?"

"Will is always worried. He feels for that family as if it was his own. He needs to enjoy his own life a little more."

"Fine words from your mouth, father of mine!" I laughed. "You who barely sit for one hour with your boots off at your ease. So, Will has no special worries about the Trenthams—or Thomas?"

"No. Are you missing them?" He did not wait for me to answer. "We are here now, Alice, enjoying the sunshine, enjoying the sight of our newly betrothed girl and her fellow, and you and I are talking together, dear girl. Forget about the Beauchamps family and enjoy your own, eh?" He kissed my cheek and wandered off to the tavern for another beer.

"He needs a wife, Alice!" he called back to me. "Will needs a nice wife!"

Did my cheeks flame for him to see?

Lizzie, Matt and both sets of parents arranged their wedding to coincide with Harvest Home. The Wallace family worshipped over the crossroads at St. Etheldreda's church in the parish of Little Steynes. Tansy Wallace came from over there and they preferred their vicar's less ranting style. Lizzie's marriage service was going to be there, which suited me and my family very well.

It was another happy wedding. Everyone was well pleased with the match. We had a wonderful sense of holidaying as the harvest was safely gathered and the orchards were full of cherries, apples and plums. We could enjoy a rest before the fruit gathering and Josiah Barnes was nowhere to be seen.

As we moved into autumn, we heard rumours that Cromwell's army was flexing its power in Warwickshire on the march again, against the Prince of Wales, and coming ever closer. People came back from markets and taverns full of alarm. We braced ourselves for more troops galloping in to grab at our harvest and make themselves free with our property. How sick we were of all of it.

"Every time the soldiers leave and we restock our holding and set things straight, horror stalks through the place again. Why can't they discipline their men? Why can't they accept that they have won and leave us to ourselves?"

Father slammed his chair back and stamped out to the orchard. Mother tightened her lips and sighed."Come, Alice. We had better hide some of our stores again."

"Make more medicines as well?"

"I suppose so. No one has mentioned battles but—"

"I know, Mother, even skirmishes kill men. There will be wounded, I suppose."

We trained young Miriam in which herbs to collect and chop. We tore old sheets and rolled more bandages. We packed fruit in preserve jars, chopped and made pots of pickles and hung bunches of herbs to dry. We hid stone jars of flour in the woodstore behind a pile of logs, took hams to hang among the rafters and steeled ourselves for the next horsemen to arrive.

We saw no Royalist soldiers, but sections of Cromwell's men rode over the crossroads towards Worcester which, we heard, was under siege yet again.

Daniel called to see us about the Parliamentary compensation.

"Have you taken yours in yet, Father? I took the Lane End Farm one in yesterday."

"What? I didn't think it would really happen. Are they really going to give out money? Will they believe what we ask for? How am I supposed to itemise all that we have lost since 1640? And are we to make a charge against Cromwell's men also or just the Royalists? What do I have to do?"

"I have kept records of some of the monies, Samuel," Mother said. "If we all sit down together and discuss it and make a note, I am sure we will be able to compile a fair assessment."

"Fair! *Fair* assessment? When were *they* fair? When were the marauding, thieving bully boys who came onto my land and stuffed themselves on our hard-won produce ever fair?

Daniel pulled a rolled-up broadsheet out of his coat. "Look."

INVENTORY OF INSULT
As many as can claim
*to have **suffered great loss** of Beasts or of Goods
or of Produce by the actions of the Army*

*or were **forced to pay** monies to the King's forces,*
*such may **submit their bills** to the **Mayor** and his*
***Council** and make appeal for a grant of money.*

"Samuel, don't work yourself into a rage. We need clear reason here. Go off and finish your work. We will talk about it later. Daniel, will you come and help your father and I compile our claim?"

"Of course. Don't upset yourself, Mother. You will calm Father. You always do." Father grunted and Mother pulled a face but my brother was right.

Mother sent Miriam home to the Smithy early so all was peaceful and supper waiting for Father's return. I had the accounts book ready and pen and ink so, after supper we poured beer for Daniel and sat as a family to make our 'inventory of insult' until we agreed an amount which did not appear greedy but still asked for a decent sum.

"It will be very welcome, *if* we get it." Father pushed back his chair and stretched himself.

"They would hardly offer it openly to the people if they did not intend to award it to them, Samuel."

"Some greedy beggars will stick all sorts of wild demands in there, you'll see."

"Oh, Father! All our neighbours have suffered. Every landowner and every farmer here knows what their neighbours are worth. Just believe that other people will be as fair as you have tried to be?"

It was unusual for my father to be so full of ill-tempered complaints. Torn between anxiety in case his claim was refused and the indignity of having to ask for it shook his pride. However, urged by Daniel, Father agreed to make the claim and took it to the Parliamentary Commissioners in Stratford.

he came back waving a folded letter. "I saw Simon Morton as I passed the Waggoners Inn. He was waiting for me with this. He said he was going to send a lad to Netherfold with it. Some traveller come from Bristol handed it in."

"Must be news from Luke," said Mother, wiping her hands on her apron and sitting down to listen.

Father read the usual greetings and assurances that business at his quayside inn was thriving, then went on:

'My Susan's brother Nathan has been working with me. His wife, Esther, is a dear girl expecting their first child but she is sickly with it and, unfortunate for her, was born with a withered arm. She will not be able to do her work in their household and tend their baby without Nathan's help. Susan and I are overwhelmed with business here. We cannot offer her the help she will need. The pair live in daily fear of Nathan being pressed into the Navy as the war with the Dutch churns on.

Now atop this, heavy news spreads through the city that Oliver Cromwell is preparing to ship troops to Ireland to quell the Catholics there. Bristol docks are choked with ships in need of crew. When you see Nathan, for he is of a prodigious size and strength, you will understand their fear.

Esther is vulnerable. She begs to keep her husband with her. I am asking, Father, if you and Mother will take them in at Bournbroke and keep them safely away from the Bristol port until the navy sails away. I hope too that my sister-in-law might have her child under your roof, for I know of your skill, Mother, at the childbed."

My duty to you from your loving son,
Luke Sanderson

"He softens me, Samuel. He knows how to play a tune on my strings, that boy."

"Do we agree, then? Another two mouths to feed."

"If Nathan is so strong, he will be an asset to you, Samuel. And the feeding will be no different from when Daniel and Lizzie were still here, never mind when Luke himself and Martha lived at home."

"I am happy to help them in their trouble, of course, but it will be more work for you if his wife is maimed and sickly."

"Yes Samuel, dear, but you know we will do it. You will always do anything your children ask of you."

"Will you write back, Alice? Say we will welcome them as soon as maybe." Mother reached over and kissed Father on the cheek.

It was a red-gold autumn day when Nathan and Esther were set down by a carrier from Evesham into Bournbroke's front street and were helped to find our house.

"This is very kind of you, Master Sanderson. You will prove our lifesaver I think." Nathan shook hands with my parents and brought his wife in to sit by the fire as though she was made of glass. There was no sign that she was pregnant, but she did look pale.

Father and I carried their bundles up the stairs while Mother prepared something hot for them to eat and drink.

"It has been a slow journey from Bristol, Mistress Sanderson, now by coach, now by public carrier, changing at every town on the way."

"Costly too, I expect," Mother said.

"Yes, but we can pay you for our lodgement." Nathan spoke eagerly, reaching for the purse at his belt.

Esther sat hunched and exhausted. She did not say a word. She was dressed soberly, in the Puritan manner, in black with a broad white collar that still looked clean, despite the journey.

I hoped she would not prove to be of Josiah Barnes's stiff-necked, preachy brand of the faith. I need not have worried. In only a few weeks, she opened like a woodland flower, talking to us in a low voice, happy to help and she was an adept cook, despite her one dead arm.

Troop after troop of horsemen from the Model Army rode through the village. Sometimes they filled The Rose Bush tavern and the Waggoners Inn. We all held our breath in case they

238

would demand quartering from us or empty our barns of hay, even thieve candles from our kitchens, as we heard had happened in Lavrock, but they behaved well and rode on.

"Even if the Roundheads came in here, Esther," Mother said, "they would not be interested in the navy or in recruiting Nathan. We have had soldiers riding backwards and forwards here for nine years now."

"Are they violent?" she asked, eyes wide.

"Sometimes," I replied.

"Oh, not so much these days," Mother said, giving me a warning look. "Don't you fret yourself. Keeping calm is best for mothers and babies." She went on stirring her spicy mixtures in preparation for the Christmas Feasting. She looked across at Esther. "Tell me, dear, what do you think of Christmas? Did your family observe the banning of it?"

Esther folded her good hand over her dead one and looked steadily at my mother.

"My parents stopped attending to those festivals when the first changes were announced."

"Ah. Here in Bournbroke we like the old traditions."

"But your minister is an eager Puritan. At every service we have been to since I came here it is the same as at my church at home."

"Yes, it is just not quite our way here at Netherfold. Now it is allowed, we walk to the next parish church. We prefer the services there."

"But you have always taken me to St. Andrews."

"Yes." I said. "We thought that you and Nathan would like it. We wanted you to feel at home."

"That is kind of you," she smiled.

"We would not want you to take part in our Christmas festival if it will make you uncomfortable, Esther, dear." Mother continued, "but we will want to celebrate as usual."

"I will not interfere with your ways. I will just sit quietly by."

"You will eat with us, though, on the day?"

"I am sure Nathan will be eager to eat your delicious food. My appetite is not, as you have seen, very great at present."

Mother reached over and patted her arm. I just hoped we could enjoy our holly and ivy, our yule log and our mince pies without my brother Luke's relatives sitting between us, gloomy as tombstones.

I need not have worried. Esther was right. Nathan ate and drank as merrily as we did and although his wife pecked at her food like a chicken, and avoided the mince pies, she smiled at us pleasantly throughout the day.

We all went out for the new year bonfire and drank the health of our neighbours and toasted our hope that 1650 would be a year without war. For weeks the weather froze and blew. Snow piled up, then rain washed it into flooded pools. The ground was clay-heavy and sodden. We did no work beyond tending the animals and Nathan cut and carried logs.

Esther's child grew within her. Nathan helped Father repair the roof and they built a new lambing shed. Daniel came up to visit now and then and helped Mother and Father down through the snow to see their safely arrived new grandson, Joseph.

The first signs of a tentative spring crept in with snowdrops, birdsong and pale sunshine to lift our hearts until the day a large company of Roundheads rode into the village. The familiar sound of horses, harness and dismounting officers shouting orders told us they were here to stay.

The men billeted here in Netherfold were, on the whole, polite and well-behaved. They did not annoy my father apart from the fact that they were on his land. But one day I was chatting with Patience from the Dairy and Tansy, outside the smithy when a gang of raucous soldiers turned into our road, staggering and rolling into one another. Tansy ushered us into her house and closed the door. The troopers stood outside, shouting for the blacksmith to come out and "Grind a sharper edge to our king-cutting swords!"

George Wallace eventually put his head out of stable door. "Come back when you are in a fit state for business!" he shouted. "You are not safe around us with those blades."

The men swore and shouted filthy oaths back at him. One picked up a rock and threw it at George's head. Watt, who had been watching from our own yard, ran, head down and butted the rock-thrower to the ground. They rolled over, arms flailing. Two of the soldiers tried to grab at Watt to drag him off but were uselessly unsteady. Nathan saw the fighting and hauled them off their feet. Three village youths rounded the corner from the front street. They ran and flung themselves into the fray, punching heads and wrenching arms. Blood flew. One of the drunken soldiers threw himself aside and was sick over George's anvil. Shouts and cries filled the street.

The officer billeted with us, drew his sword and stalked out into the middle of the road. He roared at the heaving rabble of men. "Troopers here! Stand to! Stand to! Hanson! Craythorn! Bentley! I'll have your ears for this. Stand to! Do it now!"

The village youths pulled their friends away as the soldiers struggled to their feet, wiping away their spit and the blood from their pulped noses and cut cheeks.

"Stand to attention, you snivelling gutter-rats! You shame this Model Army, shame Oliver Cromwell your commander, and, worse for you this day you—" he faced the tallest of his men and shoved him backwards on his heels "—you shame *me*!" He looked over to George Wallace.

"Master Blacksmith, I would beg of you some lengths of rope."

"Great Heaven, Tansy, is he going to hang them before our eyes?"

"You, young man," the officer spoke to Nathan. "Hold out an ell of rope, pulled tight."

He cut the rope with one sudden swipe and repeated this until there was a length of rope for each rowdy soldier. By this time four or five soldiers had followed their captain out of our yard and ranged themselves beside him.

"Hold out your wrists, crossed." Then, to his own men, "Tie their hands tight! You riff-raff, will stay thus until I come to cut you loose. You will not, at least, drink yourself stupid and behave like swilling pigs! Now, back to your billets and hang your heads. I hope all the people of this village pelt you with horse shit and mock your shamed heads. Get out of my sight!"

They straggled off, sullen, stained and torn about. The officer apologised to Master Wallace and gave him money from his own purse.

Patience Waywell bustled into her dairy and returned with a bucket. We helped her swill away the mess the drunken soldiers had vomited and spat about the place and cleaned George's anvil. Mother ran out with salves for Watt and the tavern boys, to ease their cuts and bruises.

"I do not think their officer will send for soothing ointments for his mob of drunks," I laughed. "Well done, Nathan, you were the hero of the hour." He grinned and we made our way back to the house.

"Nathan! My dear! I was afraid for you, you were outnumbered!" Esther fell upon her husband with the most overt demonstration of love I had seen from her since they arrived. I watched their tenderness with a chill of envy, remembering Will's gentle lips, his arms holding me to his chest the way Nathan was holding Esther. I turned away.

Later that night, Esther clutched the table, stood and bent herself. "I think, Sarah, I think the baby may be coming. I have a new, a different pain—a gripping, I—" She lost her breath, stood still, holding on to the table rim until the feeling passed.

"Don't be afraid, dear. We have talked about what you must expect. We will take you to your room and prepare. Nathan, there will be hours to go. You may hear shouting, but do not be afraid. All women shout as men do when they chop down trees, to aid the exertion. Once we have her arranged and in her bed for

242

birthing, I want you to come up and set a fire in your room, fill two buckets with water and carry them upstairs. Alice and I will leave you with her while we prepare a caudle for her to drink to give her strength. Then you and Samuel can keep down here until the baby is delivered."

"You will save my poor girl, Sarah. I love her so."

"Come, Nathan. You waded in to strike five drunken soldiers not an hour ago, show your mettle now. She will need such strength to push this child of yours into the world. You will have to show some strength for her. Just take heart. It happens every day, everywhere. All will be well."

We went up to Esther as I tried hard to put out of my mind the images of Will's sister bleeding and weeping for her baby that died.

I repeated Mother's words inside my head: 'Every day, everywhere. All will be well.'

Joyfully, it was! Esther's baby boy, after some hours of shouting and grunting, was safely born. How happy I was to take that tiny slip of humankind and hold it while my mother cut the cord and rid Esther of the after-birthing. "This must come away, Alice, always remember, or the mother will develop deadly fever and infection, as I fear Nell Franks did, if you remember."

Oh, I remembered, and told Mother I never would forget her lesson. We swaddled the baby tightly in his bands, cleaned Esther and gave her the baby to suckle.

"Please bring me Nathan now," Esther said. "He must see his son."

"Has he a name, this lovely boy?" asked Mother.

"Joshua, because it says in the Bible, when God called Joshua, He said, *'I will not fail thee or forsake thee.'*"

"A fine promise for his birth, my dear. I wish him and you long life and joy together."

I enjoyed having the new baby in the house. It was a marvel to watch his bodily perfection, his minute finger nails and the tiny creases at the knuckles of his miniature fingers. I loved to

243

watch the soft delight that spread over Esther's face as she suckled her Joshua, so different from her usual solemn look. I watched how his eyes began searching for the light. I watched him focus on his mother's face as though he was about to ask her a question. Mother went about the house humming to herself and Father would peep into the cradle as soon as he came home from his work, making funny noises to amuse the baby.

While Esther was still in her confinement, we all went to St. Andrews' church with Nathan to have Joshua baptised. Minister Barnes' ceremony was quick and simple and afterwards we drank a toast to the baby's life and health and Father presented Nathan with a bone and silver trinket, capped with coral, "For him to chew on," Father said.

"An heirloom for our family, Samuel. We have so much to thank you for, you and Sarah and Alice, here."

"It is our delight to have a baby here again. Is it not, sweet boy?" chuckled Mother kissing the baby's cheek.

"I will go up to Esther now, and show her our new-christened son and this pretty gift of yours." Nathan went up to his wife and we sat round the fire, reminiscing about our younger days when all my brothers and sister lived with us at Netherfold.

At last Esther's confinement was done and she came down to work beside us once again.

"Shall we all come with you for your churching, Esther?" Mother asked. "I still have my veil wrapped up safely. You can borrow it. It is nice old lace."

"Oh no, Sarah! It is not a Puritan practice. The baby has been baptised, that is enough."

Mother opened her mouth to argue but thought better of it and turned back to her bread-making.

"I hope I have not offended you but we regard that as a superstition. The Bristol priests ask money for it. My father was annoyed at that. He hoped when I had my own child I would never agree to it."

"Yes, yes, we understand, Esther. It is your way."

"I am sure you are right, Alice," Mother said. "Now Esther, are you strong enough to do some kneading of this dough with your strong hand?"

They smiled at each other and I admired my mother for her 'judge-not' heart.

Another week of harmony and baby-delight went by when a horseman rode into our yard. We looked at each other with some alarm. Was this another troop arriving? I heard Father's voice and a familiar voice replying.

The kitchen door flew open.

"Thomas!" Mother and I exclaimed together. We all began to talk at once. He was as pleased to see us, as we were to see him but I could see there was something on his mind.

Mother brought refreshments. Father, Nathan and Watt came in and we all sat together.

My parents introduced Nathan, Esther and their baby and explained their relationship to my brother Luke in Bristol and why they had come to live with us. All of this took time and I wanted to say, 'For Heaven's sake let Thomas tell us why he has come.'

At last, he took a deep breath and began his tale. "I am come a-begging for your help again, Alice. My mother has fallen ill. She is asking for you."

"Of course, I'll come. I'll come back with you now."

"Does it need to be at once? So suddenly?" asked Father.

"What is the matter with Her Ladyship?" my mother asked.

"She had a fainting attack, pains in her arm and her chest. She was so pale; I was afraid she was going to die. We laid her on her bed. Her hands were so cold." He could not go on.

I waited for him to recover his voice. "Has she rallied now? Can she speak to you?"

"She speaks in a whisper. She opens her eyes and looks at us. She replies to what we ask her, but otherwise she just lies there, unmoving, her eyes closed yet not asleep. I am afraid."

"Have you sent for the apothecary?"

"Yes, Dick has ridden into Stratford, but she keeps saying Alice's name."

"She had better go, Samuel. Alice, take with you some hartshorn shavings to make a reviving syrup. And make her the same caudle we gave to Esther to build up her strength. It is useful beyond just in childbirth and might bring her to her more normal spirits, at least until the apothecary comes."

"I am fully recovered now, Alice," Esther said. "Nathan and I will help your parents."

"And happily," said Nathan, "not always to be receiving charity but to show it too."

Father followed me up the stairs and closed the door of my bedchamber.

"Are you sure you want to go there again, girl? You came back unhappy and preoccupied after your last time and I don't like the way the Trenthams hold you at their beck and call. You are not a servant, Alice. We are a prosperous yeoman family and I say with some pride we have gained our standing in the world, despite these wars and alarums. You do not have to rush to Beauchamps to do their bidding."

"Ah, Father, I am happy to go there, truly. I like the family and they like me. They do not treat me like a servant and the true servants are my friends, too." I stopped folding my clothes. "If I was unhappy when I came back home it was because Will and I had quarrelled. I loved him. There. Now you know. And I was almost sure that he loved me. I thought he was about to speak to you about our marriage."

"But then, you quarrelled?"

"Yes, and he would not speak to me. Events crowded upon the household, persecution, priest-hunters, sickness. We had no opportunity to talk about our misunderstanding. Circumstances forced us apart."

"Will Franks is a good man. Fair. He must be ready to listen to you. I tell you, Alice, I would be happy if he were to ask me for your hand."

"I was almost sure it would be so, but I have lost hope. I fear we are too broken apart. However," I roused myself, "I have to be there, near him if I am even to try to heal our rift. And even if that is impossible for me, I cannot refuse to help poor Lady Trentham. I must go, Father. Don't forbid me."

My father took me into his arms and held me gently then kissed my forehead.

"You will have my blessing, whatever you choose, my dear. You will always behave in the right way."

He left me to prepare myself. '*Whatever I choose*,' he said. Nothing in my life lately had been what I chose. I saw myself like a blown feather, a leaf caught in the stream.

I went back to Thomas. "I am ready to go."

"Thank you, all of you," Thomas shook my father's hand and kissed Mother. She bundled together herbs and lotions and the new season's syrups and I packed them into my own medicine chest with my grandmother's herbal recipe book. We strapped everything to Thomas's horse, I climbed up behind him and we left.

"Why did your mother collapse, Thomas? Did something else happen?"

"I was away visiting Kathryn's family and the priest hunters came back. I think the strain of that, on top of all her other griefs suddenly overwhelmed her. She had a seizure."

"But why did she not use the Certificate of Safety to get rid of them?"

"Mistress Carey said she swooned almost as soon as they barged into the house and the rest of them were too busy attending to her to think of it."

As soon as we dismounted at Beauchamps, Thomas took me to see his mother.

"How is she?" I asked Aimee, who sat by her bed.

I bent closer to Lady Trentham and felt her skin, her hands. Far from being feverish, she was cold, despite the fire in the grate. Her eyes fluttered open.

"Ah, Alice, I need some of your physick, dear."

"What happened? Did you faint?"

"Yes, I think so. The floor reached up to hit me. I cannot clear the fogs that cloud my head. Have you a potion?"

"I will do all I can, My Lady."

She groped for my hand. Her finger-ends were icy.

"I am happier with you here." She let out a long breath and closed her eyes.

I left Thomas watching his mother and talked to Mistress Carey about boiling water, to mix my hartshorn syrup and which spices to add to some warm wine to make a caudle.

"A caudle? Her Ladyship is not in childbed, Alice!"

"My mother said it is a good strengthening medicine, not only for use at the childbed. I have seen her use it to such good effect with my cousin, trust me."

"Bless your heart, of course I trust you, Alice Sanderson. You drop your life and come to us at once. You are a good woman."

"What happened to Her Ladyship? Did you see?"

Anne Carey groaned. "The priest-hunters came back. Battered their way around the house, the cupboards, under beds, all the usual mayhem. They even threw open the linen chests, and searched the privy and stabbed swords into the manure heap. They kept shouting, 'Where is the Spanish spy? Where do you hide your traitor priest?' Lady Abigail just dropped to the floor. Aimee and I lifted her into a chair and tried to revive her but she just sat there, still as the tomb, even when they shouted in her face. Of course, they found no one." She dropped her voice. "Father Francis is long gone, I think you know. Well, after they left, she just sat up all night. Every time I asked her if she would take anything or go to her bed, she did not reply. She was, shaking. I could see it."

I went back up to her chamber and persuaded Her Ladyship to drink my potions.

At last Dick arrived back with the apothecary. Thomas brought him straight to her. He quizzed me about the medicines I had given to his patient then sent me away.

I was in the solar embroidering an unfinished nightgown I found in the work box when Thomas and the apothecary came back down. He explained the care and diet Lady Trentham was to be given.

"I have bled her of her excess of cold blood to reduce the melancholic humour that infects her. She needs to be given hot foods and wines to dispel her chills and to warm the purer blood now left in her. There should be music and pleasant thinking all about her. Keep the troubles of the estate away until the sanguine humours regain their balance within her."

He left the house and Anne Carey, Aimee and I discussed together how best we could help the mistress recover. Thomas joined us.

"I wish we had news of my sister and Cousin Francis. My mother lies there worrying about the safety of them both."

"Your sister will be well cared for by Will Franks until she joins Father Francis, Sir," said Anne Carey. "I should think Her Ladyship is easier for knowing there are no priests in the house when her enemies come searching. I was thinking, perhaps you should ask Elizabeth to come and visit. She could play her lute. Music is soothing. She could bring little Tom with her. He would amuse your mother"

When Elizabeth came I watched her smiling up at her husband and her little boy clambering over her knees and I felt the sourness of my own empty heart and turned abruptly to stare out of the window, wondering if Will was safe on the road.

Not In Single Spies

When sorrows come
They come not in single spies
But in battalions.

'Hamlet': William Shakespeare

L ady Trentham worried herself with the same unanswerable question every day following her recovery. "I wonder how Isabella fares?"

"She will be safe with Will," I said, "I am sure we will hear from her soon."

"I knew she believed herself called to take vows but I did not think she would leave us so soon."

One day Thomas came to join us in the solar. Almost at once she repeated her daily enquiry. "Why do you think Isabella left so abruptly, Thomas? I thought she would take time to think over her choice."

"It was Francis's decision to leave that hurried her, Mother. Much safer for her to travel with him than alone. You know he had to go. It was never safe for him to stay anywhere for too long."

"To journey in company with a priest, Thomas. How can that be safe? What if he is uncovered?

Thomas patted her hand and went away, coming back almost at once with a letter which he held out to her.

"Isabella left you this," Thomas said. "I have kept it until you regained your strength. Perhaps it will reassure you."

"Read it to me, Thomas, my eyes feel full of grit."

"Beloved Mother,

I send you greetings from a place of rest on my journey to my new life in Christ. I am sorry if my sudden departure grieved you, but you know how important it was for Cousin Francis to leave and I was happy when he said we should travel together.

Will Franks takes me to join Francis at a house of Catholic shelter in Cambridge from whence we shall journey to the coast. Pray for our safe crossing on calm seas so that we arrive at our several destinations where we may live to the glory of God and dedicate ourselves to worship and prayer

Do not weep for me. I am happy to give myself to God and to His Blessed Son.

You will have all the worldly love you need from my brother and sister.

I commend you, Mother, to Our Lord and pray that the Holy Virgin and the Blessed Saints protect you from the wickedness that surrounds you in the country of my birth.

I M T

Lady Trentham took the letter, re-read it and let it fall.

"May God protect her, Thomas. She has chosen her way. And your cousin Francis. He may be safer and left us safer too but I will miss him." She sighed. "I will shelter no more priests, God forgive me. I am too weary of living in fear."

"I hope that is the end of danger for you, Mother. But—" he hesitated,

"—ever since they killed the King, Parliament has been afraid of insurrection. Rumours of plots in support of the Prince of Wales are all over London and spreading. They say Catholics are being dragged from their houses."

"Thomas! Stop! Tell me nothing more about plots or fear of plots." She grabbed his hand. "Promise you will not leave me to join in any further fighting. I am beset by troubles on every side. Grief upon grief has exhausted me. Your sister has chosen her way and Francis has chosen his. Your father chose his way and died for it. You chose to fight and I rejoice that you cheated death, but I—I—" she struck her chest, "I want to choose now. I want to have you here with me as head of the family and let me rest. For God's sake, let me rest."

Thomas kissed her tenderly. "I promise Mother, I will stay with you. They would have to tear me from your side. I will

251

marry Kathryn Norton and we will live here beside you and have ten children so that you may be grandmother to a dynasty." He kissed her hands and nodded over to me.

I gave her my prepared draught. "Drink this, My Lady," I said, "it will send you to sleep." She drank and fell back against her cushions.

"Don't leave me alone."

Thomas sat down again beside her. I threw some dried lavender on to the fire and soon the room was fragrant and she fell asleep.

Calmer days followed during which Thomas gave himself over to estate business. At last Lady Trentham asked Aimee and Beth to help her bathe and dress. Refreshed, she began to walk about the room. By the end of the week, she asked to be helped down to the solar. Her progress down the stairs was painful to watch. Even Lady Eliza in her last days had not looked so frail.

She ate her meals on a small table near the fire although she ate little. I made hot milky possets mixed with egg, nutmeg and honey. Sometimes I added brandy to vivify her. Gradually she began to smile more. She talked more and, at last, picked up her embroidery.

Whichever of us sat with her, we talked only of cheerful things. Thomas rode across to Elms Barton and brought Elizabeth to visit with her little boy, which pleased Lady Abigail. Elizabeth was expecting their second child and asked her mother and me to help her sew and embroider a Christening gown, some cradle coverlets and baby caps.

Lady Trentham walked the length of the solar every day, until she was able to progress down to the hall without feeling overtired. Thomas even helped her to walk in the garden when the day was warm.

One such day they had been in the rose garden and retired to the hall to enjoy a cup of wine, when that beating on the door which we had all come to dread, filled the house.

252

Anne Carey and the others ran from the kitchen to find Ruth and to tell Dick to fetch some of the estate men to protect the house. Thomas unlocked the front door and five priest-hunters, all in black shoved their way into the hall past him. Simultaneously, another two kicked open the door from the garden and came in behind us.

"Nothing in the stables, Brother Levens. Hickston is searching the cellar."

Him again! My heart sank.

"You, Lady Trentham! You understand our mission. Give up the priest. And do not pretend to me. I have Stephen Barkswell's oath that a priest hides here."

"You will find no priests here," Thomas stepped between Levens and his mother. "Save yourself the search."

"You said so once before. Your mother said so, yet, behold, a priest I found here. We dragged him kicking and shrieking in fear—from *here*!"

"Lieutenant Selby, tell these papists what judgement lies in store for the priest Barkswell." His face twisted into a grotesque smile. "He is to be put to death, Brother Levens, in Warwick marketplace. And tell Her Ladyship how he is to die, Lieutenant."

"Hanged by his neck, Brother Levens, until he dies and goes to Hell."

Lady Trentham and Thomas crossed themselves. Levens shouted,

"Stop that" He swiped Thomas's arm aside. I thought Tom would punch him but he stood rigid, fists clenched, eyes ablaze.

Anne Carey confronted him, "So Father Barkswell told you we shelter a priest, did he? You are a fool, Sir, if you believe what that coward says. He would denounce his own mother if it would save him."

"Oh, I agree that he stinks of a coward's piss where his red blood should be. It is no more than I would expect from a traitor. Be sure we will wring both out of him before we are done." He moved closer to Lady Trentham and thrust his face into hers. "You stubborn woman! Give up the other priest! You can save yourself!"

"There are no priests hiding here. How many times do I have to tell you? How many times must you ransack my home?"

"Until I am satisfied. For I have fresh business with you, Lady Trentham. The traitor Barkswell's last attempt to save his miserable skin was to confess that he had stolen all the altar silver from his parish church at Throstleford and while hiding here, under your protection, hid those papist baubles on your land. Waste no more of my time. We need this silver to melt down. Our army must be paid."

Thomas looked around at Dick and the gardeners. "Mother? Do you know about this? Dick, has anyone spoken here about buried altar plate?"

The blood sang in my ears. I was the only one left who had seen the sacks of silver. I knew where Francis had buried them and I knew he had taken them away.

"Captain Levens!" With a dry mouth and my heart thumping, I stepped forward. "I saw Vicar Barkswell on the day he came here from Shipscarden's burning. It is true he had two sacks with him which he clung to. I saw My Lady's nephew, Master de Paul, order Barkswell off the estate. He said it was too great a danger to his aunt for him or his silver stuff to stay here. He forced Vicar Barkswell to leave. I saw him smack the vicar's horse to drive him off."

"Barkswell came back, though. I found him here. He must have brought the plate back with him. In any case, why would I believe you, a self-advertised adulteress?" He snorted his disbelief. "Under interrogation he told me that he had hidden it here."

"Of course, he did, man," said Thomas "to throw you into confusion and earn more time to live. As long as you were searching on our land you were not hanging him."

"You did not find him hiding in my house, said Lady Trentham. "He was riding away when your men captured him."

"My mother is right. And if he had had any of that plate he could have taken it anywhere, Stratford, for instance or back to Throstleford to hide it in the ruins.

Levens hesitated, looking about him. "We will make sure before we leave. Hickston, go around the house again. Look for a priest hole, secret entrances, anything. Go up into the servants' attic."

"Selby, take the men and search the stables, the cellars and among that stand of trees out the back."

He took his last man aside. They muttered to each other, heads together. My knees were trembling, my finger ends icy cold. I had drawn their attention to myself again. I hoped I had not laid myself open to interrogation.

They swarmed about the house, the gardens and the copse all the morning, reconvened, consulted, then went about again. Each of the men came back empty handed.

Levens smashed his fist against the table. "Nothing! Nothing! By God, they confound us. I have a mind to arrest you, Lady Trentham for further questioning."

"Wait, Sir!" Thomas opened an ornate chest he had brought to the table. "I have something here to show you." He unlocked it and took out the Certificate of Safety.

"Look at the signature on this document. Colonel Sir Bartholomew Elliot of Cromwell's high command. Look at the seal! See! Cromwell's seal. Satisfy yourself it is genuine. Now you have searched for hours, you have been told all we know. This should be the last proof you need to leave us be. Read it. My mother is to be kept safe from your harassment."

Levens snatched it. I was afraid he would tear it, spoil it, throw it in the fire, but he stared at Colonel Elliot's signature, then at Cromwell's profile imprinted in the crimson wax. At Cromwell's name his eyebrows shot up.

"Why would Lieutenant General Cromwell's commanders give you such a document? Why would Colonel Elliot even come here to this papist, king-loving place?"

"The gentleman came here because he was sick. We helped him. He was grateful. He gave my mother this consideration in thanks. Look! You see the seal is genuine, or are you so insignificant a commissioner for your Parliament that you have never seen Lieutenant General Cromwell with your own eyes?" Thomas spoke with bitter scorn.

Thomas reached between his mother and Levens, took the certificate in both hands and lifted it out of Levens' fingers.

"You have seen our proof. You have searched and found nothing. You and your insulting manner to my mother offends me. I want you gone."

"You want me gone? Must I tremble before you, boy?"

Thomas glanced about the hall. The rest of Leven's men were all over the house, only the lieutenant stood beside him. Dick and the estate men came in at that moment, through all three doors. They surrounded Levens and Selby, flexing staves and thick branches. Levens looked around, licking his lips. Selby stood transfixed.

"Call the men, Selby!" Levens shouted, then began yelling himself: "Jenkins! Coulson! Hickston, here!" Each name was almost a scream. "Selby, draw your weapon, man!"

"No ye don't!" said, Hal Fisher. He swung his stave and struck Selby's sword arm with such force the weapon flew across the room.

Thomas and Dick seized Levens by the arms and frogmarched him out of the front door as the rest of the priest hunters ran into the hall. The estate men closed in around them.

"Off my land. Master Levens," said Thomas. "I will tie you to your horse if we must, but you *will* leave. Now."

"Cromwell's comrade, Sir Bartholomew thanked us for our hospitality!" Anne Carey shouted after him. "He was a good man and knew good people when he saw them. Your heart is too black with hate to do that."

Levens spat in her direction and mounted his horse. Selby slunk out behind him. The others hurried after, grabbing at the reins of their horses that capered and stamped, agitated by the shouting.

"I will not forget this." Levens said. "Or you, Trentham. You have a sister nearby I think. That will be another house for us to examine. Imagine, the hanging, Your Ladyship." He raised himself in his saddle, shouting towards the hall. "Imagine your priest Barkswell dangling from his gibbet, kicking out his last gasping breath as the devil reaches up to grab him down to Hell!" He jabbed his heels into his horse and galloped off.

A chilling gust of wind followed Dick and Thomas back into the hall.

"Father Barkswell to be hanged! Oh, God have mercy! When? Tom! Tom! How can we find out? Follow them and ask. And now he threatens Elizabeth and her family. Oh, my God."

"Shush, Mother. I will ask that man nothing. I will ride into Stratford myself and find out."

"His sentence will be posted up at the Town Hall. I will come with you, Master Thomas." Dick was already moving out to the kitchen for the stables.

"The Carters have no need to fear, Mother, they have no one and nothing untoward there, I know that."

Lady Trentham took out her rosary and began to pray. Anne Carey joined her. I left them on their knees and went to help the others in the kitchen.

"God's Blood!" Thomas slammed the door in his fury "Let that be the last of them!"

It was dark by the time Thomas came back from Stratford and took the news of Barkswell's execution straight up to his mother. Dick stabled the horses then joined us.

257

"It is to be this coming Saturday at noon in Warwick market place." He paused and looked from one to the other of us. "He is sentenced to be drawn through the lanes of Warwickshire strapped to a hurdle all the way from Stratford's Guild Hall door."

"Merciful Heavens, that is horrible!" I spoke.

"They used to do it in Queen Elizabeth's time, Alice, but I have never heard of it done since."

"As far as I ever heard those things never happened in King James's time, did they, Dick? My mother and father said Catholics were left alone in those years. We had some peace, then. Not like now." Luce shook her head. "Dragged on a hurdle! Cruel!"

Dick took her hand and kissed it. They stood together, holding one another. I envied them their closeness.

"Will people go out into the streets to watch it?" Ruth asked.

"I cannot imagine anyone would willingly go to watch such a thing, traipsing through country lanes to witness the poor wretch's suffering. Who would do that?" I asked.

"Other fanatics, I suppose," said Dick. "And those people who enjoy cock fighting and watching bears baited."

"We will just not go near Stratford on Saturday," said Luce. "We will market in Evesham or Shipscarden."

We were all sitting at breakfast when Thomas brought his mother in to us. Mistress Carey gave her a chair and we all waited for her instructions.

"I have thought all night about what I am about to say to you and I must tell you my son does not agree with me about this, but I have determined I will go to Warwick on Saturday to bear witness to Father Bardswell's execution."

"No!" Anne Carey and Beth spoke at once. Lady Trentham held up her hand.

"He was our parish priest. He came to me to beg for shelter."

258

Thomas was angry. "And despite Cousin Francis sending him away, he came back and you gave him shelter and look at the trouble he has brought down on our heads. You discharged your duty to that man, Mother, and he has sought to denounce you."

"He is dying for the faith, Thomas, as other martyrs have done. I must go to bear witness to his sacrifice and pray for his immortal soul."

"But he was a coward, My Lady!" It was not my place to speak, but the words were out.

"We all heard him betray your nephew."

"You are right, Alice. He was prepared to drag Francis to the gallows with him and you yourself to prison or worse. Mother, you cannot—"

"I can Thomas. I must. It is my duty. Now, Aimee, please lay out my mourning clothes and a warm cloak. Anne, prepare refreshments for us to carry with us. Dick, I want you to drive the coach and Thomas, you to sit in with me. I intend us to travel through the night on Friday, counting that as a vigil for Father Barkswell's soul."

She took a deep breath and looked at the others in turn. "If any of you who are Catholics wish, you may accompany me but I will not blame any of you who do not want to make so repellent a pilgrimage. Let me know your intentions privately."

She left the kitchen. I would have agreed to go with her for her support, however much I loathed Barkswell, but I was not invited; neither was Ruth nor Molly.

The household was in sombre mood when the day of departure for Warwick arrived. We helped to stow refreshments, cushions, blankets and lanterns into the old coach. It was a squeeze for all of them, even with Dick and Thomas riding outside but off they went.

I went about the empty rooms with Ruth and Molly, refreshing all the beds and strewing all the floors with crushed lavender to scent the house. We set out trimmed candles and a

259

large water boiler over the fire so they would have hot washing water on their return. Then we cooked the supper for us all.

When they came home, all of them silent and pale, Lady Trentham went straight up to her chamber. Aimee took her hot water and Anne a tray with her supper and wine.

"She has taken a little of the soup," she said, when she came back to the kitchen. "Aimee is preparing her for bed. She said we must all drink wine tonight."

Thomas came and ate with us. "Thank you all," he said. "This has been a terrible day.

I hoped they would keep quiet about what they had just witnessed. Ever since Levens had mocked that Barkswell would be left kicking on a gibbet, terrible images flared and flickered in my head.

For a while no one spoke but the events of the day brooded over everyone. At last Beth said: "There was such a crowd, wasn't there? All standing there in silence."

"No one cheered or jeered," said Mistress Carey, "yet they could not all have been Catholics."

Dick looked around at the others. "I think, the crowd disapproved. I heard some cries of 'Shame!' when the horses galloped into the market square with poor Barkswell spatchcocked on that hurdle."

"Yes, I heard that and a small group of Protestants began to sing a psalm, that gentle one about walking through the valley of the shadow. Did you hear them?"

"I did, Beth," said Anne Carey, "And others joined in."

I set out the sewing in the solar next morning in the best of the light and Lady Trentham joined me. She picked up a baby-cap and threaded her needle ready, but the work hung idle from her hand. She sat, closed in on herself, staring at nothing. I went on stitching blue and yellow flowers across the yoke of a small gown for Elizabeth's expected baby.

260

"Alice," she said, after a while, "downstairs, did they talk about what happened yesterday? Did they tell you how Stephen Barkswell died?"

"They did not say much, just that the crowd was shocked."

"I went to bear witness to the death of a martyr, Alice, but Stephen Barkswell was no such thing. He did not die a holy death. He did not die for his faith at all. He died shouting out my name as a Catholic traitor, in the public square. He died denouncing Francis, denying any allegiance to the Pope. He even denied the sacredness of Mass. He renounced his faith, for all of them to hear, pleading with them to set him free. Did they not tell you that he died an apostate? Did Thomas say nothing? Nor Anne?"

"They barely spoke about it at all, just that the crowd disapproved, that some Protestants sang a psalm. Some cried, 'For shame!'"

"The greatest shame was Barkswell's and mine. I took my son and my faithful servants there and they were forced to watch their own beliefs disgustingly denied. They would not have attended if I had not asked them. It was wrong of me." She cried bitterly, her hands over her face.

Over her heaving shoulders I saw Thomas come in to the solar and stop, shocked at the sight of his mother so broken. "Here is Tom for you, look. Let him comfort you."

"Mother, my dear." He took both her hands and kissed her forehead. "No one in the house regrets going to support you yesterday. It was all done for love of you. Barkswell was nothing to them. He was nothing but an apostate doomed to Hell, Mother. Come." He took her hands from her face and held them between his own. "Force him out of your mind. You did a duty to the faith he rejected. He deserves no further thought from you."

"I can't get those scenes out of my mind, Tom, such terrible blasphemous words. The accusations he made. He named me, in that place. With Levens there."

"If he dares to take a step on this estate, I will kill him, I swear."

"No ! No more killing. No more death. I have had my fill. I am beginning to think I should follow Isabella's example and retire to a nunnery."

"Oh, but think of your grandson, Lady Abigail!" I should not have interfered in this family scene, but there I was. The words were out. Thomas seized on the idea.

"There, Alice is right. Elizabeth and her son need you, and the new child coming. *I* need you, Mother. If I am to take over the estate, I need your guidance, especially until Will comes back. I will flounder and make wrong decisions."

Lady Trentham gave a weak smile and stroked his face, then turned and gripped my hand. "Well, my dears, I will work to clear my mind of all this business. But I need strength."

"I will go," I said, with a deliberately cheerful voice, "and make you a strengthening drink at once, something powerful from my grandmother's herbal and if I can persuade Mistress Carey to unlock the cupboard at this time of day, I will lace it with some French brandy to add a little warmth to your blood." I left them sitting together and went to find Anne Carey.

There was a market at Shipscarden Magna and Thomas went with Dick and Luce to buy necessary supplies. He visited Kathryn and returned to Beauchamps with news.

"Sir Sheldon Norton has had letters from Harry, smuggled out of Worcester. The Prince of Wales has set sail from France for Scotland. He is going to raise a fresh army among them and fight to regain his throne."

"War again?"

"Harry said there is a plan to raise all the Royalists spread throughout the Midlands to attack Cromwell's forces and ease the way for the coming of the King."

"A plan, Thomas, or a plot? Tell me the truth."

"Well, it will be an insurrection Mother," he shifted his eyes, "but it will be an organised military plan."

"You promised me! On your oath you swore you would not become involved in any plots. Henry Norton was trying to recruit you, was he not?"

"Yes he was. He knew my name had been linked with a plot before. He thought I might be willing."

"And you said?"

"I said I had promised you I would stay to run the estate and told him my forearm has not healed well and that I have no sword-strength left."

"He will accept that?"

"Of course. He must. But he also sent the King's plea for funds. Sir Sheldon says all the local Catholic families are sending money or valuables. The Lyttlejohns from Dryden have sold their timber, the de la Salles at Houghridge have sold off land and the Langholmes have melted down their chapel silver. It made me wonder, Alice, if you told Levens all you knew about the Throstleford plate? Tell me the truth. Did Francis really take it away and do you know where?"

"Francis definitely took it away."

"For God's Sake, Alice, can you not tell me where it is? I need it!" He was shouting. He had a tight hold on my arm, shaking me. "I am desperate to donate something from Beauchamps to the cause and that silver belonged to our parish."

Lady Trentham saw how shocked I was. "Thomas! That will do. Don't bully Alice. She has told you Francis took it off our land. Barkswell is dead and your cousin has gone. No one may ever know what happened to the Throstleford plate. Accept it. Alice, please leave us."

I hurried downstairs, trembling. I did not want to join whoever might be in the kitchen, so I darted into the estate office to be alone. I sat at the table, rested my head on my arm and wept. Thomas had never been angry with me before.

In a short while I heard doors open and close, footsteps came and went. The estate office door opened and Thomas came in. I stood up to leave.

"There you are. I have come to find you, to beg your pardon, Alice."

He came close. "I am sorry I spoke to you so roughly. I did want the plate from our church to go into the King's funds. It is humiliating that other families are donating and we have nothing left to give."

"I told the truth, Thomas, I promise you. The Throstleford silver is not anywhere on your estate any longer. Barkswell did bring it here. They hid it in the copse, yes, and I stumbled across its hiding place. I told Francis I had seen it and if *I* had found it so easily, the priest-hunters certainly would. He realised it was too much of a risk to your family so he took it away himself. Then that day we were all at Shipscarden, the day he left for France, I watched him ride off with the sacks strapped to his horse. Remember he said he had an important place to go before he went to Cambridge? That's why Isabella had to travel with Will. Your cousin was taking the plate somewhere it would reach the king."

"So it was our church silver he rode off with?"

"Yes."

Thomas took hold of my hands. "I am sorry, Alice. I was unkind to you. Forgive my rudeness." He lifted my fingers to his lips and kissed them.

"Oh, Tom, of course I do," I smiled up at him.

The office door swung back and banged against the wall.

"Will!"

Tom strode across to Will and threw his arms around him. "Dear friend, welcome home. Does my mother know you are back?"

"Not yet, I have just stabled my horse." He threw his saddlebags on to the chest-top and gave me a curt nod.

"I will come with you, Thomas and tell your mother about Isabella."

Without another look at me, he followed Thomas and I was left alone. That was that. After all these weeks without him. Will was closed and shuttered to me still, his eyes cold, so severe.

I went into the garden to cry.

Never False of Heart

O never say that I was false of heart
Though absence seemed my flame to qualify
Sonnet 109: Shakespeare

That night, over dinner my eyes strayed back and back to Will but I never once caught him looking my way. I was cast down. He obviously still thought badly of me. I had fondly hoped that by the time he came back from his journey to Cambridge he would have regained his confidence in me. But there was no affection in his look and no sign his feelings had mellowed. He simply ignored me.

"Come, Will, tell us how you fared on the road with Isabella." Dick said.

"Tell us the tale, Will, come on!"

Will took a drink from his cup of wine and began: "We had to keep making detours to avoid being questioned by Roundheads. Then we were held up by flooded roads and mud near Bedford. Just outside Cambridge I asked around for a respectable inn. Isabella said her cousin had told her she must stay only at The Red Fox so we went there. This gentleman, who called himself Lamport, approached and led us indoors. He asked if the lady and I had travelled far and had we by chance passed anywhere near a place called Saxonford, where he had friends."

"Did that not make you wary?" asked Luce. "That he should ask about a place so near to us, that it was perhaps a trap?"

"To my amazement, Luce, Isabella was all smiles to him and said, 'Yes, she loved the beautiful fields near Saxonford.' Then she said something in French, I think. I was dumbstruck. She had said barely a word the whole ride. Suddenly here she is talking to this stranger! But it was a sign. Lamport was sent to watch for us."

"I would have feared a trap, Will. You were trusting."

"Isabella told me Francis de Paul had arranged everything. Lamport took us to his home. His wife gave us a hot supper and took care of Isabella after which Lamport drove us in a modest coach to a great stone house behind tall gates on the far side of Cambridge."

"How did this man know you would be at The Red Fox and when you would arrive?"

"Francis had told Lamport to wait at The Red Fox from midday to dark every day after his receipt of Isabella's letter telling him we were on our way."

"All this intrigue," Anne Carey said. "How did she know where to send her messages to Francis?"

"She refused to tell me anything except that the house was owned by a relative of the Duke of Norfolk who offered refuge to fleeing Catholics. I left Isabella there and came away."

"Was Francis de Paul there?" asked Dick.

"If he was, I did not see him but he left me a note of thanks and a purse."

"So, you got there and back without any trouble," Anne Carey. "That was good fortune, Will."

"I toast you, Will," said Dick. Everyone in the kitchen rapped the table and raised their cups. "So how did you come by that black eye?"

"Ha! Ha! I was peacefully quaffing my beer in this Bedford tavern when a burly pair of fellows came up and dragged me to my feet calling me a Kill-joy Puritan," laughed Will. "Black hat, black coat, big mistake."

"Black eye as well, then! Did you beat them?"

"I'm here, am I not?"

Dick slapped him on the back and Will grinned happily. How I loved that smile! I wished he would smile at me.

"Would you like me to put some salve on your eye, Will?"
He did not answer. He did not even look at me.

"Come, Dick," he said, "Serve me more wine, there's a good fellow."

267

Dick looked from him to me and back again, then got up to pour the wine. With burning cheeks, I reached down to the floor, as though I had dropped something.

The talk continued. The others told Will about the raids by the priest-hunters, how they had bullied Lady Trentham and about the dreadful day Stephen Barkswell was dragged through the county on a hurdle and hanged at Warwick. Nobody dwelt on the detail. Will frowned but asked no questions. At length Anne Carey told Beth, Aimee and Ruth to go down to Will's gate house to light the fires in all the rooms, prepare his bed and carry his larder provisions.

"You just sit there at your ease, Will," she said.

"Thank you, madam." He stood and made a comic bow as the women went out of the room. I envied the good humour between them all which was closed to me.

"I will come with you," I said, "and help carry things." I wanted to get away from Will and his kitchen companionship that left me out.

I joined Aimee, helping to carry a basket.

"What on earth has gone wrong between you and Will?" she asked. "We were all sure there would be another wedding among us, yet suddenly, he seems, well, hardly to know you are there."

"Oh, Aimee. Ever since he walked into the hall that day and saw me kiss Father de Paul and declare I slept in his bed, Will has shied away from me. He can't forgive me for it."

"I can understand that he was shocked. We all were. We could hardly believe our eyes or ears."

"But you must have realised I was lying to save him. It was an impulse. I thought everyone would understand."

"Mistress Carey did, straight away. And once she spoke up the rest of us realised she was right. I suppose that just made Will think we all knew something he did not—women gossiping together. But surely you told him the truth of it, after Levens was gone."

"I tried, of course I did, but he just shut me up. He would not hear a word. He said he had seen and heard all he needed to and he had been made to look a fool before the whole house."

"And that was all?"

"That was all."

"You must have tried to talk to him since he got back, surely? Have you not seen him alone?"

"No. He came into the estate office and saw Thomas kissing my hand. He was just thanking me but Will—I don't know what Will thought but he turned away, ignored me with such a look of disdain, and as you've seen tonight, not a spark of warmth. Not one."

Aimee put out her hand and stopped walking. "I am sorry for it, Alice. You know before you came to Beauchamps we used to think Will was too serious, quite cold-hearted really with us girls. He used to laugh and joke with Dick of course and with Philip until he turned Puritan with Jane Martin, but he would never flirt with any of us. No mistletoe kissing, no Midsummer Night frolics. One St Valentine day, Mistress Carey asked him why he didn't find himself a wife. She said, "You're far too handsome to waste away as a bachelor, Will Franks."

"How did he react to that?"

"He just laughed and said most women found him too glum for love. I think Mistress Carey is right. It is a waste. I think you would make him a fine wife, Alice. And he has a lovely smile." Aimee widened her eyes and grinned, knowingly.

"Oh, don't Aimee. Don't you think I love his smile?" A tear rolled down my face.

"You love him, don't you?"

I dashed away the tear-tracks. "I am too sad and sore to talk of loving him. I feel heavy-hearted and I miss him. I have done all these weeks and I still do."

"What will you do?"

"Go home to Netherfold. Neither Thomas nor his mother needs me any longer. I will just go home and pick up the threads of my life there."

Aimee reached over and kissed my cheek and we went into the gate house to ready it for Will.

I looked around at the places where he and I had held each other close, where we had talked together. I remembered my pleasure in making his home warm and welcoming for him. I remembered his strong arms, his hands gentle in my hair. Tonight, his hearth stood empty and cheerless.

I busied myself telling the others where Will kept things. It did not take long to make the place warm. We set pottage to simmer over the fire, lit the lanterns and set them in place, we made his bed. Just as we were all at the door ready to leave, it opened and Will came in.

"This looks wonderful, thank you," he smiled.

Last time it was I who had made this place into a home, me alone he thanked. This time it was everyone *but* me he smiled on.

"Glad to do it for you, Will," said Aimee and touched his arm as we left. "Sleep well."

"I could sleep for three days after that journey," he said. "Goodnight."

We were a little way up the road back to the Hall when I heard Will call my name. My heart jumped.

"Go back, go back!" Aimee turned me around and gave me a shove towards the gate house.

"I have something of yours, Alice." He turned his back and walked in.

"Come in and close the door. Sit for a moment." He gestured to the chair at the fireside where I used to sit when Lizzie and I stayed here. He held his hand out, open. "Here."

"It's Lizzie's necklet." I took it up. "Our sister Martha gave one to each of us when she left home after her marriage. Lizzie will be so happy to have it back. Thank you." I looked up at him, searching his face.

"Good. Right, then." He stood up. Was that all? He walked back and forth between the dresser, the door and back to the fireside. I stood up too.

"I'll have to run to catch up with the others."

"I'll walk up with you if you are nervous in the dark."

I stopped with my hand on the latch and faced him.

"Will, you have not forgiven me for what you heard me say about Francis de Paul, despite my explanation. I thought you knew I loved you. I thought that you loved me and would at least trust me and see what I was trying to do. It is heart-breaking to me that you could not and that you have treated me with such disdain ever since. I am leaving here tomorrow, Will, wretched. Thomas is taking me back to Bournbroke."

I threw back the door and dashed away from the gate house, not looking back. I wondered if he would call me, but I did not hear him if he did. I wondered if he would run after me, catch me up in his arms and we would be reconciled at last, but he did not come.

I went straight up to my bed and feigned sleep before any of the others came up the stairs.

Thomas joined us all in the kitchen just after dawn for an early breakfast.

"We will take the small cart, Alice. Are you ready to go at once?

"Yes, I will say goodbye to your mother and join you in the stable." I hugged them all; Anne Carey, Aimee, Ruth, Beth and Molly. "Give my affectionate farewells to Dick and Luce."

I ran up to Lady Trentham's chamber.

"Alice, my dear." She looked tired and thin. She had not yet recovered her bloom.

"I understand your desire to go home," she said, "but I wish you would not leave us. I am afraid you have sacrificed more than your time here, have you not? You and Will have been at a

271

disjoint ever since you bravely saved my nephew. Will has misunderstood. I will speak to him."

"No, My Lady, please say nothing. I spoke to Will in private last night. Sadly, there is nothing to be rescued between us. But do not distress yourself, because I believe what I did was right. I acted, recklessly, but I cannot regret it, even if Will and I are broken apart."

"Will is a dignified man," said Lady Trentham. "He takes his duties and his loyalties seriously. I have known him so long, I wish he could be happy and loved. I look at him and I look at my son. Thomas has always believed himself to be loveable. Will, I fear, less so." She pressed my hand. "God bless you, Alice. I wish you would be happy too." I felt my tears prickling, so I gave a hurried curtsey and left for the stables.

Thomas and I drove off at once. As we passed the gate house I saw the smoke rising in a column from his chimney, but there was no other sign of Will. We turned onto the Roman road and drove to Bournbroke.

It was a pleasant enough ride, with no troops on the road to trouble us. I was weary of the sad thoughts that chased around in my head so I opened the conversation with a general question.

"They say there is fighting again, in Scotland," I said. "Have you had news from Henry Norton?"

"Taking up positions, from what I hear, not fighting yet. The Prince of Wales has been declared King by the Scots. He is begging them for help but they told him he had to renounce his faith and promise to be a Presbyterian."

"Would he do that, Thomas? You would not."

"Who knows, when it comes to politics and war and thrones and power? I don't think I would, but I don't think I could go to the stake for my beliefs either."

"You went to fight. You risked death then."

"I was young and hot-headed. Would I still do it, even if I could?" He held up his damaged arm.

"If the King asked for soldiers down here in Worcestershire, you would do it, I'm sure you would, if you were able."

"Henry's letters say it's a stalemate up north. Cromwell's men laid siege to the castle at Edinburgh but it failed. Prince Charles will have to ride back to England. It is England's crown he wants."

"Well, maybe they will not come this way again. Let some other place have a taste of the billeting and stealing and mopping up the bloody wounds."

Thomas grinned at me. I knew I sounded bitter. I just did not think I could face them all crawling and brawling around Netherfold for another year.

As we turned into our lane, my mother was outside the house. She rushed to hug me. "It's Alice! Alice is home!"

Esther ran out with baby Joshua in her arms, beaming.

"Thomas, dear boy, come inside for some refreshment."

"Thank you Mistress Sanderson, but I am going a-courting to Shipscarden."

"Are you home to stay, Alice, or is Thomas coming back for you?"

"To stay, this time. Now take me in, I have been up and about since before dawn."

While Mother put out bread and cheese, Esther showed me all the clever things her little son could do. He squealed and gurgled with delight at the attention and extra kisses. Their welcome soothed my raw-scraped heart.

At midday Father came home. He gasped my name when he saw me at the table. I stood and went to him. He hugged me and I inhaled his familiar smell of straw and sheep and the open air. I kissed his whiskered chin and felt myself safe at home and loved.

Mother's keen eyes followed me about all evening and when Father went to lock up the outhouses and Esther and Nathan went up to their chamber, she took hold of me and scrutinised my face.

"You aren't happy, Alice," she said.

273

I sighed. "No, Mother, not happy."

"Will Franks?"

I looked round at her sharply. "Of course, you would guess. None of us has been able to keep anything from you, Mother."

"I know my children. Every shadow that crosses your faces, even Luke's and he has been gone Heaven knows how long. Do you want to talk about it?"

"Nothing to talk about. I loved him. I thought he loved me. There was a drama at Beauchamps with the priest-hunters. I took action to help the family and Will walked in on it unprepared. He misunderstood and was too hurt and angry to let me explain."

"And you were angry with him because you expected him to understand."

"Understand and trust me. Of course. I think I must have been mistaken about the strength of his feeling for me. I have lost confidence in him. I cannot love a man disposed to jealousy. I have never witnessed that between you and Father or between my brothers and their wives. I do not look for it in a husband."

"So, you cannot forgive him and he cannot forgive you and you are both made miserable."

She shook her head. I waited for her to say something, give me some advice, but she said nothing, just reached for me with her open arms. I wept on her breast as I had done as a child.

Father came in and stopped stock still. "What is this? What has happened to you, Alice?"

"Love-sadness, Samuel, nothing else." She led me to sit beside her on the settle. Father stood, watching anxiously.

"No crisis, Father." I said, sniffing. I felt my tears well up again and drip down my face.

"She and Will have fallen out and they are both unhappy."

"Hmph. Pity." He sat down opposite us by the fire and took off his boots. "I had hopes of welcoming Will Franks as my son-in-law. Such a fine man, Alice, surely—"

"Samuel!" Mother interrupted him with her 'shut up!' look. "Let the lass find some peace here in her old home away from the Hall. Perhaps time apart will help things become clearer to both of them."

"Don't hope for it," I said. "Our last conversation left me in no doubt Will and I will not be reconciled. It is spoiled."

"Enough for tonight, both of you. Bed!" Mother stood up and grabbed Father's hand. "All of us."

I went up to my old room, warm with a fire and my bed freshly made and lavender everywhere. I curled up into it and cried out the recent weeks of strain, fear, watchfulness and disappointment. I fell asleep devoid of hope for my future.

There was no more talk about my time at Beauchamps or about Will. I joined in the routines of home, both in the house and on the holding. I watched little Joshua whooping and staggering about, plopping into mud and trying to eat balls of horse dung, to Esther's constant squeals of warning and our laughter. The three of us spent much of our day scooping up the little boy out of harm's way.

The autumn passed with all its work in the fields. The orchards and the gardens produced an abundant harvest. The fields yielded well and the village rejoiced at Harvest Home.

We shivered on through winter to Christmas. On the night of the new year village bonfire, we learned that the glovemaker down our lane had died. He had no family that we knew of so we, his neighbours, buried him, paying into Minister Barnes' parish fund for his coffin and the services. An Evesham lawyer came and searched the house but no will was found. It took weeks of posters to find a distant relative in Birmingham who claimed the worth of the cottage and the paddock behind, but did not want it.

I could see that these recent months of peace in our area had allowed my family to prosper. The compensation paid by Cromwell's government and a good harvest meant Father had gathered in some extra money.

"I have decided we should buy Glovers Cottage for Nathan, Esther and Joshua," he said. "They can have their own home and a small piece of land but Nathan can still work with me here and I can afford to hire another hand. We might even be able to hire day labourers if we need them." He beamed at my mother. This progress made him whistle about the place in great good humour and Mother sang.

A few weeks into January one of the Netherfold estate men arrived on horseback with a letter for me from Lady Trentham.

My dear Alice, I have a parcel of good news to tell you. First, we have heard that the Prince of Wales has been crowned King by the Scots in a place called 'Scoone', somewhere ancient and holy for Scottish kings. God be praised, we have a new King Charles, the second of that name and although you are not of our beliefs, you are enough our friend to understand how glad this makes us.

Thomas came back from Stratford with a broadsheet warning of a plot to raise rebellion here in England and there were many conspirators named and arrested. I was gripped with fear again that my beloved son would be denounced and once again imprisoned. But thank God, the list of names the ringleader gave to the parliament was posted on the Town Hall door. Dick and Will rode in to read the names. They wrote down every one of them and to my great relief Thomas's name was not there. He swore to me he had taken no part in plots but I was afraid of false witnesses. Once again we have been sufficiently blessed to avert a disaster.

I have had a letter from my daughter Isabella, now Sister Agnes Maria. She is accepted as a postulant at the English convent and says she is happy and at peace. I rejoice and pray for her. I have also had a letter from my nephew Francis, He is safe in the Jesuit college in Douai. He says he prays for your soul daily.

276

Elizabeth and Edward rejoice at the safe delivery of their second child, named Carlton Edward after my dear husband. And finally, perhaps my best and happiest news, Thomas is betrothed to Kathryn Norton, whom you know. I hope I can prevail upon you to come and help me stitch some of our wedding finery.

The arrangements for the ceremony are not yet complete but I invite you to join us and take part in the marriage celebrations as a dear friend and sometime saviour of us all in times of trouble.

Give my affectionate respects to your revered Father and Mother.

Abigail Trentham.

I was relieved that Lady Trentham was lighter of heart and pleased that she wanted me back to do sewing when there were no threat hanging over Beauchamps Hall. I was flattered, too that she invited me to Thomas's wedding. The new year boded well.

We helped Esther and Nathan scrub out and limewash Glovers Cottage and we were all relieved that the work was done and they were safely settled in before the February snows fell. The weather put a stop to outside work so Nathan and Father spent their days making improvements to the cottage and stopping up the drafts that howled through their neglected windows and doors. They transformed the old place into a warm and pretty home.

We had good news when Lizzie and Matt came to tell us she was expecting a child. She often came to sit with Mother and me in the afternoons so all three of us could help her make the cradle clothes. We enjoyed some happy family hours, while it was light enough to sew, gossiping and laughing about times gone by, Lizzie's plans for her baby and the changes she wished she could make to the Lane End manor house under her mother in law's nose.

One bright day when we were sewing together and Mother went out to lock up the chickens, Lizzie confessed to me how afraid she was of her coming confinement.

"I can't forget how you and I listened to Nell Franks' groaning and crying." She lowered her voice, afraid of her own fear. "All that blood, Alice. The blood! I am terrified."

"Talk to Mother. She had five of us safely and look how healthy she is. Nell Franks's childbed was not well attended before ever we saw her, Lizzie. She developed the fever afterwards and that is why she died."

"But the baby died! How can I go through all these weeks of waiting and worrying?"

"All the babies we have seen born here in the village have thrived from their first moments Yours will be just the same. But talk to Mother. Talk to Daniel's Joan. They know about it; they have been through it before you. They will be able to reassure you, Lizzie."

"I talk to you better than anyone. I wish you had already been through childbirth, Alice. I would believe you."

I sighed. "I sometimes wonder if I will ever have babies of my own to hold, Lizzie."

"Still not heard from Will?"

"No. I fear that affair is completely over. There will be no going back."

"What, not back to Beauchamps? I thought you were invited back for Thomas's wedding"

"I don't mean back to the house; I mean back to Will, as if we were a couple. Don't let us talk about it."

"Too sad? Still?"

"Too sad, still."

The snow melted and the spring sun grew warmer. We celebrated Eastertide, choosing, this year to go to St. Etheldreda's for the services. We walked there with Lizzie, Matt and Matt's family while Nathan and Esther, Daniel and the

278

Fletcher family stayed with the Puritanical Minister Barnes at St Andrew's.

The weather after Easter Sunday was fine and warm so the whole family went to Stratford market. The men went on their farm and garden business while Lizzie, Mother and I bought more linen for Lizzie's layette and lace trimming for the baby's baptism gown and cap.

As the crowds milled around the stalls, I noticed men gathering at a news poster mounted on the tavern wall. Whatever was there was causing a hubbub of consternation. I left Lizzie and Mother and went to read it for myself.

Notorious Conspiracy Uncovered.

Plotters arrested in many towns throughout England.

Under questioning by the Lord Protector's Commissioners one Robert Capstick has confessed his part in an armed rebellion against the people's Parliament. He has named his fellow-conspirators.

These are to be arrested and tried for

TREASON.

I turned away, chilled. Lady Trentham had been so sure in her letter to me that all persecutions and plots were over.

Lizzie read my expression. "What is it? The news sheet?"

"It is a notice about a Royalist plot. They have names. They are arresting people."

"I thought the fighting was all settled and we had the Lord Protector and the Parliament in place and the wars were over." She watched me closely. "You are worried about the Trenthams again, aren't you?"

I nodded. "Any danger to Thomas is a danger to Lady Trentham. I do not think she has the strength to stand the shock. She has suffered so many alarms."

"What alarms? You have never told us what went on at Beauchamps. We have all had to put up with soldiers billeted on us, all the marauding and despoiling. The Trenthams are not the only ones to suffer."

"Hush, Lizzie! You don't know anything about what happened there."

"Well, I won't, if you never tell me anything."

"They are not my stories to tell. I will just say they have had to put up with extra persecution because—"

"—because they are Catholics. They always knew what would happen to them. They knew the law."

"Their religious life goes deep with them. They risk their lives and their property for it. We have never been tested so."

"No and would not be. They should just obey the law like we do, then they would keep out of trouble."

"You don't understand." I saw Mother coming towards us through the crush.

"You two look very serious. What has happened?"

"Alice has just read a news sheet about Royalists plotters and she is worried about Thomas Trentham again."

"Thomas?" I glowered at Lizzie. Mother looked worried now.

"I grew fond of Thomas during the time he was with us," she said. "But they found him innocent last time. Why would they be after him again?"

"His name was talked about. That is enough for some prisoner to spill the names of every loyal king's man he knows to save himself. We will just have to hope he has never heard of Thomas Trentham."

"Well, I am not going to 'hope' anything about it, Mother," said Lizzie. "It is none of our business. And you are not living there now, Alice, so it should not be any of yours either."

"You sound hard and heartless when you speak so, Lizzie. Your sister is very fond of the Trentham family. They have been good to her."

"I think rather it is she who has been good to them, Mother, running back there at their every call."

I grabbed Lizzie by the arm. "I am treated with friendship there."

"Oh, don't make a fuss, Alice. Just take care. Some people might think you are sweet on Thomas Trentham."

"What? Which people? You? It is ridiculous."

"That is enough, the two of you!" Mother snapped at us as though we were children again. "Come away!" She stalked off through the crowd and we followed. My sister was right, I was no longer at Beauchamps, their business was not my concern.

Every time Father or Watt came back from one of the markets I asked them if there was any news or any mention in the broadsheets of the Royalist plots but they heard and read nothing.

One warm summer day Mother and I were sitting outside the house enjoying the sun and shelling peas for bottling when the cart pulled into the yard with a horse tied behind it.

Someone was sitting in the cart with my father.

"Will Franks!" Mother exclaimed with pleasure, jumping to her feet. She almost upset the bowl of peas in her eagerness to greet him. I stopped dead, pea pod in hand.

"Come in dear, How lovely to see you again. It has been an age!"

Father nudged Will towards the house.

"I met him in Shipscarden market, Sarah. I insisted he came back for supper. It's a light night. He'll have plenty of time."

"Sit down, Will, I'll bring you both some beer. Alice, come and help with the food. We will ready it early."

I did not even catch Will's eye. I had no way of knowing if he was reluctant to accept Father's invitation or if he was happy to. I could hardly scrutinise his face. I felt my cheeks burn. My hands shook so I buried them among the peas. I thought my mother would hear my heart beating from where she stood.

When everything was ready, Watt, Will and my father came in for the meal. The conversation was good humoured. I joined in where I could. I wanted Will to understand that I was happy to see him and be in his company again.

At last Watt went out to close up the animals. We took our beer outside under the plum trees and sat together enjoying the evening sun. Father gave me a studied look then said to Will.

"Alice here keeps asking me if there is any news about Royalist plots and such. Have you heard about arrests or searches near here? Alice and her mother worry about the family, you know."

"I grew fond of Thomas, Will," said Mother. "When I nursed him here."

"I am afraid things have taken a turn for the worse. The Parliamentary Commissioners from Stratford arrived at the Hall and took Thomas away for questioning."

"Arrested!"

"Lady Trentham sent me to the Town Hall to ask after him, but they would tell me nothing."

"How is she bearing it?"

"Eats nothing. Barely drinks. Sleeps hardly. Someone is with her all the time."

I opened my mouth to offer to go back with him to help care for her, but the things Lizzie had said to me in Stratford market stopped my mouth. No one asked for me. It was not seemly for me to push myself forward.

"There is Sir Bartholomew Elliot's Certificate of Safety with Cromwell's seal. Can't he use that?" I asked.

"I pushed it up his sleeve as I gave him his cloak. I just hope they don't take it away from him. It does not mention him by name I'm afraid. So, they might not take note of it."

"But the Trentham name is on it, Will is it not?" my mother asked. "Poor woman. I'm sure all Thomas and his mother want, all any of us wants, is to be left in peace. It should not beyond the wit of these men to make an effective peace as well as to make effective war."

"Well said, Sarah!" said Father. "And I say 'Amen' to you. We should have you in the Parliament."

"If we women can run households and be responsible for estates and heal great sword slashes, why should we not be able to share in the governance of the country? We could hardly do worse, Samuel Sanderson."

"Woman, you need not harangue me. I agree with you. Netherfold would be near a ruin if not for you keeping me right."

"Ho hum. Well, since I cannot rule the whole country, I will rule here." She stood, brushing down her apron. "Too much war for too long. Families divided. Lovers divided." I gave her a pointed warning look but she paid me no heed.

"Look at poor Alice here and her Jack—away a few weeks then dead and back here on a hurdle, and that, Will, was nine years ago and a king dead, the new king in exile, villages ransacked, Shipscarden House burnt to ashes, church windows smashed that folk have loved for hundreds of years. Wicked! It is not men at their best, Will. It is shameful!"

"I agree with your every word, Mistress Sanderson, but we are just worker bees in the great hive. What can we do to change anything beyond our own fences?"

"You helped, Will," I said. "You intervened. You found the money to pay the fines. And you took Isabella on her journey."

Father and Mother stared at me. This was the first they had heard me speak of the dangerous events at Beauchamps.

"These are great dramas Will, and you a principal player, my friend."

"He was, Father. He drove Isabella all the way to the Cambridge under the eyes of Roundheads on the roads. And you were beaten for your pains."

"Just a tavern brawl, nothing significant. A black eye. A bloody nose. No, I think the family witnessing the Throstleford priest being hauled on a harrow then hanged at Warwick scarred them all."

"Drawn and hanged! Great God above! You were not there, Alice, were you, at such an event?"

"No, Mother, only the Catholics from the household went. Ruth and I stayed behind. But Lady Trentham was never the same after that day."

"Hmm. Great God, what times!" She stood up. "Will, I will go and collect some useful medicines for you to take to her."

"And some of your caudle recipes, Mother, to build up her strength, if she is not eating. I will come and help you."

"No, Alice. You stay and talk to Will about your friends. You have been anxious enough for long enough."

"I will go out to bed the horses," said Father. "It is a lovely evening. You two take a turn about the orchard before Will has to leave." He walked off and we were left alone. Their kindly contrivance embarrassed me.

"A good suggestion, Samuel," Will said and took my hand. He kept hold of it too as we wandered under the dappling sun setting beyond the orchard fields. I wondered if he could feel me trembling.

We walked under the plum trees as far as the cherries where father had moved two facing logs as shady seats. Will took my hand and pulled me closer. He looked deep into my eyes.

"Your father asked me to come back with him, Alice. I was unsure because you were so angry with me the night you left Beauchamps. I smarted under everything you said."

"You would not even listen to me when I tried to explain why I acted as I did that night. I tried to tell you again when you came back from Cambridge but you left me in no doubt that you had lost all regard for me."

"I was sure you had lost all love for *me*, that I had killed it."

"Your pride was hurt, Will. You felt I had humiliated you in front of the whole household. You were jealous of a *priest*. How could you believe that of me?"

He dropped his head and ran his hands over his hair.

"I know, I know. I was an ass, but, dear Alice, one full of fear. I wanted to be your lover. When you shouted to those Puritans that you had been in de Paul's bed, I was murderous with jealousy. I wanted to have you as my wife, Alice. I was afraid you were lost to me." He stopped. We looked at each other, thinking, both thinking...

"Is it too late to mend us?"

"To marry a jealous man, Will, to marry a man who will lose his faith in me at the first challenge? It made me miserable. The future I had imagined with you was gone."

I looked away from him. Tears came that I did not want him to see. My voice broke but I did not want to cry in front of him. I did not want it to look like a girlish trick to influence him.

"When I met your father today he told me you were unhappy. He said he and your mother believed you were grieving, and I grasped at his words, wondering if you were grieving *for me?* God Knows, dearest Alice, I have grieved for loss of you. I miss you in my life. I want you back beside me." He ran his hands across his face. "God's Bones, this begging is unmanly of me."

"If my parents had not stirred themselves in this matter, Will, would you have come?"

"Would I have dared?"

"Pride, then cometh before a lover's pleading?"

"Cometh before a fall, before a failing of my last hopes if you tell me you cannot love such a proud, jealous fool. Aimee told me I had broken your heart. Lady Trentham herself called me before her and recounted all she owed to your bravery" He shook his head and held me by the shoulders "The more I heard, the more ashamed I was. I determined to come and plead with you to renew our love. But—"

"—but what? More doubts, Sir? You did not come."

"When I walked into the estate office on the night I came back from Cambridge I was determined to find you and speak to you. But I saw Thomas kissing your hands and you gazing up at him."

"So you were jealous again?" I jumped to my feet.

"Hopeless more than jealous, Alice. I was sure I was too late. The Trentham heir had fallen in love with the beautiful, brave saviour of him and his family. He was a far more fitting husband for you than a weak-livered stick of a widower who was just the Trentham's servant."

I sank down again on the log, examining his face. I listened in silence. Words jostled to escape me but I could not speak.

"Alice, you are courageous, independent, loyal and tender. I am in awe of you. I can only offer you such as I am, flawed but full of love and angry for the time I have wasted. I throw myself on your mercy."

Tears dripped unattractively from my chin. Will smoothed them away. He took up my hand and kissed my fingers. Could we heal the rift between us? I wanted to feel his arms about me, to feel his body close to mine.

"I love you, Will," I said. "I love you. I want to live with you, bear your children and live close-bound together till we grow old."

He made to take me in his arms but I stopped him.

"Wait! Each of us has scarred the other. I have been wilful, impetuous and stubborn but I will never be a dimity wife, subject to questioning about my friends, told what to think, where not to go. I have the pattern of my mother and father before me. They are partners, not a master and his servant."

To my surprise he laughed. "You sound like a trader selling me a spirited mare, one I am already falling over my feet to take home with me, rejoicing. I want to claim you, Alice, if you will have me and cherish you all my life."

He opened his arms and I burrowed myself into him, pressing my lips into his neck as he covered the top of my head with kisses. My world blended in joy, desire and love. We folded our arms around each other and stood there, heart to heart, in the last red-gold blaze of the evening sun.

When we returned to the house, my parents were waiting patiently for us to come back. They smiled as we walked in, arms entwined.

"A good understanding, I see," Father said.

"We are very pleased for both of you, my dears. Now, a drink before you leave, Will."

"Before we sit," Will faced my father and mother. "I must I ask you, formally, for Alice's hand, Samuel."

Father beamed at us. "Content, dear girl?"

"Content and very happy."

By Just Exchange

September 1651

My true love hath my heart and I have his
By just exchange one for the other given.
'Arcadia': Sir Philip Sydney

Will and I parted tenderly.

"I will carry this memory of you, Alice, with the darkling orchard behind you, cascading with blackbird song in the glory of the setting sun. You look like a haloed saint in a church window."

"Not a window that villain Levens would have put his fist through, I hope," I laughed.

"No more of those days, darling girl."

"Will!" I ran over to him as he mounted his horse. "Thomas is still in danger, isn't he? Is there not a way to save him?"

"I am going to Stratford on market day. I will make enquiries about Tom at the Town Hall, the Guild Hall—anywhere they send me. I will find where he is being held, even if I have to go to Warwick—or even London. I will remind his gaolers about Colonel Sir Bartholomew Elliot's Certificate of Safety for the family, with Cromwell's seal. I just hope Thomas has still got it with him—that they haven't taken it off him."

"What if they have?"

"Then I will make sure they know how it was well known hereabouts, seen and approved by Parliament's representatives in Stratford several times already. I will take myself in front of Cromwell himself if I have to, as Her Ladyship's steward. I'll carry her letter directly to him and Colonel Elliot and get another certificate. Even if I have to blunder into them both in some Scottish battlefield! This estate has endured enough."

"Great heavens, Will! Do not let it come to that. I do not want to be widowed again, before I can be wived! Surely they will be too busy with the Scots to bother their round heads about the likes of you or the Trenthams. In any case, if Cromwell's Army is all the way up in Scotland as you say, that's too far for you, surely? You wouldn't know where to look."

"Let us not run out to meet trouble before it comes calling, Sweet-heart. But I will go there if I have to. We need that certificate."

"Promise me, if it comes to that, you will not leave me without messages. Send word to me somehow. Now I have hold of your heart I cannot be without it for long."

He bent down and kissed me then chuck-chucked the horse and rode off.

Back in the house Mother said not a word but folded me into her. Father joined us.

"We are so happy for you, dear girl. He is a fine man and a right choice for you. I am sure of it."

That night there was nothing more in the world I wanted, save to be married to Will and sleeping in his bed. I lay alone in my own with the shutters open listening to the night owls calling and trying to count the summer stars.

At the end of the week we all went to Stratford Market to buy lengths of damask for my wedding dress. I half hoped I might catch sight of Will.

We wandered between the stalls, Mother buying the household goods she needed while I indulged myself, fingering the cloth, the lengths of lace and ribbons. I spoke to the merchant and after a time of gazing and rejecting, unfurling and rolling up I chose a bolt of the palest green damask, a length of cream for the underskirt and cream lawn for the sleeves.

I was delighted with my purchases and moved on happily through the crowds passing the Town Hall. I wondered if Thomas Trentham was being held there or had been moved to

Warwick or even down to London. It added to my fears when I saw a wall- poster denouncing conspirators and rebels.

All Rowdies *causing*
Insurrections
will be
imprisoned
And
Rioters will be **punished.**

Another one had been torn over. A third showed a hanged man dangling from a gibbet. Could Thomas be in that kind of danger? How fervently I wished he was free and back at Beauchamps where he belonged and that my beloved Will would not have to ride about the country trying to save the heir to the family estate that he was pledged to.

Alongside these warnings, another poster had been over-pasted.

God Save the King
His Majesty King Charles II by God's grace
restored to his throne by his loyal Scottish
subjects
orders all true Englishmen to rise in arms,
defend his throne and
all our English Liberties.

Outside the Town Hall a table had been set under a canopy where sat two recorders collecting land-levies. The Parliamentary Commissioners had ordered property owners in every English county to pay a compulsory subscription to the army for *"defending their several holdings from marauders, vandals and thieves."*

I groaned. Once father spotted them, he would use up the whole of our journey home complaining that Parliament's Army had done nothing to protect Netherfold from damagers or scroungers but rather added to both and would again, despite what he would be forced to pay. It would sour the happy mood that had prevailed at home these recent weeks.

As we walked among the stalls we met Esther and Nathan. We went to the pie shop. I showed my cousin the beautiful green and creamy stuffs I had bought. How I loved it!

"I am going to make a lace partlet to cover the yoke," I went on.

"I am sure it will be very fine," she said with her gentle smile. "You look very happy, Alice. You must be much in love and impatient to wed. I know I was. Nathan changed my life. He made me feel beautiful and safer although I am plain and I have this." She held up her shortened arm. "I wish you great joy. Has your father decided a date for your ceremony?"

"Yes, at the Harvest Home feast in September when all the hard field work is done and everyone can celebrate together."

"Will Minister Barnes marry you then?"

"We will not ask him. We will have our betrothal and our wedding at St. Etheldega's."

Esther nodded but said nothing further. She rejoiced for me but her Puritan ways did not lead her to praise dress or lace.

"I wish you a blessed union, Cousin Alice," she said, "And the joys that children bring."

She laid her hands on her own belly and I realised another child was on its way. I wondered if Mother knew. Little Joshua was a sweet boy and they were a happy family, just what I wished for myself. The thought of carrying Will's babies sent a warm churn around my womb that took me by surprise and set me smiling. I held Esther's arm and kissed her.

As Mother and I left Nathan and his wife and went towards our meeting place at our waggon, Father suddenly appeared before us at the open door of The Three Swans.

"Alice! Sarah!" he called, "Come! Look inside." He beamed at me, "Come and see what is to be seen." I searched his face for his reason, but all I could read was his smile. I stepped inside and looked around.

Sitting in the settle by the tap room was Thomas Trentham and, doubling my joy, Will.

Will jumped to his feet and swept me into his arms. The taverners cheered and beat their ale pots on the tables. He steered me outside, followed by Thomas.

We all embraced and talked at once. "Tell me how you got him out. Is he free? Thomas, are you finally free? Tell us all, Will."

"I did nothing, Alice. All I had to do was enquire. They had already decided he had no part to play."

"Part to play in what? What are they talking about, Alice? What is all this business? Thomas, what, now?"

"You saw the poster, Mother, about the plots of rebellion, for the new King."

"That was a London plot though was it not?"

"Mistress Sanderson, let me explain for you. Because I was imprisoned before, after the fall of Oxford, my name was known. During these late troubles, someone spoke my name again, so I was hauled in to be 'examined' as they put it."

"Goodness, your poor mother! All this again!"

"Well, I was called before a very thorough Commissioner who took his role seriously. He sifted through his wallets of documents, his lists of names, the charged conspirators, the dates of secret meetings, dates of my comings and goings, arrests and releases, on and on. He examined my wounded arm, tested my useless sword-hand grip. He wrote down every word, numbered, checked and countersigned, every why and where-to-for."

"Then, reasonable pen-pushing hero that he was," Will interrupted, "he examined the Certificate of Safety that Thomas pulled out from his undershirt."

"And they believed it? They did not rip it to pieces?"

"Believed it completely." Thomas smiled. "The Commissioner was especially reverent when he saw Oliver

Cromwell's seal with the portrait on it. He recognised Old Noll's face. Praise be! I thought he was going to kiss the very wax."

"So, you are properly safe now, and your mother will be able to breathe again?" I said.

Tom nodded and seized me by the shoulders, "Will tells me you and he are to follow Kathryn and me to the altar. We will all have happy occasions to celebrate at last."

He waved a letter he was holding and went on. "There is something else for you to know, Alice. Will brought me this from Kathryn. You remember how grieved I was that we had nothing left to give when the young king was appealing for funds? I was ashamed that so many of our Royalist neighbours, made a contribution when we could not. Well, Kathryn tells me in here that Henry sends thanks to me for the large stock of silver rescued from our own parish church. It *was* hidden on our land, Alice." He gave me a knowing look. "My cousin made sure it was safe-delivered to a royal destination. I am satisfied that Beauchamps has been able to lend aid to the king after all."

He took a deep breath. "Now I will turn my hand and mind to sweet-hearting. Will, since I am horseless, you must take me to see my beloved Kathryn and from thence to my dear mother and, if God grant King Charles his English throne, all will be right in the world."

Will embraced me and they left. We mounted our own family waggon and drove home, my spirits soaring higher and freer than for months past.

At the end of August Will and I exchanged our betrothal vows. Mother and Lizzie, Miriam Wallace and Daniel's wife, Joan decked the church porch with bunches of trailing ivy, hedge-berries and late blush roses tied with plaits of straw. There were stands of corn-dollies threaded through with fiery poppies and field cornflowers.

Will gave me his pledge with a gold ring studded with one clear moonstone, like a raindrop caught in sun. He placed it on the finger of my right hand. It would not be long before he would put it on my wedding finger and we could go back to his gate house as man and wife.

After the ceremony, we walked back to The Rose Bush in procession to the music of the fiddlers, playing the new love song heard on every Stratford street:

> *Come live with me and be my love*
> *And we will all the pleasures prove.*

We joined the revellers on the village green. Father called for beer for the whole village and my mother and I brought a pig roast, rabbit pies, spiced mince pies and honeyed cherry cakes to the neighbours' harvest supper. Nathan and Esther with little Joshua joined us for the feasting and the musicians played the jaunts and jigs we all loved and danced to at every Harvest Home. Everyone made merry until dark.

Will and I lingered over our last farewell. Everyone else had gone to their beds but he and I lay together on the orchard grass, oblivious to the rising dew, close-entwined.

"I don't want to wait another three weeks to be your wife, Will," I said, pressing my hands into the muscles of his back, his shoulder blades, the hollow of his spine beneath his shirt.

"How you make free with my body, woman!" he laughed. "If I was so forward with you your father would horsewhip me through the village."

"My father is long a-bed, and out of my sight, while you, my darling Will, are very much here."

He closed over me and the weight of him was the pleasure I wanted to know better. But he rolled over and stood up, dragging me after him.

"We torture each other here, darling girl, I promised, this very day, to observe the forms—"

" '—and practices of Christ's church and to present ourselves…' Yes, yes, we made the promises, and they are very well for maids of seventeen, but you and I are almost elderly. We should seize our pleasure before we need our slippers and our gruel."

"Wicked woman!" he lifted me into his arms. "Have I pledged myself to an insatiable she-devil? Will I ever be able to satisfy your lust, Alice Sanderson Franks?" He kissed my neck.

"As completely as you will satisfy your own, I have no doubt at all."

He carried me to the house, rattling the latch ostentatiously then stood me on my feet at the staircase.

"That lets your mother know I have brought you back in a decent time," he whispered, then raised his voice, directing it up the stairs and winking at me. "Goodnight sweet Alice. Tell your parents I will borrow the small Trentham coach and come back to collect you on the morning of Thomas and Kathryn Norton's wedding so you need not ride across my horse in all your finery. Now, goodnight." He made a great deal of noise with the yard door while we held each other, lingering over our kisses. "Goodnight." I whispered and sent home on his way.

It was the end of August and we were at our morning's work when we heard horses riding along the front street; lots of horses, a troop, a whole battalion! Mother and I looked at each other in dismay. We had fondly thought the days of warring armies riding through the village were over. The young King Charles was up in Scotland and Cromwell had taken his army up there to close the fight at last. Who then were these horsemen riding, riding?

None of them stopped or turned into our lane. In the end our curiosity took us up to the front street to see a column of Cromwell's army, riding four abreast towards Evesham.

As the cavalcade rode on, men stopped work and leant on their pitchforks, women came out of their cottages holding their babies or wiping their hands on their pinafores. We had never seen such a force. Little boys ran alongside with sticks for swords, holding imaginary reins. The cavalrymen raised their voices singing.

> *My help cometh from the Lord;*
> *Which made Heaven and Earth.*
> *He will not suffer thy foot to be moved:*
> *He that keepeth thee will neither slumber nor sleep*
> *The sun shall not smite thee by day,*
> *Nor the moon by night.*
> *The Lord shall preserve thee from all evil.*
> *He shall preserve thy soul.*

Four troopers turned their horses into our lane, one leaning to ask something of a woman standing on the corner. She pointed to the blacksmith's. Lizzie ran ahead of them to warn Matt and her father-in-law that business was coming.

We saw the horse column end and a company of foot soldiers followed, all carrying their pikes at the same slant.

"However many does Cromwell need?" exclaimed Mother. "Hundreds have passed here, just while we have been watching."

Esther's eyes were shining. "How brave and well-ordered they are. And such singing."

"But, Esther, they are marching to kill other Englishmen. That is their intent."

Mother had hoped so fervently that the war, after all these years, was over. She and Father were prepared to accept the rule of Parliament and an established Commonwealth, so long as peace was the result, but when Father had brought home the market-place news that the Prince of Wales had been crowned in Scotland, he had predicted woe.

"Fighting will break out again, here in England, depend upon it. We will be back to having them all on our land, eating us out of board and trampling our gardens. Wait and see."

Despite Father's gloom-laden predictions, months had passed by peacefully. That, together with my own happiness, led me to forget about war, but then came more Royalist calls for money. The factions were preparing to fight again. I hoped it might all happen far away from our Vale, but here they were again, horsemen at our doors. I turned back to the house, dejected.

"Go across to the smithy, Alice, see if Lizzie needs your help."

I crossed the street to the forge. The Roundheads were leaning against the wall, supping beer while the their horses grazed the verge. The men were quiet enough, just talking to each other. Matt worked on the horse that had cast a shoe and Lizzie brought out bread and cheese. I helped pour beer.

"We thought the King's army was in Scotland. Why so many troops marching this way?"

"We 'bin marchin' for weeks an' months it seems like. Horses tired. Men tired. Yet on we march. Mile on mile."

"If you hate it so, why do it? Could you not just run back to your homes, if you are tired of war?"

The four soldiers laughed heartily. "Ah, poor, simple Missy. You have no idea what rough usage we would have for that."

"We'd be hauled back with ropes about our necks and strung from yon oaks!" said another.

A third spoke more quietly. "Some of us believe in the new Commonwealth and want a hand in putting down the Stuart tyrants, son as father."

"And some of us," the fourth gestured with his beer mug, "keep on marchin' for love of Old Noll and the beer money he gives us."

"Aye, we give a toast to Oliver Cromwell, who helps us to the Promised Land."

"But by your blood, Sirs, or risk of it."

"'Tis paid work, like any other." said the last man.

"'Tis faith-work, too, Rich," the quiet one added.

"Well, I pray safety for you all," I said. "And I pray you all keep moving on and on to Evesham."

"Worcester, Missy. We march on Worcester to rid England of the other Charles Stuart once for all."

"We will have twenty-eight thousand men to our army, Missy. Noll told us that himself. He rallied us troopers, didn't he? Roused us."

"He is a man of faith," the quiet one went on, "He tells us, he believes it too, that God is at our side. We have defeated a Stuart tyrant once. He will help us do it again."

"Ha! Ha! Ha! Twenty odd thousand pike and musket men will help us do it!" The two beer drinkers touched pots in a toast to victory.

"Here!" Matt thrust his irons hissing into the water trough and stroked the horse's, leg, setting it down. "Lead him about while I look at his gait, then have your money ready."

The trooper did as Matt asked and the others fished about in their pouches and gave Lizzie coins for their refreshments. They paid the blacksmith bill without a grumble and mounted up.

"Has King Charles so many soldiers to fight on his side?" I asked, remembering Henry Norton's plea to Thomas to rally to the King's side.

The soldier who spoke of 'Old Noll' laughed. "Not at all, Mistress, not half so many is what we hear and most of them are wild Scotchmen who cannot be put to order like our army. They will run amok in all directions and we can pot them off like pigeons in a field."

The four of them joined in the laughter and waving to us, rode away to join the cavalry formation.

Later that day Daniel came. He had been into Evesham selling fruit. He was full of the Roundhead troop numbers that had swamped the town.

"The townsfolk lined the streets to watch them ride in," he said. "Thousands of them. They took over every tavern, small holding and merchant's place for their officers and the mass of men made camp along the river meadows."

"Lizzie and I talked to four soldiers who stopped at the smithy for shoeing." I told him. "They said Cromwell is at the head of twenty-eight *thousand* men to lay siege to Worcester."

"They say young King Charles rode into Worcester last week for his stand. There were news sheets in the Evesham taverns asking the local men to rally to the King's side."

"Did people say they would go, Daniel? To fight for the King again?" Mother looked worried.

Daniel shook his head. "People just grumbled that they'd have to put up with soldiers whether they wanted to or not, just when they'd got their places put straight, and beasts bred up again. Then there was this. Look." He handed us a broadsheet roughly printed and the ink mushy. "From Oliver Cromwell himself, it says."

In the name of Parliament
and under the Authority of the Commonwealth of England
I do hereby offer and grant a
Free Pardon
to all who once raised their swords in support of the Stuart Kings, if they now turn their swords to defend the right of Englishmen to live under Parliament Free from tyranny and march under the banner of the Lord.

"Is he there, then? Oliver Cromwell, in Evesham?"

"I would not know him, Alice, if I did see him. You would be better to tell *me* that. You have seen his face on that seal of the Trenthams, haven't you? The gossip is he is going to sleep at The Troute Inn.

Mother and Father turned to stare at me. "What does he mean, 'You have seen Cromwell's face?'"

"It was when I was at Beauchamps. Cromwell's deputy, Sir Bartholomew Elliot and his officers came into the Hall for shelter. The rains had flooded the place and Colonel Elliot was sick. They asked for physic and a warm bed."

"And you gave him the medicines—made them up for him?"

I nodded. "He was very pleasant. And grateful."

"What ailed him?"

"A fever, congestion of the lungs. He had been soaked for days, and he was exhausted. Lady Trentham made them comfortable, they stayed a few days then left for Scotland."

"Did he pay her before he left then? I would have thought he scorned staying with Royalists who were Catholics to boot. I wonder they didn't think Lady Trentham would get Will or Dick to slit their throats in the night."

"No, Father, he was polite. He was a nobleman and a landowner like her. He was grateful and he gave Her Ladyship that Certificate of Safety with Cromwell's own seal on it, showing his face. That is what Daniel was talking about. It was very valuable to them all. It saved Thomas's life and saved his mother from mighty fines or worse."

"I remember Will and Tom talking about it in the Stratford tavern. I did not know you had been there in the midst of it all. Well, well, honour and gentlemanly conduct among the warmongers! Still, I suppose these nobles look after their own. We were never given any certificates of safety for all our hospitality or your mother's nursing."

"Fancy you having to do with such great men, you Alice! You will come one of these days and tell us you have kept company with King Charles himself."

"It will do us no good if she does, Sarah. These nobles, from whichever pitch of the battle, will only treat gently with their own sort."

Daniel gathered up his hat. "Well, I must leave this exalted company where I have sisters who mingle with the nation's great ones and go back to Lane End's pig sties." Laughing, he kissed us all. "Think how galled Great Oliver and his deputy the baronet would be to know that his nurse had saved the life of a clandestine Jesuit priest."

300

Father and Mother stared at me again. It was another story I would have to tell them.

At the beginning of September, the day came for Thomas Trentham's wedding to Kathryn Horton. Dressed for the festivities, I sat in the sunshine waiting for Will when two tired and bloodied soldiers astride a single horse rode into the yard. Mother ran out.

"Sit where you are, Alice. I will deal with the wounds here. Don't you spoil your finery."

Father and the men crowded round them. Neither of the King's men were badly wounded but sat, exhausted clutching a cup of ale. The older one was eager to tell their tale.

"We was on the city walls, Jacob here and me. Beautiful day, sunny. Quiet, weren't it?"

Jacob, now the blood and muck was washed from his face, was just a boy. "I could hear larks trillin' an' warblin' over my head. It were peaceful." He paused, sadness clouding his eyes, "til it wasn't."

"Lookin' out below the city walls, ranks an' endless ranks o' Cromwell's men kneelin', holdin' their weapons ready."

"We was waitin' for our order for to fire, but—"

"—the skies split from north to south. Cannon balls smashed into the stone beneath us. We were shaken to the teeth, weren't we, lad?"

"Threw me down. Stones and grit rainin' on me where the larks' song had been before. It's still in my hair. Look you, Joseph, a bit of Worcester City in my hair." He fanned some strands of hair with trembling fingers. Poor young Jacob was still in battle-shock, his eyes staring in the distance at the scenes he could still see.

"It were rainin' musket balls, an' all through it half them Roundheads was singin' psalms about the sword of the Lord and Gideon."

"Gideon? Don't know no Gideon. Who was Gideon, Joseph?"

"Never bother, Jacob, we are all safe now, lad. Just drink up then you can sleep."

"How did you escape?" asked Father.

"The cannons blasted the wall by us apart. Great hole—our men started fallin' through, pushin' an' shovin' and gettin' away."

"Steppin' on our dead men, Joseph, they was standin' in their blood."

"Well, Master, I grabbed young Jacob here and we ran. The fine officers in their frills and feathers, they was runnin' so why was we to stay and have our heads blown away by cannon balls, eh?"

"I saw a man without no head. Just blood where his neck used to be." Jacob sobbed.

My mother took him in her arms and rocked him as if he had been seven, not seventeen.

"Deserters were throwin' down their pikes and muskets, both ours an' theirs. The river was washed red."

"Blood! Everybody's blood," sobbed the boy.

"I saw one of our captains yellin' to another on his horse that the King and his beggarly Scots ruffians were finished and the city lost. So, me and Jacob ran and ran till we come to the woods an' waited. I found a grazin' horse. We climbed on it an' rode away an' kept on ridin' till we fetched up in your village. An' grateful we are for your kindness, Master."

Worcester fallen. The King's army defeated. What a blight this would cast upon the wedding party.

My father and Watt went on asking the older soldier about the battle, while Mother took Jacob indoors away from the talk.

To my relief Will rode into our yard to collect me and I hurried over to prevent him hearing the whole terrible story. I wanted to preserve the happy day for now.

302

The small coach door handles and the horse's bridle were tied with white ribbons and posies of marigolds, rich with the glow of autumn sunshine. As we rode through the vale to Shipscarden, the whole countryside beamed gold; the stubble, the haycocks, the leaves just turning. The Cotswold hills shimmered a gilded blue.

The church of St. Mary Magdalene in Shipscarden was full. Generations of the town's families had worked for Sir Sheldon Norton in the wealthy wool town. They had mourned the burning of the manor house and were determined to show their loyalty by turning out to rejoice at the wedding, toasting a future they hoped would be their assured future too.

The estate workers and wool weavers, dressed in their best clothes, lined the street waving posies of rosemary and myrtle. I could smell the roses that spilled over the lych-gate and filled the church before we reached it. Every shop and inn sign and overhanging bough was hung with the yellow and white banners of the family crest.

Inside the church, the lace-covered altar reminded me of the Beauchamps secret chapel, but no one here was afraid. Candlesticks and a crucifix were polished and on show.

Sir Sheldon walked to the chancel steps with Kathryn on his arm, herself in white taffeta worked with dandelions symbolising faithfulness and happiness, joined by a border of trailing orange blossom worked in green and gold thread.

She carried a nosegay of myrtle, rosemary and yellow roses and wore a coronet of the same among her fringing curls.

Thomas Trentham looked courtly and fine in a suit of oyster satin trimmed with silver lace and pinned with his bridegroom's favour of rosemary, myrtle and yellow rosebuds. I had never seen him look so grand. Neither had I ever seen him look happier.

The priest spoke all the service in the accepted forms of the English Protestant church I knew, but as the new-made husband

and wife knelt to write their signatures in the church record book, they crossed themselves and their priest bent low over them, whispering. I looked across at Lady Trentham and Anne Carey, Aimee and Beth. They knelt and crossed themselves too and whispered their own prayers, as did most of the Shipscarden congregation.

Sir Sheldon's feast, the food, the wine and the music were all of the finest. I danced with Will, delighting in the thought that the next time we danced would be on our own wedding day.

Servants came around with baskets of sweetmeats and gifts of fine kid gloves for every guest, some trimmed with lace and others with cords of leather. Dusk gathered and the first stars appeared. Two blackbirds were calling loudly across the street from church roof to tavern roof as Will and I stood among the revellers under the open arches of the market arcade. It was lit now by torches and fire baskets and the two noble families sat at the long table, nibbling the last candied fruits and sipping their wine. I had not seen Lady Trentham look so carefree. I smiled across to her. A smile she returned, her eyes dancing. How sad, I thought, that all this happiness would vanish into tears once the news of Worcester's fall reached the ears of these families now rejoicing.

The violin players and the pipers struck up again and the music filled the street where all the locals danced and drank the free beer doled out from The Eagle Tavern's open door.

Across Will's shoulder I saw the Norton family steward push his way through the dancers, his eyes fixed intently upon Sir Sheldon.

"Will," I stopped dancing and turned him to look at the family table. "Something's wrong."

Sir Sheldon took his family into the house and urged the Trentham people to follow him. Indoors there stood Henry Norton, blood-stained, his cloak torn to rags, a cut to his cheek.

"Henry!" his mother cried and ran to him. They led him to a chair. She smoothed his hair away from his face. "Are you worse wounded?"

"No, no more than this. The battle of Worcester is lost, Father. His Majesty's force is routed. Cromwell overwhelmed us. Everything is lost."

"The King, Harry, what of the King? Is he dead?" asked Sir Sheldon.

"No, not dead, but disappeared. No one saw what happened to him."

"Was he wounded, has he escaped? For God's sake, tell us all you know." Thomas ran to his friend with a cup of wine.

"Everything was confusion. Chaos. Roundhead soldiers, at every turn. So much blood." He shook his head and wiped his face. "They are rounding up our men and penning them in with farm hurdles."

"They cannot hang them all, imprison them all."

"One of the officers was yelling at them, saying they were going to be transported to the Americas."

"Do you think King Charles was helped away?" Sir Sheldon looked ready to go to the rescue himself.

The revelling outside had ceased. There was no more music. Voices called the news from street to street. A man rushed into the house, knocked on the inner door and cried, "Here's more news! Sir Sheldon, Sir. "He ushered in another Royalist soldier, battle-worn and limping.

"I claim sanctuary, here," he shouted. "They say this house supports the King. I am one of his men, lost and hurt."

"Come in and welcome, man," Sir Sheldon led him to a chair and gave him wine. "What do you know of King Charles?"

"Escaped. Bundled away under wrappings and tied to a horse."

"Thank God," Henry crossed himself, as did most of those listening. "Are they putting our men to the sword?"

"No, no. It was better ordered as I left. They are keeping the Scotsmen, as foreign invaders, they said. And they have tied up our officers, such as they could stop from riding off, but they ignored us common men. They watched the likes of us go without stops or threats."

"Come, then," said Sir Sheldon "We will organise quarters for you and as many of our side as make their way here." He called his steward and the estate workers to ready the barns and camping grounds. He sent others to beg room in the inns and taverns for the fleeing, tattered remnants of the King's defeated army.

Lady Agnes took her son to his chamber to be bathed and bandaged. Thomas called Will and Dick to take the Beauchamps people home.

"I should come home with you, Will, to prepare the place, for we will have our share of the King's escaping men. But God help me, it is my wedding night."

"You must not spoil it, Thomas. Dick can take charge of the vehicles. I must see Alice safely back to Bournbroke, then ride on to Beauchamps. Everything will be organised as you would wish."

I could have said there was no need for Will to take me home, that I would stay with the Nortons or let them send me with one of their men, but I wanted to go with Will, so I said nothing.

Will and Thomas embraced then he and Kathryn left together for their marriage night, although I feared it would be less carefree than their happy wedding day had promised.

Will came for me. "You will have to ride pillion with me back to Bournbroke, Alice. Thomas has commandeered all the waggons and carriages for the Hall." He borrowed a horse from the Norton stables and I climbed behind and clung to him.

As we turned off the crossroads into Bournbroke I leant forward and spoke into Will's ear. "It is not quite dark yet. Leave me at the top of our lane. I can trot into Netherfold safely and you can turn round and hurry on your way."

"I must see you safely in, Alice."

"It is completely quiet and deserted. There are no strangers to be seen. I will be quite safe. Stop here."

At our gate Will reined the horse and I slid down and lifted my face for his kiss. "Don't come in," I said. "Father will insist on you staying to drink a mug of beer with him and tell him all the news about the fall of Worcester. You just go, but go safely."

He bent down and touched my lips. He gave a soft groan. "Leaving you is harder every time. I want to see you indoors."

"No, no, darling. It's hard for me to send you away, too. The closer you are to me the more I want you to stay. Just let me get in. I will go straight to my lonely bed and dream of you. Go." I gave his horse's flank a gentle tap. He turned its head, mouthed a parting kiss and rode away.

Farewell King!

4th September 1651

> 'What must the King do now?
> I'll give my jewels for a set of beads
> My figured goblets for a dish of wood.
> My sceptre for a palmer's walking staff'
>
> 'Richard II': William Shakespeare

As I hurried into our yard, I was puzzled by the sight of a grazing horse tied to a cherry tree in the darkening orchard, its bridle hanging loose.

'Father must have a visitor, not one of ours.' I thought it strange. Father would have put up a visitor's horse in our barn.

I lifted the latch of the house door and stepped in. A fire was blazing in the grate. Mother sat in her usual place facing the door but the smile faded on my lips. Her eyes were plate-wide with fear.

"What?"

A rough hand clapped over my mouth and I was heaved off the floor and thrown down into the settle. My head crashed into the wood. Pain shot through me, flashing and spinning. There was shouting and noise. I think it was me who was screaming.

"Shut your mouth, woman, or you'll get a worser slap."

I forced my eyes open. A ragged-haired cavalier, bloodied, with swollen lips and days' growth of whiskers stood over me.

"What is it you want, for God's Sake, money? What?"

"Food, bed, money. You, old woman, get up and get me some eats. No more complaining. And you!" He grabbed my wrist and hauled me to my feet

"Ugh!" I shook my head, struggling to make sense. My blood hammering. "What is this? Who are you?"

"Go with your mother there. I want food. Be quick. And don't try resistance. Your father there tried that and I flattened

308

'im, see! The old hag there said you had no food, no nothin'. Well, you look mighty plump and well-fed to me, so she is a lyin' drab! An' your old fool dad thought he could set about me so I felled him. I haven't survived a bloody siege-war at Worcester to be flapped down by an old pantaloon and his whoreson wife and daughter, so get what I want."

He shoved me in the direction of the pantry door. I almost lost my feet again but stumbled upright, shaking with fear and fury. 'Why did I send Will away?' I thought, 'What a fool, I should have let him come in. He would have saved us.' Useless. He was gone. We were alone with this ruffian.

"Hurry yourself, you harlot, don't make me have to come after you in there!" I heard him pouring more beer into his cup, gulping and belching.

I lifted out some pork, not yet properly cured but it would have to do. I collected a lump of cheese, a couple of raw onions and a loaf. I looked at the butchering knife hanging from the beam over the salting barrel. I unhooked it and hid it under the kitchen cloth in my hand. I carried everything back into the parlour and slammed the food down in front of him. He tore at it all, one thing after the other, stuffing it into his mouth.

I looked over to Mother. She sat in her chair, rigid, fuming. I could see she was hatching a plan. She made a tiny, careful gesture towards Father and frowned. He was slumped in his chair, bleeding from the nose and mouth.

"I shall see to my father now."

He slammed his fist on the table. "Stay where you are!"

"Shut up, you stupid oaf. What, are you afraid of two old folk and a maid. Just eat and try not to open up that wound in your side that I can see is bleeding into your sash there. If you want my help to see to your wound, you should bully me less."

"Huh! What are you, a woman-'pothecary? I don't need no midwife, which is all you two are good for. What do you think a maid like you could do?"

"I could deliver you to Hell as soon as help you, and just leave your wound to fester and putrefy until you die a slow way. No matter to me, but I *will* help my father."

I went over to Father and looked at his bruised face. He was dazed. I flared my eyes towards Mother, in alarm. I ladled some hot water from the fire-pot and I bathed away the blood.

Mother stood up and straightened herself. "Here, Alice, the medicine chest. I will stop this ruffian's bleeding which is more than he deserves. You see to your father."

She went to look at his wound and pressed on the blood stain.

"Aagh! Give over!" He swiped Mother's hand aside.

"Do you want help or bleed to death?" she snapped.

He swore and groaned so she came over to Father. I spread some salve on his cut lip while Mother made a cold-water press for his eye and the bridge of his nose. She stroked his head and he opened his eyes sufficiently to give her a wan smile then groaned and slumped back; his eyes closed

Her voice was small and tight. "His nose might be broken, Alice. We will have to wait to see when the swelling goes down."

She turned to the soldier with more hatred in her face than I had ever seen there. "You!"

Her voice was almost an animal growl. "You ask our help. You want a bed. Why should I lift a finger for you? Look what you have done to my poor husband!"

"Shut your caterwaulin', woman! You, Missy, you strap my wound and give me more beer to kill the pain. You do it, not that old witch." He unwound his blood-soaked sash. "A pox-ridden musket ball. Don't think it went in there, just sliced it, but it's bled plenty. Bloody Cromwell's bastards! Guns! Do something. Get to it. Same as you did for the doddering old man."

He pulled aside his shirt. The musket ball had glanced a long groove along his waist. I tried to part the wound to see if the ball was buried in there. As I bent with my hands on his bare flesh, he groaned and closed his arms around me. His mouth scraped up and down my neck, his breathing hard and heavy as he slobbered over my skin this way and that.

"A nice, plump bit of woman's flesh, eh? Eh?" He pushed his face into mine. I smelt the beer and onions on his breath and pulled away. His fingers grasped my neck and he pulled me to him, rasping his chin around my mouth.

"A kiss or two for a weary, warrior, my lass." His mouth was slick. I writhed and bared my teeth. I bit his lip. He yelped and slapped me hard, spinning sparks and flashing lights into a ball of pain behind my eyes.

"Long time, since I had a clean and dainty woman. You would be the best salve for my body after all the death and screamin'. Oh God, Wench!" He stood and pulled me to him, pressing wet kisses over my mouth. One hand held me fast while with his free hand he groped my throat, kneaded my breast. I twisted and struggled.

'Not this! Not him! Not when I have waited so long for Will. This one will not—' My mind was racing. I scrabbled for the kitchen cloth where the pig-knife lay, closed my hand around it and lifted it up and under his chin, threatening to pierce his jaw. He roared and swiped the blade out of my hand. It clattered to the floor and skittered under the dresser. As he turned his head to watch where it fell, I twisted and bent myself at the same time as my mother leapt around the table behind him. We rammed his wounded side into the table edge. He shrieked in pain and loosed his hold on me. Mother picked up the stool and cracked it across his back. As he fell she sat on the backs of his knees. I knelt on his upper torso while he bucked and flailed. I retrieved the knife. And stuck the point against his neck.

"Do not think I will not dare to cut you if I have to. You can die one way or another. I do not care. But if you want to live, you need to have your shot-wound dressed."

Mother unrolled her stockings, knotted and tied the soldier's hands behind his back as I had seen her tie the legs of the winter pig before cutting its throat to catch the pudding-blood. The

311

soldier swore and cursed but his body gave up. Heavy and sagging, we dragged him up against the wall, propped him up and stripped him to the waist.

"There *is* a musket ball in here. It will have to be got out or it will kill you."

"Here." Mother pulled me aside and pressed his wound, making him yell. "I have done this before for comrades of yours. I will do it for you but you have to do as I say."

"You will kill me, you witch. Both of you, witches. She stuck the knife at my neck."

"She could have killed you then, and I could kill you now."

He groaned. "Why would you help me?" he muttered.

"Because," she gave a weary sigh. "Because I am sick to my bones of war and cruelty. Because I am better than you. Because you are some mother's son. So, let us get on with it, Alice, before I change my mind"

"This," I said, giving the knife at his neck a final light jab," is more than you deserve."

Father began to mutter behind me, then sat up in a fright. "Sarah! Where's he gone, that—ugh!" He lay back in the chair again, groaning and holding his head.

"We are in charge of him now, Samuel. I have tied his hands. Alice is here."

"Alice?"

"Yes, Father. Mother and I have the man at our mercy here. We are treating his wound as a bargain for his better behaviour."

We set about the soldier with the hot water, a cleaned blade, the crochet hooks and the linen to sop up the blood. Despite his shouts and oaths and father's continual waking to ask what the matter was and who caused all the noise. Mother and I succeeded in cutting out the musket ball as he yelled and cursed in pain. We bound him tight to staunch the fresh bleeding.

"I am going to make you a draft to ease the pain," I said.

He looked at me, his eyes screwed up in pain. "You goin' to dose me with poison now?"

312

I shrugged. "As you please, then, suffer the pain and do not sleep. I don't care."

"How do I know what you give me will be safe?"

"You don't. You may take the help or endure." I began to pack away the herbals and cloths into the chest.

"Wait! Here."

"Wait, Alice. Show him. In fact *I* will show him how we make up your Grandmother's poppy potion." She went round to him. "I will make it before your eyes. Watch me put in every ingredient then you can be sure of it."

She dusted the poker and thrust it into the hot coals, then held it in a goblet of small beer. She took out the poppy seeds and, showing him every move, she ground them in the mortar I handed her. She added them to the hot ale with some hyssop and stirred. I caught her eye. I knew she had put far more powdered poppy into the dose than she should. He would be near-dead asleep soon, very soon.

Once we saw his head drop to his chest, the goblet drop from his hand and all his limbs flop useless, Mother and I went to help father. We part walked, part carried him up the stairs and put him into bed. We then took a spare blanket and lay it on the floor and heaved the drugged soldier aside and covered him. Mother put a basin by his head.

"If he vomits in the night, "she said, "I don't want it stinking all over our floor."

I scrabbled under the shelving in the pantry and found some twine that Father and Watt used for tethering the winter pig. With that Mother and I bound the soldier's ankles and fastened his right wrist to the shutter hinge.

"Pig-twine," Mother snorted. "Very suitable."

All of that done, we hugged each other with relief and cried a little.

"Bar your chamber door, Alice, and I will ours, just in case."

"He has no knife; I have searched him. He cannot escape the bonds."

Mother nodded. "Tomorrow, first thing, we will run across to George Wallace, get him and Matt and Watt to put the fellow on his horse—tie him on it if need be—and ride him out of Bournbroke."

At first light I sat up. My body flushed with fear again. I dressed, ran across to my parent's chamber and tapped. Mother opened and we went down the stairs together.

"Is Father better?"

"Still asleep. But he slept better than I did." We peered into the living room. The cavalier was still there, in a tumble on the floor, breathing heavily. We busied ourselves with the essential chores, boosted the fire and set water to boil and bread to bake. I ran across to the smithy to get help from the Wallace men and ran further down the lane to fetch Nathan too. George collected the soldier's horse, fed and watered it for its journey while Nathan, Watt and Matt came inside carrying cudgels. The soldier came to, moaning.

"Well, Sir, we did not kill you, as you now can see. You have great cause to be grateful to my mother, that she found that deep-shot musket ball before your side turned altogether bad."

He grunted but made no reply.

"I will re-dress your wound, "said Mother, "and give you salve enough and bandages to tend the wound yourself as you travel on, and a small flask of the tincture to drink at night if the pain is severe. Keep yourself clean and without exertions which might open up the gash again."

"How am I to do that on the road? I will stay here."

"That you will not do," said Watt. "My neighbours here and I will think naught of beating you to minced meat for attacking these friends of ours." He lifted his stave to make his threat clear.

"Puritan pig!"

Nathan shoved his cudgel against the bloodstained sash at the man's side. "Will you speak so again? I will revenge myself."

314

"Hush, Nathan" my mother said. "I want a quiet morning. Yesterday's violence was more than enough for me. I just want him gone. Watt, go and ask your father to fetch the soldier's horse back in an hour and a stout rope to tie him to the saddle. I will have this devil fed and treated by then and you can all help bundle him out to the crossroads and on his way."

We did all as she said and afterwards, the soldier sat with us, docile, his ankles still tied together. We ate the morning's new bread with plums and autumn apples waiting for George Wallace to fetch the horse.

"You escaped from Worcester, then?" I asked. "They say the siege fell, that it was a rout and the King's Scots soldiers did not help him much at all."

The soldier snorted and shook his head. "Cromwell's men came on and on, waves of 'em. We was hopelessly outnumbered. I just ran. The rumour went round that the young King had cleared out himself. Smuggled away in disguise they said. So, everybody ran." He wiped his mouth. "None of us wanted to hang around and die for a King as wasn't goin' to pay us, nor wasn't even goin' to stay there alongside us. Devil take 'im!"

"I should think you have had your belly full of fighting, "Mother said, "What will you do, go back to your home?"

"Home? I haven't had a home since—" He shrugged. "Just the army. I've been in France, in the Low Countries, for the money."

"Fighting other men's wars for money?" Mother was disbelieving. "You are finished with that now. You have escaped the devil's claw with this musket ball. Next time he will have you, certain. So where will you go?"

"London. Probably." He drank, looking at us, frowning. "Why have you done this for me? I beat your man so he keeps still to his bed; I terrified you. I nearly dishonoured the girl." He nodded in my direction. "You had me at the knife point. Why did you not kill me?"

"Because we are not like you, any of you. We do not live by killing."

"My mother and I defended ourselves against your raging last night but, once calm, you are a man like any other. We want to do all that is needful to get you away from our house."

"You could have killed me, though."

"We still could. You could have killed us. *You* still could."

"But" said Nathan, standing up. "You would have to kill us first." Watt and Matt stood over him, staves in hand. Silence.

The soldier wiped his mouth and nodded. "Untie my feet then and I'll clear out." I cut the twine and he stood and walked unsteadily out to the yard.

George Wallace had tied the soldier's horse to the barn door. The men watched him mount, awkwardly, gasping in pain but no one moved to help him.

I heard Father clomping down the stairs. He came out with his fowling gun in his hand. He lifted and levelled it at the soldier's head, his eyes glittering.

"Samuel! No! I have not spent half the night tearing a musket ball out of his guts for you to put another one in there. Let him leave."

"He broke my nose, Sarah. Drew blood, by God!"

"Enough! "Mother took hold of the gun and pushed it aside. Only Mother could have intervened with my father in that way when he was so ominously still with anger. He threw the gun to the ground, his face thunderous. He stalked over and struck the horse's rump. It squealed and galloped out of the yard.

It was not until afterwards we discovered that the cavalier had stolen my silver baptismal cup from the dresser and Father's pewter tankard. The pig-knife, too, was gone.

That day the neighbours held a meeting in the street and decided to take turns to act as sentry at the corner of the front street to watch for beaten Royalist stragglers sneaking into the village.

Nathan and Watt, already armed with their staves, took the first day shift and the landlord of The Rose Bush and his pot boy watched overnight, huddled over a bonfire.

Battered and weary soldiers trailed through Bournbroke on horseback but seeing our watchmen, they either rode on through or stopped at one of the taverns for ale and food. For a wonder, they paid for it. Nevertheless, quarrels and brawls broke out. The men talked about stretching sheep hurdles across the village entrances, both from Evesham road and from the crossroads, but others complained they needed to move their carts and their flocks without waiting to be let in or out of their own home place. After more arguments and voices raised, the idea was thrown out on condition that all the village men took a turn on guard.

Not all the retreating soldiers were aggressive. Some came in on foot, and not all were Royalists. Some Roundheads came too, exhausted and begging for help. They gave money if they had it or offered to stay and work on the land if they had none in return for bread and shelter. The Roundheads moved on, having homes near Coventry or Warwick or in some of the Puritan villages outlying. But it was clear to us that all that the fight had gone out of the abandoned King's men. They, like the rest of us, were sick and tired of war.

"I no longer care who rules us," George Wallace said, "so he leaves us in peace to do our work, eat our dinners and never see another billeter ride into my yard."

"You're right, George. And I want to go to my church in my black hat and white collar and not be vilified as a traitor."

"You and Esther, are quiet Puritans, Nathan lad," Father said. "It's the ranting ones I object to. A man's prayers should be betwixt him and God, not the business of Parliament Commissioners or priest hunters or such."

"I don't even agree with them tormenting Catholics," said Tom Waywell from the dairy. "My cousin married a Catholic over in Lavingham. His manor lord there was a fair enough man, yet when they rounded him up they took all his estate people as well and my cousin was dragged up, questioned for treason and all sorts. Terrified they were, yet he knew no more about Rome or the Pope than I do. He just wanted his beads and his statues in the old way. What's the harm there, eh?"

They muttered and debated this way and that. I could have told them a hair-horrid story or two about priest hunters, secret chapels and hanging and drawing through streets but I kept my counsel and served stew to the watchmen at our corner.

About five days after the last battle and the fall of Worcester, one of the sheep boys ran into the village from Oxley Field shouting, "The Roundheads are comin' along the Evesham road! Noll Cromwell's army's comin' through here! The Roundheads are comin' now!"

As word spread everyone ran out of the houses and gardens to watch them ride through. Mother and I, Lizzie and Esther, Joan and Primrose Fletcher all stood at the corner while the watchmen stood lining the street-edge, staves in hand.

"I hope they keep on riding through," said Lizzie. "I don't want Matt trying to wield his staff at those helmets and getting a sword stuck in him."

"And I don't want them camping here and eating us all out of harvest home." Joan Fletcher craned her neck to see along the Evesham road. "I'll take my brass skillet to their heads, I swear."

We heard the horses coming. We heard the men's voices singing a psalm in unison. It sounded rather fine. At last they came in our view. A huge troop, two abreast, banners flapping, trotting steadily singing in triumph. The officers wore those cage-wire helmets, their buckskin jerkins looked unstained, their sashes bore no blood. They were the winners of the war.

I stared at the leading horsemen but saw no face that looked like Oliver Cromwell.

Bringing up the rear came waggons carrying tousle-headed ruffians with their hands tied together.

"Scotsmen," said Daniel, who had come to join us. "You came a long way to get your heads broken!" he jeered. The nearest one snarled something we did not understand and Joan knocked Daniel in reproof. "Don't draw attention to us, Daniel. Shut up!"

After they passed, we were about to wander back home when The Rose Bush pot boy ran along with news that four officers had stopped at the tavern to buy food and beer.

"They'm waitin' to follow the last an' close the train." He said. "They were sayin' them Scotch 'uns is bein' sent across the seas to the Americas for punishment."

"They are not sending all the captured Royalist soldiers to the Americas are they? "I asked. "As punishment? Why the Scotsmen?"

"Them officers said as they was foreigners meddlin' in English things against our proper rulers and comin' over our borders like what the Dutch men or the Frenchies do so they'm bein' sent where they can't not do it never again, meddlin'. There." He pointed back int the village. "Him, see, him with the orange sash, that's him as was in our tavern. He'm stayin' to the end, he says."

Four officers rode towards us in the opposite direction from the main procession.

"God save Oliver Cromwell!" someone shouted. A few of our neighbours cheered. The officer raised his hand in acknowledgement.

"God save King Charles!" came another voice, followed by cheers then long shushing and catcalls. Their chief looked neither to right nor left but as the last waggon passed us, he and his fellows, wheeled their horse's heads and rode back through Bournbroke, bringing their guard of the troop-passage to an end. Nothing more to see, we all went back to our homes.

"Do you think that is really the end of all of them?" asked Lizzie. "That the war is over altogether at last?"

319

"I hope to God it is," Mother shoved the door open with more vigour that necessary. "I want peace and quiet for a long, long time."

"Amen." Esther was serious.

"Yes, Amen," I smiled. "I can concentrate on thoughts of my wedding, my dress, my home with Will."

As we sat to supper the sound of a horse in our yard, froze us all mid- mouthful. Father strode to the door and threw it open, fowling piece in hand.

"Ha! Alice has conjured you up by wishing!"

"Will!" I ran to him and flung my arms around him. Mother made another place for him at our table and we told him the tale of our battle with the Royalist runaway.

"My God, Alice! I should have come in with you, not left you in the yard. He could have killed you all! A terrible mistake, sweet-heart. Samuel, I am sorry for it."

"Ahh; you were not to know. I was flattened and of no use. It was these two harpies of ours who saved us. My beloved wife here struck him down with yon side stool, your betrothed thrust the butchery-knife at his gizzard and then they fished out a musket ball from his side and left him quivering and grateful."

Will turned to me and kissed my hand. "Is your bravery never-ending, woman? You persist in doing the office of protector in every house you are in. I will have a charmed life, Samuel. You have given me a greater bargain than I knew."

"*Father* gave you?!"

"I could not have tried to *'give'* this daughter of mine to any man. She's like a wild bird, goes where she will."

"Believe it, Sir." I said. "But I come gladly to *your* tender hand."

Will cleared his throat. "I came to ask for a favour, I hardly dare ask now I know I left you in danger of your lives."

"Oh, gladly, man," grinned Father. "What do you want done?"

320

"Can you spare me Alice and her mother for a few days to prepare my house for my new bride? I fear it is a bachelor nest of cobwebs and snails in damp corners. The bed-curtains…the kitchen pots… I can't take Beth and Ruth and the others from their duties, however much I know they would be glad to help." He turned to my mother. "I thought, Sarah, you and Alice could go marketing for what you think is needful for our house and—" he looked at me and flared his eyes naughtily, "—bedchamber, so it is fit for our bride-night."

It was agreed that he would stay with us that night then take us in the small coach to stay with him at Beauchamps. We took our sewing boxes, pots of beeswax, polishing rags, brooms and cut lavender. I was never so happy at the prospect of such work, because this was to be for my own home, with Will.

Mother and I slept together in the bedchamber while Will made up the truckle bed in the parlour and slept there alone. I slept but fitfully, my thoughts straying continually to the thought of him, so near.

We swept, scrubbed and polished. We beat the wall hangings and bed curtains and spread them out on bushes in the September sun.

Mistress Carey came down to greet my mother.

"The mistress has sent me with an invitation to dinner in the Hall tonight, Mistress Sanderson. She wants to make you welcome and to tell you in person how happy she is at the prospect of this marriage between Alice and her steward. Will has been like a son to her and Sir Carlton and has been her right arm since her husband was killed."

"I am sure we will be happy to join you all. Alice has spoken so fondly of all the household, almost as her second family."

"Dick will bring the waggon down to the gate house ready for market."

When they arrived Will was with them. I ran out, delighted. "Are you coming with us?"

"Yes, sweet-heart, but I want you to look at these broadsheets young Joshua picked up in Shipscarden last night."

Evaded Capture!
Charles Stuart
Reward *of* £1000

*For any who find or can lead to the Arrest
of he who claims to be England's King against the
weal of Parliament
and the People's good.
He is black of hair and eye and
above the height of most Men.*

"A thousand pounds!" I was astonished. "Will! That really is a king's ransom."

"That's more money than most men could amass in a life of work," said Mother.

"Do you think, if they do capture him, they will cut his head off too, like his father's?"

Will shrugged. "Who knows, Alice. They are the victors. They have the power."

Will and Dick did not think there would be trouble in Stratford.

"If we see anything we don't like, Mistress Sanderson, we will ride straight on through," said Dick, so off we went.

In the market place the crowds were already jostling between the stalls to gather at the steps of the market cross. The Town Crier was mounting the steps ringing his bell. Dick halted the waggon, so we could hear him cry his news.

"I here announce to all men news of the great victory at Worcester which God's grace has granted to the forces of Parliament. The complete destruction of the last royalist army ended the siege of that city where the first battle of our late wars' miseries was fought and marks the people's triumph and ends the sorrows of our broken nation. Thanksgivings to God are ordered in every parish church on the first Sunday after this September 6th in the year of Our Lord 1651."

He finished speaking and gave his scroll to a servant to paste up on the door of the Town Hall. The proclamation was received with a buzz of talk, some cheers and a catcall or two. There was no outbreak of rage or unrest. I thought that what he said about the end of the sorrows of our broken nation must have been welcome to everyone who heard him, even if the land would take time to heal.

The marketing folk drifted back to the stalls. We dismounted and took our baskets to the shopping with lighter hearts.

Stratford Market was rich with stalls full of autumn fruits and harvested vegetables; bales of jewel-bright dyed woollen cloth; rolls of bleached linen. There were tables of lace trim, beads and hose; plumes for hats, velvet bonnets, white close-caps and bundles of ribbons and ready-tied bows. I was in a whirling coloured haze of bride-minded happiness.

Near noon I saw Will's curly head above the crowd, coming to find me and felt only joy.

"Baskets all well laden, I see. I suppose you have had a successful market day."

"I have been a spendthrift and I glory in it, Sir."

"Whatever brings that smile to your dear face, Sweetheart, and takes us nearer to our wedding day brings delight to me.

"I do not see packages of silken suiting or fine velvet caps for you, Will Franks. I hope you are not coming to my side dressed in your farmyard jerkin and cellar-apron."

"I can dress the gentleman when I have a mind, Madam. You will be full of admiration."

That evening, dressed for feasting, we set off for the big house. Will took us into the kitchen to remove our cloaks. There was such a turmoil of stirring, mixing, baking, setting plates as my friends perfected the feast.

"Come Sarah, Alice," said Will, "You are guests tonight, I'll take you in to Lady Trentham."

"Wait, Will." Anne Carey laid a hand on Will's arm. "We have newcomers here. A cousin of Her Ladyship, Mistress Crane from Tacklenden Hall, up Wolverhampton way. They asked to rest their journey here. They are going on to Bristol. Sir Robert Drayton is the gentleman with her. So here we are, rushing to make extra of everything, for they are to stay."

"Is this Sir Robert a soldier? A Royalist escaped from Worcester?"

"Well, he might be, but the others are just the cousin, Mistress Margaret Crane and yon fellow, her steward, Master Christopher Something-or-other." She gestured to a tall, brown faced man with soot black hair and a black moustache sitting on a stool by the table. He was chatting and laughing with Ruth and Beth while they worked.

He looked up as he heard us speaking about him and nodded his head in our direction.

"We—my mistress, I should say, has a permit to travel to Bristol to attend a pregnant relative. Sir Robert and I go for Mistress Crane's protection. There are so many ruffian soldiers on the roads."

"Was this Sir Robert Drayton in the Worcester battle?" Will asked. "Is he in danger of arrest if they find him? There are rewards posted for Royalist escapees and the broadsheets say there is a huge reward for the capture of the King. A thousand pound! They will be searching for his likely shelterers, I'm sure."

"So much?" muttered Christopher.

"What!" Anne Carey looked as amazed as I had been. "A thousand pound? That's a fortune!"

"More money than we will ever see," Dick exclaimed. "Has your Sir Robert got a price upon his head also, Master Christopher? Our mistress here has had a deal of torment from priest-hunters and Roundheads because she offered protection to the King's men and to priests."

"Ah, so loyal, then?"

"Wholeheartedly loyal," Anne Carey cried. "Our late master, Sir Carlton Trentham, died at Worcester. And My Lady has taken great risks to her own safety. Thomas her son was wounded, thrown in prison and accused of plotting. We have suffered in this house for the poor late King and his son."

"My mistress must know the family's loyalty, that is why we have come here."

Mistress Carey pursed her lips. "We do not want to see more troubles on our poor family's head." She turned back to her work. "Sit you down, Mistress Sanderson, away from the steam and flour. Will, you can go in and discover if they have finished their private talk."

"I'll sit here with Aimee and help peel these pears," I said, covering my dress with an apron from the wall-hook.

Mistress Carey bustled about giving tasks to the kitchen boys. The young spit-turner was new to me.

"He is an orphan Dick discovered asleep under the haystack," she said. "We have taken him in. He says his name is Eli. He runs about like a terrier trying to be helpful to everybody at the same time. Eli! Go down to the cellar with Master Franks and help carry up the wine." The boy followed Will at a run. Then she turned to Mistress Crane's servant. "Here, you Christopher! Don't you sit chattering to my women, slowing up their work. Make yourself useful. Turn that spit-jack and earn your supper."

The steward stood up, so tall, and hung his hat on the back of a chair and shook loose his long black curls. He moved his stool nearer the spit-jack but just sat there with his hand on the lever. He did nothing. Mistress Carey, not hearing the spit clanking, turned to look.

"Get on with it, man or the chickens will burn!" She glared at him, her mouth set. It was a look that we all knew boded ill for Master Christopher. She stalked over and shoved him aside with such force he half tumbled off his seat. "Mind away!" she snapped. "What sort of servant are you that you don't know how to wind up a spit-jack! Watch! Here! Get busy!"

"Ah, Mistress, I was merely the son of a poor farm labourer, we could hardly ever afford to eat meat and when we did, why, we never used such a fancy machine as this. I can see it is a clever contrivance."

"Does your mistress not have such a thing at Tacklenden Hall then?" Beth asked.

Christopher grinned. "I am the steward, Mistress, kitchen work is for the lesser servants, as I am sure your steward here would allow, but see, I am a willing hand." He cranked the spit-jack furiously, sending the chickens spinning.

"Oh, slower, steadier, you ham-fisted oaf! God's Beard! Ruth, run to the cellar and send young Eli back to turn the spit or we will have no supper fit to eat. You!" Mistress Carey rapped Christopher on the shoulder with a ladle, "Move out of the way. Steward or no steward, you are not commander here, I am. Get you down to the cellar with Ruth and help Master Franks. You can carry wine bottles safely, I dare say."

"Oh yes, Mistress Carey, wine I do know about."

Anne snorted and gave him another swipe with the ladle on his retreating back.

When he came back from the hall after delivering the wine he carried on addressing Anne Carey with a wily good humour we knew would annoy her.

"Her Ladyship and her good steward have sent me back to assist you, Good Mother Carey. Tell me what I may do for you to avoid your fiendish ladle."

We all looked at Anne Carey. She never took humour kindly when the dinner preparations were reaching a climax. She pursed her lips and shoved a bowl of peeled vegetable skins and tops into his chest.

"Take this lot and empty it into the pig pen. I daresay you will find that without help. Just follow your nose." He took the bowl with a grin and went out to the yard.

"Watch yourselves around him," said Mistress Anne as he closed the door. "That one is over-familiar. He needs to know his place better. He fancies himself a fine gallant, I think. Take care you girls are not caught alone with him in a dark corner. He will take liberties."

Ruth grinned at me and lifted her eyebrows as though she would not mind that at all.

"He is a handsome one, Mistress Carey, you must admit."

"Is as does, Beth. A wise old saying."

Christopher came back in and flourished the bowl upside down. "Task complete. Pigs happy. Now what work for me?"

"Take that whetstone on the shelf there and sharpen the table knives. I assume Tacklenden Hall has knives."

"And a lowly kitchen boy to sharpen them, Mistress." He reached down the whetstone, positioned it and laid a cloth across his knees, the knife-carrier beside him. "I will sharpen keenly, although I am better acquainted with the sharpening of poigniards and, erm, Sir Robert's sword blades."

I watched him. His eyes rested on each of us girls in turn, his gaze travelling from breast to ankle. He watched us move about and when his eyes turned to mine I felt a little wave of heat. I did not want to blush for him, but my, he was handsome and a charmer.

He smiled at my self-conscious look. "Very pretty, Mistress Alice Sanderson," he said, softly.

Anne Carey cleared her throat loudly and clattered pewter plates together.

"Here, Sir, carry these plates and set them around the table in the hall with the knives between. Alice, you and Aimee take the wine cups and beer mugs, Ruth the napkins. Set all ready at our best. Beth, you place table nosegays beside each candlestick. Tell Will the food will be ready in a few minutes, then we can all wash, carry in and sit to join the dinner.

In the hall Thomas and Kathryn sat close to Mistress Crane and Sir Robert Drayton, by the fire. The steward Christopher stood by them, within their circle, heads together, speaking privately. Every so often there would be short bursts of laughter. He seemed familiar with them, I thought. Will always kept a respectful distance between himself and Lady Trentham, despite his life-long service with her. I found it hard to make sense of Christopher's demeanour.

As we sat to our supper I spoke quietly to Will. "I wonder if that Christopher is actually an escaped nobleman or one of the King's generals under a disguise."

Will looked over at him. He was flirting with Aimee on his one side and Beth on his other. "Hmm. He is mighty sure of his power to charm. I caught the palm of his hand as I passed out the wine bottles to him. Very soft, Alice, not a servant's hands. Feel mine."

I took his hand in both of mine. "Rough but manly, Sir. Perfect. And the hand for me."

He took my hand and kissed it, screening it with his wine cup, but not before Christopher had caught us and grinned.

Will and I used this shared mealtime to talk together about our wedding, our plans for the gate house and my ideas for a flower and a herb garden. I smiled at the sight of my mother and Lady Trentham talking eagerly together.

During a lull in the hubbub, I heard my mother talking about the exasperating untidiness of her sons when they were young, the mud they brought in on their boots, the risks they took, the tree-climbing.

"And making boats, Mistress Sanderson, to sail the fishponds here, that was Thomas's mischief; sinking and having to be dragged out by his hair."

"Luke, my oldest, was once nigh trampled by a cow he tried to ride."

I watched Christopher Greenleafe lean closer to them. "Tree-climbing, now, I am something of an expert there." He dropped his voice and went on speaking, making them laugh. He caught my eye and nodded, lifting his cup of wine.

At the dinner's end, Thomas stood and bade welcome to Sir Robert Drayton and Mistress Crane, even mentioning Christopher by name and nodding his way. He said how pleased he and his mother were that they had chosen to stay at Beauchamps Hall to avoid the packs of troops and the flooded Roman road

"We have ordered this dinner to honour Mistress Sanderson and, especially Mistress Alice, her daughter, for everything we owe to them; our safety, perhaps even our very lives."

He recounted my part in smuggling him out of the house when the Parliamentary Commissioners threatened a search and how my mother nursed his wounds. Without going into detail, for which I was glad, he reminded the company how I had saved Francis de Paul from the priest hunters. Everyone applauded. Will took my hand and squeezed it.

Thomas went on. "And that same priest, my cousin, knowing of the new king's plea for funds, risked his life to rescue a hoard of silver plate from the sacking of our parish church so it could be used for King Charles's good."

Everyone hammered the table. Christopher the steward stood up and raised a toast to Tom.

Lady Abigail rose to her feet. Everyone fell silent. "I ask all here to join in a prayer for those killed at our defeat at Worcester and, to beg God's blessing on His Majesty."

Everyone stood. Some crossed themselves, others simply bowed their heads. I prayed too, for the King's safety, for the peace of our countryside and for a fair government in future by Oliver Cromwell and his Parliament.

"Now," said Thomas, "we will drink a health to His Majesty King Charles the second. God save the King."

Christopher was rather late to stand on his feet I thought, but his mistress did not glare at him, and neither did Lady Trentham. I rather thought they lowered their heads.

"God save the King," he said.

The meal over, Lady Abigail and Thomas led their visitors upstairs. Aimee and Beth followed carrying their candlesticks. Anne Carey caught my arm.

"Please, Alice, will you carry up the hot water can Sir Robert has asked for. My knees are so painful tonight."

With a smile I took the brass can from her and made for the staircase.

"I will collect our cloaks Alice," said Will, "and your mother and I will wait for you by the garden door."

I climbed the stairs and crossed the solar towards the guest rooms. Sir Robert Drayton's door stood open but he himself was climbing up to the menservants' sleeping quarters carrying a bedcover and a pillow. In the room, with his back to me, Christopher Greenleafe was sitting on the bed without his jacket, removing his boots. I tapped the door.

"I have brought the hot water Sir Robert asked for, Master Greenleafe, but he seems to have gone up to the servant's quarters. Is there anything else he needs?"

Christopher came to the door and, to my amazement, took up my hand and kissed it, then took the hot water can.

"Thank you, sweet Mistress Alice, and not only for the water, for all your efforts for, er, the royal cause. Mind you," he crossed the room and put the water can on the mule chest, "I hear you also tended my Lord Protector's deputy when he was sick here in the hall." His eyes twinkled. His cheeks dimpled.

"Yes, they were trapped by floods and he had a congestion of the chest."

"And the Kings forces have done their best to kill him while you strove to keep him alive. What times we live in, eh? Good night, Mistress Alice." He closed the door behind me and I felt I

330

had been quite charmingly dismissed as though by the lord of the manor himself

Will, Mother and I were at breakfast discussing our wedding arrangements when there was a rapping at the door. It was Dick.

"The mistress has asked if the three of you will join her in the solar when you are ready. Sir Robert and Mistress Crane are leaving to travel south. Her Ladyship wants me to ride them through our east track on to the Stow road to avoid the Roundhead packs. I am to set them on their way."

"When do you leave?" Will was already on his feet.

"At once, they have a distance to ride."

We followed Dick up to the house. Everyone was assembled in the hall.

Eli was holding the horses at the front door. There was a buzz of light-hearted chatter inside and Lady Trentham stood to address the company, but before she could speak Dick turned back.

"The men in the sheep field have just seen Roundheads turning in to the estate road! I've told Eli to move the horses."

Lady Trentham looked alarmed. "This way!" She hurried the three visitors and their steward Greenleafe, up the stairs.

"How many?" Thomas asked.

"Thirty, forty."

"To the kitchen, everyone. The usual measures. Mistress Sanderson, will you and Alice sit by the fireplace with my wife. I will go and see what they ask for. Will, please come."

As they approached the door, a Roundhead officer in a lobster pot helmet, sword and breastplate came inside followed by three more officers. One holding a useless, crooked arm, another in a blood-soaked jacket and breeches, white and sick. They half dragged, half carried the blood-drenched man and laid him on the floor, grabbing cushions off the window seat.

"Major Fletcher, Sir, lately ridden from the Worcester battle. As you see we have severe wounded officers here. Our captain is very sick with fever and blood-loss. We need your help and shelter."

"I wonder you did not stop for aid sooner. We are a long ride from Worcester."

"The Captain ordered us to go on to Stratford headquarters but there is damage to the bridge. They are working at repairs. We are forced back and he is worse. Dying maybe. At least give us your barn."

Thomas sighed. "How many do you need to billet?"

"Thirty active horsemen. Two badly wounded and five others who need smaller wounds cleaned and bound."

Will faced the major "Follow Master Page there and carry your officers to the kitchen. I will go out and direct your men to the Larch Barn. But, let me warn you, Sir, Sir Thomas and his mother expect you to conduct yourselves as gentlemen and show due gratitude to the household. See to it or I will personally deal with whoever steps out of line."

The major stared, reading Will's face, testing his determination then nodded and helped lift the sick captain.

Thomas led me to the staircase, speaking softly. "Run up to my mother and tell her what has been agreed. Mistress Crane will have to have her safe-passage letter to show them. Say to take great care. None of them should come down. We will try to get her away as soon as I think it safe."

As I delivered Thomas's message Christopher Greenleafe was nowhere to be seen. I remembered the way Francis de Paul used to disappear at times of danger. If there was a priest hole used by de Paul, why would they be using it to hide Christopher Greenleafe who was no more priestly than a cheese?

Mother was speaking. "Your Ladyship, by your leave, Alice and I will go down and see to the wounded. You know we are used to it and at least the officer was polite and not bullying for help."

"Well, if you are willing. It will be safer if we give them what we can and quickly, so they leave, although we cannot mend the bridge for them." Lady Trentham was twisting her fingers together. She kept glancing toward the fireplace.

I took Mother down to where we stored the herbals and the linen cloths. We chopped and mixed our wound preparations while Anne Carey and the others made huge pots of soup and bread for the troops, anticipating their demand for both, hoping to preserve our chickens and pigs.

"How can we still be doing this for men who have murdered one King and defeated the other?" Aimee slammed spoons about on the table.

"Don't glower," said Beth. "Being sweet and outwardly obedient is the quickest way to get rid of them."

"Well, I am not going to be smiling at them. God's Blood!" She stuck a knife into a turnip with as much hatred as if it was a Roundhead's heart.

We tended to the captain first. He was in a stupor, moaning in pain when he came into consciousness, then passing out again. His hip had been smashed by what must have been a ball from a cannon. The bone was exposed and ragged. As she washed away the blood she could not pull enough flaps of skin together to close the wound. All she could do was lay a pad covered with salve over the gape and bind it tight then dose him with the poppy medicine and hope infection would not set in.

"Will he live?" asked Major Fletcher.

Mother shook her head. "He is in danger of infection. He cannot travel with you. He must lie still."

I moved on to the lieutenant with the hanging arm. It was obviously broken. He was in great pain too. I sent young Eli out to the yard to cut two short staves which I strapped around the lieutenant's forearm for a splint. I gave him some pain-killing medicine too.

"I can't move this," he grumbled, "It's my working arm. How will I do?"

333

"You need to keep it still to give the bone a chance to grow together again. You will just have to do the best you can."

"Think yourself lucky you have had Mistress Sanderson here to mend you. Some camp surgeon would have probably cut off the broken bit altogether and you would have had to live with half an arm. How would you do then?" Ruth snapped.

The soldier took the poppy draught with his free hand, looking sick. Mother and I moved out to the Larch Barn with Ruth to dress the minor injuries.

It was dark before the frenzy of feeding, bedding, stabling and wound cleaning was complete. Will came to the barn to find us and carried the medicine chest back to the house. We threw the blood-soaked rags and torn clothing into the campfire in the yard where a huge pot of soup was bubbling. Will barred the kitchen door and all the shutters.

"All secured downstairs, Mistress Anne. I will take Mistress Sanderson and Alice back to the gate house now."

But outside the front door, Dick bent close with his hand on Will's arm. "Lady Trentham has asked me to take her visitors over Lavrock way after midnight and set them on the road south. She wants them away before the Roundheads are up and about in the morning."

"They will have posted sentries. They'll hear the horses."

"I already moved the horses and packs through the copse to my house. Sir Robert is waiting there with them. I want you go towards your house and look about. If the coast is clear, stand by the stile at the sheep field and take your hat off. I will go back in and take Mistress Crane and the steward out through the copse to my house, join Sir Robert Drayton and be off."

Will nodded and steered us outside. The three of us stood together by the stile looking about. There was no moon but there were no sentries, no movement, not a sound. Will took off his hat and held it aloft. As we left the Hall behind, we saw three cloaked figures come out of the garden door and disappear among the trees.

Back in the safety of Will's home, we lit candles, while he raised the fire and we settled comfortably together talking over the night's events.

At last Mother went up. Will and I exchanged our last kisses and tearing myself out of his arms, I joined her in bed and lay thinking about the escaping threesome Dick was leading away.

Their planned journey to Bristol was a journey into more danger I thought. I knew from Nathan and from my brother Luke's letters that Bristol port was packed with Roundhead troops. I only hoped if Christopher Greenleafe *was* a fugitive nobleman, they were not riding into trouble, rather than away from it. But there was nothing more to do. My time of mixing in the affairs of men at war was over.

'I am going to be a bride,' I thought, 'and sleep in Will's arms and bear his babies, that is enough.' I smiled myself to sleep.

Next morning the Roundheads were calmly going about their camp business so it looked as though Dick had got the visitors safely away. Will took Mother and me up to the solar to bid goodbye to Lady Trentham, who was sitting alone by the fire.

"Ah, here you are. Welcome. Come and sit. You too, Will. I want to make a wedding gift to you both as a measure of our family's affection and respect for you."

"You have been so faithful a servant. My husband loved you like a son and we owe the survival and prosperity of this estate, in large measure, to you." She unwrapped a chamois cloth and held out a large silver goblet to Will. "This was my father's, from Queen Elizabeth's time. It has our family crest on it but I have had it engraved with your monogram on the other side, see." He took and turned it, smiling. It was beautiful. A treasure.

"And Alice, as Thomas said at last night's dinner, we are greatly in your debt. Will, you are marrying a pearl among women. And, if I may presume to do it, Mistress Sanderson, I want to congratulate you on your brave and resourceful daughter." She opened her sewing box and took out a small parcel, wrapped in silk which she handed to me. I shook out a necklace of garnets with a central drop: a pearl set in silver filigree.

"I thought you might like to wear it on your wedding day, in remembrance of me and my family so you may feel our prayers are with you. It is a pleasure to me that Will here will be bringing you to live at Beauchamps Hall so we will see you often. And you, Mistress Sanderson, will always be welcome."

At that moment, Anne Carey climbed the stairs and approached us.

"Major Fletcher would like to take his leave of you, My Lady. He waits in the hall."

"Tell him to come up."

The Roundhead officer lowered his head respectfully and thanked Lady Trentham for her hospitality and turned to my mother.

"Captain Porteal had a calmer night, Mistress Sanderson thanks to your treatments. I understand your advice of yesterday but he is urgent to leave. I have requisitioned a cart from your stable Your Ladyship, and lined it with straw for his comfort. We will take him with us as carefully as may be." He held out a purse. "Here is payment for the cart and I thank you for your help. Lady Trentham, Master Franks. Ladies." He nodded and left.

We heard the hooves passing under the window as they rode towards the Roman road.

"Can they get across the bridge today, Will?"

"I sent two of the lads out there this morning to find out. The river is high but the bridge looks safe enough. The water over the meadows and the road is fetlock deep but passable. They will get through, so young Eli said."

336

"Good. And has Dick returned from setting our friends on their road?"

"Not yet."

"Come and fetch me as soon as he is back. Ask Anne to prepare a breakfast for him and send for Luce to come up here to wait for him. He will be tired and hungry and she will be so anxious."

I was reluctant to leave for Bournbroke until I knew Dick was safe.

Mother, Will and I sat in the kitchen talking to the others, even Thomas and Kathryn came down to wait. Luce arrived with her smaller children and the smell of warm bread made us feel comfortable.

At last, the kitchen door flew open and Dick clattered in, windblown and tired. Luce ran to embrace him.

"All safe, Dick?" asked Thomas. "Fetch my mother, Aimee."

Dick nodded, eagerly drinking the hot mulled ale and tearing his bread and cheese.

"Dick! They are all safe?" Lady Trentham stood at the door.

"Yes, all safe, but it was a near thing. I got them down the east track towards the road and, Devil take them, they had put sentries at that gate."

Lady Trentham's hand flew to her mouth. "No!"

"They were mighty suspicious, demanding to know why we were setting out at such an hour. I was trying to think of something convincing to say when Mistress Crane exploded in a coughing fit and that Christopher Greenleafe shouted to stand clear because they feared they had caught the plague at Bromsgrove and had been ordered off the estate. The sentry still held my bridle. 'You will be infected yourselves!' he says. At that Sir Robert clutches his scarf over his mouth and yells at them, 'Do you think we don't know that, Damn you! She wants to go to her sister's in Stow.' Then Mistress Margaret starts to wail, 'I want to see her before I die.' She coughs and sobs and coughs again with such violence that the sentry drops the bridle. The other one drags him out of the way so Sir Robert spurs his horse and we ride off. We don't look back. That was it and here I am."

Lady Trentham crossed herself. "Thanks be to God and the Blessed Virgin," she said. "And thank you, Dick."

I felt relieved too. I reached for Will's hand and squeezed it.

"I bid you goodbye, Mistress Sanderson, Alice. Thomas," she laid a hand on her son's arm. "Take me up to the round room. I must pray. Join me."

I took leave of all my friends, taking their good wedding wishes with me. When I came to Beauchamps Hall again it would be as Will's wife.

Calming the Storm

September-October 1651

You frame my thoughts and fashion me within,
You stop my toung, and teach my hart to speake,
You calme the storme that passion did begin
'Amoretti': Edmund Spenser

I opened my eyes, wondering what woke me. The cockerel crowed in the still Vale air. and was answered by a fellow at Lane End Manor farmyard. George Wallace's dog barked lazily, probably chasing a late butterfly. I got out of my bed and threw open the shutters. Bright. Dry. Blackbirds pecked at the few ungathered cherries, beak-tasty despite the wasp-holes. I breathed the morning air, my last in this beloved place. Tomorrow I would be in my own home with Will.

Mother was crossing the yard to the house carrying fresh water. The smell of the morning's bread was already rising. She was my pattern for a wife.

Watt moved from stable to pig-house, feeding the animals, refreshing the straw. Little Abel Fairleigh from The Rose Bush worked with him now as helper. Father wanted all the work done early. He had more important things to do today, at the church. It was my wedding day.

After our early bread and milk, Mother, Lizzie, Esther and I arranged all the food we had prepared over recent days then baked fresh pies. We peeled, decorated and arranged the plates and boards on every shelf and sill ready to be carried out to the tables that stood waiting in the orchard for the guests to our wedding feast.

Once everything was ready, the others ran to St. Etheldreda's to decorate the door-arch, the windowsills and chancel steps with training ivies, scarlet hips and haws. They wove rosy crab-apples and late-glow roses through the garlands of green.

I stood alone and bathed myself in hot scented water by my chamber fire. I washed my hair, rinsed it in vinegar and rosemary to enhance its copper glints and brushed it dry with long, lazy strokes. I had never lingered so long over my appearance. I heard Lizzie on the stairs, come to serve me, the bride. She wound and twisted my hair into two long ropes and pinned them into a double top-knot and fastened a posy of rosebuds between the two. I uncurled two long strands by my ears and pinched my cheeks pink.

Lifting the layers of lavender-scented linen, I put on the wedding dress Mother and I had made. Lizzie fastened the garnet necklace Lady Trentham had given me and polished Will's moonstone ring, soon to be moved to my marriage finger.

Lizzie held the mirror-steel, moving it up and down for me to see the effect of my gown, my gemstones, my decorated hair.

"You look lovely, Alice," she said, giving me a kiss. I grinned, hoping today, for once, I might be beautiful.

I stood there in my chamber looking out on our orchard, the outbuildings, the new-swept yard and remembered our dread of the horsemen arriving at the gate: strangers who disturbed our peaceful farming days, who ransacked our fruited harvests. I remembered their shouting, their blood and filth, their violent hands, their slobbering, repulsive mouths. The fear I felt then, cast up a whirl of other jolts of danger; how I stumbled upon Francis de Paul and the secret chapel; Stephen Barkswell jabbering with fear; Brother Levens spitting out his bigotry and threats. I remembered Cromwell's noble deputy, coughing and weak, submitting to my hand and lately the Royalist travellers, their strange steward Greenleafe, flirting with his dark-pool eyes and kissing my fingers.

I shook my head to rid myself of these tumbling daydreams and nightmare images. Today was my day, a family day, not a time for public events. A day for my happiness, and Will's.

I closed the shutters and walked down the stairs in slow measure, so I would not tread on the finest silken dress I had ever worn. Afraid to sit down and crease it, I stood waiting until all my family came tumbling through the door to lead me to the church, exclaiming and praising me until I felt like a great beauty.

We carried our posies of rosemary, myrtle and roses in procession past the Bournbroke cottages. Villagers came out of the doors to wave us on our way. Children skipped behind us. Father, brushed, trimmed and wearing a broad-brimmed hat with two wagging pheasant feathers stuck in at a jaunty angle, held me on his arm as we approached the crossroads. The bells of St. Etheldreda rang out. Friends and our near neighbours crowded the church path. All the Beauchamps company stood together by the porch door; Sir Thomas Trentham, Kathryn, in their best lace-trims and as I drew close to Lady Trentham she touched her neck, pleased to see me wearing her gift.

Then there was Will. Everything spun away in a swirl of colour and faces and sound. There was only Will, sunlit, filling my sight. There was no one else. Only his eyes. My eyes. His heart showing in them. Mine answering. There were words. Vicar Page spoke from the Book of Prayer. I spoke. Will spoke. We made vows.

The old church whirled with autumn lights, hedgerow-green and orange-berried. The honey-coloured walls glowed and the scent of rosemary filled my head. Dust motes danced in the sunbeams that warmed the ancient stones and beloved faces whirled around me, smiling at every turn.

Will moved my ring on to my marriage finger and we sealed the promise our hearts had made long ago. We left together, hands held fast, to live our new life in a Vale at peace.

The After Word
Summer 1661

'Whom the King delighteth to honour."
Esther v.6: King James Bible

I woke. What woke me? Not the children. Not the baby's cry. There were sheep bleating, but it was not that. Horsemen! Galloping here. To the door. I leapt out of bed, the old dread surging.

"Will! There are riders here!" There was a loud knocking.

Will jumped up and threw open the casement.

"What is it? What is the matter?"

"Is this the gate house for Beauchamps Hall?"

"Yes. Who wants us?"

"Urgent message. Come down, Sir. Come down!"

Will pulled on his breeches and thrust his arms into a shirt as he ran down the stairs. I followed.

"I have letters for Sir Thomas and Lady Trentham. Take me to them at once."

"What? Is there trouble for the family here?"

"Nothing to fear, just take me to Sir Thomas."

Will gave me a long look and reached down his keys. "You are mighty early, for a visit."

"Not a visit. Court business. Lead on."

"Will?"

"If it is a message from the royal court, it cannot be anything bad." He went down to them.

I roused the children. As I watched them, Edward, now eight years old, Sarah, six, Eliza with her unruly black curls and baby Luke, I thought back over the events of the last nine years.

Oliver Cromwell had died and there were rumours of renewed fighting, but the Vale had stayed quiet. One day Thomas and Kathryn came back from a visit to her brother in

Shipscarden with amazing news. Thomas called us all into the hall to hear it.

"My brother has a friend with the King's court in the Netherlands," Kathryn told us. "Some of the Parliament have met with the King. They are asking him to come back!"

"What? Parliament asking for a king again?"

"But they ruled against monarchy years ago?"

"Can it be possible?"

Thomas said, "General Moncke wants to bring back moderate ways. He has been abroad to see the King and offered him the crown."

Lady Trentham said if she could only live to see the King restored to the throne, she would die happy.

King Charles indeed came home.

What a festival day, the coronation! Thomas invited all the neighbouring villagers to the estate. He ordered the roasting of a coronation ox, with chickens, ducks and legs of lamb. Beer and wine were poured and health was drunk to His Majesty many times and we all danced around a house-high bonfire under the stars until the children fell asleep where they sat.

Now the King was back on the throne, a fragile peace restored, and here, this morning, there were horsemen at our gate again. What urgent news could officers be bringing so insistently to the Trentham family? A knock roused me from my thoughts. The children scrambled over each other to see who was at the door. It was young Eli from the kitchen.

"Master Franks says you'm all be wanted up in the hall. You'm to bring the children."

"Is there trouble, Eli?"

"No Missus, Everyone be smilin'."

I smoothed my hair, put on a fresh white cap and examined the children for clean hands and unsmutted faces. We walked up to the big house together, baby Luke nodding himself to sleep in my arms.

As we arrived at the door of the Hall, the morning horsemen who had battered our door were taking their leave. Their officer swept a bow, flourishing his plumed hat in such a manner that Edward and Sarah sniggered at him. I sent a frown their way as Will came out to us.

The whole household and all the estate workers were gathered together. Lady Tennant sat in her usual chair, smiling. A hush fell as Thomas stood beside his mother to face us, holding a large document in his hand, at the base of which was a huge red seal.

"Dear Friends. We have travelled long and far together through tears and joys. I am only sorry my father could not be with us to hear what I am to tell you. The rider who just left was a courier from—" He paused to heighten the effect of his words, his eyes twinkling

"—the King himself with this letter for my mother and me and, as you will hear, to all of you."

We looked, one to another, raising our eyebrows or whispering questions. Thomas began to read:

"To my good and faithful servant Sir Thomas Trentham and his gracious mother, Lady Trentham, greetings.

I praise Almighty God that I am restored to the throne of my sainted father and as I am come into my own, I fulfil a happy duty in sending you my heartfelt thanks for your loyalty during these years of bitter war .

I recognise that your husband and father, Sir Carlton, gave his life fighting for my father's cause from the first and that you, Sir Thomas, suffered wounds and imprisonment in his service and in mine.

I honour you, Lady Trentham, for the dangers and humiliations you suffered at the hands of cruel men. You have the gratitude of your king.

I thank all of you at Beauchamps Hall for opening your doors to our wounded and exhausted troops, for their healing

344

and care. I send, herewith, a purse of gold as a small reimbursement for the substance your estate outlaid.

As I passed from Worcester in the darkest days of my defeat, I was sustained by many brave friends. I am happy to count the Trentham household among them. You took me in when I was a fugitive and a huge reward for my betrayal was offered."

At this people exchanged looks and murmured under their breath.

"*We* took him in?"

"Wait," smiled Thomas, "Hear the rest." On he read:

"*So it is that I thank Mistress Carey for her instructions on operating a spit-jack. The royal cook has been amazed at my expert handling of the same in the palace kitchens! And I thank her for shoving me towards the pig pens but not head first into them."*

Anne Carey's hands flew to her mouth. "God's mercy!" she cried, "I have laid hands on His Majesty the King and called him 'Oaf' to his face! I even clattered him with my soup ladle!" We all laughed and clapped our hands.

"He writes more." Thomas read on:

"*I rejoice that I proved myself so excellent an actor, that I convinced even Mistress Carey's sharp fool-finding eyes that I was merely Christopher Greenleafe, an over-familiar servant.*

I must also thank Master Page for braving the Roundhead sentries at the last, pretending to boot us off the estate as plague-carriers and helping us on our last long journey to safety."

We burst out with more applause and laughter.

"His Majesty ends:

I give all of you my good wishes for a King's peace in a kingdom united under God with fair rule and care for each other. Pray you Amen."

This time everyone called out, "Amen!"

Thomas held aloft the letter so everyone could see the royal seal and the King's very handwriting and his signed name.

As people talked excitedly among themselves, Thomas asked Will and I to follow his mother to the solar. Leaving our children with Luce, who took them all out to romp in the garden, we went upstairs. Dick followed.

We watched, full of expectation, as Lady Trentham smoothed out another letter on her table.

"I have gifts here from His Majesty. Dick, the King asks me to give you this gold as thanks you for defending his escape from the Roundhead sentries."

"Alice." She held out two small velvet purses. "The King sends your family these silver medallions from his coronation as mementos of his gratitude for the nursing and sheltering of my son. And this is for you, a reward for your brave intervention rescuing my nephew, Francis, from certain death and, he writes, 'And for your discretion, for I think you suspected I was not a serving man.'

That night, sitting by the fire with the children at our feet, Will told them the story of the King's escape and our part in it, dwelling only on the excitement and the happy outcome.

Later, lying in each other's arms, Will stroked my hair.

"I cannot think I earned the King's praise and his gold, Alice. It was you who did all that for Tom, and the nursing and you who saved de Paul while I behaved like a jealous ox-headed fool. I almost lost you."

"Hush." I kissed him. "Enough of that old business. We were both fools and stubborn for not speaking out clearly. You doubted I could love you. I doubted you loved me. We both know better now, four children later! But, Will Franks, you must promise me you will not prove jealous once again when I show you my own gift from the King."

I sat up and shook the velvet purse out onto the bed. Among the coronation medallions lay a miniature portrait in a golden case of a 'tall man, black of hair and eye'; Charles Stuart, King, bringing with Parliament's consent peace to the quiet orchards, villages and fields of our English Vale.

The End

Acknowledgements

With thanks to Ivan, my editor and wielder of the blue pencil, for all his work and his constant encouragement.

Thanks to Andy Allen for the cover design.

I am grateful to the many works of reference I consulted, especially to The Open University for its study course: *"Seventeenth Century: An Age of Change" (1982)* and to *"The Civil War in Stratford upon Avon: Conflict & Community in S. Warwickshire 1642-1646"* by Philip Tennant, published by Alan Sutton Publishing. & Shakespeare Birthplace Trust 1996, both of which fired my enthusiasm to write this book.

I am grateful to Doug Sharp and Solihull MBC Education Authority for the teacher's living history project at the National Trust property of Baddesley Clinton. I had the unforgettable experience of hiding in costume with 25 pupils while other costumed children, dressed as priest hunters, hammered on the doors. It gave me an idea of how it would feel to be dragged into danger by the decisions of remote rulers.

Printed in Great Britain
by Amazon